In The Lan
The One-Eyed Man Is King

A famous movie star found dead on the set of his latest picture...

Drugs hastily disposed of at the scene of the crime...

It's the stuff of Tinseltown scandal—and could ruin the investment Harry Bannock made in the dead man's library of films.

For help, Bannock turns to Mark Clayburn, a one-eyed private eye with his own history of scandals. But can Clayburn uncover the truth about Dick Ryan's murder before time runs out for Ryan's co-stars...and for Clayburn himself?

"Robert Bloch is one of the all-time masters."
—*Peter Straub*

Robert Bloch was the legendary author of PSYCHO and a true Hollywood insider, writing scripts for numerous movies and TV shows including ALFRED HITCHCOCK PRESENTS, Boris Karloff's THRILLER, and the original STAR TREK. You haven't see Hollywood's dark side till you've seen it through Bloch's eyes...

Shooting STAR

by **Robert Bloch**

A HARD CASE CRIME NOVEL

A HARD CASE CRIME BOOK
(HCC-042)
April 2008

Published by

Dorchester Publishing Co., Inc.
200 Madison Avenue
New York, NY 10016

in collaboration with Winterfall LLC

ISBN 0-8439-5960-6
ISBN-13 978-0-8439-5960-4

Cover design by Cooley Design Lab

Typeset by Swordsmith Productions

The name "Hard Case Crime" and the Hard Case Crime logo
are trademarks of Winterfall LLC. Hard Case Crime books are
selected and edited by Charles Ardai.

Printed in the United States of America

Visit us on the web at www.HardCaseCrime.com

Chapter One

My private eye was a little bloodshot this morning.

I focused it on the mirror, then wished I hadn't. There was somebody in the mirror I didn't care to see: the tall, thin guy with the graying hair; the man with the bloodshot eye. He bothered me. I didn't like the way he looked today. He'd shaved and dressed too carelessly, and with that black eyepatch and the ridiculous little mustache, he bore a mocking resemblance to the man in those shirt ads of a few years back. Besides, his good eye was bloodshot.

We nodded at one another in the mirror though, just like old friends. Why not? I knew all about him and he knew all about me. Maybe I didn't approve of my own reflection but, who knows, perhaps my reflection didn't approve of me, either. We were even on that score.

Maybe my reflection remembered the days when I had two eyes. The days before the hair started to turn gray and the collars began to fray a little at the edges. The days when I was *Mark Clayburn Literary Agency,* with an office on the Strip.

Well, I remembered those days, too. Perhaps that's why my eye got bloodshot—from too much remembering, from drinking too many toasts to the past. But it couldn't be helped. I was stuck with my reflection and my reflection was stuck with me. Me, Mark Clayburn, still a *Literary Agency,* but not on the Strip any more.

I thought about that for a moment, thought about the long road leading from the Strip to Olive Street in downtown L.A., and of the things I'd lost along the way. The eye went in the accident, and most of my savings were gone by the time I got out of the hospital. Then I found my clients had disappeared, and my help, and the big office.

So here I was, starting all over again. Just a part-time tenpercenter, really, with a typewriter, a telephone, and a couple of small clients. Plus a license as a Notary Public and another one as a Private Investigator. Anything to make a buck. Not a very fast buck, either.

My bloodshot eye did a fast pirouette around the office. Nothing much to see there: a desk, files, a few chairs. No beautiful bra-breaking blonde secretary, no top-shelf rye in the bottom drawer. It was just a walkup office, the kind nobody ever comes to unless they've been kicked out of all the better places first.

I went over to the desk and sat down. This was no time to feel sorry for myself. Save that for tonight. Right now I had work to do: a science-fiction yarn to send to Boucher, for a client; another to try on a confessions mag, and a true-detective job to revise.

That was still my meat—the true-detective yarn. I picked it up and started to read it over, wondering for the ten thousandth time why so many people are interested in crime and its solution. How many of them identify themselves with the detective and how many of them identify themselves with the criminal? Yes, and how many of them subconsciously identify themselves with the victim? Come to think of it, you could divide all society up into those three classes: the potential investigators, the potential criminals, and the potential victims. Might do an essay on it some time, stressing the fascination people have for reading about murder. Call it *Five Little Peppers And How They Slew.*

But right now, my job was to read the manuscript, read it and correct it, sitting in the dingy little office that nobody ever visited. I picked up the pages, bent my head, then jerked erect.

The door opened.

He stood there, big and bluff and blond, bulking in the

narrow doorway so that his tweeded shoulders almost touched either side of the frame. His eyes and teeth and rings sparkled and he said, "Hello, Mark. Long time no, *si?*"

"Harry Bannock! Come on in!"

"I am in." The big man walked over and pumped my hand. First he looked at me and then he looked down. They all do if they haven't seen the eye-patch before. "Great to see you! You're looking great. How's business?"

"Great," I told him. He seemed to like the word, always had.

"Glad to hear it. Been meaning to look you up now for a long time." He sat down. "But I've been rushed."

"Sure," I said. "I know how it is."

"You had a pretty rough time of it, from what I heard—losing the agency and all. But you're back in business, and that's the main thing."

"That's right." I riffled the pages of the manuscript. "I'm back in business. And you didn't come all the way downtown just to tell me how great it is either."

Harry Bannock leaned forward. "You don't like me, do you?"

I smiled at him. "I wouldn't say that, Harry. You and I used to be pretty close. We worked on a lot of deals together. I sold my clients' stories to the studios and the networks. You sold your clients as actors. We did each other a lot of favors, tipped one another off whenever there was a lead, made some money together. And you used to phone me at least once a week and ask, 'What are you doing for lunch, sweetheart?' Good old Hollywood custom—everybody's a 'sweetheart' or a 'darling' or a 'lover' or a 'doll'.

"Then I had my trouble, and you didn't phone me. You didn't come to see me, or write me, or anything. Neither did anyone else I knew. They had their own affairs to handle, and they just forgot about me. Good old Hollywood custom." I shrugged. "No, I'm not sore at you—sweetheart."

For the second time, Harry Bannock looked down at the floor. "I'm sorry, Mark. Honest to God, I'm sorry."

"It's all right. Forget it. Now that I've said my little piece, I feel better. But what can I do for you? Business? Want to buy a story?"

"That's right, Mark." He took out a cigarette case, flipped it open, extended it. "I want to buy a story."

"For one of your stable? Looking for a vehicle for a picture, is that it? I've got a few originals knocking around here that you might—"

"No. It's a true story I'm after."

"You mean one of those true-detective yarns?"

"In a way. Only it hasn't been written yet. And it's never going to be written. I don't want to see it on paper, either. I want you to tell it to me."

"Don't be coy, Harry. What's this all about?"

"I told you. I want to buy a true story from you. The story of a man named Dick Ryan."

"Dick Ryan?" I took a deep drag and let the smoke out slowly. "But I was in the hospital when it happened. I read the papers, and that's all I know about it."

"That's all anyone knows about it," Bannock said. "I want the facts. And I'm willing to pay you to find out for me."

"Ryan was murdered," I told him. "There was a big scandal. The police investigated but they couldn't pin it on anybody. That was six months ago, and now you show up and ask me to solve it. Why?"

Bannock grinned. "Call it curiosity."

I shook my head. "I don't buy that. Come on, let's have it, was Ryan a client of yours?"

"No."

"Then what do you care? He got his name smeared in the news, but it's all over with now, and forgotten. Why bother?"

Bannock stood up. "I want his name cleared, Mark. And solving the case will do it. I think he was framed as well as murdered. I think—"

"Save it for the cops," I said. "Which reminds me. We *do* have a police department here, you know. Understand they even have one of those newfangled Homicide Bureaus. Why don't you ask them for a little help?"

"Believe me, I have. But they couldn't do anything. Or *said* they couldn't. And meanwhile, there it sits. Ryan's dead; they can't find the killer; his name is mud all over town, all over the country. I'd like to set the record straight."

I rose and faced him. "Big-hearted Harry. Fighting to defend a dead man's honor! How like you that gesture is! Yes, and how dark it is here in the pig's hinder."

"Wait a minute now…"

"I'm waiting," I said. "I'm waiting until I hear the real reason. Just where are you tied in on the Ryan murder, Harry? Did you do it? Does somebody suspect you? Do you know who the killer is?"

"All right." Bannock sat down again. "I'll show you the cards—the whole deck."

"You'd better. I've got a right to know what you want me to get into."

"It's like this. I don't know who killed him, or why. Actually, I don't much care. Ryan was a louse, for my money. Everybody knew he played around, and there were probably a dozen husbands who'd have put a bullet into him, *and* two dozen wives. That part's all right with me. But it's the tie-in. You know, when they found him they found those reefer butts. And that's what hurts. They began to talk about a dope ring, say that he was on the stuff. It isn't true. Everybody who knew Ryan swears he never monkeyed around with weed or anything else. But the story's out and nothing will change it except the facts. The police can't give them to me, and I need them, bad."

"Why, Harry? If he wasn't your client…"

"He *is*, now."

"But he's dead."

"Dick Ryan's dead, yes. But *Lucky Larry* lives on. Or can live on. When this murder came out, when the scandal broke, Ryan's studio yanked all his pictures back from the exhibitors. The whole *Lucky Larry* series was put on the shelf. Poison at the box office when a cowboy star gets that kind of publicity. At least that's what Abe Kolmar thought, over at Apex. You know him, don't you, Mark?"

"I know *of* him, yes. Little indie producer, isn't he?"

"That's right. The *Lucky Larry* flicks were his biggest grossers. When he shelved them he was hard up for dough. But he figured there was no other way because of the stink being raised, and I didn't try to talk him out of it. Instead, I went there and I bought the whole business, outright: lock, stock and negative."

"*You* bought—?"

Bannock nodded. "Thirty-nine *Lucky Larry* pictures, at five grand apiece, with the rights to the name and future production thrown in. One hundred and ninety-five thousand dollars I paid. And in *cash*."

"You're crazy!"

"That's what everybody told me, including my ever-loving wife. Until I told *her* that See-More TV Productions were willing to buy the series for three hundred and ninety thousand. Ten Gs apiece, plus five percent of all future rentals. Now do you get the angle?"

"I get it. You double your money, and then some. Because westerns are hot stuff for TV rental. And the *Lucky Larry* name will sell."

"Right. That's exactly how I figured it. But at the time, I didn't figure there'd be quite as much of a stink raised. Now See-More keeps stalling me. They're leery of buying and using a star who's tied in with dope addiction. You know the angle: kids see westerns, parents object, they write to the sponsor, sponsor cancels out. It's a rough deal all around."

"And that's why you want Ryan's name cleared."

"Now you've got it, sweetheart."

"But why do you come to me? If the cops won't or can't help, there are plenty of big private investigation outfits you could work with."

"Too risky." Bannock ground out his cigarette. "Why do you suppose the case died so suddenly? One day the papers were full of it: big investigation planned on all this dope ring stuff. Next day, nothing. You ought to be able to figure the answer, Mark. It means things were getting a little too hot. Getting a little bit too close to some of the big wheels in the industry who were mixed up in narcotics. We've got a couple of stars who carry a monkey on their backs, and a few producers and directors, too. Somebody passed the word along to lay off."

"You mean they fixed the cops?"

"Of course not. But they did the next best thing, they clammed up tight. And they've stayed clammed up ever since. Do you think they'd talk to a big-time investigating outfit? You know better than that.

"But a little guy—a guy who's known in the industry—he can get around and nobody will bother him. Particularly if he gets to them under false pretenses—say he wants to discuss a story, or something. I need a little guy, Mark. An honest little guy. So I came to you."

I shrugged. "Very touching. But let me remind you of a few things. I'm still a writer's agent. Sure, I've got a permit to carry a pistol and a license for private investigation, but I only use it when I'm working on a true-detective assignment. It helps me to get in and go after material for an article. I don't know anything about narcotics. I've never tangled with a murderer in my life. With this eye-patch I couldn't use my pistol to shoot Charles Laughton in the belly at five paces."

"But you're honest."

"Sure. I'm honest. Like you say, 'an honest little guy'. And you're a big-time operator. A big-time operator who thinks he can walk in on an honest little guy and buy him body and soul for a big hello and a five-dollar bill."

"Listen to me, Mark. I've got a hundred and ninety-five thousand dollars tied up in this deal. Almost every penny of cash I could scrape together. I mortgaged the house on it. I've got to clear Ryan's name so I can unload. And we're not talking about five-dollar bills." He gripped my arm. "I'm offering you this assignment, to handle in your own way. It may take a day, it may take a week, it may take a month—though I hope to God it doesn't. But I won't be paying you on a time basis. I offer a flat deal."

"I'm listening, but I haven't heard anything yet."

"A thousand dollars cash right now, and five thousand if you find me the murderer and let me turn the information over to the police. Plus *another* five thousand if I sell the films. That's eleven grand in all."

"I used to get good grades in arithmetic," I told him. "But I was just thinking—"

"Good, I want you to think. That's what you're being paid for." Bannock took out his wallet. It was big and fat and bulging, like Bannock himself. He opened it and started to lay down hundred-dollar bills. One, two, three, four, five, six, seven...

I used to get good grades in arithmetic, and I was figuring what a thousand dollars would buy: Three months' rent for the office, for the flat; three months' groceries and gas supply. And five thousand more would give me a full year. Another five thousand might mean a chance to open up a real office again, with a little front to it, a girl receptionist, my name on the door, a few ads in *Film Daily*. Eleven thousand dollars cash meant a new start with a good push.

"What do you say?" Bannock asked.

I walked over to the mirror and stared for a moment. And I said to myself, *What do you want to get mixed up in all this for? It's one thing to write about murder and another thing to go out and find it. You couldn't kill anyone because you're not the criminal type. And what makes you think you're an investigator? The way you look, with that damned patch, you're more like a potential victim. Are you going to risk your hide for eleven grand?*

I took a good long look at what I was risking. The grayed, frayed figure didn't impress me. Eleven grand was a good price. The bloodshot eye stared at me. Then it winked.

"All right," I said. "You've got a deal."

I walked over to the desk, scooped up the money, then opened the bottom drawer and took out my pistol.

"Where you going with that?" Bannock asked.

"Public library," I said. "I always carry a pistol when I go there. Never did trust those stone lions."

Chapter Two

I'd been kidding about the public library, of course. They don't have lions. But they do have a very pretty little feline in the Reference Room who purred at me when I asked for the newspapers. She didn't look as if you'd have to use a pistol on her, and I doubt if she was carnivorous. At another time I might have been willing to take the chance of finding out, but right now I wanted to see those back issues.

I gave her a list of dates, as near as I could recall.

"Not again!" she said, checking them over on her pad.

"Somebody else ask for them?"

"This morning. Look, here's the old sheet—same dates. I know, because I had to haul them out."

"Happen to know who it was?"

"Why?"

"Just curious." I leaned over the counter. "Confidentially, I happen to be a writer. The reason I want those papers is to check up on a story I'm doing. And I wondered if somebody else might have the same idea and plans to beat me to it."

"Oh." She smiled. "You know, the minute you walked in here I said to myself, he's a writer!"

"How could you tell?"

"I just *knew,* that's all. We get a lot of them in here."

"I'll bet. And the person this morning?"

She shook her head. "I didn't see him. I just went and got the papers. Mae filled out the slip, but she's too old to go hauling around in the files. Wait, I'll go ask her."

My little feline friend padded off. Presently she returned.

"Sorry. She says she can't remember who it was."

"But if she tried…"

"She *did* try." The girl gestured toward the room. "Look,

mister, we get a hundred people an hour in here, eight hours a day, six days a week. Who bothers to remember all those faces? Mae's been here twelve years."

"Bully for her," I said. "And thanks, anyway. Now, can I take a look?"

The girl brought me the stack and I took them over to a table. I pulled out a pen and a notebook and went to work. For the next hour I was up to my neck in murder.

The newspapers told it their own way—with headlines, with pictures, with feature stories, even with editorials. But gradually I got the facts sifted until I could tell it in my own way, to myself.

Dick Ryan was a pretty boy. He had black, curly hair and clear blue eyes and stood six feet two in lounging pajamas. He had a great following among the youth of America; in the 6-to-12-year-old group with the boys, and the 16-to-36-year-old group with the girls. The boys thought he looked good on a horse. What the girls thought I really couldn't say. (I *could*, but there are limits).

Ryan had played in oaters for about five years before his death, working for two or three studios before he tied up with Abe Kolmar at Apex and starred in the *Lucky Larry* series. Although he didn't sing, play the guitar or twirl a baton, his pictures were highly successful; particularly in the rural areas, where his protrusions of jaw and biceps were equated with manly cleancut heroism. He did not smoke, drink or indulge in amorous advances on the screen.

But when the cameras stopped grinding on the evening of April 2nd, Dick Ryan held a little party in his private trailer. He was on location at Abe Kolmar's ranch out in the San Fernando Valley, and he might easily have chosen to drive into town or stay at Kolmar's place. But Ryan preferred his trailer, a handsome, custom-built job that accompanied him whenever he was shooting away from the studio. It had a built-in bar and a number of other conveniences which made it ideal for parties.

This particular party started out in a small way, as a

matter of fact with just Ryan and a bottle. But shortly after the dinner hour at the Kolmar ranch, the celebration grew. Polly Foster came in. This wasn't unusual, because Polly Foster played opposite Dick Ryan on (and some said *off*) the screen. Tom Trent, who did the villain in the series, accompanied her. Both of them were staying at Kolmar's place overnight, as were most of the principals in the cast.

According to their story, Ryan was already high when they arrived. He was cursing Joe Dean, and that wasn't unusual either. Dean was his stooge, valet, chauffeur, masseur, and one-man audience. At the moment, Dean was driving Abe Kolmar into town for a preview. The visitors gathered that Ryan did not approve of this.

They partook of their host's hospitality nonetheless, endured his curses, and waited for Dean's return. He came back about nine, accompanied by Estrellita Juarez, a minor player in the film.

What happened during the next two hours came in four separate versions: Polly Foster's story, Trent's account, and the evidence of Joe Dean and Miss Juarez. Put them all together and it spelled something like this.

Ryan took a drink. Then he fired Joe Dean. Ryan took another drink. Then he called Estrellita Juarez a dirty greaser and told her to get the hell out of there. Ryan took another drink. He punched Tom Trent on the jaw. Ryan took another drink. He pitched Polly Foster bodily from the trailer and told her to take her goddam blubbering someplace else because he was expecting company.

Joe Dean said he left right away and he didn't see any muggles being smoked. Estrellita Juarez said she left right away and she didn't see any muggles being smoked. Tom Trent said he left right away and he didn't see any muggles being smoked. Polly Foster said—

Anyway, they all left. None of them knew about marijuana. None of them came back. Dean took his car and drove Estrellita to a motel. Trent went home and let his doctor work on his black eye. Polly Foster drove back to town herself.

And that's all there was to it. Employees on the ranch noted that Ryan's trailer lights were out by eleven. Nobody woke up during the middle of the night to see or hear anything.

But in the morning, Ryan was dead. Dead as a doornail, if you can picture a six foot two doornail with one bullet in its head and another in its hips.

That's the way it went, according to the newspaper reports of the testimony at the inquest. But there was a little bit more to it.

The reefer butts, for instance. There were four or five of them, lying on the floor and in the ashtrays. Homicide found them right away, and it seemed odd none of the guests knew anything about the matter.

Then there was the little business of Joe Dean getting fired. Did he or did he not threaten his employer? Nobody seemed to recall that he did, but the police wondered vaguely, inasmuch as their records disclosed that Joe Dean had once been a naughty boy back in Detroit. Some years ago he'd enjoyed a reputation as a strong-arm artist, and the authorities thought he might not have taken his dismissal so lightly.

And this incident of Ryan punching Tom Trent on the jaw. That was all right, as far as it went, but how could a mere punch on the jaw produce a black eye, plus a broken chair, two broken glasses, and a ripped shirt? The police wondered, not quite so vaguely, if there hadn't been a bit more of a fight than was first mentioned. And if Tom Trent couldn't have left the trailer in a rather unpleasant mood.

They also speculated on just how Miss Juarez might have reacted to being called a dirty greaser (the more so because dirty greasers are notoriously hot-tempered) and how Polly Foster felt about being tossed out of the trailer.

But nobody could help them there, it seems. Everybody stuck to the story, everybody had an alibi, everybody suggested hopefully that since Ryan said he was "expecting somebody later" he was, *ergo*, murdered by "somebody later."

"Somebody later" smoked the reefers, of course. "Somebody later" smashed the furniture. It all added up. Added up to the "death at the hands of a person or persons unknown" verdict which was reluctantly delivered and even more reluctantly received.

There the matter rested. But not for long. The follow-up stories began to appear: stories about Ryan and his previous escapades; stories about the reefer parties he'd held with other well-known cinematic celebrities, where everybody got stark, staring stoned.

A couple of columnists sniffed pay dirt and began to excavate for golden nuggets of gossip. They came up with a series of *exposés* on life in the film capital. Up in the editorial department they decided to lay off Russia for a day and consider the matter of Hollywood hi-jinks, from Arbuckle to Zukor (though what they had on Zukor nobody could possibly imagine).

And the authorities, chasing down lead after lead, let a few hints slip about a narcotics ring. That was enough. The press took up the "Ryan murder scandal" all over the nation.

Took it up, and then dropped it with a dull thud.

Seven full columns in three papers on April 24th. Not a line on April 25th. Or thereafter. Three full weeks of sound and fury, and then the nothingness. *Dig* that crazy, mixed-up case! Yes, *dig!* And I dug, but there was nothing more to read. Ryan was cool. Ryan was gone.

And, a few minutes after I satisfied myself about the newspapers, so was I. I stopped in at Clifton's for a bite to eat and a chance to chew over what I'd learned. There was no time at present to digest it.

Still indulging in mental mastication, I stopped back at the office long enough to check the mail. Two letters. Tilden took a story and Browne bounced one. I made a note to call my clients later. Right now I had a thousand dollars' retainer on a case and ten thousand riding. Right now I'd better go to the bank and make a deposit before two o'clock closing. Right now—

The phone rang.

I picked it up. "Hello?"

"Clayburn?" I didn't recognize the voice, but it recognized me.

"Yes. What can I do for you?"

"You can lay off."

"What's that?"

"Lay off, Clayburn. Lay off the Ryan case."

"Who is this?"

"A friend, Clayburn. But you'd better lay off if you want to keep me friendly."

"But—"

He hung up.

I held the phone in my hand for a moment, then dropped it in its cradle.

There it was. This morning I'd been feeling sorry for myself. I thought I didn't have a friend in the world. But I'd been wrong.

I had a friend, after all. A friend who seemed to have my best interests at heart. Somebody who would rather see me dead than get into trouble.

It was something to think about. I thought about it all the way downtown. And by the time I walked into Al Thompson's office, my mind was made up.

Chapter Three

Al Thompson used to be on the Vice Squad until he lost his hair. In his younger days he looked a good deal like Stewart Granger and specialized in jobs around Pershing Square. When he started to get bald, they transferred him to Homicide, and he's been there ever since.

I once asked him how he liked the change. "Just fine," he told me. "You meet a much better class of people in Homicide."

If I remember rightly, I quoted the remark in one of the true-detective articles I worked on with a client. That's how I met Thompson originally: I went to him for material. Since that time I'd got into the habit of calling on him whenever I needed help along the article line.

And now...

Thompson was sitting at his desk, going over some post office pinups when I came in. He looked up and nodded, thus acknowledging my presence and indicating that I should sit down. I took a chair and waited. After a minute or so he pushed the stack of pictures aside.

"Hi, Clayburn. What can I do for you? Another yarn?"

I smiled. I didn't really want to smile. I didn't really want him to think it was another yarn. But that was the way to play it.

"That's right. I was thinking of doing a piece on the Ryan murder."

"Dick Ryan?"

"Seems like a good idea," I told him. "Unsolved mystery angle."

"But we're still working on it." Thompson hesitated. "A story like that doesn't do the Department any good."

"Don't worry, I'm not going to use the police-are-baffled approach," I assured him. "That's why I came to you. I wanted to check my facts and clear them, seeing as you were on the case."

Thompson sat back. "You know the regulations. I'm not supposed to talk. And I haven't got the authority to okay anything. Maybe if you went in and saw Captain—"

"Never mind." I lit a cigarette. "This visit is off the record. Just thought you'd be interested."

"All right. What've you got?"

I recited what I'd learned from reading the newspapers. He listened shifting around in his chair and staring up at the ceiling. When I finished he grunted and said, "Is that all?"

"Sure. That's all the papers carried. Why? Is there more?"

Thompson smiled, and despite the bald head I could see why he'd been the fair-haired boy of the Vice Squad. "You hope there is, don't you? That's why you came to me now, right?"

"Well…" I paused. "Since this is all off the record…"

"Just how long do you think it would stay off the record if you broke a story containing facts known only to this office? They'd come running in here for my scalp."

"Little late for that," I said. "Come on, give a guy a break. We've worked together before."

"Not on something like this."

"Well, can't you tell me anything?"

Thompson hesitated. "Let's see, there's a few things you missed in the papers which might not sound out of line. That gun, for instance. It was a .38 revolver. The same gun Ryan used in the picture. Ordinarily it was loaded with blanks, but that afternoon Ryan had loaned it to Trent. He was doing a little target practice out there on the ranch, and that's why it had real bullets in it. He claims he was called to the set in the middle of his shooting—just after reloading— and gave the gun back to Ryan, forgetting to tell him it was loaded. Anyway, Ryan must have taken it to his trailer and left it there without examining it. So right there you have an interesting question. Did the killer know the loaded gun was there, or did he just happen to come on it by accident? In other words, was the murder premeditated?"

I made a note, just for effect. "What about fingerprints?"

"There weren't any. Not on the gun. Whoever did the job saw to that. Lots of other prints around, all over. Polly Foster's, and Trent's and Joe Dean's, Estrellita Juarez, even Kolmar himself. But nothing that helps us establish anything."

I made another note. "About the killing," I said. "The paper said all six shots were fired. One in the head, the rest in the hips."

Thompson shook his head. "I can tell you that much, too, I suppose. The newspapers had to say hips. On account of the family audience. But the murderer didn't shoot Ryan in the hips, Clayburn. Between them, that's where."

"You mean?"

"Jealous husband, boyfriend, lover? Homicidal maniac, sex pervert? We've thought about all the angles."

"How about someone who'd flipped? Loaded on reefers or—"

"The reefer angle's out."

"But they found those butts. And the whole things points to some kind of narcotics tie-up."

"I don't know anything about that."

"Don't know or won't tell?"

"Suit yourself. Either way, I got nothing to say about the reefer situation. Ryan didn't go in for that sort of thing. He got his kicks in a different way."

"And the alibis all hold up? Dean, Juarez, Foster, Kolmar, Trent?"

"If they didn't, we'd have made an arrest."

"Why haven't you made any since then?"

"We're still working on the case."

"There hasn't been a line in the papers. Did the drug angle scare you off?"

Thompson stood up. "Sorry, that's all I know. If you want to talk to the captain, now, maybe—"

"Never mind." I rose. "I guess I've got enough for my story. But I hate to leave it hanging in the air like this. I hate to let the readers think that maybe everything isn't exactly on the up-and-up."

The detective put a fatherly hand on my shoulder, and squeezed it in a most unfatherly way. "You write anything like that and I'll kick your teeth down your throat," he muttered. The grip relaxed. "No, I didn't mean it. Forget it. It's a free country. Write what you please. But I can't tell you any more. Except one thing." He paused.

"What's that?"

"If I were you, I wouldn't write the story. I wouldn't write anything at all. I'd just forget it."

"Forget it?"

"If it's a yarn you're after, I can give you a dozen better ones. Complete with solutions and pictures of the guilty parties. How about a nice, juicy torso murder? We got one where the guy burned this dame's arms and legs off with a blowtorch, and then he got to work on her head with—"

"You really don't want me to write this, eh?"

"I really don't."

"And you can't give me a good reason?"

"That's it." Thompson walked me over to the door. "But you're a smart guy, Clayburn. You're a writer, you've got an imagination. Maybe you can dream up a reason. Like say, if there was something like a narcotics ring mixed up in the case. And they didn't want anyone nosing around, trying to uncover clues that could lead to them or to their very important customers. Figure a reason like that, if you like. And then, like a smart guy, forget the whole thing. Including the fact that you talked to me."

"I'll think about it," I said.

"You do that."

"Thanks for the help. And the advice."

"It's all right. You know I'm always glad to do what I can. But…think it over."

I thought it over all the way back to the office. Then I called Harry Bannock.

"Hello. Bannock here." He must have picked that up from some English movie.

"Mark Clayburn. When can I see you?"

"Business?"

"Yes. But I'd rather not talk over the phone."

"Right." He hesitated. "You free tonight? How about coming out to the house for dinner? I'll call Daisy. Good. Make it seven, then. See you."

I made it seven.

Bannock had a big layout in the foothills, not far from Laurel Canyon. I leaned on the doorbell and watched the sunset over the hills. The sky was a deep orange.

Her hair was a deep orange, too. She wore it long, over bare shoulders, and it contrasted with the creamy tint of her skin. The chartreuse garment she wore was what is generally called a hostess gown. Seeing it on her, I could easily understand why.

"Mr. Clayburn?" She smiled. "I'm Daisy Bannock. Come right in. Harry said we'd be expecting you. He phoned just a few minutes ago to say he'd be a little late."

I followed her perfume down the hall, into the parlor.

"Fix you a drink?"

"Thanks." I nodded. She walked over to the bar in the alcove.

"What'll it be?"

"Oh, I don't care. Whatever you prefer."

"I don't indulge." She shook the orange curl from her forehead. "But you needn't worry, I'm supposed to be a very capable bartender."

"In that case, make it a Manhattan. No—an Orange Blossom." Why I wanted an Orange Blossom I didn't know. Until I looked at her again. Then I knew.

Her fingers flew in deft deliberation. From time to time she paused and shook that single unruly curl back into place. Harry's wife. And he was delayed at the office. If I had a wife like that, I wouldn't be delayed. Maybe I wouldn't even go to the office at all.

"Here you are."

"Thanks." Yes, thanks for the drink, and thanks for letting your fingers accidentally (was it accidentally?) touch mine. I sat down on the sofa. She took a chair, and through the window the sun set fire to her hair.

"So you're Mark Clayburn. Harry's told me quite a lot about you."

"Is that so? Well, he never told me anything about you. Not that I blame him."

She laughed. "Harry never mixes business with his domestic affairs."

"Then I'm sorry I butted in like this. Because I'm here on a sort of a business matter."

"Yes, I know."

"You do?"

"Of course. Harry told me." She leaned forward. I offered her a cigarette. "No, thanks. I'm afraid I don't smoke, either. But you go ahead." I lit my cigarette and she continued. "The poor guy's so worried he doesn't know what to do. And I can understand how he feels. All that money tied up, and just on account of a no-good heel like Ryan." She shook her head. "Even when he's dead he makes trouble for Harry."

"Trouble? Harry never told me he had any dealings with Ryan before."

"He wouldn't. Harry isn't the type to talk about it. But he used to be Ryan's agent. When he came out here, from New York."

"When was that?"

"About seven years ago. I was working in Harry's office then. He'd just gotten started in the business and didn't handle any big names. When he saw Ryan he thought the guy had possibilities, and he knocked himself out trying to get a break for him.

"Ryan must have hung around for a couple of months before he got his first assignment. Harry even staked him until the opening came along and he got his first billing."

"What kind of a guy was Ryan in those days?" I asked.

She shrugged. "Nice kid. You know the type. Fresh out of dramatic school, a few bits in New York, some radio work. Thought he was all ready to set the world on fire out here. But Harry wised him up. Made him take riding lessons, fencing, dancing. Taught him how to handle a gun. Harry was the one who groomed him for westerns. Said he'd have a better chance there than in juvenile stuff for the Bs."

"What did you think?"

"Well…" She shrugged again. "I didn't like the setup. Harry and I weren't married yet; we were waiting until he got himself set with the agency, had the business going good. And here he was shelling out dough to keep Ryan eating, to pay for his lessons. Of course, Harry expected he'd get it all back, and then some, if Ryan clicked. But I didn't feel so sure about it."

"Why?"

"Oh, I don't know. Call it a hunch. I told Harry he couldn't trust him, asked him to stop subsidizing Ryan. We almost had a quarrel over it, once."

I finished my drink. "You say you had a hunch about Ryan. Why? What kind of hunch?"

Daisy giggled. "How can you explain a hunch? You've heard of feminine intuition, haven't you?"

"I've heard of it, but I've never believed in it," I told her. I leaned forward. "Could it have had anything to do with women? Was Ryan a chaser in those days?"

Daisy giggled again. "I never saw him go for a girl under twelve, and I never saw him get interested in a woman over fifty. But anything in between—oh, brother!"

I smiled at her. "Then I take it he also made a pass at you?"

She wasn't giggling now. Two vertical lines formed in her forehead above her eyebrows. "He tried. But Harry put a stop to that. That's when they had their big fight. Ryan walked out. Walked out cold, just like that. We never saw him again. About two months later we heard he got a role in one of Kolmar's horse operas. And he was on his way."

"You haven't seen him since?"

"No. And Harry never got his money back. Oh, it was only a few hundred, and it doesn't matter. But the louse never came near us after he made good. He hooked up with another agency. And last year he cut Harry dead at the Academy Award banquet."

She stood up. "Fix you an encore?" she asked.

"Wait a minute." I stood up, too. "Does Harry hate Ryan? Or did he hate him when he was alive?"

"He didn't like him, if that's what you mean."

"That's not what I mean. There's a difference between not liking a guy and hating him." I was close enough to her to smell her perfume. "If I were Harry and I took this kid on, staked him, trained him for a career, and then had him walk out on me, I'd dislike him. And if he never paid me back, gave me the freeze after he became successful, I might hate him a little." The lines in her forehead, between her eyebrows, came back now. I stared at them as I continued. "But if I was Harry and I found out that Ryan was making a pass at you, I'd hate him a lot. I might even hate him enough to—"

She raised her head and now I was staring straight into her eyes. "You're crazy," she said. "Harry didn't kill Ryan. He wouldn't wait almost seven years. Besides, Ryan never got to first base with me. And what kind of sense would that make, putting you on the case, if he did?"

"No sense at all," I answered. "But you can't be too careful."

"How right you are," Daisy murmured. "And if you'd only thought of that, you might have bothered to check up on what Harry was doing the night of the murder. He was in

the Mark Hopkins at San Francisco, at a conference with
some of the people from Twentieth Century. And there are a
dozen witnesses to testify he never left the hotel all night."

"Where were you?" I asked.

"You really *are* a suspicious type, aren't you?" The giggle
came back again. "Just for punishment, I ought to make you
look up the record yourself. But if you must know, I was at
Dr. Levinson's Clinic. I checked in at dinnertime. I was
under observation that night and the next day. They almost
yanked my appendix out. There are witnesses for that, too."

"All right," I said. "Sorry I got so nosey. I'll take that
drink, now."

She crossed the room, then halted.

"Harry's home!"

I heard the door slam, listened for the footsteps. Bannock
stood in the doorway. Daisy ran over and put her arms
around him. He stood there. She said, "Darling, we've missed
you." He stood there. She kissed him. He stood there.

Daisy stepped back. "Honey, what's the matter?"

"Nothing," he said. "But just before I left the office, I got
a phone call. Somebody whose voice I never heard before.
He told me that if I didn't lay off the Ryan case, he'd kill
me."

Chapter Four

The maid announced dinner. She served roast duck with wild rice, and it looked good enough to eat. None of us ate very much, though. We just sat there and stared at the table like one big happy family. Sat there and talked about the phone calls—the one Harry got and the one I got.

For the third time Bannock said, "But *who?*"

"Think," I suggested. "All you have to do is remember everyone you talked to about this business. Who overheard you mention you were coming to see me? Who knew you were interested in finding out about the murder?"

"I am thinking." Bannock sighed. "There's the three of us. Your friend Al Thompson, in Homicide."

"You can check him off," I told Bannock. "He's not the type."

"But he asked you to quit the case."

"Of course he did. Only he didn't know I was after anything more than a story. The question is, who does?"

"Sarah." Daisy gestured toward the kitchen. "She heard us talking this morning, before Harry went to the office."

"Really, now, Sarah's not the type, either." Bannock grinned.

"What about the office, then? You tell anyone there what you planned?"

"Not a soul."

"Did your girl listen when I called this afternoon?"

"Perhaps. But you didn't say anything that would give her a clue. Besides, we both heard a man's voice. The same man, we must assume."

"Maybe he's psychic." Daisy smiled, then frowned. "I'm sorry. This is nothing to joke about."

I looked at Bannock. "Do you know Tom Trent's voice over the phone?"

"Yes. I'd thought of that. It wasn't Trent."

"What about Joe Dean?"

"Never met him. Do you think perhaps—?"

"I don't think anything perhaps." I sat back. "We've got three possible courses of action, as I see it. First, we can call the police and tell them we've been threatened. And why."

"That's out." Bannock shook his head. "I don't want anyone to know this. If the news got out, it would queer my deal with See-More for sure."

"Our second alternative," I continued, "is to take these threats seriously and drop the investigation."

"Drop a hundred and ninety-five grand, you mean? Not me, sweetheart."

"But suppose somebody means business with these threats?" Bannock scowled. "I'm not chicken. Are you?"

I pulled at my mustache. "No."

"Well, *I* am!" Daisy put her arm on Bannock's shoulder. "I don't like this, Harry. You know I was angry when I found out you'd bought those films and tied all our money up. I said it was a big risk, and that's how it worked out. But risking money's one thing, and risking your life is another."

"Don't get panicky," Bannock said, "Just because some lunatic makes a crazy threat—"

"Lunatic?" Daisy's face was pale. "Ryan was murdered. Whoever killed him is still at large. Maybe he's just crazy enough to kill you, too."

"But the money—"

"I'd rather see you lose the money than your life. Please, Harry, lay off, for my sake."

"For your sake." Bannock nodded. "Listen, Daisy. It's you I'm thinking about. What do you think I've worked for all these years, built up this business from a two-bit hole-in-the-wall? So that you'd have something. And I made the grade. Now everything I own is tied up in this deal. I've got to go through with it."

"We could get along," Daisy said. "You've got your clients, there's money coming in."

"I'm not going to let an anonymous phone call trick me out of the biggest deal I ever made," Bannock declared. "Don't worry, we'll be careful." He cocked his head at me. "That's why we've got Mark here."

I smiled at him. "Which brings us to our third alternative," I said. "We can go through with our plans. As carefully as possible and as quickly as possible."

"Right." Bannock pushed his chair back from the table. "We've got to work fast. I take it you have some idea of where you want to begin?"

I nodded. "Best thing to do is take each suspect in turn," I told him. "And I'm going to start with Ryan's girlfriend, Miss Polly Foster. Can you get me lined up with a studio pass for tomorrow?"

"Now you're talking. Sure, I'll fix it for you." He led us into the other room, stepped over to the bar. "What'll it be?"

"What are you drinking?"

"Straight rye."

"Make mine the same."

"And me." Daisy smiled at him, then at me.

"I thought you didn't drink," I said.

"I don't, as a rule." The smile never left her face. "But right now I could use one. I'm always a little bit uncomfortable when I'm around corpses."

"Daisy, please!" Bannock sighed.

"I can't help it." She went to him and put her arms around his neck. "Harry, I'm scared. There's something wrong with this whole thing, I know it. It isn't just a murder, there's more to it than that: something we don't know; something we aren't supposed to find out. You talked about a lunatic. Maybe it's that, maybe worse."

"What do you mean, worse?"

She walked around him, found a bottle and a glass, and poured herself a stiff hooker. "Hollywood," she said. I watched her neck go back as she lifted the glass and downed the drink.

"What kind of a remark is that?"

"You ought to know," Daisy answered. "You've been out here long enough to have heard the stories. Thirty years ago a director named Taylor was murdered. Nobody ever found out who did it or why. But you've heard rumors, haven't you? About big names who hushed things up with other murders?"

Her voice lowered. "Didn't you ever hear the rumor about Tom Ince, the producer? They said he died suddenly of poison, but there's another story, too. About a murder, and about a big fix, because of the big names involved. And there are other cases—plenty of them.

"Harry, listen to me. Whoever killed Ryan *must* be crazy. You heard what Mark told us, what the detective said about *how* Ryan was killed. Anybody who'd do that wouldn't be afraid to strike again, if necessary. And suppose there are others involved, who want him to strike? Please!"

Bannock shook his head.

Daisy stared for a moment, then returned to the bar and poured herself another drink.

I walked over and waited as Bannock filled our glasses. "About Polly Foster," he said. "You can tell her you're there for an interview. Figure out some kind of a story."

"Right," I answered. "I'll handle it."

We raised our glasses. "Here's luck," Bannock said.

"Luck," I echoed.

Daisy stared at both of us over the rim of her glass. "Don't forget," she whispered. "There are two kinds of luck. Good…and bad."

She drank quickly and left the room. "I'm going to bed," she told Bannock. In a few moments we heard the sound of a radio drift down from upstairs.

"Sorry," Bannock said. "It's her nerves." He reached for the bottle, chuckling a little. "Can't say that I blame her, at that. I feel a little edgy myself." He looked at me. "Have another?"

"No, thanks. I'll be running along. Got a big day tomorrow. Shall I stop by your office for the pass?"

"Right. If I'm not there, Harriet will give it to you."

He walked me to the door. "Look, Mark, I've been thinking it over. Maybe Daisy's right. This could turn out to be dangerous."

"Change your mind?"

He stood in the doorway and looked out at the night sky. "No. I'm going ahead with it because I have to. The business is in hock and it's not as easy as she thinks. Didn't want to worry her, but if I can't clear up this murder and make my TV sale, it's curtains for me. I've got to take the risk, no matter who threatens me."

"I understand."

"But I'm thinking about you. No sense getting yourself killed over a thing like this."

"Don't worry about me." I said "I'm going through with it."

"Good boy."

"See you tomorrow." I started down the walk. "And don't worry, we aren't ready for Forest Lawn yet." I smiled and headed for the car.

Driving away, in darkness, the smile slipped off my face. It hadn't been glued on very well in the first place. Because I really *was* scared.

Daisy's notion made sense to me. I remembered all those stories about unsolved killings and mysterious suicides and sudden deaths. Everybody who has anything to do with the industry hears a dozen of them. I could understand why, too. If you're mixed up in a billion dollar business and your success or failure depends on publicity, you'll take steps to see that the publicity is good. You won't hesitate to frame and fix in order to protect your good name or the good name of your product.

Not that Hollywood is any different than any other city, or the motion pictures different than any other industry. Detroit has its scandals and its unsolved murders, too. The automotive business holds secrets and so does steel and the railroads and the mines. You can't indict the automobile industry as a whole because of a few black marks. And you can't indict Hollywood because of the few exceptions.

On the other hand, the exceptions do exist; the black marks crop up from time to time. Ugly black marks, like the smudging X where the body is found. And if somebody threatens to rub you out, make another X, it's worth thinking about.

I thought about it a lot during the long drive back across town. Suppose Daisy was right, and a lunatic *had* killed Ryan? Thompson spoke about the possibility of a pervert or a sex fiend at work. Such a man wouldn't hesitate a moment. He'd be ready to kill again, and again if necessary. And he'd be clever. Clever enough to find out (he *had* found out, somehow, what we were planning) and clever enough to act.

Wilshire was welcome, with its bright lights. I headed east, through MacArthur Park, cutting off a way, then back and down to Columbia. My apartment was around the corner, on Ingraham. Darker, there. I parked in the shadows, then hurried across the street towards the safety and security of the well-lighted lobby.

I climbed the two flights, reaching for my key as I got to the second landing. At the same time I couldn't keep my hand away from my coat pocket. It wanted to feel the gun nestling there.

I opened the door. The apartment was dark, and I switched on the light. Everything was in order. I stepped inside, but when it came to closing the door behind me, my hand wasn't having any.

It wouldn't cooperate. It insisted on leaving the door open as I stepped across the room to peer into the kitchen and the bath. Nobody there, of course. And nobody in the closet, when I went to hang up my coat.

"Silly," I told my hand. And took it over to the door again. This time, reluctantly, it reached down and closed the door for me.

I turned. And my hand reached out and pointed. I followed it over to the armchair, next to the table. It brushed the top of the table and scooped up the little white card resting against the ashtray. The little white card I'd never seen before, the little white card I'd never propped there. But my hand held it up so that I could read the brief message scrawled with a common ballpoint pen.

"LAY OFF!"

That's all the card told me.

I wasn't frightened. My hand was frightened, though, because it trembled.

Then I looked down in the ashtray and I saw the butt. The coarse, crumpled butt of a hand-rolled cigarette. My fingers closed around it, and even before I brought it to my nostrils I could smell the harshly sweet scent of marijuana.

He'd been here. He'd been sitting in my chair, in my apartment, smoking weed. He'd given me another warning, and if I didn't take it, he might come back. Only this time he wouldn't bother to warn me. You get high on weed. It was a crazy thing to risk leaving a butt like this. But then, he could be a maniac.

All at once my hand stopped trembling. It dropped the butt back in the ashtray, picked up the card again, and shredded it to bits between my fingers.

Maybe I was up against a lunatic. Maybe I was up against somebody bigger—somebody who didn't want his secrets revealed. Maybe I was just a little guy, like Bannock said, and a scared little guy at that.

But nobody, sane or insane, big or small, was going to push me around. I needed that eleven grand as badly as Bannock needed his big stake. Besides, I had a prejudice against murderers. It was so easy for me to put myself in the victim's place.

And that, of course, was exactly what I was doing...

Chapter Five

I don't like the smell of reefer butts.

I thought the air might be purer at a hotel, so the next morning I moved. I didn't give up the apartment; just packed two suitcases and checked in at a room in the smallest and cheapest hostelry across the Park.

Then, just to keep the smell out of my office, I went to a hardware store and bought a new lock for the door.

By the time I'd finished changing the lock and holding a treasure hunt with the mail, looking for checks, it was close to noon.

I lunched, then drove out to Harry's office to pick up my studio pass.

He was out, but his girl had news for me.

"Mr. Clayburn, you're here about a pass, aren't you?"

I nodded.

"Well, Mr. Bannock called this morning. They're doing retakes on Miss Foster's scenes, and they're behind schedule, so the set is closed."

"I see."

"But he said for me to tell you he reserved a table at Chasen's for you and Miss Foster tonight. Eight o'clock."

"Thanks. And thank Mr. Bannock for me, will you?"

The girl smiled. "Gee, Mr. Clayburn, you're an interviewer, aren't you? Mr. Bannock says you see all the big stars. How does it feel to be in your line of work?"

"Feels good," I said. "As I was saying to Marilyn Monroe last night, though, there are times when I get so embarrassed because Jane Russell keeps telling me things Ava Gardner shouldn't know."

"Are you kidding?"

"Could be." I leaned over the desk. "Funny thing," I said. "Here you are, right on the inside, seeing Bannock's clients. And you're still movie-struck. I've never been able to figure that one out. All the smart little chicks in Hollywood going for the phony glamor. Suppose you'd like to get in the movies yourself?"

"Would I?" Her eyes widened. "Why, I'd give anything to land a job." Then she grinned. "Come to think of it, I *did*, about two years ago. But I never got the job."

"You're lucky," I told her. "This is steadier work."

"I'd still trade places with you any day," she sighed. "Imagine, interviewing Polly Foster at Chasen's."

"Which reminds me," I said. "I've got a lot of time to fill until eight o'clock. We interviewers have to keep busy. Does Harry still run a spot-check on current assignments?"

"Yes. Why?"

"Be a good girl and find out if Tom Trent's listed for anything today."

"I'll ask Velma."

She buzzed Velma and waited for a reply.

"No, Mr. Clayburn, Trent isn't down on today's schedule."

"Good."

"Are you going to interview him, too?"

"Why not?" I said. "It's a free country. Thanks for the help. If you want, I'll bring you Trent's autograph. I'm not sure if he knows how to write, but they say his horse is very intelligent."

"Could you...could you get Polly Foster's autograph for me?"

I shrugged. "I'll try. See you."

Then I went away, wondering about this whole whacky business of hero worship. Even here in Hollywood, where you'd think they'd know better, the crowds still jam the prevues, still mob celebrities, scramble for buttons and souvenirs. Crazy. Crazy, but profitable.

That's what made it important. It was profitable to give people what they wanted. If they wanted heroes and heroines, Hollywood must provide them. And that's why I was on this job. I had to take the battered, bullet-riddled body of Dick Ryan and prop it up on a pedestal again.

And the first step was to see Tom Trent.

Wrong. The first step was to stop at a drugstore and hunt up his address. I might have guessed he'd live out in the Valley.

But I had time to spare. I took the scenic route and pulled up in front of his place around three.

It hardly surprised me to find that Tom Trent lived in a regulation, sure-enough ranch-house, complete with true Western air-conditioning, a trusty station wagon, and an ol' swimmin' hole lined with turquoise tile and surrounded by umbrella tables at which a quick-shootin', redblooded hombre could set hisself down and have a shot of fire-water—bonded, of course.

I pulled into the driveway but didn't bother to ring the bell, because I could see little ol' rough-and-ready, two-fisted Tom Trent out yonder at one of the tables. I went thataway.

I'd recognized Trent's face, of course, but he was the kind who doesn't depend on that alone. As I got closer I noted the white terrycloth robe thrown over the back of the chair so as to display the *TT* monogram in gold. A few steps nearer and I could see the same *TT* on his towel, and reproduced on his trunks. When I reached the table he raised his left hand in salutation, and I saw the silver identification bracelet dangling from the wrist. Three guesses as to what was engraved on it.

For some reason or other, he hadn't bothered to tattoo his initials across his chest, though they *may* have been elsewhere, hidden by the trunks.

Trent was watching a white bathing-cap bobbing in the pool. The cap contained a brachycephalic head which now popped over the edge of the pool as I approached. The face stared up at me. Trent turned and saw me coming.

"Yeah?" he said.

"Hi. I'm Mark Clayburn, Mr. Trent. I'd like a few minutes of your time for an interview."

"Interview? I didn't get any word on an interview." He glanced over at the pool. "Hey, did the studio call about any interviews this morning?"

The face moved from left to right.

"Sorry," Trent said. "You know the rules. No story without a clearance from the front office."

"I really should have checked first," I told him. "I didn't mean to barge in on you like this. But I happened to be in the neighborhood."

"Who you with?"

I shrugged. "Freelance. But I've got a sort of roving assignment for features from *Photoplay*. You know, profile stuff, with a picture spread."

"You can get anything you want from Higgins, in Publicity," Trent informed me. "If you get together with him, he'll set up the whole deal."

I smiled. "I understand that, Mr. Trent. But what I had in mind was something a little different."

The big man scratched himself under the arm. "That so? What's the angle?"

"Well, it's rather confidential." I shot a look at the face hanging over the pool. Trent followed my gaze.

"Hey," he called. "Swim underwater for a while, will you?"

The face disappeared.

"Sit down and help yourself. What were you saying about confidential, now?"

I sat down, ignored the bottle and glasses, and concentrated on smiling and keeping my voice soft. "Well, it's like this. I'm trying to work up a series of interviews with dead stars."

"Huh?"

"Novelty idea. For instance, I'm going to contact the Barrymores about a yarn on John. You know, intimate details, little bits of personal reminiscence, things like that. I'd like to do one on Beery and maybe Dix. Get the dope and then write it up in question-and-answer form, in the first person, just as if they were talking."

"Sounds screwy if you ask me." Trent scowled. "Besides, I ain't dead." He poured himself another shot.

"Of course not. But you happen to have been associated with a star who died recently. I thought you might have some interesting material I could use."

He'd started to lift his drink, but put it down again now. The sun sparkled on the initials cut into the side of the tumbler.

"Who you talking about?"

"Dick Ryan," I said.

Trent looked at me. Then he raised the glass, emptied it and lowered it to the table again, all in a single continuous motion. He stared at me again before he spoke. "Never heard of him."

"What's that? I'm talking about *Lucky Larry*."

"Never heard of him, either."

"But you played in a whole series together. You were with him the night he died."

Trent stood up. "I told you," he said. "I never heard of Dick Ryan. End of story."

"Well, if that's the way you want to be."

He wasn't letting me finish my sentences. "That's the way it is, Clayburn. And let me give you a tip for what it's worth to you: you never heard of Dick Ryan, either. And you don't want to write a yarn about him, or ask anyone else."

"Mind if I ask why?"

Trent scowled. "How'd you lose the eye?" he asked. "Poking it in other people's keyholes?" He was a big man, and he had a big hand. It felt like a ton, resting on my shoulder.

"What's wrong with asking?" I murmured. "Who knows, maybe I can find a few interesting angles. Since you didn't know this Dick Ryan, you might be surprised to learn that he was murdered." I paused. "Then again, you might not."

Trent's hand began to clamp down. I reached up and

batted it off. He made a sound in his chest. "Why, you!"

There was the sound of splashing from the pool. Both of us turned and saw the face beneath the bathing cap bob up. The head shook again, a slow, grave movement.

"All right." His voice shook with the effort at control. "I'm giving you a break. I'm leaving you the other eye, if you get out of here right now. But get this, Clayburn. You aren't doing any story on Dick Ryan. You're not asking anyone else about him, either. He's dead. Let him stay that way. You're alive. And if you want to stay that way—"

The hand gave me a shove. I moved back.

"Thank you for the hospitality and the advice," I said. "You've been most gracious." I gestured toward the pool. "Now I'll leave you to your goldfish."

Trent made a suggestion which I didn't care to follow, due to certain physical limitations that rendered it impossible.

I walked away, and he stared after me. So did the face in the pool.

Then I climbed into the car and drove back to town.

The lights were coming on, twinkling in Glendale, flickering over Forest Lawn, sparkling along San Fernando Road. Los Angeles, that gaudy old whore of a city, was putting on her jewels for a big night.

It was time for me to get to the hotel, to put on a few jewels of my own. I thought it over and settled for a shave, shower, soft shirt and striped tie. What the Well-Dressed Interviewer Should Wear.

According to me, that is. Tom Trent would probably prefer to see me in a shroud, nothing fancy, of course, but he'd be willing to let me have my initials embroidered on it.

I thought about Trent as I drove over to Chasen's. A very aggressive gentleman, Mr. TT. What had his alibi been? Home with the butler, nursing his black eye; something like that. I wondered if the butler had been in the swimming pool. Somebody was calling signals. Maybe I'd better follow them, because it seemed as if the game was getting rough.

My table was reserved and waiting at Chasen's, but Polly

Foster hadn't arrived. I glanced at my watch. Just eight. Perhaps I had time for a before-dinner drink.

I took it at the bar, and it tasted good. Felt good to be there again, after all this time. Used to spend a lot of evenings here, a long while ago. But of course, none of the crowd at the bar remembered me. Too much time had gone by. Almost a year.

And a year, in Hollywood, is an eternity.

I remembered the old legend about Orpheus and Eurydice. Orpheus went to Hades and got permission to take Eurydice away, on condition that he didn't turn around and look at her during the return trip. But he looked back, and the bargain was cancelled.

Nobody here in Hollywood would ever be guilty of making Orpheus's mistake. Because in Hollywood, no one looks back. What you did, what you were yesterday, doesn't count. Nobody cares if you won the Academy Award last year; the big question is, who's going to win *next* year?

I raised my glass and drank a silent toast to Mr. Orpheus, who'd never get in the Musician's Local out here. I knew just how he felt.

I spotted three or four familiar faces down the bar, including a man named Wilbur Dunton who was still working out at Culver City on the strength of a contract I'd landed for him when he was in my stable.

Nobody looked at me. The freeze was on. Everybody was talking about tomorrow, and I belonged to yesterday. And so did Dick Ryan. Nobody wanted to look at him, either, or talk about what had happened. *De mortuis nil nisi bonum,* if you'll pardon the expression.

I ordered another drink and wondered about Dave Chasen. Did he ever look back, now? Did he remember the days when he played stooge for Joe Cook in all those wonderful shows—*Rain or Shine, Fine and Dandy, Hold Your Horses?* I hoped he did. Somebody should remember old Joe Cook. A great comic. And Chasen had been a great stooge, too.

How long ago was that? Less than twenty years. And now Cook was ill and forgotten, while Chasen was a big man out here on the Coast.

There was a moral somewhere in all this, and I was just looking for it at the bottom of my glass when I happened to see Polly Foster come in.

I'd seen her on the screen several times, of course, and that had been enough to make me look forward to this evening with a certain mild anticipation. Recognizing her now, my anticipation changed immediately from mild to wild. Polly Foster in the flesh was quite something else again. Nor is that "in the flesh" merely a figure of speech. The figure she cut had nothing to do with speech.

White-gold hair over white-gold shoulders; her dress was robin's-egg blue, and where it left off beneath her neck, any resemblance to robins' eggs ended.

She halted just inside the door and looked around for a moment. Heads turned, which wasn't hard for me to under-stand; she'd just turned mine. Several people nodded, and she nodded back. But all the while she was scanning the crowd.

I got off the stool and prepared to walk over. At that moment she spotted me and came into the bar. She walked right up, without any hesitation, and she smiled.

As she stood before me now, I could see that her lips were full, too. Her eyes were something rather special. They were smiling along with her lips, and all for me.

"Hello," she murmured sweetly. "Are you the one-eyed bastard who wants to pump me about Dick Ryan's death?"

Chapter Six

"My dear Miss Foster," I said. "There seems to be—"

"I'm not your dear Miss Foster. And I don't give a damn about what there seems to be. What I want to know is why you're sticking your big fat nose into somebody else's business."

"Tell you about it at dinner," I said. "Come on, our table's ready."

"Do you think I'd actually have dinner with you?"

"Of course." I grinned at her. "You didn't come here just to call me names. You're just dying to find out what I know. So you'll just have to pay the price."

"And that price is having dinner?"

"Half of it."

"What's the other half?"

I winked. "Tell you about it later."

"Well, of all the nerve—"

But she had dinner with me. Steaks, New York cut, and baked Idaho potatoes and one of the special salads. Plus Manhattans. A quick one before we ate and several during the meal.

The drinks helped a lot. Let's give credit where credit is due. She got the first one down fast before she started to go after me.

"I suppose this is Bannock's idea of a joke," she said. "Pulling that interview gag. Wait until I get hold of Costigan tomorrow morning."

"Who's Costigan?"

"Publicity. Bannock set this up with him. I'll tell that cheap flack a thing or two."

"Why? It's not Costigan's fault. How could he know? And Bannock really thought I was after a story."

"The hell he did."

"What other reason would he have?" I asked.

"I don't know. But I intend to find out. And fast."

"Be reasonable," I said. "Bannock was just doing me a favor. He's not involved in this at all."

"Then who is?"

"It's my own idea. I'd like to do a story on the Ryan case."

"That's not what you told Tom Trent."

"Oh, so he's the one who tipped you off."

Polly Foster made a face which might have surprised her fans. "All right, so he called me. And I said I'd find out what this was. So start talking, Mr. Clayburn. A bargain's a bargain."

The steaks arrived with the second round of Manhattans. "I already told you. I want to do a story, for the true-detective magazines."

"Why don't you go to the police?"

"I did that little thing, but they can't seem to tell me what I want to know."

"Which is?"

"Who killed Dick Ryan?"

She put down her fork and picked up her drink. For a moment I thought she was going to throw it at me. Instead, she gulped.

"Level with me," she said. "Are you a cop?"

"No. Just a literary agent. Do a little writing of my own, now and then."

"In other words, all you're interested in is a chance to make some money."

"That's right. I could use a little dough, and this seemed to be an excellent lead."

The big gray eyes narrowed. "So that's it. I'm beginning to get it, now. How much?"

"What do you mean?"

"How much are you asking to lay off?"

I looked at her. Then I put down my knife. I put down my napkin. I stood up.

"Hey, where do you think you're going?"

"Home," I said. "I've been insulted."

Polly Foster looked around hastily, then reached out and grabbed my wrist. "For God's sake, sit down!"

I smiled, but didn't move.

"Come on, everybody's looking."

"And you don't want anyone to see me walk out on you, is that it? Imagine the gossip! 'Who was the unknown escort who staged a public walkout on glamorous Polly Foster the other night at—' "

"Sit *down!*"

"Say you're sorry."

"I'm sorry, damn you!"

"There's a sweet girl." I sat down again. "But don't ever accuse me of anything like that again. Poor but proud, that's me. I'm no blackmailer."

"Sorry."

"I understand. Easy to make a mistake. The woods are full of them out here. Come on, let's have another drink." I signaled the waiter and ordered.

"Trent guessed you were after shakedown money."

"Trent's a slob."

"Isn't he, though?"

"What about Dick Ryan, was he a slob, too?"

"*Must* you drag him in?"

"That's what I'm here for, lady. Do you think I enjoy working evenings?"

This time she nearly got up. "Well, of all the!" She dug her nails into the tablecloth. "There's a million men who'd be damned glad to trade places with you right now."

"Sure." I nodded. "I know all about that. Your Mr. Costigan has done a good job for you on the glamor angle. Now, about Dick Ryan—"

"You don't like me, do you?"

"I never said that."

"What's the matter? Are you a qu—"

"Careful," I told her. "Want me to get up again?"

"Oh, hell!"

"You know what I'd do if you were mine?" I said. "I'd wash your mouth out with soap. You swear too much, young lady." I smiled. "Outside of that, I like you fine."

"Well, that's certainly a load off my mind." But she relaxed and lifted her glass. "You know, you're kind of attractive, the way you get mad."

"Thanks. How about Ryan, now. Was he attractive when he got mad, too?"

She groaned. "For—"

"Careful!" I said. "No profanity. Not before dessert. Or will you settle for another drink instead? Good."

I ordered, and the waiter went away.

"All right. You win. I'll tell you what I can. But it isn't much. Suppose you've read up on the case?"

I nodded. "Got everything they printed. And I checked with Homicide on it, too. I don't expect you have anything to add to the story you told them. What I'm interested in is a new lead."

The drinks arrived.

"Seems to me the way to figure things out is to find out more about Ryan himself. What kind of a guy he was, what was eating him that made him get loaded that night, things like that."

"I see." Polly Foster twirled the maraschino cherry in her glass. "Ryan was a louse from the word go, if you must know. Strictly a bad casting. He was a conceited ham, he was a tomcat who'd prowl anybody's back fence, he was a lush, he was a double-crosser, and—"

"He was also your lover," I said, softly.

She made a gesture midway between a shrug and a wince. "All right, if you want to be blunt about it. He was. I suppose you can't figure out why."

"Yes I can. I've seen his pictures."

"Funny." She stared down into her drink. "You get so

used to the type that after a while you forget there are any right guys left. And of course, there's always a line, some kind of phony front to fool you. Then afterwards, when you find out, you figure what the—" She smiled. "Whoops, nearly got the soap there, didn't I?"

I picked up her glass and held it out to her. "Wash your mouth out with this, instead," I said. "I'll order another."

She was beginning to get a glow, and that was good. "You know the last time anybody told me that?" she said. "Fifth grade. Old lady Perkins. Kid in back of me dropped an eraser down my neck and I hollered at him."

"I'll bet they were all trying to drop things down your neck," I told her. "Even when you had brown hair."

"How'd you know my hair was brown?"

"Just guessing. Complexion. Am I right?"

"Right." She lifted the new glass. "You'd make a good detective."

"Don't know about that. I'm not getting many leads on this case."

"But there's nothing to tell. Honestly." She leaned forward. "You know it all. Ryan went to his trailer that night, after we finished shooting."

"Anything happen during the day to make you suspicious?"

"You mean, to make me think he was in trouble? No. But he acted kind of sulky. I knew what that meant."

"What did it mean?"

"He wanted me out of the way. Some other woman on the string."

"Who?"

"How would I know? He had plenty of choices. That boy played the field."

"What about Estrellita Juarez?"

"Could be."

"And you think he was just putting on an act, pretending to be angry so that you'd leave him alone that night?"

"Yes."

"You didn't actually quarrel or anything like that?"

"Of course not."

"Did he quarrel with anyone at all before he went off and started drinking?"

"No. He said something to Tom Trent, but I don't know what it was. Nothing serious, because Trent was willing to come with me when we went over to the trailer after dinner."

"How did Ryan greet you?"

"He didn't talk much. Just offered us a drink. We sat down and talked."

"What about?"

"Trent was trying to get him to lay off the bottle. Because of the next day's shooting schedule."

"What did Ryan say to that?"

"If I told you, you'd wash my mouth out with soap."

"Did Ryan seem nervous or upset?"

"Well, he kept looking at his watch."

"As if he were expecting someone?"

"He said he was waiting for Joe Dean to get back. Joe was his valet, you know. He'd driven Abe Kolmar into town for an early preview. When Dean showed up, he brought Juarez with him."

"Do you think that was the deal? Dean had been told to bring Estrellita Juarez to the trailer for Ryan?"

"The way it looked, she was Dean's girl."

"Could that have been for your benefit?"

"Maybe. But if it was, Ryan went too far. Because he got a skinful and fired Dean, and he kicked Juarez out. But you already know that."

"Sure. And he hit Trent, too."

"Hit him? He damned near broke him in half."

"Why?"

"He had a skinful, like I said."

"But there must have been some reason. Was it because Trent objected when Ryan threw Estrellita out?"

"Partly. But I guess it really started when he tried to pitch me out, too."

"In other words, they had a fight over you."

"I don't know. There was so much noise, and then they started swinging, and I got out of there."

"Statement says Ryan told you to go. Said he expected company."

"I don't know. I was crying, it all happened so fast."

"Were you drunk?"

"No more than I am now." Polly Foster stared down at the new Manhattan. "Hey, you're getting me loaded!"

"Sorry. You don't have to drink it."

But she did. "Who cares? Feels good. You treat a girl right, Mr. Clayburn. Mark, isn't it? Person'd never know you were just being polite, that you hated every minute you had to sit here with little old me."

"Don't rub it in," I said. "I apologize. I know I have a temper."

"Temper? You don't have any temper. You're a lamb compared to boys like Trent and Ryan. They're the kind that haul off and clout you one. That lousy Ryan hit me on the arm when he threw me out."

"Then he did toss you out?"

"Sure. What the hell. I didn't want to say it, but that's what happened. Tossed me out on my can. And Trent after me. Trent was looking for his gun, he was so damned mad."

She stopped.

"Go on."

"I don't remember. We were all high, and I was crying. Of course, Trent was only talking. He didn't have his gun anyway. Ryan did—in the trailer. And Trent went back to town to get patched up."

"Are you sure?"

"He's got an alibi."

"But couldn't he have come back later?"

"The way he was beat up? No. And with all that liquor in him?"

"You're sure it was just liquor?"

"Of course. What else? He went back to town, and I was mad so I drove back to town myself."

I nodded. "So I heard. You didn't by any chance happen to turn around, did you?"

"Why?"

"Well, Ryan said something about expecting company. And it occurs to me that you may have been curious, that you might have sneaked back to take a look at his visitor."

"Look, I was so damned mad at that louse, I never wanted to see him again. I wouldn't have cared if somebody blew the top of his head off."

"Somebody did," I said, softly. "And that's not all they did, either."

She opened her mouth, but no sound came out.

"Somebody knew Trent's gun was in Ryan's trailer. Maybe you all did. It doesn't matter. What matters is that someone came there and killed him—killed him in a horrible way, a way that deserves to be punished. I want to see that he gets what's coming to him, and no matter how you feel about Ryan, I think you do, too."

"But I don't know anything," she murmured.

"I think you do. I think you know, and you were afraid to talk, because your name would be involved. You didn't want to get mixed up in any scandal. There's that reefer tie-up in it, I know."

She drained her glass. "Go on," she said. "I'm listening."

"If that's the way it is, I don't blame you. But remember this. I'm not a cop. It's safe to tell me. I can put my information into a story without revealing the sources. And you have my word for that. Wouldn't you like to see them get the killer?"

Polly Foster set her glass down.

"I'm getting woozy," she said. "Think I'll go home."

"But you haven't told me—"

"Bright boy. I haven't, have I? I'm going home."

"Let me drive you."

"No. Taxi."

"Look, don't rush off. It's early yet. I promise, I'll drop the subject."

"Like hell you will. You'll just keep pouring drinks into me until you get what you want." She sighed. "I know the routine. Only usually, when a guy does that he's after something else."

"There's a thought," I said.

"Skip it. You aren't even interested, are you? I can tell. And if you pretended to be, it's only for your goddam story."

"Please, this is important. Haven't you ever stopped to think that there's a murderer running around loose? Maybe it's someone you know. Surely it's someone who knows you. It's dangerous to let—"

"Never mind." She stood up, accomplishing the act without swaying. "I do a lot of thinking. And all I know is, I'm alive, and I want to stay that way."

"Sure you won't let me drive you home?"

"I'll manage." She turned, and I came around the table and took her arm.

"One thing more," I said.

"What's that?"

"I told you I had another favor to ask you. For a girl, a fan of yours. Will you autograph this menu?"

"Very funny."

"I mean it." I took out my pen. "Here."

"Sorry. No autographs. No answers, either. You aren't getting anything more out of me, Mr. Clayburn."

I picked up the menu and wrote on the margin of the cover.

"All right," I said. "If that's the way you feel. But take it with you. If you change your mind—about the autograph or anything else—you can call me at the number I wrote down. I'll be there tonight."

"Don't hang by anything until," Polly Foster said. She favored me with a ravishing smile, and I beamed back at her as we moved toward the door.

I watched her enter the taxi and waved goodbye. She noticed the stares of the couples on the driveway and blew me a kiss for their benefit. But all the while her lips moved, and I knew she was saying something suitable for washing out with soap.

Then she was gone, and I was left alone. Left alone to reclaim my car and drive back to the hotel.

By the time I got there my glow had faded. I bought a pint at the drugstore and took it up to my room; not in any hopes that it would restore the glow, but merely to keep me company.

I needed company right now, needed it badly, because I'd goofed.

Sitting there on the bed, I opened the bottle and took a drink on that. Then I reviewed my record so far.

Goofed with Trent this afternoon. Goofed with Polly Foster tonight. Two foul-ups in one day. Quite a record for a novice. I hadn't learned one solitary new fact. All I'd succeeded in doing was to make enemies out of the best possible leads in the case. Maybe Miss Foster had something there: I *was* just a one-eyed bastard who didn't know his way around.

I took another drink. Might as well get blind. In the kingdom of the blind, the one-eyed man is king...

How long had I been sitting here? An hour, two hours? It didn't matter. The bottle was half empty and I was more than half full. Might as well kill it. Everything else was dead. Dead as Dick Ryan. Dead as the case.

Tomorrow morning I'd have to call Bannock and tell him the deal was off. No soap. No soap to wash out the mouth that wouldn't talk. No soap, no leads, no clues, no case—and no eleven grand for me, either.

Pity. It was all a pity. I could cry over it. Cry with one eye. But that's the way it was. No sense in trying to fool Bannock. I'd goofed, and I didn't have any idea what else to do.

If I saw Joe Dean or Estrellita Juarez or Abe Kolmar, I'd wind up with a blank again. Nobody was talking. The reefer angle had them all scared. So they laid off.

Or was it something else?

I sat up.

Laid off.

Had they got what I'd been getting? Had somebody gone to them directly and told them to lay off?

I'd forgotten about my phone call, the visitor to my apartment.

Sure, I could tell Bannock I was through with the case. But who'd tell the *other?*

I stared at the phone, sweating, wondering whether or not it would start to ring, if I'd pick it up and hear that flat voice once again.

Then I grunted, remembering that I wasn't home any more. I was in the hotel, I was safe. *He* didn't know, couldn't call.

That called for more than a grunt. It called for a grin. In fact, it called for another drink.

I was just reaching for the bottle again when the phone rang.

No drink now. No grin. I was sweating again, and my hand wavered as it went to the phone.

But I picked it up because I had to pick it up, said "Hello" because I had to say "Hello," and listened because I had to listen.

"I changed my mind. You can have that autograph."

"Miss Foster!"

"Polly, to you. I came home and had a couple drinks here all by my lonesome. Now I'm Polly." Her voice was slurred, low. "Been thinking about you, you know that? Want to 'pologize again."

"You don't have to apologize."

"Want to. In person. 'Bout that autograph—how's for you coming out and picking it up?"

"Well—"

She laughed. "I know. Old one-track mind. Wants his information. All right. Told you I been thinking, didn't I? Thinking, drinking. Lonesome. Come on out."

"You say you're alone?"

"Just little old me. Don't be scared. Won't bite you. Not hard, anyway." She laughed again. "You're too smart. You guessed, didn't you? When you said maybe I went back. Well, you're right. I did go back. Saw somebody, too. You come out, maybe I'll tell you all about it. If you're nice."

"I'll come out," I said. "Leaving this minute."

"Good. Hurry up. I'll be waiting."

I went out.

She hadn't lied. She'd autographed the menu. And she was waiting, waiting for me with her lips kissing the signature. From the way she sat there with her head resting on the table, you'd think Polly Foster had hung up the receiver and passed right out. There was only one little detail which made me think differently...

The bullet in her back.

Chapter Seven

"All right," said Al Thompson. "This is for the record."

Leaving out Bannock, I gave it to him straight: about going after a story, seeing Trent, interviewing Polly Foster at Chasen's, coming home, getting the call.

"What time did you get out here?"

"Eleven. Few minutes before. I parked in the drive. You saw my car when you came in. Rang the bell. No answer. I went around the side."

"Why? You figure on busting in?"

"Of course not. But I told you, she'd been drinking. I had a hunch maybe she was sick, or passed out. So I looked through the window and I saw her with her head down on the table."

"Could you tell she'd been shot?"

"No. I thought I was right, she'd passed out."

"So you went in anyway. Why?"

"I explained that before. I glanced down and noticed the window was open. I couldn't walk away and leave her like that—after all, she'd invited me." I paused and stared at him. "This is straight, Thompson."

"Nobody said it wasn't. Keep going."

"That's all. I went in, walked over to her, and then I saw she was dead. Didn't touch anything. Came right to the phone and called you."

"Let's go, then."

"Where?"

"Downtown. You'll have to tell it all over again, you know that. This time we'll want your signature."

"All right."

We left. Thompson wasn't in charge. A man named Bruce

was running the show. I didn't envy him the job. In a little while the press would be there, and the studio people, and there'd be a devil of a mess.

There'd be a devil of a mess in tomorrow's papers, too, but I wasn't worried about that. I had my own mess to consider.

Thompson considered it for me in the car going down. "So you couldn't take my advice, eh?" he mused. "Had to get that story. Well, you've got one now, all right. And I just hope for your sake that it holds up."

"It'll hold," I said.

"How come you're living in a hotel?" he asked me. "Give up the apartment?"

"Neighbors. Objected to my typing late at night. Got a few rush assignments I had to get out in a hurry, so I decided to take a room for a week or so."

"Why not use your office?"

"They lock the building at nine."

"Couldn't you get a key?"

"Never thought of it. There's no law against moving into a hotel, is there?"

"All depends."

"On what?"

"On what the boys turn up in your room."

"They won't find anything."

"They'll try, though."

"Damn!" I said.

"What's wrong now?"

"Just happened to remember. I left half a pint of good liquor up there."

"This isn't funny, Clayburn. We're inclined to take our murders seriously, you know. And knocking off a name like Polly Foster is a very serious matter. Which reminds me. That autograph on the menu—what did you say was the name of the girl you were getting it for?"

"I didn't say. I don't know her name. She works in Bannock's office. Harry Bannock, the agent."

"Heard of him. But how come she knew about your date with Foster?"

"I told you. I went to Bannock because he's got an in with the studio. Asked him to get me a pass. Instead, he arranged this dinner date. I got to kidding with his girl, and promised her an autograph."

"I see."

"You can ask Bannock if you like."

"Thanks." Thompson nodded. "I was planning on doing just that. With or without your permission."

"Look," I said. "I'm trying to be nice, you know. I haven't made any trouble."

"Oh, you haven't, eh? You just blew the lid off the Ryan case all over again, and piled a new killing on top of it. And you haven't made any trouble."

"You think the two cases tie together, too, then?"

"I'm not thinking out loud right now," Thompson said. "Let's get this over with, first."

We got it over with.

There's no sense dragging anybody else along on that part of the trip. It was bad enough for me, what with statements and questioning and more statements, and a call to Joe Fileen, my attorney. Coffee, cigarettes, and then another quiz show.

They held me forty-eight hours. No, fifty-eight, counting the first night. I saw everybody and his brother, including the little guy at the liquor store who sold me the pint. And the man on the desk at the hotel, who—believe it or not—remembered me leaving to go out to Polly Foster's place.

So that gave me an alibi, of a sort. Except that I *could* have gone out there and shot her, then phoned immediately. She hadn't been dead long enough for the coroner to establish any exact time for the murder.

But they couldn't find a gun, and they couldn't find a motive. They looked. I don't know where they searched for the gun, but I know where they pried for a motive. Right inside my skull, that's where. Working in batteries, in relays.

I'm not complaining. Thompson was my friend, and the rest of them were doing a job, a job they had to do, with the pressure bearing down on them from the D.A.'s office and the newspapers and public opinion.

There was plenty of the latter around, although I didn't see any papers until after the second day. Headline stuff, this Polly Foster slaying. Headline, front page, feature story, even editorial stuff. And me, right in the middle. In the middle of the yarn, in the middle of a ring of fugitives from *Dragnet*.

They were looking for a candidate for the Grand Jury, and they were looking hard. They dragged up everything I'd ever done, checked my accident, went into my files and questioned my clients. A very thorough job. I had no objections, but I got awfully tired.

And I wasn't the only one who went through the mill. Tom Trent had his little session, although somebody swung enough weight to keep it out of the papers. Harry Bannock and Daisy were called in, too, but both of them stuck to their. story. They'd just been doing me a favor.

Which was all I expected. I saw them at the inquest, and everybody testified all over again. There was nothing to go on, and that's why they let me out after the inquest.

That gave me twenty-four hours to prepare for the funeral, twenty-four hours to rest up, get myself straightened out.

I rested, but not too much. First of all, I had to read the papers and catch up on the case. Everybody was doing it; everybody wanted to know who killed Polly Foster. Everybody except the guy who did it.

I wondered about him. Was he reading about the case, too? And was he reading *my* name? Was he going to start calling up at the hotel now? Maybe I'd better move out. Maybe I'd better not attend that funeral after all.

"Of course you will." Harry Bannock told me that, when I finally drove out to his place to see him. "Mark, I know what it's been like these past days for you."

"No, you don't," I said. "Nobody'll ever know."

"Well, I can guess. And I appreciate it. Here."

He pulled out a roll.

"Never mind that. It's not necessary."

"Of course it is. I want you to have it."

"Yes," Daisy Bannock added. "Please take it. You were swell, keeping Harry's name under cover and all."

I pocketed the bills. "Maybe it will help some after all," I said. "With this killing, they can't just walk away from the Ryan tie-up. They may find the murderer, clear your boy. I hope so."

"So do I." Harry sighed. "I haven't dared go near the See-More outfit since the news broke, though."

"It shouldn't be too long. The whole Department'll be out on this."

"Not enough."

"What's that?"

"I want you to keep on, too."

"Now wait, you don't need me. You've got what you wanted, the authorities are interested again."

"That's not what I wanted. I wanted Ryan's killer. I wanted his name cleared. And the authorities may not do the job. But you can."

"Me?" I laughed. "Know what I was going to do the night Polly Foster died? I was going to call you up and resign. Because I didn't get anywhere. I goofed the works. I'm no investigator, Harry."

"I'm betting you turn up the murderer."

"Why?"

"Because he's interested in you, now. Whoever he is, he knows you've been talking to people involved in the case. Chances are, you'll hear from him one way or another."

I smiled at Daisy. "What a coffin salesman your husband is," I said. "Certainly knows how to make a deal sound attractive." Then I turned to Harry. "It's no use. I want out of this."

"He's right," Daisy said. "Mark's already done more than anyone could expect in covering up for you. You can't ask him to run any more risks."

"I'm not asking him to. He's in this thing whether he likes it or not, as far as the murderer is concerned. So it doesn't matter if he chooses to cooperate. The killer will keep an eye on him, either way. And all I'm asking him to do is keep an eye out for the killer—in case he runs across a clue."

I tapped my eye-patch. "From now on, this is the only eye I'm keeping out for anybody."

"Suit yourself. But I intend to go right on paying you, because I know if you turn anything up, you'll tell me." Bannock chewed his cigar. "Seems to me, you'd be anxious to do what you could to get this thing solved. The sooner the murderer is behind bars, the sooner you'll be safe. Until then—"

"One more crack and I'll probably pack up and leave town," I told him. "Besides, what makes you so sure it's the same party?"

"The police think so. The papers think so. And what other motive would he have?"

"I'm not so sure," I said.

"You aren't?" Daisy cupped her chin with one hand. "What makes you say that?"

"He's just saying that to be contrary," Bannock grunted.

"You keep quiet! I want to hear Mark's ideas. So far he's made sense."

"Thanks," I said. "Well, here's my guess. And it's just a guess. You know how Ryan was killed. Take the way he was shot, add the reefer butts, and you've got something a little bit special. Whoever murdered him must have really hated the guy. Went a little whacky, too, on the weed.

"But Polly Foster's death was different. This was just pure, cold-blooded, premeditated murder in the first degree. Somebody wanted her silenced, and did the job, and did it quickly and efficiently. You were at the inquest; you heard the theories. Whoever killed her could have been there when I called. Or seen us together at the restaurant. Maybe I was on the list, too—if the killer could have found me at home in the apartment. But the chances are, it was someone who came to call on her; someone who knew her, knew her house, sneaked in and caught her while she was phoning. Waited until she hung up, and then—"

"Did Trent have an alibi?"

"I thought of that. And I asked Thompson. He was home, with his sister, all night. Double checked. Don't worry, I asked about everybody, including you two."

"That was smart." Bannock grinned. "We get a clean bill of health?"

"I know you were playing cards with the Shermans, yes." I grinned back. "By the way, you satisfied with my story, or do you think *I* killed Polly Foster?"

"Touché," Daisy Bannock muttered.

"One thing more," I said. "Maybe it's a minor point, maybe not. Whoever killed her might not have gone there with that purpose in mind. He carried a gun, yes, but that could have been intended merely for effect—when he threatened her about keeping silent. Let's say it was that way. Somebody saw us at Chasen's, or she told somebody about meeting me before she kept the date, and that was enough of a tip-off. The killer went there to warn her about talking too much.

"Suppose he wasn't sure she'd be alone, though. Suppose he thought I might be there with her, or somebody else. Then he might take a sneak around to look through the window. Let's say it was when she was phoning me.

"The window was unlocked. He might have opened it and heard—heard enough for him to come inside the moment she hung up. And then…"

"Sounds logical," Daisy said. "Doesn't it, dear?"

"I don't know. I'm trying to think who could possibly be involved."

"I'm willing to play my hunches," I murmured. "And my hunches say it has to be a friend of Polly Foster's. Somebody close to her."

"Then your job is clear," Bannock said. "Start working on her friends."

"Just like that, eh?" I scowled. "What should I do, run an ad and call a meeting?"

"No need for that. You'll see them all tomorrow afternoon at her funeral."

"Maybe," I said.

Bannock put down his cigar. "Please, Mark! You know how important this is to me. I wouldn't ask you if it wasn't."

"All right," I answered. "I'll go to the funeral. Unless something happens to interfere."

"Such as what?" Daisy asked.

"Such as another killing." I smiled. "In that case, I'll probably be going to my own funeral instead."

Chapter Eight

You can talk about Zanuck. You can talk about Dore Schary, Ford, Capra, Mervyn LeRoy, all the rest of them. But for my money, the top producer in Hollywood is Hamilton Brackett.

No matter how you look at it, he's got what it takes. Talk about grosses; he's never turned out a job yet that lost him money. Talk about art; he knows every trick in the business. His casting is superb, his handling of crowds is perfect, he knows how to wring the last ounce of drama from every situation and every scene.

And what a production staff! Some of his settings are really out of this world; his props are all genuine; his costumes beat anything Adrian ever dreamed up; his makeup artists have it all over the Westmores. Terrific public relations, too. No wonder he draws the crowds whenever one of his jobs has a showing.

Of course, he knows the real secret of production. You've got to build everything around a star. And when he gets the right lead for a part, he can run rings around any outfit in town.

Hamilton Brackett was doing his finest work today, but then he really had a hot attraction to feature.

Polly Foster never looked lovelier.

Wardrobe must have had a touch of genius when they suggested that simple black strapless gown, so symbolic and yet so photogenic.

Brackett's staff must have spent hours on her makeup job: getting just the right touches to the hairdo, concentrating on the precise poignancy of her smile. Of course, they were working with a cooperative subject. Say what you will about

Polly Foster, she was a trouper. She'd realize the importance of making the best appearance in her big scene.

And the scene was big. Hamilton Brackett's stage was almost an auditorium set, with a big pipe organ, just like they used to use back in the days of the silent movies. He actually rolled out the red carpet for the center aisle, and his juicers furnished a light-setting that was colorful and effective. Whoever thought of throwing an amber spot on Polly Foster's face deserved a bonus.

Brackett always did have an eye for color, though, and today he could give it a real workout. He was hitting with red, blue and green spots, all over the flowers. Because the flowers really made the scene. They banked the stage and the sides of the hall on both walls. You wouldn't see a bigger display at the Tournament of Roses.

Brackett made good use of the crowds, too. He had about twenty assistant directors in formal afternoon wear, running up and down the aisles playing usher. Actually, they were grouping the audience to the best advantage. Those who had contributed the best floral offerings got the front seats. Everything according to protocol, everything to keep the distinguished guests happy and place them where the press could spot them easily.

Outside the set, on the curb, Brackett made equally good use of a dozen volunteer assistant directors wearing police uniforms. They handled the mob scenes, holding the crowd back behind the ropes strung along the sidewalk, and keeping the curb clear as the cars drove up.

Oh, it was a genuine Hamilton Brackett production, all right. His funerals were always the best show in town.

I won't review the performance itself. Everything was flawless. No original score by Dmitri Tiomkin, but the organist knew what to do with the oldies he played. And the guy Brackett had cast for the sermon part was sensational. He had Laughton beat for delivery any day, and whoever wrote his script did a bangup job. Even managed to work in some religious stuff—that always goes over big with audiences—but mostly he kept building up to the big scene. Plugging Polly Foster, all the way. How beautiful she was, how charming, how intelligent; what a personality she had. He told about her life; made you see her as she actually was, radiant, ravishing, poised on the threshold of achievement. Then he turned on the agony, worked that old tragedy angle. By the time he finished, he had them crying. Their tongues were hanging out for a sight of her, for a great big close-up.

That was the deal, of course. The whole gang began to file past the coffin for that close-up.

I went along with the rest. I was way in the rear, naturally, but I kept my eye open. I saw Bannock and Daisy, and the little girl from Bannock's office who wouldn't be getting her autographed menu unless the police released it from the exhibits they were holding as evidence.

I was looking for other faces, though. Gradually, as I worked my way up the line approaching the casket, I spotted a few.

Tom Trent was there, in a black suit minus the monogram initials. He was accompanied by a small brunette I couldn't identify, and he didn't see me. Near the head of the procession was a chunky little redfaced man with a hairline receding almost to the back of his neck. I recognized Abe Kolmar, from Ace. He'd been Polly Foster's producer, and Dick Ryan's too. His eyes were red, and he kept twisting a big handkerchief in his hands.

I saw Al Thompson, too—or, rather, he saw me. He wasn't in line, just standing there leaning against a floral arch as I went past. He nodded.

"What brings you here?" I whispered.

"Same as you. Looking around." He joined me in the file. "See anybody?"

"Whole town's here."

"What about Estrellita Juarez? Joe Dean?"

"Dean was here, but he didn't stay. We questioned him, you know."

"Clean?"

Thompson shrugged. "He's out, if that's what you mean."

"And Juarez?"

"Can't locate her. We're trying." Thompson scowled. "Quit needling me. That's official business."

"My business, too. You might say I have a personal interest at stake now."

"Well, I wish you'd lay off. Before you're laid out."

"Is there a flip to that record?"

"Never mind the repartee. If you'd listened to my advice at the beginning, you wouldn't have had any trouble. And maybe Polly Foster wouldn't have had any trouble, either. Ever think about that angle, Clayburn?"

I'd thought about it, all right. I'd been thinking about it ever since the murder.

That's why I kept trying to kid myself along, building up a line about this being a Hamilton Brackett production. Anything to take my mind off the facts, the cold, hard facts of the case.

Now it was my turn at the casket, and I couldn't pretend any longer. I was looking down at the cold, hard facts in the silver case. The cold death mask, the hard death mask with the smiling lips. The lips I'd threatened to wash with soap. The lips I could conceivably have kissed.

But that was gone now. That mouth had been washed out for the last time. And when I thought about what would soon be kissing those lips...

My fault, all my fault.

Like hell it was!

I hadn't killed her. That was the murderer's responsibility, and neither Thompson nor anybody else was going to make me take the rap.

I looked at Polly Foster a long time. At least, it seemed like a long time because I thought of so many things. I thought about a little girl with brown hair who was always bothered by the boys. Who grew up and was still bothered by the boys—the wrong kind of boys—until she got the wrong kind of slant on things. I thought about a woman who swore too much and drank too much and probably slept around too much, and I thought that maybe she did it because she was afraid too much. Afraid of a world that valued her only for her beauty. A ghoul-world, always after her body; wanting to photograph it, wanting to see it, wanting to paw it. Afraid, perhaps, of one particular ghoul who wanted to destroy it. And who succeeded.

I was sorry about that, but I wasn't to blame. And as I took my final glance, I wasn't even sorry any more. I was angry. "Lay off," Thompson had said. That's what all of them wanted me to do, including the guy who had sat in my apartment with a monkey on his back.

I stared at Polly Foster for the last time and if the dead can read minds, she knew that I was telling myself—and her—that I would never lay off now.

Then I moved on.

Thompson went over to talk to Abe Kolmar. He and most of the other big shots were going out to the cemetery. I didn't feel like it. This new, sudden feeling of anger made me want to slug somebody. For the first time I was beginning to understand the meaning of murder.

Sure, like the hammy preacher said, it was tragic to see someone ruthlessly trample a white rose. But it's always a tragedy, even when someone tramples a weed. No one has that right. And who is even fit to sit in judgment, to separate the weeds from the roses?

Weeds. Marijuana was a weed. A weed that made some people high, made them feel that they *did* have the right to judge, made them feel like trampling. I knew.

And I was going to find out more. Somehow, some way, I'd find out.

I headed for the door, almost bumping into a tall man who stood in the outer entry, talking to a girl.

"Excuse me," I said.

"So it's you again," the man said. "The snooper!"

I stared into Tom Trent's face.

"I ought to let you have it," he said. "I ought to beat your brains out."

"You've got the wrong party," I answered, softly. "Save it for the killer."

"One more word out of you and—"

"I know," I said. "I know how you feel. I'm sorry. And I'm going to do something about it. Can't you forget what happened long enough to help?"

"I've talked to the police. Any help I can give they'll get. Now beat it, snooper, before I change my mind. I don't want to be caught dead talking to you."

I turned away.

Harry and Daisy Bannock came up to me as I reached the door.

"Saw you talking to Trent just now," Harry told me. "Did he have anything to say?"

I shook my head. "He's still sore. But he'll cool down. At least, I hope he does. Because I'm positive he knows something about this business."

"You suspect him?" Daisy asked.

"Of the actual killing? No. But there's something he knows that he didn't want to leak out. That's why he called Polly Foster and warned her not to talk."

"What's your plan?" Bannock asked.

"Nothing definite. But I intend to have another visit with Trent, and soon. I'll get the story out of him some way."

"You sound pretty determined all of a sudden," Daisy said. "Yesterday you wanted to quit."

"I've been thinking it over. When I saw Polly Foster lying there in the coffin…"

Harry Bannock stared at me. His voice was deliberately lowered when he spoke. "Don't tell me you went for her? That little tramp?"

I shook my head. "No. I didn't go for her. But she wasn't a tramp. She was a human being, a kid who came up the hard way, maybe even the wrong way. But she came up, and she deserved to live. Everybody does. Nobody should get a slug in the back. And then a bad name on top of it. Harry, you're the last person I'd expect to talk about Polly Foster. You want Dick Ryan's name cleared, don't you? Well, so do I. I want everybody's name cleared."

"Dig the shining armor," Harry said. Then he reddened. "I'm sorry, Mark. You're right. I'm talking like a heel. Forget it. Do what you think best, and I'll back you up all the way. You want me to smooth things over with Trent for you?"

"Never mind, let me handle it," I answered. "I'll work things out. The sooner I can get him to help, the better."

"Coming out to the cemetery?" Daisy asked.

"No. I'm going back to my place and rest up. You driving there?"

"I guess not. Daisy's got a headache. Allergy."

"Smell of lilies, I think," she said. "Wasn't it awful in there? Stuffy. I hate funerals."

"Me too." Bannock put his hand up to his pocket, reaching for a cigar. Then he remembered and his fingers withdrew. "Call us tonight, Mark, if you hear anything."

"Right. I may have news for you."

"Hope so. Want a lift?"

"Brought my own heap. But thanks just the same."

I walked out, into the late afternoon sunlight. The crowd had moved over to the side entrance around the corner, waiting for the casket to come out. The photographers were setting up their paraphernalia in the driveway.

My car was parked two blocks away. I walked toward it slowly, and it was like walking through water because of the recurrent waves of anger and confusion and pity which impeded me. I had to get rid of them, I knew. This was no time for sentiment or sentimentality. A clear head, that's what I needed. I had to keep my mind, my eye, my ears, open.

I kept my ears open.

That's how I heard the staccato clattering behind me. As I turned, a voice called, "Mr. Clayburn! Wait!"

I stood there, waiting until she came up, waiting until I

could take a good look at the face of the girl who'd been following me. The girl whom I'd seen in the chapel, talking to Tom Trent.

"Don't you remember me, Mr. Clayburn?" she asked.

I shook my head.

"The goldfish," she said.

"Goldfish?"

"Yes. The one you noticed the other day at my brother's pool."

I looked at the face carefully now, trying to visualize it encircled by a bathing-cap. It was entirely different today: pertly piquant in makeup, framed by a brown pageboy bob, and surmounted by a small black hat. The girl was young, but there was something familiar about her features. Come to notice it, she looked a little like Tom Trent himself, in a feminine sort of way.

Apparently she read my thoughts, because she nodded quickly. "That's right," she said. "I'm Billie Trent. Tom's sister."

"Pleased to meet you."

She glanced over her shoulder. "Never mind that now. Where can we go to talk?"

Chapter Nine

I led her to the car.

"Hop in," I said.

She paused. "I can only stay a few minutes. I told Tom I had to go to the ladies' room."

"Might as well sit down."

"All right." She climbed in. I got behind the wheel. She kept peering around.

"I'll keep my eye on the rear view mirror," I told her. "Don't worry."

"Thanks." She looked relieved, but I noticed her hands kept moving restlessly along her lap. "Mr. Clayburn, I heard you talking to my brother just now, and of course, the other day, out at the house. I...I'm sorry for those things he said."

"You needn't be. He has a right to his opinion."

"But that's just it. He didn't tell you what he really thought. At least, I don't think he did. Tom hasn't been acting natural ever since Dick Ryan was killed. It worries me."

"You aren't the only one," I murmured.

"I feel foolish, coming to you like this, but I've just got to talk to someone. And since you're in on this, I thought maybe you could help me."

"All depends," I said. "On the other hand, there's always the police."

She stiffened. "That's just it. I don't want to talk to the police. I'm...I'm afraid."

"Why?"

"Oh, it's not because of myself. It's Tom. He's got his career to think about. And ever since Dick Ryan was murdered, he just sits around and gets drunk. He used to drink a lot, but not this way, not every night."

"Drink," I said. "Is that all he does?"

She looked at me.

"Skip it," I told her. "You say your brother seems to be worried. What about?"

"That's what I'd like to know."

"Is it his contract, something to do with the studio?"

"I don't think so. He's under personal contract to Mr. Kolmar, and they're starting another picture next month. It isn't that."

"Do you know Kolmar?"

"I've seen him. He's come to the house a few times."

"Lately?"

"You mean, since Ryan was murdered?"

I nodded, and she went on.

"Once or twice. I wasn't home, though."

"Then how did you know about it? Did your brother tell you?"

"Yes. In advance. I…I always got out."

"Don't like Kolmar, is that it?"

"He offered me a screen test once." Billie Trent stared at her twisting hands. "I never told Tom anything about it, because he'd be furious. So, please…"

"I get it. Kolmar made a pass at you, eh?"

"Well, not exactly. He just…suggested things."

"I can imagine. But is there anything else, anything that might tie him in with these killings?"

"No. I don't think so." She was silent for a moment. "His chauffeur might know, though."

"His chauffeur?"

"A man named Dean—Joe Dean. You must have heard of him; he was there the night Ryan was murdered."

"I know. But he worked for Ryan, didn't he?"

"Yes. He's working for Mr. Kolmar now. And he's always coming over to talk with Tom. Tom says he's all right, but I don't like his looks. I don't see why Tom would want to make friends with such a man."

"Did you ever ask Tom about him?"

She nodded. "He says Dean's a good person to know because he hears all the studio gossip. He can tell about things before they happen."

I sat back. "Do you happen to remember if Dean talked to your brother any time before Polly Foster was killed?"

"I don't think so. I know Tom made some phone calls, but he didn't say who he was speaking to. I went out for dinner that night, and I didn't pay too much attention."

"Out for dinner? But your brother told the police he was with you at home all evening."

"He was. I came back around eight-thirty. We played Scrabble."

"Was he nervous?"

"I told you, he's always nervous. He kept going to the phone, trying to call Polly Foster."

"Did he say why?"

"No. But of course, I read about it in the papers later. He'd called Polly Foster and told her not to see you. I guess he wanted to make sure she hadn't."

"What did he say about me?"

She put her head down and I could see the pink flush creeping along her neck.

"Never mind the adjectives. I mean, what did he think I was doing?"

"He thought you were trying to pull a shakedown. He thought I'd talked."

"Talked?"

"Told someone. What I'm going to tell you now." She turned to me and now the words came so fast I had difficulty following them. "I'm taking a big chance, Mr. Clayburn, but somebody ought to know this. Maybe they can help. There's nobody I can trust. And I wouldn't dare go to the police, because it might get Tom in trouble when he didn't deserve to be. But if you're investigating, you can find out the truth, can't you? It may be nothing at all, and then again...I'm afraid."

I put my hand on her shoulder. "Slow down! What is it you're trying to tell me?"

"The night Dick Ryan died, he and Tom had a fight. And Tom came home. Gibbs—that's the butler—taped him up and put something on his eye. Then Tom went to bed. At least, that's what Gibbs thought, and that's what Tom told the police. But he didn't stay there, Mr. Clayburn. My room is down the hall, and I heard Tom get up and go out again. Around eleven o'clock. He was gone for over two hours."

"Does your brother know you're aware that he went out again?" I asked.

"No. I never dared mention it. The whole thing's so awful."

I patted her shoulder, then let my hand lie still as I looked at her. "What do you think?" I murmured. "Do you think he killed Dick Ryan?"

Her eyes fell. My hand tightened its grip. She jerked away, then slumped. "I don't know, Mr. Clayburn. That's what's so terrible, can't you see? I don't know."

I smiled at her. "Cheer up. It's not that bad. He may have had a perfectly legitimate reason for going out again that night. Perhaps he was too shaken up to sleep. But you can understand, under the circumstances, why he wouldn't want the police to know he left the house later on.

"At any rate, I'll do my best to find out for you, if that's any help. And I must thank you for telling me what you did. I know it wasn't easy."

"You've got to find out," she whispered. "You've got to. I can't stand thinking what I think, day after day. Can't stand seeing him this way. There must be something wrong, or else why would he drink like this?"

I sighed. "You mentioned his drinking before, Miss Trent. And I started to ask you something else, then dropped it. But I'd like to ask again, because it could be important. Very important."

"Go ahead."

"Don't get me wrong, now, but have you ever noticed your brother taking anything besides alcohol?"

"You mean—?"

"That's right," I said, gently. "Is he a narcotics addict, have you ever seen him with a reefer?"

She shook her head.

"All right. You've been a great help."

"I must go. He'll get suspicious, I've been away so long."

"I understand. But from now on, I'll keep in touch with you. You live at the house there?"

"Yes. But don't call. He'd be furious. Let me call you. Where can I reach you?"

I hesitated, then gave her the office number. "Give me a day or two," I said. "Maybe I can find out something. I'll do my best."

"Thank you."

"Thank *you*."

Then she was out the door. I watched her trot up the street, watched her through the rear view mirror. Cute kid. And she wanted to help. A refreshing change from the old buttoned-lips routine I'd been getting. Nothing like a new routine to brighten the day.

A new routine.

I frowned. Could this be a routine, too? A different kind of one? Sure, she might be on the level; just a mixed-up minx with a problem and no shoulder to cry on. Then again, she could be a plant. Hell, how did I even know she was Trent's sister?

I tried to expel the notion with a sigh. Mustn't let this get me down. The way I was going, I'd end up trusting nobody. The world wasn't all phony. There were still plenty of ordinary people around; ordinary, straightforward people who asked straight questions, gave straight answers.

Like this guy with the crewcut who stopped at the side of the car now and stuck his head through the window.

"Hey, Mister," he said. "Can you tell me how to get over to the LaBrea Tar Pits from here?"

"Why, I guess so." I slid over in my seat and pointed south. "You take Western Avenue down to Wilshire Boulevard, then turn west on Wilshire and—"

I turned my head. Somebody had opened the other door, next to the wheel. A small man slid into the driver's seat next to me. He nodded and reached out, and I felt something hard press against my side.

"Sit still," he said. "No bright ideas."

I sat still. I didn't have any bright ideas. No bright ideas about ordinary straightforward people who asked straight questions and gave straight answers.

"Come on, Fritz."

The guy with the crewcut opened the door on his side and crawled in. I sat there wedged between the two of them. All at once the pressure was gone from my left side. It was replaced by pressure on my right, as the man called Fritz took over.

The small intruder started the car.

"Mind telling me where we're going?"

Apparently he did, because he didn't answer.

"Would you pull down that visor? The sun's in my eye."

Nobody pulled down the visor. Nobody stirred, or said a word. The small man drove, the big man sat there, and I could feel something pushing hard against my ribs.

"Sure you boys aren't making a mistake? I don't get this."

"You will." Fritz spoke, and the little man uttered a short bark.

We drove west on Sunset, into the sunset. The car stopped for the lights a half-dozen times. I could look into other cars, see the people passing on the sidewalk, even stare as a squadcar passed us on the left. But I couldn't utter a sound or make a move. Not with Fritz on the job, not with that constant reminder against my ribs.

Then we turned off down a side street and headed south through a tangle of traffic. The little man drove slowly, as though he were out for a leisurely pleasure trip. Who knows, maybe this *was* pleasure for him? Anyway, he took his time. And all at once I realized why.

He was waiting for it to get dark.

Now I watched the light dimming. I watched the shadows

lengthen on the streets of Santa Monica when we turned west, then south again. I watched the street lights of Venice, glimpsed dusk descend over the ocean. Then we were speeding along the coast highway, heading for Long Beach.

Somewhere, we turned off. Somewhere we turned off and headed for the hills. Oil country, with derricks, dotting the dunes here and there. Some of them were working, others were deserted, pumped out.

It was quite dark now. We were jolting along a back road that was no better than a trail. The dunes rose all around us. No houses out here, just empty space, and the gray dunes looming beneath a black sky.

Abruptly the road came to an end in the middle of nowhere. But the car didn't stop. We drove on, across the sand. Drove straight ahead into more nowhere. Drove until we rounded the side of a dune and came up against a derrick. It was old and rusty and the wind whistled through the scaffolding.

The car stopped. "Out you go," said Fritz.

I thought, *This is a hell of a place to die.* But I got out. Fritz was waiting for me. He took my arm and held it while the little guy came around the front of the car. I had trouble seeing either of them in the dark, but I could feel the big hand squeezing into my arm.

This isn't happening, I thought. *I'll close my eye and when I open it again, everything will be different.* I closed my eye and put my head back.

When I opened it again I could see a single star shining up above. I wished on it. Believe me, I wished on it. But I was still standing there, Fritz still held my arm and the little guy was saying, "All right, Clayburn. Let's have some answers. Who you working for?"

They'd been fooling me. The thing against my rib hadn't been a gun at all—just a sap. A long leather sap with a steel handle. I could see it now in the faint light, hear it thump against Fritz's left palm as he held it in his right hand.

"Come on," said the little guy. "Give."

I looked up at the star. Then all at once there were a million stars, and I felt something hot running down the side of my face. Fritz caught me before I fell.

"Sample," he said.

"Who you working for?" the little guy repeated.

I grunted. "Trade you. You tell me who you're working for first."

Crunch. I could hear it this time, hear it as well as feel it. Something hit the other side of my head.

"Who is it? Names."

"Who are you?" I panted. "Joe Dean, by any chance?"

The wind whistled through the derrick. The sap whistled. The back of my neck went numb, but only for an instant. Then it was a red-hot iron bar that burned and burned, and the sap was whistling again, and I went to my knees but the little guy held me and he said, "Who you working for?" and I tried to make my tongue move.

"Do you smoke reefers?" I wheezed.

Crack. The sap made a sound like a wet towel smacking up against a board, but it wasn't a wet towel and my lower spine wasn't a board, and nobody could hear it anyway because this was out in the middle of nowhere. Nobody could hear it, but I could feel it. Feel the fire flooding my kidneys, feel the blood on my knees as I went down, feel the hand tearing at my hair.

"You better talk soon," the little guy said. "Fritz gets mad easy." I saw the sap rise in rhythm with the little guy's voice. "Who you working for?"

"Who are *you* working—?"

I never finished the sentence. The sap came down, and I tried to twist my head away. I felt a jarring wrench, but no blow.

"Goddamn you!" the little guy howled. "You hit my hand! Jesus, I think my wrist's busted."

He let go of me and stood there, moaning and holding his right hand.

Fritz scowled. "Get out of the way," he said. "I'll finish

this." The small man stepped back, letting his partner advance. He crouched before me, and the sap went back.

"Listen," he said. "I ain't got all night. This is your last chance. Either you tell us what we want to know, or—"

I swayed there, watching the sap come up again.

"All right, then!" Fritz moved forward and swung the sap down.

I swung with it, dropping to my knees. At the same time I pushed forward, catching him just below the belt with the top of my head. I put all my weight behind it, and he felt it.

At first, when he opened his mouth, I thought he screamed. But he couldn't scream. It was the other one who made all the racket. Because the big guy fell on top of him.

I raised my head, located the hand holding the sap, and twisted. Then I put my foot down on the fingers and jerked the sap away. I got it free and raised it. I brought it down once, twice, three times. Fritz stopped moving. The little guy beneath him stopped screaming. I wondered if he'd passed out, too.

Well, I'd know in a minute. Now the trick was to lug them both into the car and take them back to town.

I moved toward Fritz, trying to summon up energy for the effort. My knees were wobbly, and I wondered if I could manage to support myself, let alone a big man like Fritz.

I never found out.

Because the little guy wasn't unconscious. And he wasn't unarmed, either.

As I stooped over Fritz, the little guy moved. He rolled out from underneath, his left hand dipping towards the coat pocket, then emerging. He groaned and rose to his knees. The hand pointed towards me.

One red burst, and a million echoes, bouncing off the dunes.

One red burst, and then I was running, dodging and weaving as I tried to outguess the gun, outrace the second shot.

The echoes exploded again, and I turned sharply, veering

off to the right. It was hard to run, hard to just keep on my feet, even hard to breathe.

Another shot. My head throbbed, my heart was pounding, the back of my neck ached. But I had to get away. I had to.

Then I mounted a rise and looked back. I saw the spurt, but never heard the echoes.

I took one more step and fell into the middle of nowhere.

Chapter Ten

The middle of nowhere isn't such a bad place to be. The trouble is, you can't stay there very long. Sooner or later, something starts to throb. At first it's just a far-off motion you're aware of; then you begin to react to the throbbing, feel its effects, realize that it's your head.

Then the pain comes in waves, like the tide washing its way up a beach. The beach is your body, and it lies there and lets the pain ebb and flow, ebb and flow, over your head, over your neck, over your shoulders and arms and chest.

Finally you decide to do something about it, something hard, like opening your eyes.

That's what I did, eventually. I opened my eye and found myself lying at the bottom of the dune. I'd pitched off the top, apparently, and slid down. The bullet hadn't hit me, the fall didn't break any bones. It was the sapping that caused the pain, and that was enough. I ached all over.

I lay there, moving my hand over my limbs and torso. I stretched my legs, sat up, steadied myself against a long moment of dizziness, and then I listened.

No sound. Nothing to hear. And nothing to see, either, in the dark. I gazed up at the rim of the dune, towards the sky beyond. The first star was still twinkling.

Damn you, I thought, *I'll never wish on you again.*

I wondered about my little playmates. Were they still looking for me in the dark? Well, I could join the game. Hide-and-seek didn't exactly appeal to me at the moment, but I knew I'd better play along.

The dune was high. I started to stand up, then decided it would be more comfortable to crawl. I inched forward, upward, until I clung to the dune's lip, peering over towards the derrick.

By this time my eye was adapted to the light, or the lack of it. I gazed at the ground, looking for Fritz. He was gone. And the small man wasn't there, either.

More important, and more convincing to me, was the realization that my car was gone, too.

Of course, they might be waiting down the road. But I'd have to chance it.

I stood up, took a deep breath. My ribs protested, but my lungs enjoyed it, so I took another. And another. Gradually my head cleared. I found I could walk.

Making my way into the shadow of the derrick, I examined the sand. Plenty of footprints, and the imprint of Fritz's body, plus my own. And the car tracks, two sets of them. They'd turned and gone out the same way; there was no other choice.

I followed the tracks, moving slowly and cautiously. I wound my way along until I could see the road. It was clear. Then I started walking. It seemed like forever before I hit the highway. It seemed like forever before I thumbed a ride. I guess nobody was interested in picking up a bleeding stranger with an eye-patch who stood on the highway in the middle of the night. Nobody except an ambulance driver.

But as luck would have it, I got the next best thing. The car that finally halted contained a Dr. Engebrusher, of Santa Monica. He took an immediate professional interest in me. I regaled him with the story of my mysterious assailants as we drove to his home.

Once there, he patched me up. I don't know if he believed me at first, but he patched me up. And when I asked to use his phone, I guess he realized my story was straight. He listened while I dialed the L.A. police and reported that my car was missing. Then I told them about the assault. They were very courteous; told me to stay right where I was until they signaled a squad car to pick me up and bring me in.

I asked for Thompson, then. My luck was holding. He was on duty, late as it was.

"Hello, this is Mark Clayburn. I just gave your people a report. Want to hear it?"

His groan was audible over the phone. "Now what?" he said.

I told him what it was now. All of it. All of it except *why*. That I had to change to protect Bannock. I made the reason appear to be that they were trying to find out what I knew about the deaths. Which, in a way, was still true enough. Then I described my playmates, in rich and, I fear, somewhat profane detail.

"Recognize the little guy?" I asked. "Sound like Dean, by any chance?"

"A little. In fact, more than a little. But it wasn't," Thompson answered.

"Why do you say that?"

"According to your story, you were picked up around four or four-thirty, right?"

"Right."

"And they drove you south and jumped you about an hour and a half, say two hours later?"

"That's about it. I figure seven o'clock, thereabouts," I said.

"Well, at seven o'clock, thereabouts, Dean was sitting here in this office, telling us he didn't know anything about where Estrellita Juarez had run off to."

"Must have been two other guys," I told him.

"Must have been. But don't worry, we'll check the files. Probably have lots of pictures waiting for you by the time you get down here."

"Thanks."

"Don't mention it. We aim to please."

I hung up. I was just forcing ten bucks on Dr. Engebrusher when the squad car arrived for me.

After that, we went into action.

I've got to hand it to the boys; maybe they were having a

little trouble finding a murderer, but there was nothing wrong with their methods.

They didn't take me right in. They took me back to the place where I got slugged. They made me reconstruct the action, took down a full description of everything. They contacted the State Highway Patrol about covering the scene in daylight to look for the bullets. The bulletin about the car and the description of Fritz and his little friend had already gone out.

There were three men in the car, and we had quite a chat as we finally drove downtown. They wanted to know all about the Foster case, of course. One of them, off the record, seemed to disagree with my theory that the killing was the work of a cold-blooded, calculating murderer.

"He must have been nuts," he told me. "Anybody that breaks in on a dish like that Polly Foster just to *shoot* her has to be crazy."

He turned to me. "You're the one who found her, isn't that so? What kind of a story is that, about going out there to get her autograph?"

"It's the truth," I said. "So help me."

"What kind of a dame was she? I mean, on the level."

"Sorry. I only met her once. And our relations were strictly vertical."

He didn't get it, but the cop who was driving laughed.

"I guess they're all alike," he said. "All them Hollywood people. Bunch of screwballs, in one mess after another."

"You know better than that," I answered. "There's hundreds who never get into any trouble. Lots of nice, decent citizens in the movie colony, just as there's lots of nice, decent citizens down on Olive, or Main. But the few exceptions, the wrongos, are the only ones you ever hear about. That's what gives a bad reputation to the whole bunch."

"Pretty funny talk, coming from a guy who's just been beat up the way you have."

"Maybe so, but it's the truth. What about your Department? There've been cases where a couple of cops went off the deep end. But does that mean you're all crooked?"

"He's right, Evans," said the man sitting next to me. "And I'm sorry I sounded off that way about Polly Foster. But you know how you get after a few years in this game."

We reached our destination, but I didn't see Thompson waiting for me. My business was with another department. They had everything ready for me to swear out a complaint, and they took down the story and the description again, and then a sergeant brought out the file and I started to look at faces.

As I said before, all very efficient and quite polite. It was nice to be on the other side of the fence for a change, after the grilling I'd taken when they heard about Polly Foster.

I was even beginning to relish the attention a little, enjoy the way they hovered over me as I checked the photos. Then they took the play away from me. Somebody buzzed the sergeant and he hit the phone.

After a minute, he turned to me. "They've found your car," he said.

"Huh?"

"Highway Patrol located it backed off the road near the gun club, below Santa Monica. Right near Washington Boulevard. Everything's okay, I guess. You can check and see if anything is missing. They'll be bringing it in later."

"Nothing on the two men?"

"Nothing so far. They're on the lookout. Meanwhile, here's some more pictures."

I looked at pictures. As I looked, I began to wonder about my previous remarks concerning the integrity of the citizens of Los Angeles County. There seemed to be no end to the number of malefactors.

I stared at scars, briefly noted broken noses, carefully eyed cauliflower ears, scanned sneers; most of these men had their history written in their faces and there was no need to read a description of their misdemeanors. I know Lombroso's theory is discredited, but there's still something about physiognomy that registers with me. I'd seen too many faces like these in my time to discount them, seen them at the edges of dark alleys, seen them peering through the dirty, fly-specked windows of the dives, seen them staring up from the gutters of grim streets.

So far, though, I hadn't found Fritz, or the man who looked something like Joe Dean but wasn't. I reached for another stack when the door opened and Thompson came in.

"Hi," I said. "Wondered whether you'd come down. Want to hear about it?"

He didn't return my smile or my greeting. He just looked at me and shook his head.

"No time," he said. "Leaving this minute. Just thought you might be interested in the news."

"What news?"

"Call just came in. Tom Trent's dead."

I blinked.

"His sister found him in the garage five minutes ago. Shot through the heart."

"Murder?"

"Don't know. Could be a suicide." He turned. "Going to find out."

"Let me come with you."

"You know the regulations."

"But I—"

"Somebody'll be around to see you tomorrow. We'll keep in touch."

I nodded at his back as he went out.

Then I started to look at pictures again, but I didn't see them. All I saw was Tom Trent lying dead in his garage. It would be murder, I knew that. And he'd been shot through the heart.

The room started to spin a little, but the scene before my eye never wavered. It was so clear I could notice every detail. There was one detail I had to verify, though.

I stuck around for over an hour until the reports started coming in. Then I needled the sergeant until he told me.

"You were wrong," he said. "Looks like suicide, so far.

Had the gun in his hand and everything. Shot himself in the chest."

Then I asked about the detail that interested me. The sergeant looked puzzled at my questions, but he told me what I wanted to know: what Trent had been wearing, and just where the bullet had entered his body.

"Thanks," I said. "And you can tell Thompson or whoever is in charge that it wasn't suicide."

"No?"

I shook my head. "I'm positive. Even if Trent wanted to kill himself, there's one thing he'd never do. He'd never shoot himself through the monogram."

Chapter Eleven

I didn't find the pictures which would identify either of my attackers. The car came, and I checked it. Nothing was missing but the gas they'd used. Of course I wanted to stick around and hear the reports on the Trent case, but they told me to go home.

It was late, so I went. In spite of Dr. Engebrusher's handiwork, I felt as if I needed a rest. The hotel bed looked good to me. I'd rather sleep here than out in the dunes, or in a casket like Polly Foster, or on a garage floor, like Trent. Only he wouldn't be on the floor any more. He'd be occupying a slab somewhere, while the coroner's little helpers played ring-around-the-bullet-hole.

Yes, I was lucky because they hadn't got me. Hadn't got me *yet*.

I started to review the events of the day, searching for angles I might have overlooked. Those men had been sent after me, but by whom? Somebody who knew I was going to the funeral, or who had actually seen me there. He or she. Billie Trent, perhaps? Maybe her story was a gag. Maybe she'd come and talked to me as a stall, to see that I stayed put there until the two hoods arrived. Maybe she was in with her brother on the deal. Maybe *she* killed *him*.

Plenty of possible alternatives there. After all, what did I actually know concerning her, outside of what she chose to tell me? She didn't look like a murderess in my opinion; but then, Mr. Lombroso's theory isn't supposed to be valid. Come to think of it, what did old Cesare Lombroso himself look like? I made a note to look up his picture in some encyclopedia when I had a chance. Perhaps he had the face of a criminal himself, according to his definition. Who knows, maybe *he* was the murderer? Not likely, seeing that he died almost fifty years ago. Everybody appeared to be dying off lately: Ryan, Foster, Trent. And they tried for me, and threatened Bannock too. Bannock. I'd have to talk to him tomorrow. But what could I tell him, really?

I didn't know. All I'd actually learned today was that it isn't safe to direct strangers to the LaBrea Tar Pits.

On which thought I drifted off to sleep. I went to the LaBrea Tar Pits and visited some of the prehistoric monsters. They were alive in my dreams, and I saw them all. Saw them over my shoulder, mostly, because they kept chasing me. Not an herbivore in the crowd. They had big teeth, every one. I saw the Kolmarsaurus and the Deanosaurus and the Estrellitajuarus; the Fritzopodus, the Bannockactyl and the ten-tentacled Trent, the Sabretoothed Thompson, and the Marijuanus Rex. The latter was a big white worm shaped like a cigarette. Smoke came out of its mouth as it crawled after me and tried to smother me in its poisonous fumes.

Oh, I had a delightful rest. Funny part was that I woke up around ten in the morning and felt fine, hardly stiff after a shower. By the time I went out for breakfast I was ready for anything.

But most of all I was ready for the morning papers. I read them over coffee. I read them when I went to the office to check my mail.

There wasn't a line in them about any murder.

It was straight suicide, all the way. Grief-stricken actor kills himself after Polly Foster's funeral. Love-crazed star suicide over sweetheart's death. Details on page two.

I ignored the fake romance leads the reporters had so avidly exploited and went after those details on page two. These made less lurid reading, but better sense.

Trent and his sister had gone to the cemetery. They left about five and ate at a restaurant. Then they went home. According to the girl's story, Trent seemed depressed but not spectacularly so—not enough to justify the headlines on page one. I wondered if Kolmar's publicity staff had planted the romance notion in an attempt to tie things together. But no matter now; the important thing was what actually happened out there in the Valley last night.

Trent took a few drinks and Billie decided to go up to bed. She didn't undress immediately; she lay down and read for a while. It was almost midnight when she glanced at the clock and realized she hadn't heard Trent come up.

She went downstairs and asked Gibbs, the butler, if Trent had gone out. Gibbs said he'd left about an hour before, following a phone call. He hadn't paid any attention, just assumed Trent took the station wagon which was parked near the gate.

Billie Trent looked out the window. The station wagon was still standing there. Either her brother had never left, or he had recently returned. She was about to comment on the fact when they both heard the sound.

Neither of them recognized it as a shot, at first. The garage was behind the house, and its solid brick walls would muffle a backfire.

Their first reaction was that somebody might be prowling around outside. Gibbs volunteered to take a look, but Billie refused to stay in the house alone.

They went out together, down the walk between the trees. Gibbs tried the garage door and found it locked. Billie's feminine indirection led her to the side door. It was open.

She went in. Tom Trent lay on his back. He was still warm. So was the barrel of the .32 he held in his right hand.

Billie called Gibbs. Gibbs called the doctor, then the police, then the studio. Trent wouldn't have approved of the order; he'd probably have wanted the studio called first. But that's what Gibbs did. He also verified Billie Trent's story, *in toto*.

Which meant that it was true. Or that they were in on it together.

The paper didn't say so, of course. That's just what *I* conjectured now. All the papers said was that neither of them had seen anyone, neither of them knew who might have called Trent, neither of them could definitely identify the gun as his. He had a big collection of pistols and revolvers, kept them in the garage, as a matter of fact. Some were on wall racks and some were in drawers. Plenty of ammunition was around, too. An ideal setup for suicide.

Or for something else.

Well, Gibbs was being questioned and so was Billie Trent. And the police were investigating...

It was a big story, all right. So big it had crowded out any possible pitiful little squib about my own adventures. A forcible abduction and a beating were just peanuts compared to cowboy-actor-suicide-in-garage-for-love-of-beautiful-blonde-star.

I put the papers aside and began opening my mail. About time I paid a little attention to my work. I'd almost forgotten I was still an agent after being kept so busy running around getting beat over the head and finding bodies. This private eye business can be very wearing.

It was a relief to open envelopes, to return again to the reality of the treasure hunt which constitutes a literary agent's daily life. A treasure hunt in search of little blue pieces of paper. Some of them are checks. Some of them are just slips saying, *"Sorry, not for us."* But you never know what's going to turn up next. After a while, the mailman becomes Mercury, bearing messages from the gods. And every time the phone rings, you jump.

I jumped.

"Hello."

"Hello yourself. Bannock. Did you read the papers?"

"Just now."

"Just now? Where the hell were you last night when it came over the radio? I called and called."

I told him where the hell I was last night.

He listened through it all without interrupting.

"You'd better come over to the office," he said. "We've got to figure things out."

I paused and watched my door open. "Can't make it right now," I told him. "I've got company. Get in touch with you later."

Then I hung up and turned to face Al Thompson.

"Sit down," I said. "You got here sooner than I expected."

"Never mind that. Who you talking to just now?"

"Friend of mine. Harry Bannock."

"Him again? What's the tie-up, Clayburn?"

"No tie-up. He wanted to find out what I thought about the news."

"What *do* you think?"

"Rogers."

"Roger?"

"No, Rogers. Will Rogers. He used to say it, didn't he? 'All I know is what I read in the papers.' "

"You sure that's all you know?"

"Why?"

"Last night you made some kind of crack to Sergeant Campbell. Something about you didn't believe this was suicide, because Trent was shot through the monogram initial of his jacket."

"I remember."

"You have anything else to go on when you made that remark?"

"No. Why?"

Thompson didn't answer. I leaned forward.

"It *was* murder," I said.

"Yeah. It was."

"Who?"

"Do you think I'd be sitting here now if I could answer that one?"

"Then how do you know?"

"Did a little checking. In the first place, it wasn't Trent's gun. We found a list, complete inventory of his stuff, with the permits and purchase dates. He was a careful, methodical guy when it came to his hobby. No such gun was listed. He wouldn't go in for an ordinary thirty-two pistol anyway." Thompson lit a cigarette. "Also, he wasn't killed standing up. He was killed lying down, on the floor. The bullet went through."

"Neither of those things rule out suicide," I said.

"That's right." Thompson blew smoke at my telephone. "But it seems mighty funny for a guy to lie down before he shoots himself in the chest that way. Mighty funny for him to buy or borrow a strange gun when he has a small arsenal on hand. Mighty funny for him to register every weapon he owns, and then file all the identification off the pistol he uses to kill himself with."

"Circumstantial evidence."

"So's the rest. Guy named Keasler driving past about the time of the shooting, near as we can establish it. Said he saw a car pulling away from Trent's place. Not out of the driveway; it was parked under the trees adjoining the property."

I nodded. "I remember the spot. You could put a car in there, back from the road, and nobody would notice it at night, unless they were looking for it."

"Right. We found marks there, too."

"Tire tracks?"

Thompson groaned. "No. It's never that simple when I get a case. This fellow Keasler didn't jot down the license number for me, either. Just saw a big black car pull away. A big black car just like a hundred thousand other cars in town. But that's enough for a lead."

"What about the butler, and Miss Trent?"

"They're clean."

"And that phone call?"

Thompson waved his cigarette. "Who knows?" He reached out and found an ashtray. "I didn't come here to make an official report. I came to find out if you had any basis for your suspicion about this being murder."

"No basis at all. I was serious about the monogram, though. Trent was a pretty conceited character."

"He was a pretty worried character, too. I talked to his sister."

"What'd she say?"

Thompson grinned. "She didn't know about your little caper last night. She suggested maybe you killed him."

"Why, the—"

The grin never left his face. "So come clean, Clayburn. She doesn't exactly seem to trust you. Why trust her? You saw her yesterday afternoon. What did she tell you?"

"I already gave my story."

"Sure. But I'm not convinced you gave us all you know. What did she say about Trent? Why did she come to you in the first place?"

"She was worried about him. He'd been drinking too much."

"Since when are you supposed to be interested in that? You the new head of Alcoholics Anonymous?"

I shook my head. "She came to me because she knew I'd seen Trent. Wondered if there was some connection."

"Was there?"

"No."

"All right, boy." Thompson stood up. "If that's the way you want it."

"That's the way it is." I walked him to the door. "Don't worry, if I turn up anything, I'll let you know."

He stopped grinning. "You'd better not try," he remarked. "You've turned up more than enough already. Clayburn, this whole business smells. Everywhere you go, there's murder. If I ever find out you've been holding out on us, I'll—"

"Put a tail on me if you like," I answered. "Just to save you the trouble for the moment, I'll tell you where I'm going right now. Over to Harry Bannock's office, to discuss the case. Is it all right if I mention it's murder? Or must I wait until the afternoon papers scoop me?"

"Suit yourself." He opened the door. "But please, I'm not

fooling. Keep out of this mess. Everything I told you at the first goes double now. This is big. And we don't want it to get any bigger. Unless you're shilling for some undertaker's union."

"I'm not shilling for anybody."

"Good. Just keep your nose clean, Clayburn. If you don't, somebody's going to be patting it with a spade."

Chapter Twelve

I drove over to Bannock's office.

He had a new receptionist. Could be that the other girl quit when she knew she wouldn't be getting Polly Foster's autograph.

I gave my name and asked for Harry.

"Mr. Bannock has left for the day."

"Home?"

"He didn't say."'

I didn't offer this girl any autograph-collecting services. I went out, got in the car, and drove to Bannock's place. The sun was shining over Laurel Canyon, but I wasn't in the mood for Nature appreciation.

There was too much to think about. Tom Trent was dead, and Hamilton Brackett was probably getting ready to declare another dividend to his stockholders on the strength of it. There was a notion—maybe Hamilton Brackett was the killer, on the loose, out drumming up business.

But why would he pick on Apex Studio players? I wondered about that. I wondered how Abe Kolmar must feel, losing his talent right and left. I wondered a lot about Kolmar, wondered so much I nearly ran into a coupe as it turned out of Bannock's driveway. It wasn't Bannock's car, though.

I turned in, parked, and went up the walk. The door opened before I had a chance to knock or ring, and I smelled that old familiar perfume.

"Hello," said Daisy.

"Is Harry home?"

"No. Why, were you expecting him?" She looked puzzled.

"Well, I talked to him this morning about getting together.

Then I took a run over to the office, and they said he'd left for the day."

"He didn't tell me anything about it." Daisy frowned. "Come on in, Mark."

I followed her into the front room. "Fix you something?"

"No, thanks."

"Mind if I have one, then? I've got the jumps."

"Getting you down, eh?"

"Can't you tell by looking at me? I'm a fright."

That was *her* opinion. To me she looked good. I'd thought I wasn't in the mood for nature appreciation, but that was before I saw Daisy. Today she was wearing white sateen lounging pajamas, and when she sat down on the sofa, drink in hand, and started to lounge...

"Mark, where do you think Harry went?"

"How should I know? Some studio, probably. You know how he operates."

"I know how he used to operate. Before all this started." She must have had the jumps after all. The drink disappeared before my eye, and she was on her feet already, mixing another. "But now he doesn't even call and let me know where to reach him. I never know what time he's coming home."

"Maybe the police are questioning him about Trent's death."

The liquor slopped over the edge of her glass "I—I never thought of that."

"Where was he when it happened, anyway?"

She mopped up the tabletop. "Why—home, home with me. That is, he *came* home. He'd gone out earlier in the evening to see some client, down near Pacific Palisades."

"But he was here most of the evening?"

"Of course." She began to work on that second drink. "Mark, you keep asking questions about Harry, almost as if you didn't trust him."

"Do you?"

She bit her lip. "Of course. He's my husband."

"I know. I keep reminding myself about that."

Daisy smiled. "Do you?"

I nodded. "Yeah. But that's not what I came here to talk about."

"Why not?"

For a minute I didn't think I was hearing straight. Apparently she realized this, because she stood up and walked over to where I was sitting. And then she put her drink down very carefully, and lowered herself into my lap.

I didn't move.

I didn't have a chance to move, because her arms were around me and her head was on my shoulder, and I could feel the weight and the warmth of her quivering against me. The perfume was rising all around me, and her voice was rustling into my ear.

"Oh, Mark, I'm glad. I'm so lonely, so frightened. I don't know what to do. If you only knew what it's been like, just sitting here day after day, wondering what was going to happen next."

"Please, Daisy."

"Don't talk. Let's not talk now. Let's forget all about what's happened. You'll do that for me, won't you, Mark? You'll help me to forget?"

I twisted my head away. "That's not my job, Daisy. I'm here to help you remember." Her pajamas had a tendency to gape. So did I. But I didn't move.

"Mark. Darling. Try to understand…"

I wasn't letting her finish her sentences, or anything else she planned on starting. I reached out and held her at arm's length. "I understand, Daisy," I said. "You don't go for me, really. You're just scared."

"All right. I'm scared. I said so, didn't I? How long do you think I can go on this way, watching people getting murdered, knowing that Harry's been threatened too?"

"So you went into a big vamp scene," I told her. "Which would end up by you getting me to promise that I'd quit the investigation."

She got off my lap so fast I thought she'd hit the ceiling. Literally. Figuratively, that's just what she was doing now. "You're going to quit!" she snapped. "You've got to! I'm not taking any more of this. They killed Foster, they killed Trent, they tried to kill you. Where's it going to end? Do you want to see Harry dead, is that it?"

"Calm down," I answered. "Take another drink. Take two drinks. Get yourself loaded, for all I care. Do you good."

"Nothing does any good. Not as long as this keeps on. Mark, you've got to lay off. Can't you see this is all your fault? If you hadn't stirred things up again, there wouldn't have been any trouble."

"My fault?" I shook my head. "Harry hired me, in case you don't remember. And have you forgotten why? Because he has to clear things up in order to swing his deal. You've got a big stake in this too, Daisy. You know that."

"Not enough to risk our lives—his and mine. Mark, be reasonable."

"I'm reasonable."

"I'll talk to Harry. I don't know how much he promised you for doing this, but I'll see that he pays you every penny, in full. You don't have to keep on just for the money."

"It isn't the money alone, believe me," I said. "And I don't expect to be paid off unless I deliver the goods."

She poured her third drink. This time she was slow about it, and careful. Nothing spilled, but when she turned to face me I could see she hadn't lied. She *was* jumpy, and her voice held an unnatural edge. "Quit talking about delivering the goods. I mean it. The minute I see Harry, I'm going to get him to stop you. This has gone far enough."

"It's going further, I'm afraid." I stood up. "Listen to me, Daisy. Stopping me won't help matters now. This is a police job, because of the murders. You can take me off the case, but they'll go on."

"Let them. They haven't done anything so far."

"How do you know? Don't underestimate the police. And they may turn up something any minute now. If they do, good. If they don't, things won't change. The murderer, who-ever he is, will still be at large. If he has any future plans, he'll go through with them whether I'm involved in the case or not. Seems to me you'd want my help. The more help you've got, the sooner we'll settle this thing."

"Mark, there's something you're not telling me. Some reason why you insist on risking your life, our lives, taking crazy chances. What is it?"

I tugged at my eye-patch. "I can't tell you, Daisy. Let's just say that I'm a crusader, shall we? And let it go at that?"

"Crusader?" She slammed her glass down on the table. "Well, I'm talking to Harry, wait and see. He'll have you off your horse in no time. So you might as well stop, right now."

I shrugged. "When he tells me to quit, I quit," I said. "Until then—"

"Where are you going?"

"Got to see a guy about breaking a lance with the hea-then." I headed for the door. "Tell Harry I'll call him."

"Mark…"

She wasn't angry any more. She was very soft. Soft and clinging.

"What is it?" I asked, as if I didn't know.

"Do you *have* to go?"

"I have to go. I'm sorry, Daisy. Really, I am."

"So am I. I—I'm not putting on an act, this time. I like you, Mark."

"I like you, too, Daisy. That's why I'm going to try and save the family fortune."

She sighed. Standing where she was, I could feel it as well as hear it. "All right, you stubborn idiot! But couldn't you at least kiss me?"

"No," I said. "I couldn't at least kiss you. As you damned well know."

"Maybe you're right, at that."

"I know I am. And so do you. See you, Daisy."

"Promise me you'll be careful?"

"I'm always careful. You've just had a demonstration." I

left her standing there and went out through the hall. The fresh air outside had its points, but I preferred the perfume I'd left behind.

Driving away, I wondered what was the matter with me. Old age setting in? Perhaps; although I hadn't noticed any of the symptoms when Daisy Bannock put her arms around me.

Then what was it? Why did I deliberately walk away from that setup and head for trouble?

Why was I stopping at this drugstore? Why did I call Apex and ask for Mr. Kolmar? Why did I bother to find out he was at home this afternoon instead of at the studio? And why did I get back in my car and head off to the San Fernando Valley?

I'd already *had* the San Fernando Valley. Enough to last me the rest of my lifetime, however long that might be. Going out there again might shorten it considerably.

And remembering fat little, redfaced Abe Kolmar, I couldn't understand why I'd prefer his company to Daisy's. Daisy had red-gold hair and white sateen pajamas. Why, Kolmar was baldheaded, and I bet he didn't have a pair of white sateen pajamas to his name.

So why was I going?

Mark Clayburn, crusader, riding his rusty steed into the Valley. Into the Valley of Death rode the six hundred. Bring on your heathen, your infidels. Here comes Clayburn, ye true and parfait knight. Dig the stance of that lance. Onward, Christian soldiers!

It was hot in the Valley this afternoon. I was sweating. I didn't stop perspiring as I passed Trent's place, either. No signs of life, though. There wouldn't be. And what about signs of death?

No police cars, either. I was glad of that. Maybe I'd be sorry, later on. A police car in the neighborhood might come in handy.

I kept driving. Kolmar lived way out. He was a good five

miles away from Trent. But come to think of it, that wasn't very far. A man could cover the distance in a very short time. I might ask Kolmar about that.

Then again, I might not. I'd have to wait and see.

I waited and saw his ranch loom ahead.

This was the genuine article. Kolmar did have a ranch, and it was big enough to serve as a location for his oat operas. Come to think of it, here's where Dick Ryan died. Here's where Dick Ryan died, and Tom Trent got it only five miles away. Very interesting.

The car entered the gateway between the fence posts and climbed a long hill. The big house was set way back from the road. I could see a corral and outbuildings, baking under the sunlight.

A new Hillman-Minx was parked in the driveway alongside of a veranda. Somebody was polishing the fenders with a rag.

I pulled up behind the car and let the motor die. Then I climbed out. The car-polisher glanced up, then walked around to meet me.

"Who you looking for?" he asked.

I stared, then stiffened. "You," I said. Then I took two steps forward and my right came up. There was a dull sound, a grunt, and another sound as he flopped at my feet.

I stood there, gazing down at the face of the little man who had come after me with Fritz.

My knuckles hurt. I started to rub them, then looked up as I heard a sound. A man appeared in the doorway of the house, a chunky man with a bald head. "What's the big idea?" he murmured.

"Just squaring a debt," I said. "I've owed this guy a punch on the jaw ever since he roughed me up the other night."

"You're Clayburn, aren't you?"

I nodded.

"I'm Abe Kolmar."

"I know. I was coming to see you."

"Is that any reason for assaulting one of my employees?"

"Told you why I hit him. He's one of the two guys who tried to kill me."

The man in the doorway shook his head. "Better take another look," he said. "This man couldn't have attacked you. I happen to know where he was at the time you were abducted. And so do the police, because that's where he was—at headquarters."

I stared down. The man at my feet began to mumble and stir. I eyed his features closely. "Wait a minute," I said. "Maybe I did make a mistake—"

"This is Joe Dean," said Kolmar. "My chauffeur. You made a mistake all right."

"I'm sorry, I could have sworn—"

Kolmar nodded. "A big mistake," he said. "Suppose you come inside now and let me straighten you out."

"Well—"

"Come inside." Kolmar made an impatient gesture with his hand.

I looked at it. He was holding a revolver.

"This way," he said.

I went this way.

Kolmar kept the muzzle trained on my waist. "You all right?" he called.

The little man was sitting up now. He held the side of his jaw and grunted.

"You got him, huh? This the bastard who slugged me? Put your gun down, A.J. I want a chance at him myself."

"Come in," Kolmar told him. "We're going to settle this inside."

Dean got to his feet and charged up the porch steps. "I'll settle him," he panted. "Hit a guy without warning, huh? I'll rip his heart out, the sonof—"

"Shut up!"

Dean shut up. We walked into the parlor. Kolmar jerked the gun toward me. "Over there," he said.

Dean began to move after me.

"You stay where you are," Kolmar ordered.

"But I only want to give him a—"

"Never mind."

I turned and nodded. "I'm sorry," I said. "I apologize. I thought you were somebody else, one of the men who tried to kill me last night. You look just like him. It was a natural mistake."

"The hell it was. You come right up and socked me one. If A. J. don't let me have a chance at you, I'll—"

"It's the truth," I said. "You look enough like this man to be his brother." I paused. "Do you have a brother, Dean?"

"No."

Kolmar grunted at him. "Get out," he said.

"Now wait a minute, A.J."

"Get out."

"All right." Dean moved toward the door. "But I'm not forgetting. You got something coming to you, brother."

He went out.

"Are you sure he hasn't got a brother?" I asked.

Kolmar grunted again. "I wouldn't know, Clayburn. I wouldn't know." The gun kept watching me out of its one eye. We made a good pair, but I didn't appreciate it right now.

"Suppose I ask the questions for a change," Kolmar suggested.

"Go ahead," I told him. "But why don't you put that thing away? You're not going to shoot me."

"Don't be too sure."

"Tell you the truth, I'm not." It was hard to grin, but I made it. And he put the gun down on the desk. Not too far away, though.

"What's your interest in this business, Clayburn?"

"Looking for a story. Didn't Trent tell you?"

"Why should he tell me anything?"

"That's one of the things I wanted to find out. Trent worked for you. Polly Foster worked for you. Dick Ryan worked for you. And they're all dead now."

"So?"

"It could be a coincidence. But I don't think so."

He almost reached for the gun again. Instead his hand went to his pocket and came out with a handkerchief. He mopped his forehead. There was plenty to mop. It went all the way back.

"What are you suggesting, Clayburn? That I killed them? That's impossible. The police have my alibis."

"I'm not saying you pulled the trigger, no. But you have people working for you."

"Killers?"

"This Joe Dean wanted to do a job on me just now."

"You hit him. Naturally, he got sore."

"Naturally."

"But that doesn't mean he'd kill you. It doesn't mean he'd kill anybody."

"He has a record in Detroit."

"I wouldn't know about that. He's just my chauffeur."

"And he used to work for Dick Ryan."

"That's right." Kolmar put the handkerchief down. "He used to work for Dick Ryan and Ryan was murdered. You know what that cost me, to have that boy die on me in the middle of production? And everything he ever did went sour when the news hit the papers. Reefers, yet, they had to drag reefers into the case!"

"I know."

"You know something else?" Kolmar sighed. "Polly Foster cost me another fortune: seven reels in the can, and three to go. Now she's dead. I ask you!"

"Tough."

"Tough, he says? And Trent. We were getting ready to do something with Trent. Had a new script lined up, going to make him over into a sympathetic character. Gotten ourselves a new hero type, maybe. So what happens? Bang."

"I'm aware of that."

"Well be aware of this, then, Clayburn. You think I'd go to work and commit suicide by knocking off my own

contract players? You think I'd toss a million dollars out the
window like that? It don't make sense."

"Nothing makes sense," I answered. "Nothing. That's
why I'm grabbing at anything that looks as if it formed even
part of a pattern. Like the fact that all these people worked
for you."

"You think I haven't wondered about that? Maybe it's one
of my lousy competitors, some of those guys would murder
their own mothers. Take a fella like Sam Hague, now."

I shook my head. "That's nonsense, and you know it."

"So what else can a guy figure? Like you say, it's all
meshuggah."

"There's one other possible link," I said slowly. "And
that's what I came out here to see about."

"What's that?"

"Reefers."

"I don't know what you're talking about."

"Oh yes you do. They found evidence in Ryan's trailer,
didn't they? I think that forms part of the pattern, too. Did
Polly Foster smoke weed? What about Tom Trent?"

"You're *meshuggah* yourself, Clayburn. My people are
clean, I wouldn't have anybody around unless I was sure of
that."

"You've got Dean. He has a record."

"So maybe I'll fire him. Clayburn, take it from me, that
reefer talk don't mean a thing."

"I think it does. I think it's the key to the whole mess. And
I was hoping you'd be able to furnish some information
which might help me. If not, I'll just have to keep on
looking."

"For a lousy magazine story, huh?"

"It's a living."

"Living?" He came around from behind the desk. "You
talk about a living, after what's happened to me? I'm going
to tell you something, Clayburn. These killings cost me
some of my top talent. I lost more than a million bucks so far.

How long you think I can afford to sit still and watch this kind of stuff go on?

"You think I'm blind or something? I know what's happening. It's a conspiracy, that's what it is. You think you fool me? Maybe the cops believe that cockeyed story of yours about how you're out trying to write a yarn for the magazines. But I know better.

"It's a frame, isn't it? I was right, wasn't I? Somebody's behind all this; somebody's out to ruin me. And you know who. Because you're working for them!"

"That's not so."

"I say it is." He bent over me, shaking. "And I know what you really come for. You want a deal, is that it? Well, go ahead. I'll play ball. Tell me how much you want to lay off. But you got to promise to give me the names. I want to know who it is that's trying to knife me."

"You've got it all wrong. Nobody's out to get you, Mr. Kolmar."

"Quit stalling and tell me how much."

"I don't want your money. I just want these murders to stop."

He grunted again, turned away. I stood up.

"Where you think you're going?"

"Away," I said. "If you can't help me, I'll just have to find someone who can."

"You aren't going anywhere."

He said it as if he meant it, and when he turned again I saw that he did. Because he had the gun in his hand once more.

"You think I'm gonna let you walk out of here just like that?" he muttered. "Not me. Not until I get the truth. Not until you tell me who you're working for, what they think they're trying to do to me."

"Honestly, Mr. Kolmar—"

"Honestly, he says. Honestly! There ain't no such thing in this business. I know. For days now I been thinking about it, sitting there in my office and trying to figure it out. What's happening in the industry? Why are they out to get me—

me? I'm just an independent; why pick on me? Killing Foster, killing Trent. Wrecking my schedule. Trying to bankrupt me. They're all against me." He was shaking and the sweat poured down, rolling into his eyes and making him blink. But he held the gun, held it steady.

"I couldn't work today, Clayburn. I sat there and felt like I was going to blow my top. I had to come home. Something must of told me to do it. Because you're here now, and you're staying until you talk."

"But I don't know anything about it, I swear it."

"Swear! Go ahead and swear. But make it fast. I give you ten seconds, Clayburn, ten seconds to talk, or I shoot."

"You're crazy!"

"So I'm crazy. What difference does it make? They kill your people, wreck your pictures, take away your business. You think I care what happens now? I just want to know who did it, that's all. And unless you tell me…"

I sighed. "You win. But you better not let Thompson see you with that gun."

"Thompson? That dick?"

"Just drove up," I said. "See him coming up to the porch now." I nodded toward the window. Kolmar turned his head. "Where?"

I didn't answer. I was too busy jumping him. I got my hand on the wrist holding the gun, and then I shoved my knee against his elbow. The gun dropped. Kolmar growled and made a grab at my neck. I knocked his hand down.

Then I picked up the gun. "Sorry," I said. "There's been enough shooting around here. Sit down and cool off, Mr. Kolmar. I know how you feel, but try to understand this—I don't know who killed your people. But I intend to help the police find out. And if I do hear something, I'll tell you without asking."

He slumped into a chair, swimming in sweat. "Give me that gun," he wheezed.

"No. I'm taking it with me. You don't need a gun, Mr. Kolmar."

"Yes I do. Give it to me."

I didn't answer, just started to walk out.

"You'd better," he panted. "I'll send Dean after you. He'd like that."

"Better not, you've lost enough employees already."

There was no answer to that one.

I left him sitting there, staring and sweating.

The sun was going down when I got outside. The Hillman-Minx still stood there, but I didn't see Joe Dean around. And I didn't try to look for him.

I put the gun in the glove compartment and drove back to town. A long drive, but I'd made it before. And once again, it was dark when I arrived. It was almost six-thirty when I hit downtown.

Time to eat; but first a stop at the office. Maybe I could call Bannock from there. Maybe I'd find some mail waiting for me.

I didn't call Bannock, and there was no mail. Something else waited for me. A visitor, standing there in the dim light of the hall.

I came around the top step before I saw the figure, and then I wished I'd brought the gun. The figure wheeled, and I caught sight of a white face and wide eyes.

"You!"

"That's right," I said. "How are you, Miss Trent?"

Chapter Thirteen

"I've been waiting over an hour," she said. "When they let me out down at the station, I came right over here."

"Let's go inside, shall we?" I unlocked the door.

"Is it—safe?"

I looked at her. "Do you mean am I going to murder you?"

She blushed. "N-no. The police told you what I said, didn't they? I'm sorry about that, really I am. I was so hysterical, I wasn't thinking."

"Understandable. Forget it."

"Then when I heard you'd been beat up, I felt awful for suspecting you. That's what I was thinking about now when I asked if it was safe. I mean, nobody's following you?"

"Not that I know of. What about yourself?"

"I don't think so. They let me go."

"So I heard." I pushed the door open, switched on the light. "Just want to see if I've got any important mail. We needn't stay here."

I picked up the pile of letters the postman had shoved under the door. It was all routine stuff, as near as I could see. No need to open any of it now.

"Suppose we go somewhere and eat?" I suggested. "I'm starved."

She nodded. We went downstairs and hit the first restaurant across the street. Apparently she was hungry, too. We didn't do much talking until after the roast beef arrived.

Then I told her about what had happened since I saw her at the Foster funeral, up to and including my recent interview with Kolmar and his chauffeur.

Her eyes went wide. "They lied to you," she said. "I know they were lying."

"How's that?"

"Dean *does* have a brother. He isn't his twin, but he looks like it. I've seen him, when I went to visit Tom on location at the ranch."

"You're sure?"

"Positive. His name is Andy. Do you think—?"

"That Kolmar hired him and the other mug to beat me up? Yes, it sounds probable."

"Then maybe he's the murderer."

"I won't rule it out, no. But I'm inclined to doubt it. What he told me makes sense—dollars and cents. He's got too much dough tied up in his company to bump off his players. At least he'd wait until their picture roles were completed. And there's no apparent motive." I paused. "Did Kolmar ever quarrel with your brother over anything?"

"No. I don't believe so."

"You see? As I say, there's no apparent motive. Unless one turns up, we'll have to rule Kolmar out."

Billie Trent sighed. "But then why would he hire these men to beat you up, threaten to kill you?"

"Because he's afraid. I told you how he acted when I saw him. These deaths have given him a persecution complex. He thinks everybody's out to get him; that his actors have been murdered just in order to ruin his business."

"But that's fantastic!"

"Stranger things have happened out here. Anyway, Kolmar must have some such notion. He heard I was investigating, thought I might be tied in with the plot to wreck him. Those two characters were probably hired to beat the truth out of me. Then again…"

"What?"

"I don't know. It could be something else entirely."

Billie Trent picked up her coffee. "Yes, it could be." Her brown eyes were thoughtful. "That beating you took, did it make you decide to quit?"

"I went out to Kolmar's, didn't I? No, I'm going to stick

this thing out if it k—" I stopped and grinned at her. "Sorry, didn't mean to be morbid."

"That's all right. I understand." She put her hand on mine. It was a nice hand, and I let it rest there. A nice, tanned, healthy, outdoor-type hand that trembled only a little.

She leaned forward. "But there's one thing I don't understand," she continued. "And that's why you're doing all this."

"The article."

Billie Trent shook her head. "I can't believe that," she said. "You don't have to tell me the real reason, but there must be one. You're not interested in an article any more, and I doubt if you were in the first place."

I looked at her hand, and then I squeezed it. "That's right. Somebody hired me to investigate the Ryan death. I won't mention names, because it's confidential and it has nothing to do with what's happened, believe me. Anyway, I started out on that basis. And I'm continuing for a personal reason." I looked at her hand again because it was easier to go on if I didn't look at her face.

"You remember when I saw you the other day, I asked if your brother ever smoked reefers. Ryan did, you know. You denied it. And today Kolmar denied that any of his people ever indulged. But that angle keeps coming into this case. When Ryan's body was discovered, they found roaches— marijuana cigarette butts—in his trailer. Some viper broke into my apartment shortly after I started to work on the murder and left part of a stick there. I've reason to suspect Polly Foster was on tea herself."

Billie nodded at me. "You sound as if you knew a lot about it."

"I do. You see, I used to go off on a stick-kick myself. Oh, I wasn't an addict, but a few years back I went to a party and somebody passed the muggles around just for laughs. I tried one and liked it. Didn't get high, because I didn't know the technique of smoking. You've got to suck in a lot of air along with the smoke when you inhale.

"Turned out that this girl—it was a girl and I'd been seeing quite a lot of her—was a regular user. She taught me how to use the weed. Pretty soon I was sending myself with the stuff any time I felt down. Never bought any of it directly: she got it from a pusher, but she wouldn't tell me the source and I didn't ask.

"Don't get me wrong, now. I wasn't dependent; the drug didn't have a physiological hold on me. Marijuana works differently on different people, just like alcohol. Some people drink and get sick, others get drunk and get a glow. Some people have to drink, others can go out and get drunk and then lay off for as long as they like. That's the way it was with me and reefers. I'd pad up with this girl once a week or so and go out of this world. I won't deny I got pleasure from it, and I thought I knew what I was doing at the time. Until I found that I was starting to hit the stuff twice a week, then oftener. And not just in private, either. We went to a couple of parties when we were high. We never got into any trouble, because people thought we'd had a few drinks. Except for a few others like ourselves who knew the score because they indulged themselves.

"But you only think you know the score when you get into something like that. It creeps up on you gradually. You get careless about the amount you smoke, the frequency. Worst of all, you begin to get that smart aleck feeling, that snotty fraternity outlook, as though you were the privileged member of a secret society. Using your private language, your slang code, you think that you and your fellow addicts are just a little smarter and just a little better than anyone else. You're a solid sender, the non-addicts are squares.

"Of course, the actual smoking helps to give you that sense of false security, false superiority. When you're high you can do anything without getting hurt. Like piling into the car with your girl at two in the morning and barrelling off to Las Vegas to get married at a hundred miles an hour.

"That's what I did, one morning last year. Both of us high, and the car sailing along on a little pink cloud while we giggled at nothing and watched the road curve like a snake. That's what I told her, 'It's like driving over a snake's back.' I remember, because it was the last thing I said when we went around the curve without slowing down and I hit the side of the culvert.

"When I woke up, I was in the hospital, minus an eye. And she was already buried. End of story."

"So that's what happened," Billie murmured.

"Yes, that's what happened. They thought it was an accident, and I said it was an accident, but I know differently. I was responsible for that girl's death. Sure, I paid for it in a way: lost her, lost an eye, lost a good business. But there's still another installment due on the debt. I've quit the habit myself and I'd like to go after the source of the stuff. They peddle it all over town, you know that. Peddle it to people who are hungry for thrills, for kicks, for escape. And I know what kind of escape it brings. The kind it brought to Dick Ryan, the kind it brought to my girl.

"Now do you see why I want to go on? This thing is a racket, a big, vicious racket, involving important money and entangling important people. You've read enough about the estimates on the number of addicts in this country, the yearly take on the traffic. And you've read what addiction does to some people. As I said, not all of them turn into drug-crazed killers, the way the sensation mongers like to picture them. But plenty of them get into the kind of mess I got into. Thousands more ruin their health, ruin their reputations, ruin their lives because of the need to procure a regular supply from the pushers who bleed them white. They'll do anything to get the stuff: beg for it, steal for it, even kill for it if they have to. I'm not turning moralist on you, just telling you the accepted facts. At least, that's the way I feel about it. And it's the reefer angle in these killings that makes me want to continue.

"I've never told anyone this before. I don't quite know why I'm telling you except that maybe, if you understand, you can help me."

I stopped. Now I looked at her. The brown eyes were still grave, but this time her hand was squeezing mine.

"I'm glad you told me," she said. "Because it makes it easier for me to tell you. I was going to, anyway. That's why I came." She paused. "I—I lied the other day."

"About your brother?"

"Yes. He did smoke reefers. He, and Ryan. I don't know about any of the others. But that's why he was so jittery and upset there at the last. He couldn't get his usual supply."

"Who was he getting them from?"

"I don't know. He never talked about it to me, of course; he didn't even realize I knew. But I'd read enough and heard enough to recognize a marijuana cigarette when I saw one, and he got careless about cleaning out his room. Gibbs knew, too, because he'd seen Tom smoking."

"Did Gibbs have any ideas where your brother got his stuff?"

"No. I asked him. From Ryan, or Ryan's friends—that's what he thought. And then, after Ryan died, something went wrong."

"Did you tell the police this?" I muttered.

"Of course not. That's the part I couldn't tell anyone. You know what it would do to Tom's reputation. I was thinking of that the other day when I came to you, hoping you could find out something without the police getting wind of it. Now that Tom's dead, I don't want his name blackened."

"But you should have told them," I said. "If it helps them to find the killer…"

She shook her head. "It wouldn't do any good for me to say my brother was an addict. If I knew anything more than just that, yes. But that's all. And they already have the information on Dick Ryan; that should be enough."

"What's their theory about your brother's death?" I asked.

She shrugged. "I don't know. They just kept asking me questions. Who were Tom's friends? Did he have any enemies?"

"Did he?"

"None that I know of."

"How about him and this man Dean?"

"I don't know." She brushed her hair from her forehead. "You're just as bad as the police."

"Sorry."

"I don't really mean that." Billie smiled at me. "It's just that I'm so sick of questions, questions, questions all the time."

"One or two more, and that's all," I promised. "Did they find anything out about who called your brother that last evening?"

"No. He answered the phone himself."

"And that was the only call he got?"

She leaned forward again. "That evening, yes. But when we were leaving for the funeral, there was another."

"Did you tell the police?"

"No. Because of what I said, about Tom's reputation. She was nothing but a tramp. I hated her, and I wasn't going to—"

"Who? Tell me."

Billie hesitated. "That Mexican girl—Estrellita Juarez."

"She phoned before the funeral?"

"Yes. I heard Tom talking to her in the next room. He didn't speak to me about it after, but he let her name slip during the conversation."

"What did he say?"

"I can't remember. Something about wanting to see her, and why was it impossible. Something else, he was thanking her but he wasn't scared." She paused. "Yes, that's what he said, I recall now! He wasn't scared, and he wouldn't think of leaving. But that doesn't make sense, does it?"

"First sense I've heard," I muttered. "Don't you see now? The cops have been looking for this Juarez dame from the start. She disappeared right after Ryan's death. Why? Obviously because she knows something about it and doesn't want to be questioned. She called your brother to warn him, warn him about something or someone threatening his life. Told him to get out of town, probably.

"No wonder he was nervous; that, plus being deprived of weed. Then, sometime during the evening, he got another call. He went somewhere and the warning came true."

Billie Trent frowned. "Then you think I should go to the police now and tell them about that call?"

It was my turn to frown. "You don't want to, do you? Because your brother and Juarez were...?"

She nodded.

"All right. Let me handle it. I've got a hunch that even if the cops know she's still in town, they won't be able to find her. Even if they do, she wouldn't talk. Maybe I'll have better luck. At least, it's worth a try."

"You'll be careful?"

This was *my* day, all right. Two women in a row telling me to be careful. I gave her hand a final pat. "Sure. Careful Clayburn, that's me." We got up and left the restaurant. "Can I drop you off?"

"No. I'm staying in town, at Gerry Summer's house, until after the funeral. You'll be there?"

I'd forgotten all about it. "Yes," I said. "Tomorrow?"

"That's right."

"See you then."

We parted on the corner. I went back to my office, and read the mail. I was particularly interested in a little bulletin from the editorial office of an eastern newspaper. They were starting a Sunday supplement and indicated they were open to the submission of short stories. Their requirements specifically emphasized that they were not interested in murders, crimes of violence, sexual transgressions, marital infidelity; no profanity or drinking in the stories, and absolutely nothing offensive to religious organizations or reflecting upon the morals and integrity of any group.

I did a little wondering about what would happen if they should apply the same standards to the real life stories on their front page, and then forgot it. Maybe they had something there; maybe their readers wanted a diet of pap for escape. Maybe they felt safer if they sat back and closed their eyes to the terrifying truth all around them.

But I couldn't. I knew too much of the truth, because I'd been a part of it. And I had the rather stubborn personal conviction that the more people who knew the truth, the better. The truth about what makes people dope, and drink, and deviate and dissemble and destroy. Destroy…

I picked up the phone and called Bannock's house. The maid answered.

"Hello, Sarah, this is Mr. Clayburn. Is Mr. Bannock there?"

"No sir, he's out for the evening."

"Mrs. Bannock?"

"She's out, too."

"Thank you. Tell Mr. Bannock I'll get in touch with him tomorrow."

That was that. Nothing to do now but go home and wait for tomorrow.

I locked the office and went downstairs.

Without realizing it, I'd had my luck working with me when I called and found Bannock was out. Because if he'd been home I'd have talked to him. And I wouldn't have reached the street just when I did. Just in time to see the squad car pull up behind my heap.

I was out the door and down the street before anyone noticed. They didn't go up right away; they were opening the door of my car. It took three cops to do it. One of them opened the glove compartment and brought out Kolmar's gun. I could see him pointing at it, saying something.

He put it in his pocket and sat there in the front seat. The other two cops started for the doorway of the office building. I didn't wait to see them go in. I knew all I needed right now.

Kolmar had started something. Probably cooked up some story about me coming out there and attacking him and Dean and stealing his gun. That's a criminal offense. At least, it would be criminal enough to get me locked up. Locked up and out of the way.

So they'd come looking for me at the office. They'd be looking for me at the apartment, at the hotel. Technically now, I was a fugitive from justice.

What does a fugitive from justice do?

I know what I did. I walked over to the Hotel Mars and took a room under the name of Orville Wright. It was that kind of a fleabag. I could have brought in a blonde and registered her with me as my brother Wilbur and nobody would ask any questions. Any more than they did when they saw I didn't have any baggage. Five bucks on the line in advance; that's all they cared to know about.

I went upstairs and sat down in my crummy little room and spread my crummy little assets on the crummy little bed. Forty-four dollars and twelve cents in cash. A driver's license, but no car any more. A key to an office which I wouldn't dare to use. My own gun was up there, in the desk. A social security card, but no feeling of being socially secure to go with it.

There wasn't much security left for me now, I realized; not with my name out, and my description. This eye-patch was easy to spot anywhere. I didn't have much chance. And I didn't have much time.

That was the rub. If I intended to do anything, I'd have to work fast from now on. The police were looking for me. Kolmar and his pals were looking for me. The murderer was looking for me, or was that last remark redundant? I didn't know, but I'd better find out in a hurry. Somewhere in the streets below a siren wailed. I closed the window, pulled down the blinds and went to bed. That kept the siren out of everything.

Everything except my dreams.

Chapter Fourteen

I took a chance going out the next morning. I took a chance going into the barber for a shave, took another when I stopped off for breakfast.

But all this was only a rehearsal. A rehearsal for the big chance, when I called Bannock's office.

The girl put me through.

"Mark. Where are you?"

"That's what a lot of people would like to know. Have you heard?"

"Damned right I've heard. What'd you do?"

"Don't want to talk about it over the phone. Where can I see you?"

"Better not come out here."

"I didn't intend to. But I want to go over some things fast. I'd counted on getting together with you at Trent's funeral this afternoon. Now it looks as if I'm not going."

Bannock was silent. "Hello?" I said, jiggling the receiver.

"I'm still here. Just thinking. Look, I'm leaving around noon to pick up Daisy. We planned to eat and then go to the funeral. Suppose I tell her to eat at home and I'll come by for her later. That okay?"

"Fine."

"Where'll I find you?"

I hesitated. "You know Perucci's?"

"You mean that spaghetti joint way down near the Union Station?"

"That's the one."

"Don't tell me I've got to drive all the way down there."

"Suit yourself," I said. "It's pretty tough on you, I know

that. Me, all I have to worry about is how to dodge the police and a couple of strong-arm artists and a murderer."

"All right, I'm sorry. I'll be there. Twelve?"

"Good. Reason I picked it is nobody ever comes there at noon. And they've got a back room."

"Fine. Mark, I'm awfully upset about getting you into such a mess."

"Don't be. If you want to help, here's what you do. Try to get a line on Estrellita Juarez for me."

"But I thought the cops—"

"Sure, they looked for her. Probably called Central Casting, stuff like that. You know a few people. Get on the phone this morning and ask around. Make it sound as if you had a part lined up, or she has a check coming for back work. Say anything. Do what you can for me. I think it's important."

"You do? You mean you've found something out?"

"Tell you when I see you."

And I did.

He met me at Perucci's and we ate spaghetti. That is, he ate spaghetti and I talked. While he was busy unraveling the stuff, I was busy unraveling the saga of the past two days, including, of course, my reasons for trying to locate Miss Juarez.

He shook his head. "No dice, pal. I tried. Called everybody in town. Nobody knows where she disappeared to. I even contacted Central Casting, just for the gag of it. They said her name had been dropped from the rolls. How do you like that?"

"I don't. We need her, Harry."

"If you say so, sweetheart."

I stabbed my fork at him. "What's the matter?" I asked.

"Matter? Nothing's the matter. Why?"

"I don't know. Anytime anybody makes with that 'sweetheart' stuff I get suspicious. Level with me, Harry. Has your wife been talking to you?"

He moved his head up and down between mouthfuls.

"Wants you to drop this investigation, is that it?"

Another movement.

"How do you feel about it?"

"I don't know." He pushed his plate back. "I've been doing some thinking, Mark. About this whole setup. Maybe she's right. Maybe we made a mistake stirring up trouble when we didn't have to. Just suppose I hadn't gotten this idea of trying to clear Ryan's name. So I wouldn't sell the series to See-More for a while. What of it? In another five or six months or so, everybody'd have forgotten. I could sell it to them then, or someone else. But no. I had to play eager beaver. I had to get smart, call you in. And now where are we? With all these killings, Ryan's name has fresh mud all over it."

I tugged my mustache. "Is this you talking, Harry, or is it Daisy?"

"Oh, she gave me hell all right. But not about the business deal. It's the murders that worry her. Ever since I got this call telling me to lay off she's been frightened about it. Last night she told me about seeing you, made me promise to quit."

"Did you promise?"

"Well—"

"Do you want to fire me?"

"Mark, what the hell are we going to do? I don't want to get bumped off, and I don't want to see you get bumped off, either. If Kolmar or anybody else finds out I'm responsible for you re-opening the case, my goose is cooked all over town. Look at the trouble he's caused you already. You can't expect to dodge the cops forever."

"I don't," I said. "Just give me another twenty-four hours."

"You really think you're that close?"

"Just a hunch," I answered. "If I could only talk to one or two people."

"But couldn't the police do it? If you went to them?"

"I can't go to them. Kolmar's fixed that. They'll put me on ice so fast there won't be a chance to get a word in edgewise.

By the time they listen to me anything can happen. And you know what I mean by anything, Harry."

"I know."

"Besides, if I went to them, I'd have to go clean. Tell them the works, all about you hiring me and why. You wouldn't want that, would you?"

"No, I wouldn't."

"Twenty-four hours, that's all I ask. I've come this far. Maybe we can still save this deal for you. That's worth a gamble, isn't it?"

"If Daisy knew—"

"Don't tell her, then. No sense of her worrying any more. Leave it to me, Harry. I'll get word to you before tomorrow night. Either way."

"Where you going now?"

"It's best that you don't know," I said. "Give me a hundred on account, though. Hiding out costs money."

He gave me two hundred.

"Thanks. Now run along and pick up Daisy and go to your funeral. Tell her I called you and you fired me over the phone because the cops are after me. Tell her anything that'll make her happy. And just wait until you hear from me."

Bannock scratched his head. "The way you act, anybody'd think you had some kind of personal interest in this case."

I smiled at him. "Maybe you've got something there. After a guy gets his apartment broken into, his life threatened, his brains knocked out, and his liberty jeopardized by the police, he's inclined to take a rather personal interest in such matters."

Harry Bannock glanced around the back room, then pulled me over into the corner. "I almost forgot," he murmured. "Can you use this?" His hand disappeared inside his coat, emerged again. I caught the glint of metal on a gun barrel.

"Where'd it come from?" I asked.

"It's mine. I've been carrying it, ever since I got that call. But something tells me you'll probably need it more than I will."

"Something tells me you're right," I said.

I slipped the gun into my pocket.

"Careful, it's loaded."

I nodded. "Thanks."

Then he went out and climbed into his big car, and I went out and climbed into the nearest drugstore.

They didn't have what I was looking for, so I went to another, and another. Finally I hit a dingy little place which carried the product I was looking for. It was the City Directory.

Nothing so remarkable about that. You want to look somebody's address up, that's the first thing you go for. Even the cops use it.

But nine times out of ten, they look in the current issue. And nine times out of ten, that's all they ever look in.

That's why I tried the run-down drugstores, the ones with the dusty displays in the windows and the rubber goods counter up front. Sometimes they have an older edition of the Directory. This one did.

I turned to *J* in a hurry. *Juarez*. Plenty of names here; a lot of them right in this neighborhood, around Olvera Street. But no Estrellita. Of course, I could start calling or start hiking around. Maybe I'd strike a family sooner or later…if she lived with her family.

No, come to think of it, she wouldn't have. She'd been Trent's girl, and before that probably anybody's. Including guys like Joe Dean.

Joe Dean. I went after the *D*s now. Dean was living with Kolmar on the ranch, and he'd worked for Ryan. But where was he two years ago?

I found out. *Dean, Joseph*. And the address, on Broadway, not more than five blocks away.

Hunch, long-shot, call it whatever you like. I only knew that I had to start someplace. And it might as well be over on

Broadway. That seemed to be the right neighborhood for what I was interested in.

I walked over, slowly. The afternoon sun was hidden by smog, and the streets were gray, gray as stone. And crawling along them were what you find when you turn over a stone.

This was Broadway. Not Broadway, New York. Broadway in L.A.; just a knife's throw from Main and a blind stagger from Olive. Bumway. Skidway. Wrongway. The kind of a street you find in every big city. Even in that nice eastern city where the newspaper doesn't want to contaminate its readers with sordid stories of unpleasant people.

I saw plenty of unpleasant people during my walk, and their sordid stories were usually quite apparent. There was a girl with platinum blonde hair who somewhat resembled Polly Foster in appearance. But her dress was sleazy, her eyes were puffy, and she was walking with a big Mexican who'd never put her in the movies; at least, not in the kind of movies that would lead to stardom in anything except a public health clinic. I noted a man of the same general physical build as Harry Bannock, up to a point. *Down* to a point, rather; he rolled along on a coaster platform because he lacked legs. I saw a baldheaded little fellow who might have passed for Abe Kolmar, except that Kolmar wouldn't have been snoring in an areaway with an empty pint of rotgut cradled in his lap. A fellow resembling Al Thompson stood picking his teeth in front of a cigar store; he stepped out and offered to sell me some pictures Thompson would never have approved of, and said he could introduce me to the subjects if I so desired. I saw a man almost as handsome as the late Dick Ryan, in a Latin sort of way. He was cursing and being cursed by a fat Indian woman whose four off-spring clung to her skirts and pummelled her pregnant belly. There was a girl about the same age and complexion as Billie Trent; at least I thought so until she turned her head and I saw the purple blotch covering the left side of her face. And there was a man with a mustache and an eye-patch, just like me. Only *his* patch covered both eyes, and he held out a battered tin cup. *There but for the grace of God…*

Yes, there but for the grace of God went all of us, and there seemed to be plenty the grace of God had somehow overlooked. Everybody overlooked them, including the nice, clean family newspapers and the smug little moralists who devoted their oracular pronouncements to solving the vital problems of people who couldn't make up their minds between buying a new station wagon or taking a vacation in Hawaii this season.

I walked on, thinking there wasn't anything particularly original about my philosophy. On the other hand, there wasn't anything particularly original about a run-down neighborhood or its run-down inhabitants, either. Maybe they were happy. Maybe they pitied *me.* Most of them would, if they knew the police were looking for me. *That* they could understand.

And remembering, I kept a lookout for squads or patrolmen. My luck held. My luck held all the way to the Harcourt Apts.

That's what the grimy stone lettering read: *Harcourt Apts.,* in abbreviated grandeur. There hadn't been much grandeur to begin with when they built this old three-story block of flats, and none of it remained now. The lobby was about the size of a pay toilet and looked no more inviting. To the right on the ground floor was a liquor store; the left had been retained as living quarters by someone who'd placed a sign in the front window reading *Gypsy Horoscopes.*

I walked up the steps, into the lobby. There were twelve buzzers to ring, but only seven names to choose from in the adjoining panels. Three of them I could read; the other four were either illegibly written or had been rendered illegible by the action of time and grime.

There was nothing resembling the name of Dean or Juarez that I could read. Maybe I was the wrong guy for the job. Fellow name of Jean-Francois Champollion might have had better luck. This stuff couldn't be much harder to decipher than the Rosetta Stone. Say 50 percent harder at the most.

I was still squinting, wondering whether or not I ought to start ringing doorbells at random and going into a one-eyed version of a Fuller Brush Man routine, when somebody shuffled out into the hall and leaned against the side of the wall.

"Lookin' for me?"

She was a fat woman with almost invisible eyebrows and pale yellow hair done up in pin curlers; she was wearing a pink housecoat decorated at the throat with braid and egg yolk. I smiled at her.

"Could be," I said.

"You after a readin'? C'mon in."

I remembered *Gypsy Horoscopes*. Victor Herbert should see *this* little Gypsy Sweetheart. But I followed the un-corseted amplitude of her behind into the musty flat off the first landing.

The front room was dark, rankly odorous. She waddled over to a gas burner.

"Sit right down," she said. "First I gotta make the tea." But she didn't move away immediately. I noticed she had her paw out. "Two bucks," she said. "Advance."

I gave her two dollars. She turned away and busied herself at the stove. The tea came from a cabinet. I noticed that the better Gypsies were doing their tea leaf readings with Salada nowadays.

She put the pot on, then came over and planted herself in a chair across the table from me. A lamp switched on.

"Let me have your palm," she said. "Give you a readin' while you wait."

"Look," I said. "I'm in a hurry. I don't need a regular reading. It's something else."

Her eyes narrowed. She watched me as I put my hand in my pocket.

"What?"

"Do you have any experience locating missing articles?"

"Lost somethin', eh? What was it?"

"It wasn't a something. It was a someone. A man named

Joe Dean lived here a few years ago. I'm looking for a friend of his, a girl named Estrellita Juarez."

She stood up. "Who sent you?"

"Nobody. I just thought you might be able to help."

"Don't know the name, mister. I just moved in here last year."

"But I thought you might be able to use your divination—"

"Crap!" She stood up. "You a copper?"

"No. I'm an agent. I used to work for the same studio as Miss Juarez. She's got some money coming to her for a bit she did some while ago. They asked me to find her. All we had on file was Dean's old address."

"I wouldn't know nothin' about it." She started to get up.

I took my hand out of my pocket. "Maybe if you concentrate on this it might help," I told her.

She stared at the twenty I held in my palm, then sat down again.

"You on the level about having money for her?"

I nodded. "I'm no cop, you ought to know that. If I was, I'd have put the cuffs on you the minute I came in and took a sniff. That tea on the stove isn't the only kind you serve here."

"You're crazy." Her upper lip was wet.

I held out the bill. "Knock it off," I said. "I'm just interested in saving time. All I really have to do is start rapping on doors. But like I said, I'm in a hurry."

She reached for the money. "Yeah. But if there's any trouble."

"There won't be. I'm not even going to say where I found out."

"Crap." It must have been an old Gypsy expression of some sort, and I wondered what it meant.

"Well, if you won't tell me where to find her, at least you might be able to tell me something about her. What she's doing nowadays, and—"

"Oh, ast her yourself!" she sighed. "Number eight. Second floor rear."

I stood up and made for the door.

"You won't say nothin' about who told you?"

"No. How could I? I've never been here. Let's both try to remember that, shall we?"

I went out and closed the door on the mustiness behind me. Then I walked upstairs.

Number eight was easy to find. I knocked. There was no answer. I knocked again. Still nothing. I tried the door gently, turning the knob and pushing. It was locked, all right.

Well, there was only one thing to do—wait, sit it out. And perhaps it would be safer downstairs, across the street.

I turned and walked down the hall, started down the stairs. Somebody was coming up. There was the clatter of heels, the swish of skirt, a glimpse of a broad olive face with high cheekbones surmounted by dark curls. This was type casting if I'd ever seen it. She started to brush by me. I stuck out my arm.

"Miss Juarez," I said.

"Yaiss?"

"I've been looking for you. My name's Clayburn, Mark Clayburn."

"So?"

"Can't we go somewhere and talk?"

"I do not onnerstand. Why for we talk?"

"We've got mutual friends to discuss. Such as Joe Dean."

"You know heem?"

"He sent me."

She hesitated, then turned. "We go to my place, eh?"

I followed her up the stairs. The view was a distinct improvement over the pink posterior of my downstairs hostess.

Estrellita Juarez unlocked her door. "Come een," she invited.

Her parlor was a cut above the average for a joint like this: new furniture, and in fairly good taste. I noted the door to a closet and a bedroom, both shut. There was a kitchen and a bath in back.

"Seet down." She put her purse and gloves on the table, then turned. "Now, what ees all thees?"

"Friend of Joe's, like I say. He told me about you."

"How ees Joe? I 'ave not seen heem for long time."

"Funny. He talked like he'd been in touch with you regular. As if you'd know all about me."

"No. Heem I 'ave not seen for months."

"Quarrel?"

She didn't answer.

"Well, it doesn't matter," I said. "Main thing is, he told me you're the one to contact about the stuff."

"Stoff? What you talk about?"

I tried my hands-in-pocket routine again, but this time I came out with a fifty.

"What'll this buy?" I asked.

"I doan know what you talk about."

"Business must be better than I thought, if you can turn down this kind of money." I grinned and kept my hand extended. "All right, if you don't want to help me out, there's other places I can go. Right downstairs, for instance. She pushes a pretty good brand of weed, I hear. Or does she get her supply from you?"

Estrellita Juarez licked her lips. Then she took the money and put it in her pocket. She walked over to the closet door, opened it, and took out an upright vacuum cleaner. I watched her unfasten the dust bag attachment. She began to shake packages out on the floor.

"That's enough," I said. "This is all I need." I stooped and picked up the manila-wrapped carton of muggles.

"Bot for feefty dollair—"

"This is all I need," I repeated. "One package. So when I walk in and tell them where I got it, they'll have evidence."

Her mouth opened. "Why, you lousy, double-crossing stoolie!"

She came at me, trying to grab the refers. I got her arm and twisted it back.

"Wait a minute," I said. "You forgot the accent."

"Never mind the accent," she panted. "Give me that before I—"

"Before you what? Call the police? Or try to kill me?" I shook my head. "Better not. You're mixed up in enough killing so far."

"Who told you that? Joe?"

"No. He didn't tell me. I lied to you. Joe hates my guts." I let her arm go. "But I'm not lying to you now. And if you don't lie to me, I'll forget about going to the cops."

"So that's it, huh? Shakedown. I might of known."

"No shakedown. All I want from you is a little information, information you should have given to the law a long time ago. You'll have to sooner or later anyway, you know. They're looking for you right now, Estrellita, or whatever your real name is."

"Never mind about my real name. Suppose you tell me who you are, instead."

"I already did. My name's Mark Clayburn. Didn't Joe tell you about me?"

"I haven't seen Joe, honest I haven't. Not since—"

"Not since Ryan was murdered?" I nodded. "That's what I'm really here to talk about."

"I don't have anything to tell you. I already talked to the D.A.'s office."

"Sure you did. But where were you when they tried to find you after Polly Foster's death?"

"I had nothing to do with that setup."

"Nevertheless, they wanted to question you, and you hid out here, in Joe Dean's old apartment."

"That's no crime."

"You're sure you haven't seen him?"

She shook her head. "I tell you, not since Ryan died."

"He didn't die. He was murdered." I had to keep reminding people of that, it seemed. "Was that the reason for the quarrel? Were you afraid of Dean because you knew too much about what happened?"

"I didn't know anything."

"Yes you did. And you're still getting information from some place. Enough information so that you called Tom Trent the night he was murdered, warning him to get out of town."

"Who told you that?"

"His sister." I pushed her back into a chair. "It's bound to come out sooner or later, just like I told you. All you've got to decide is whether you want to talk to me or to headquarters."

"What's your angle?"

"I want to solve this case, that's all. I've got no axe to grind, nothing against anyone except the killer. Which means you're safe, as far as I'm concerned, unless you happen to be the guilty party."

Her hand went to her mouth. "No. I'm not. Honest."

"That's the way I want it," I said. "Honest. All right, let's get on with it. How long have you been pushing this stuff?"

"Two years."

"You work for a syndicate?"

"I don't know."

"Quit that talk."

"I said I don't know. I get it from a guy. I pay him when I make delivery. He tells me where to take it."

"You're a runner, in other words."

"That's all. I don't have anything to do with the stuff, where it comes from. They wouldn't be fools enough to tell me."

"What about Dean? Does he push, too?"

"No, but he knew about it. He saw me pass some to Dick Ryan."

"Ryan was one of your customers?"

"No. He only bought once. Said he was getting it for a friend."

"How did he know you could supply him?"

"I asked, but he wouldn't tell. He could have heard talk, though. I had a lot of customers in the industry."

"You're sure Ryan wasn't a viper?"

"Positive."

I nodded. That's what I'd started out to clear up, a long

time ago. That's what I'd wanted: a plain statement clearing Ryan of addiction, from somebody who knew.

But I felt no satisfaction in hearing it now. Even if I could get her to put it in writing, that wouldn't help. Too much had happened since I began my search, too many murders.

"All right," I said. "So he bought some for a friend. Who was it? Polly Foster?"

"No."

"Didn't she use tea?"

"Sometimes. But she knew where to get it. Right from me."

"What about Trent?"

"He dealt with me, too. And Ryan wouldn't be buying for him."

"Well, somebody was smoking at Ryan's trailer. You were all there that night."

"Nobody took anything when I was around."

"Kolmar?"

"I don't know about Kolmar."

"Joe Dean works for him now."

"I wouldn't know about that, either. I told you I haven't seen Joe since."

"But you left Ryan's trailer with Dean the night of the murder. You spent the rest of the night with him in a motel, didn't you?"

"Yes. The little rat! He was always after me, and when he caught me slipping the stuff to Ryan, he made me promise to go with him or else he'd squeal."

"That's how it was, eh?"

"That's how it was." She scowled. "In the morning I kicked him out and told him to go peddle his papers. I haven't seen the little fink since, and I don't want to."

"But you're sure Ryan didn't take weed. And you're sure Dean didn't kill him."

"Positive. Somebody else must have come to Ryan's trailer after we left. Somebody he expected, somebody who liked kicks."

"So Polly Foster said."

"She did?" Estrellita Juarez clenched her fists.

"I talked to her the night she died. In fact, I found her body. You must have read about that. She told me over the phone that she'd gone back to the trailer later that evening. She'd seen someone there. Whether or not she could identify the party, I don't know. But if she could, somebody made sure of getting to her before I did. So maybe your idea is right. Why didn't you tell the police about it when Ryan died?"

"Why get into trouble? Let them do their own figuring."

"Even if they suspect *you?* That doesn't make sense." I sat down and leaned forward. "Because they *do* suspect you, now. This business of disappearing after Polly Foster's death looks mighty suspicious. Everybody else showed for questioning and gave an alibi. Everybody but you. Why?"

"I got my orders to lay low. Changed my territory on me; I don't work the studios any more."

"You're sure it isn't because you know who killed Polly Foster?"

"I haven't any idea."

"Then why did you phone Tom Trent and warn him to get out of town?"

"I—I was worried. I liked Tom. He was on the stuff, sure, and I used to get it for him. Then I was told to hide out here and that cut off his supply. From something he said to me after Ryan got killed, I got a hunch he might know who did it. I think he must have gone back that night, just like Polly Foster. Maybe he just guessed. But I figured he knew, and after Polly Foster died, I was scared for him. I called him up and told him maybe he'd better get out of town for a while. We figured maybe he'd be safe then."

"*We?*"

"I mean, *I* figured."

"Uh-uh. You were told to warn him, weren't you?"

"You're getting me all confused."

"You're confused plenty, if you ask me. You're shielding somebody who's put you on the spot."

"I'm not on the spot."

"Yes you are." I talked right into her face. "Whoever this party is, he's got you right where he wants you, the perfect suspect. You disappear the minute Foster gets murdered. You call Trent the night before he's killed. Somebody came out to his place in a car and bumped him off—couldn't that be you? The cops think so. They know about that call."

"But I didn't."

"Don't tell me. Tell them. Tell them when they come for you."

"Nobody knows where I am. I'm safe. Unless you double cross me."

"I'm not going to double cross you," I answered. "I don't have to. Because you're not safe here. I found you in fifteen minutes. I used my head, and an old City Directory. Got your apartment number from that tea peddler downstairs. She sold you out for twenty bucks. I'll bet you another twenty the police will be knocking on your door before tomorrow morning."

"I won't be here," she said. "I'm getting out of town."

"Suit yourself. But you're a sucker if you keep on trying to protect somebody who'd line you up for a rap like this. Who is it, this guy you're running for?"

She nodded. "That's right."

"Suppose you tell me his name?"

"No. I couldn't do that—"

"Give you my word. I won't say anything about it for twenty-four hours. You've got time to clear out of here."

"I couldn't." She dug her fingers into the arm of the sofa. "He'd come after me."

"I doubt that. Because if you ask me, he won't have a chance. The police will grab him right away. Don't you see? This guy's the killer."

Her fingers stopped clawing.

"Haven't you figured that yet? It has to be that way. I'm not playing brilliant; it's just simple elimination. He's the only one left who's linked to all three of the victims: Ryan, Foster and Trent."

She stared at the wall behind me.

"Come on," I said. "Is it Kolmar?"

"No."

"Tell me his name." I reached over and shook her. "Don't be a fool. Do you want to end up like the others did?"

Estrellita Juarez stared.

"All right," she said, tonelessly. "It isn't Kolmar. The name is Hastings. Edward Hastings. He works for—"

She wasn't staring at the wall any more. I realized that now. She was staring at the door, because it was opening, fast. I turned in my seat, my hand searching for the gun Bannock had given me. I felt the butt in my fingers, started to tug it out as I tried to get up.

I never got the gun out, never reached my feet.

Joe Dean came in right behind my chair. "Here's what I owe you," he said.

What he owed me was something hard, something that cracked down to split my skull and leave me sprawling on a floor that went spinning and spinning around. It was like one of those outfits you ride in the Fun House of an amusement park, where centrifugal force finally throws you off to the edge. It was throwing me off now.

I hit the edge and dropped into darkness.

Chapter Fifteen

The rungs were slippery, but I kept climbing. That was the only way to get out of the darkness again. I had to keep on climbing. It took years.

Then I was up, back on the floor, lying there with my face pressed into the rug. My mouth was open and I wheezed.

The rug tasted awful, so I rolled over. Still the same taste. It wasn't the rug after all; it was something else. Something that clung to my mouth no matter how I turned my head. A gag.

Now I could feel the pressure of the cords on my hands and legs. They'd trussed me up, too. I opened my eye, but there wasn't much to see. Quite dark in the room now. Dark, and lonely.

My head throbbed. Those Dean brothers were great ones for rapping you over the skull. Did an efficient job, too. I wasn't bleeding, but I could tell I had been hit hard. When I rolled over onto my side, the room spun for a moment, then steadied.

I stared in the dimness. They were gone, all right. The closet door was open, and there weren't any clothes on the hangers. The vacuum cleaner was right there on the floor. Thoughtful of them to leave it. Maybe they thought I'd want to clean a few vacuums. Such as the one inside my skull.

They'd opened the dust bag, of course, and emptied it. And I knew they had taken the package of muggles from my pocket. Estrellita probably did it while Dean tied me up. I even knew what they'd used to tie me with. I could see the rumpled sheet in the corner from which the strips had been torn.

I tried to move my arms and legs. It wasn't easy. Maybe if

I rolled over to the wall I could brace myself enough to stand up.

I tried. Just raising myself made my head ache. And standing on my numbed legs was almost impossible. After a few minutes of effort it became possible, though.

Now what?

I worked my wrists. The knots held. Maybe I could follow the wall into the kitchen, get a knife out of the drawer. Better roll into there, though.

I rolled. Once again there was the business of raising myself up. I found the cupboard and the drawer, inched my way upright alongside it, stood with my back to the drawer and got the edge under one hand. I tugged. The drawer opened, then fell to the floor with a thud.

A thud, not a crash. There was no tinkle. I stared down through the shadows on the kitchen floor. The drawer was empty. They'd thought of everything.

I started to roll back, passing the bathroom on my way. Too bad this wasn't a hotel. In hotels they usually have that dojinger on the door for opening bottles and stuff.

Wait. Maybe…

I rolled back into the kitchen. I forced myself upright again. Then I saw what I was looking for on the far wall. I edged around towards it, hopping a step at a time and keeping my balance by sticking close to the wall. Then I reached the spot. There was a wall can opener and it had a bottle-opening attachment.

So far so good. But the rest was awful. The thing was set up too high for me to reach easily with my hands tied behind my back. I had to bend my arms. For a little while I thought I'd have to break them before I could make contact. Then I managed by twisting my left arm almost out of its socket.

I began to run my wrists back and forth against the knots. Of course there was no way of seeing what I was doing, and I had to be careful. The bottle opener was sharp; I didn't want to puncture my wrists. A few gashes were to be expected, but that didn't make them hurt any less when I felt them.

It took time. Quite a long time. Then I felt the knots giving. I pulled away and worked my hands. Something came loose. My hands were free.

I sat down, wrung a little circulation back into my fingers, and took the gag out of my mouth. Then I untied my feet. I rubbed my ankles, stood up again, felt the top of my head just for luck.

Then I looked at my watch.

No wonder it was dark. Almost nine o'clock. I'd been out for over five hours.

That was a long time. Long enough for the two of them to get a long, healthy head start.

I wondered where they'd run off to.

Switching on the lights, I made a brief tour of the apartment. They'd packed, all right. Taken everything, and left. I found a few ties in the bedroom, though; all were striped patterns. Dean had worn a striped tie. Which meant Estrellita had probably lied about not seeing him any more. The two of them were in this together.

All of which didn't matter now. There were other puzzlers.

My gun, for instance, or rather Bannock's gun. It was still in my pocket, I discovered. Thoughtful of them. Or thoughtless.

Well, there was nothing I could do about that. Nothing except go to the police and tell them what I knew. About Dean, Juarez, and this man Hastings. Edward Hastings. So he had to turn out to be the killer. Like those old-fashioned mysteries where everybody is suspected and it ends up that the butler did it. A fine thing. And I was a fine amateur private eye, too.

No sense looking any further. They wouldn't have left anything around that might help.

I went out and closed the door behind me. Nobody lurked in the hall. Nobody opened up to peek at me from the Little Gypsy Tea Room. I hit the street and headed for the nearest drugstore.

It was about time I turned sensible and called Thompson.

Yes, that was the only thing left for me. Call Thompson and try to work with him, for a change. We could still round up the murderer, if luck only held.

The drugstore wasn't hard to find. I went in, looking around for a phone. I couldn't see it, so I walked up to the clerk at the counter.

"Yes?"

"Have you got—?" I stopped. There was a pile of early morning editions on the counter. I picked up the top one and gave the clerk a buck. I started to walk away.

"Hey, mister, you forgot your change!"

I didn't pick up my change. I kept right on walking. Walking and reading.

It was only a box on the front page; that's all they had time for when the flash came in. Maybe there'd be an extra later. I didn't know. I didn't care.

Everything was over, now.

Hastings was dead. Edward Hastings, 42, of such-and-such an address, found shot through the head late this afternoon at…

I read the address again, read what Hastings did for a living.

Then I turned around and went back into the store.

"Where's the phone?" I asked.

"Back there, behind the counter."

"Thanks."

I didn't dial the police. I called Bannock, at his house.

"Hello."

"Yes?" Daisy's voice.

"This is Mark. Is Harry there?"

"No."

"Where is he—police?"

"Of course not. Why should he be?"

"Then you haven't heard?"

"Mark, what's this all about? Harry ought to be in soon, he had to finish up at the office after the funeral this afternoon."

I'd forgotten all about the funeral. I'd forgotten about a lot of things, apparently.

"Well, if he comes in, be sure to hold him. I'm on my way out."

"Mark, is there something—?"

"Plenty," I said. "Stay right where you are."

I hung up and went out. I hailed a cab up the street and gave the driver Bannock's address.

It was a long haul across town and I had plenty of time to think things out. No matter how I put the pieces together, they always fitted.

Over? Nothing was over. Not yet.

The moon was shining bright as we drove up in front of Bannock's place. There was a light in the window for the wandering boy, too.

I got out and wandered up the walk.

Daisy let me in. "Sarah's day off," she told me. "And me with a stinking headache."

"How was the funeral?"

"I didn't go. Harry went, though."

"Did he?"

"What do you mean?"

"I'll tell you."

She looked at me. "What happened to you?" she asked. "Is it the police?"

"No. They haven't caught up with me yet. I'm going to call them in a little while, though. But first let me tell you the whole deal."

"Come in. I'll mix a drink," I did, and she did. It was pleasant to sit back and relax in the soft lamplight, with an easy chair to rest in, a tall glass in my hand, and Daisy's presence vibrant before me.

Only I wasn't relaxing. Not yet.

First I had to bring Daisy up to date. I told her about seeing Kolmar and Joe Dean, about my interview with Billie Trent and the police finding Kolmar's gun in my car.

Then I went on and gave her a report of my interview

with Harry. I told her how I'd found Estrellita Juarez; how Dean had found me again, and finally I told her about what I had just read in the paper.

"But I still don't understand," she said. "What does it all mean?"

"It could mean several things," I said. "It could mean that Juarez and Dean were working together all along; that they killed Dicky Ryan, Polly Foster, Tom Trent. Or perhaps one of them did and the other knew about it.

"And so did this man Hastings, because Juarez was a runner for him in his dope peddling racket. So this afternoon, when things got hot, they decided to bump him off before they left town for good. Cover up the trail."

Daisy nodded. "But why come to Harry with that? Why don't you call the police?"

"I will. Only I won't tell them this theory. Because I don't believe it's true." I took a drink and felt a little better. "There's one thing wrong with that setup. The motive. You see, there isn't any. Why should Juarez and Dean, or either one of them separately, kill those three people? No reason." I sighed. "Besides, both of them have alibis to account for their whereabouts during Ryan's murder. And Dean has alibis covering him for the other killings, too."

"But they still could have killed this man Hastings. If they were leaving town, and thought he was the murderer, maybe they went to him and tried to blackmail him." Daisy took my glass and refilled it.

"I thought of that. It's a possibility. Won't know unless they're picked up, of course. Until then all we have to go on is hunches, and my hunch is they'd be too frightened, too anxious about getting out. I don't think they'd risk breaking in on Hastings cold and trying a fast shakedown."

"Maybe it's a coincidence, then," Daisy mused. "You say this Hastings was operating a reefer peddling setup. He might have a lot of enemies in that business who would want him out of the way."

I nodded. "That's so. And if it turns out to be the answer,

then we're right back where we started from. We still don't know the identity of Ryan's killer, or Polly Foster's, or Tom Trent's."

"What about Kolmar?"

"He was telling me the truth the other day, I think. Kolmar wouldn't murder his own stars. Why should he kill the geese that laid the golden eggs?"

Daisy shook her head. "Must we go on like this, Mark? I'm sick of murder and murder talk—physically sick! Didn't Harry tell you to lay off the case? Isn't it bad enough to have your life threatened, get beat up this way, put yourself on the spot with the police?"

"Sure it is," I answered. "But there won't be any more of it. Not now."

"Are you certain?"

"Positive." I sat back and put my drink down. "Because I think I've got the answer now. It was sitting right under my nose all the time, of course. I should have spent less time figuring why these people were being killed and more time wondering why these things happened to me."

"You?"

"Of course. I'm the clue to the whole business. Ryan died months ago and nothing happened. But the minute I was brought into the picture, trouble started again. Everybody who might know about Ryan's death either disappeared or was permanently silenced. The murderer got there before I did. It wasn't coincidence. The murderer must have known who I planned to see."

"But how could that be?"

"There's only one answer," I said. "I must have told the killer myself just what I was going to do."

Daisy made a little sound in her throat.

"Mark! No!"

"Yes," I said. "Who hired me? Harry. Who arranged my interview with Polly Foster? Harry. Who did I tell before-hand that I was going to have a showdown with Tom Trent?

Harry. And who knew I was still working on this business today? Harry."

I paused. "The other night, when Trent was murdered, Harry said he was with a client in Pacific Palisades. Does he have proof? And what makes you sure he went back to the office today, after the funeral?"

"That's absurd! When Polly Foster was murdered, both Harry and I were playing cards at the Shermans. The police checked his alibi about this client in Pacific Palisades. And he wouldn't dare say he was at the office. He never works there alone, someone would be with him."

"All right," I said. "Let's figure it this way. See if it makes sense. Harry killed Ryan. He got someone else to kill Foster and Trent because he was afraid they'd talk. And then he got someone to kill Hastings."

Daisy shook her head. "You're crazy. Harry wouldn't jeopardize his TV deal any more. He hired you in good faith, just to clear things up. And how would he know Hastings?"

I was silent for a moment. "That's so. He didn't have a motive, did he? And he didn't know Hastings. That leaves only one person. One person who also knew what my movements would be, because Harry wouldn't suspect anything wrong if he revealed them."

Daisy looked at me. I nodded. "That's right, Daisy. There's only one person left. You."

Chapter Sixteen

She stood up quickly.

I had the gun out of my pocket now. It felt good to be on the right end of a gun for a change.

"Sit down, Daisy," I said. "First you're going to listen. Then you're going to talk."

"You can't bluff me."

"I'm not bluffing. I've got the goods on you. Ever since I read about Hastings' death tonight. When I read where he worked, I knew."

"Where he worked?"

"The papers said he was an interne at Dr. Levinson's clinic. The clinic you went to, the day before Ryan died."

She sat down again. I held the gun on her.

"That was your alibi, wasn't it, Daisy? Hastings covered up for you the night you sneaked out to visit Ryan at his trailer. You were the person he expected.

"You'd known Ryan since the old days, when he was your husband's client. He was also your lover. Harry never suspected that, did he?

"Any more than he suspected you had the reefer habit. Or that Hastings was your source of supply. No wonder you went to the clinic he worked at instead of to a hospital. Am I right so far?"

She didn't answer.

I went on. "Ryan was drunk when you got to his trailer. You started to smoke. There was a quarrel, a serious quarrel. Something set you off. The gun was there, and you used it. Then you went back to the hospital. Hastings covered up for you with an alibi after Ryan's body was discovered. And for a while everything was all right.

"Then Harry bought those films, and he hired me to try and clear Ryan's name. You were against that from the start. You called your friend Hastings, had him phone me and Harry with a warning. Hastings even paid a visit to my place when I was out.

"That didn't stop us. Hastings also supplied Polly Foster with reefers, and one of his runners—Estrellita Juarez— knew Tom Trent. He contacted Foster and Trent right away, told them not to talk to anyone.

"But Polly Foster was frightened. She'd come back to the trailer later that night, evidently, and seen you. I don't think she actually recognized you, but she knew a woman had been there. She wanted to find out if anyone had actually spotted her, so she came to see me.

"You learned that from Harry. He told you he'd made an appointment for me. So Polly Foster was killed."

Daisy breathed hard, but she was smiling now. "Ridiculous! How could I have killed her? Ask the police—they know Harry and I were with the Shermans at their house all evening."

"Sure. You didn't kill Polly Foster. Your friend Hastings did that little job for you. I'll bet when the police check back they'll find he had a night off. He went to her place and heard her phoning me; then he came in and shot her."

"Why would he do such a thing?"

"Two reasons. The first is, he couldn't afford to have his reefer racket exposed. Must have made a nice piece of change off his big shot clients, and maybe he worked a little blackmail on the side. Reason enough for silencing Foster, but I think he had a better one. I think by this time he'd taken Ryan's place with you."

"Why, you—" Her voice quivered with indignant protest.

"No show, Daisy. You're a little late with that innocence act. You forget, after Polly Foster's death, that you offered me the same privileges if I'd lay off."

"Rave on," she said. "I suppose I also hired those thugs to beat you up out in the dunes."

"No, I don't think so. You might have, but I'm inclined to suspect Kolmar of that little deal. He was beginning to get paranoid delusions of persecution by this time, seeing his people get killed. Maybe he passed the word to Joe Dean that he'd like to know what I was up to in the case. And Dean told his brother to come after me with this other hood.

"Anyway, it didn't work. Foster was dead, your friend Hastings told Estrellita Juarez to hide out, but I was still on the case. And I told Harry I meant to interview Tom Trent again about the murder of Ryan.

"He had several hours unaccounted for on the night of Ryan's death, and you couldn't be sure he didn't know something. You had to act fast.

"Estrellita Juarez knew he was in danger and called to warn him. Then he got another call—from you. I don't know what you told him; maybe you said you knew who the killer was and wanted his advice about going to the police. Anyway, you got him to do what you wanted—to meet him off the roadway alongside his property.

"While Harry was in Pacific Palisades, you drove over to Trent's place and waited for him to come out. He climbed in the car with you. You shot him, dragged his body to the garage, tried to make it look like suicide. Then you drove off. Somebody saw the car, but didn't pay any particular attention to it. That was the riskiest deal of all, but you were panicky.

"I don't think you wanted to kill Trent, Daisy. I think by this time Hastings was forcing you, threatening to expose you, threatening to cut off your supply of muggles, making you go through with his plans and help protect him.

"He told you I had to be dealt with next. You promised you'd make Harry take me off the investigation. And Harry promised.

"Only I didn't get off the case. I went to see Kolmar, he sent the police out after me because I took his gun, and then I told Harry I wanted another twenty-four hours to work in. I told him not to let you know about it.

"But he did, didn't he? You wormed it out of him this noon, Daisy, isn't that it? And you knew I'd be looking for Estrellita Juarez or Joe Dean, because they were the only suspects left on my list. If I found either of them, the trail would lead straight to Hastings and to you.

"I think you called Joe Dean and warned him this noon. Right after you told Harry you had a headache and didn't want to go to the funeral. That would take care of me, you figured, if Dean found me.

"But there was still Hastings. Hastings, who knew the whole story, who had you under his thumb as long as he could threaten to talk. You decided to silence him. You went to the clinic—it wasn't the first time you sneaked into his room when he was off duty—and surprised him...with a slug in the head. Then you came back here, and I called.

"Sarah's gone and Harry's at the office. I wonder what you had planned for me, Daisy? Surely you must have made some plans about me, in case it turned out that I knew the truth."

She stood up again. "I was going to shoot you," she said. "Shoot you and tell Harry you were the killer, that you'd come to me and confessed, tried to get me to run away with you. That you were an addict yourself."

"You don't think he'd have gone for such a whacky yarn, do you?"

"Why not?" She shrugged. "I was going to use the gun I'd used on Hastings, and say I had gotten it away from you during a struggle."

"Where's the gun, Daisy?"

"In the drawer." She started to turn away.

"Don't go any nearer," I warned her. "I'll shoot if you do. I mean it."

She smiled at me over her shoulder.

I grinned back. "That's the only thing you didn't know about, Daisy. Harry forgot to tell you he gave me this gun of his when I saw him this noon."

She shook her head. "He told me, all right." She turned

away again, walked over to the desk, reached for the drawer.

"Stop!" I snapped. "One more step and I—"

"Go ahead."

She didn't even look around. She took the step. She opened the drawer.

I could feel the sweat run down my arm, run down my hand, wet the finger that was pressing against the trigger. I had to press it, there was no other way. In another second she'd have a gun of her own. She'd killed before; she'd kill again. It was self-defense, it was the only way.

I sighted carefully and pulled the trigger.

She took the gun out of the drawer and pointed it at me.

I pulled the trigger again.

"Keep trying," she said. "It won't work. I fixed Harry's gun a couple of days ago. Just in case."

Her smile was broader now. "Smart operator, aren't you? So smart you never even bothered to check a borrowed gun. Well, I've checked this one. So drop that and get your hands up. Fast."

I did what she said.

"Sit down," she told me. "Right there, where I can see you."

I sat down, staring at the useless weapon on the floor. She was right. I'd never even looked at the gun, just took Harry's word for it that it was loaded and set. No wonder Joe Dean hadn't bothered to lift it from me when he knocked me out. It was useless.

It was useless, and I was useless. Everything I'd done was useless, now. She held the upper hand. And her gun was in it.

"You dumb jerk," she said. "I could have taken you any time I wanted since you came in this room. But I thought I'd wait and hear what you knew, find out if you'd spilled to anybody else. You haven't, so that makes it perfect."

"Then I was right about the killings."

"Yes, you were right, if that makes you feel any better."

She took a step closer, and she wasn't smiling now. "You've got it all pretty straight. Except for a couple of things you wouldn't know about. Like the reason I shot Ryan.

"I didn't go to the clinic for appendicitis. I was pregnant. And Ryan was to blame. When I found out for sure, I went to his trailer that night and told him. I wanted him to know. I said I'd divorce Harry and he and I would get married."

Her mouth twitched. "You know what he did? He laughed at me. He laughed, like it was all a joke. Well, I showed him what kind of a joke it was. I took the gun lying there and..."

Daisy shuddered. "You think it was easy? You're wrong, Clayburn. It was hell. I went back to the clinic and had a miscarriage. And I quit reefers. That wasn't easy, either, but I did it. From then on I was going to play straight, with Harry, and with everybody.

"But Hastings wouldn't let me. Sure, I slept with him. Because he made me. He threatened to tell. About the murder, about the baby. I had to do what he said. And when this other trouble started, he told me what to do then. He killed Foster and he had me kill Trent. That was awful. Not only the risk, but doing it. I felt—dirty—inside."

She gulped. "You don't know what it's like, do you? To feel dirty. To feel murder crawling around in your stomach, making you gag and throw up. I've felt that way ever since the beginning. Until today. When I went to kill Hastings today, I felt good again. I was happy to see him die, Clayburn, because when he died, the dirty part of me died with him.

"Now I'm clean again. And I'm going to stay clean. After this is over, after I finish with you."

I shook my head.

"No, Daisy. You'll never feel that way, not if you kill me. It's too late."

"Too late for you." She took one more step forward. "I'm sorry. But I can't stop now. I can't."

She wasn't stopping. I saw the gun come up, noted the

silencer attachment for the first time, realized that it explained why no one had heard the shot when Trent died. No one would hear the shot now, either.

This was it. A silly way to die, sitting in an armchair in a big house out in Laurel Canyon, watching a woman's hand move, watching her finger squeeze the trigger on a gun mounted with a silencer.

She squeezed.

Funny. I heard the shot after all.

No, it wasn't a shot. Somebody must have thrown a stone through the glass of the front window. Yes, because Daisy was turning to look.

Wrong again. She hadn't turned to look. She'd turned to fall. And it was a shot after all, but not from her gun. Somebody had fired through the window.

I watched her drop to the carpet, watched the redness run out of her mouth.

Daisy Bannock lay on the floor, her body curled like a question mark.

I stood up. I walked over to her and started to kneel down.

Then the question mark straightened out once and for all, and Al Thompson walked into the room.

Chapter Seventeen

You never feel clean after a murder.

That's what I'd tried to tell Daisy, and that's what I found out now.

Hastings' death had been a mess. Lucky for me, because when they went through his room they'd run across a notebook inside his mattress. Names of clients, including Daisy Bannock.

That's what brought Al Thompson out to see her, and saved me.

For a while there, I wasn't even happy about being saved. Not when I had to watch them break the news to Harry. They found him at his office, and he took it hard. The poor guy had never suspected. I felt bad about that.

I wasn't rejoicing when they managed to pick up Joe Dean and Estrellita Juarez, either. They were traced to San Bernardino, where they'd holed up on a piece of property his brother Andy owned. Yes, they got Andy and this big guy Fritz, too. I had to testify against them.

They made a deal with Kolmar to drop his charges about the gun and the assault, so I was in the clear. And I did what I could to help in the weeks that followed.

It was some consolation to know that this particular reefer pushing outfit was broken up; turned out Dean's brother Andy and his friend Fritz were both peddling for Hastings, too.

But they never were able to trace Hastings' source. If there was anyone higher up, the police couldn't find him.

And of course, I never got any eleven grand from Harry Bannock, either.

I haven't seen him for months, but that's my fault, I suppose. I could call him up and ask how's tricks, sweetheart, and did he ever sell his films to See-More?

But I haven't, and I won't.

I just sit here in the office and tend to business. The literary agenting business, where all the murders are on paper and nothing is red except the ink of a typewriter ribbon.

Sometimes, though, when I happen to be working overtime, at night, I stop and stare out the window.

I can see across the city from here, and look down into the streets. And no matter what the hour, the streets are never empty.

They're always moving down there, moving all over town—this town and every big town. The pushers and their customers, the big dealers and the little squealers, the future killers and the future victims. Along with a lot of other people: guys like Al Thompson, who do their best, and the anonymous thousands like Harry Bannock who never suspect.

When I stare out the window, I see them all, realize what's happening outside. And I say to myself, *It never ends, does it? What you knew was just a tiny fraction of the whole. Somewhere out there tonight there'll be another murder. Another chapter in a book that's never finished, even though it started way back with Cain.*

That's what I say to myself when I look out the window.

And then, I pull down the shades and go back to work.

What Sordid Secrets Would He Find
In the Depths of His Crystal Ball?

Eddie Haines came to Hollywood to work in television, not to become a phony self-help guru, collecting secrets from his wealthy clients in order to blackmail them.

But that's what Eddie became, under the tutelage of Professor Otto Hermann, Ph.D., a vicious little man with dollar signs where his soul should have been.

It was a lucrative set-up—until the day the professor pushed Eddie too far...

"Perhaps the finest psychological horror writer."
—*Stephen King*

Robert Bloch was the legendary author of PSYCHO and a true Hollywood insider, writing scripts for numerous movies and TV shows including ALFRED HITCHCOCK PRESENTS, Boris Karloff's THRILLER, and the original STAR TREK. You haven't see Hollywood's dark side till you've seen it through Bloch's eyes...

SPIDERWEB

by **Robert Bloch**

A HARD CASE CRIME NOVEL

A HARD CASE CRIME BOOK
(HCC-042)
April 2008

Published by

Dorchester Publishing Co., Inc.
200 Madison Avenue
New York, NY 10016

in collaboration with Winterfall LLC

This book is a work of fiction. Names, characters, places, and incidents either are the products of the author's imagination or are used fictitiously, and any resemblance to actual events or persons, living or dead, is entirely coincidental.

ISBN 0-8439-5960-6
ISBN-13 978-0-8439-5960-4

Cover design by Cooley Design Lab

Typeset by Swordsmith Productions

The name "Hard Case Crime" and the Hard Case Crime logo are trademarks of Winterfall LLC. Hard Case Crime books are selected and edited by Charles Ardai.

Printed in the United States of America

Visit us on the web at www.HardCaseCrime.com

For
GUSTAV MARX
who gave so much of
his time to this book

One

The door was of blonde wood, highly waxed. Across its surface, in angular script, was lettered:

LARRY RICKERT
AND
ASSOCIATES

I snapped the brim of my hat, turned the doorknob, and walked into the office. A set of chimes made background music.

The walls of the small reception room were of glass brick. Torcheres gave off a soft, discreet light. There was an end table bearing the usual copies of *Variety* and *Billboard*. Two chairs and a sofa, overstuffed by a firm of reliable over-stuffers, completed the ensemble. It made me sick to look at the joint.

I headed for the ticket-window opening in the wall ahead, where a receptionist's ponytail bobbed behind a panel of glass.

When I rapped, the ponytail switched around until I got a look at a long, thin face with about three dollars' worth of fancy makeup on it.

The panel opened and the makeup cracked into a smile. "Oh, it's you, Mr. Haines."

Well, that was something. At least she recognized me, even if she didn't exactly swoon in my arms at the sight of my smiling face.

"Is Mr. Rickert in?" I asked.

"Have you an appointment?"

"No. Not exactly. But I only want to see him for a minute or two."

She nodded, closed the panel, and manipulated the intercom system, or the TV set, or whatever they used to convey trivial messages around here. After a brief pause for station identification she opened the panel again.

"Mr. Rickert will see you in a moment. Won't you be seated, please?"

I tipped my hat, smiled roguishly and hit bottom on the overstuffed sofa. The sliding panel closed again. I waited to see if she would put up a *Sold Out* sign, but nothing happened.

There were exactly three cigarettes left in my package. I lit one and watched my hand tremble. Inhaling, I leaned back and forced myself to breathe deeply and slowly. Gradually I calmed down. It was going to be all right as long as I kept a grip on myself. Sure, I was perfectly relaxed now.

I only jumped about two feet when the outer door opened and Peter Lorre came in.

It wasn't Peter Lorre, of course. Rickert didn't handle any movie talent. But the little guy in the black hat bore a fleeting resemblance to the star. He walked over to the reception window and mumbled something about an appointment. I avoided watching or listening too closely, and presently he took his place on the chair set at right angles to my sofa. Something began to burn inside my forehead. He was staring at me.

Right away, my jumpy feeling came back. It was silly, of course. Let him stare. What did he know about me? What could he know?

I was putting up a good front. Sitting down with my legs tucked back this way, it was hard to tell that the shine was on the seat of my pants and not on my shoes. He couldn't guess that the reason I came to Rickert's office instead of calling him was that my phone had been disconnected. For all he knew, I had a full, fresh package of cigarettes in my pocket, and plenty of money to buy more.

So why should I worry if he stared at me? But I did worry. I doused my cigarette and looked up. His eyes were stones set in flesh.

I could feel my shirt getting sticky under the sports jacket. And I got the funniest notion that he felt it, too. He could feel everything I was feeling, think everything I was thinking. Those stones set in flesh were magnets.

Maybe I was flipping my wig? Maybe that's what was wrong with me? All these weeks in the apartment, waiting for Rickert to call, watching the money run out. Then no phone, and nothing to do but run around and try to break the doors down myself—carrying my own photos and recordings.

Rickert had warned me that I'd get no place, fast, on my own. And that's exactly where I'd arrived. No place. You feel funny there, in no place. You feel as though you aren't really alive, or have no right to be alive. So you take a couple of drinks and wait for tomorrow. You might be somewhere else, tomorrow. But you're not. You wake up in the crummy apartment and you're still no place. Mr. Nobody from nowhere.

But that's your business, isn't it? People haven't got the right to stare at you and find it out. Damn it, there was nothing to be ashamed about. I knew what I was doing here. I had it all figured out, just how I was going to put it over. And then this little character had to come along and upset me!

I raised my eyes and looked at him. He wasn't so much. Black suit, unusual for the West Coast, but nothing special about its cut. White shirt, quiet foulard tie. Flashy ring on little finger of left hand. Probably fake stone.

He saw what I was doing, of course. But his expression did not change. He stared. I stuck my chin out, folded my hands across my chest and stared back. It hurt a little. He refused to blink, and those two stones met my gaze. You can't break stones with your fist. Constant dripping—

Sweat rolled down my forehead and I blinked first. But I wouldn't turn my head. I stared at the bridge of his thick nose. Maybe if I thought of something else, it would help.

I thought about the trip out, thought about meeting Rickert for the first time, and the fast line of con he handed

me, the buildup about what he would do for me. I thought about really getting a break, making the grade on a big show, wowing 'em. That would make my dumb brother wipe the sneer off his face for good. I'd wipe the sneer off all their faces, including this little puffy face in front of me.

But he kept staring. He knew. He knew I was a fake, he knew I was licked, that I'd never make it.

The hell he did! All imagination. Keep staring. He'll break first.

I looked into his eyes. For the first time, the stones seemed to turn. His pupils were dilating. The lids crept back. The stones glittered. Diamonds. Diamond drills. Drills that bored.

Fakes. Like the diamond on his little finger. I wasn't afraid. I stared.

All at once, his hand moved. Pudgy worms crawled into the handkerchief pocket of his coat. They emerged and carried something up to his left eye. It glittered. A monocle.

He fixed it into position without altering his line of vision. It hung there in the eye-socket and the eye behind it became huge. The distorted pupil glared at me. I thought that he looked like Erich von Stroheim. I thought that if I had to endure that wave of power beating into my brain, I'd get up and run. I thought—but I stared back.

And his mind told me something. Told me that I was really through, that it was no use, that I was washed up. I'd better get up and leave now. Yes, that's what he told me, and he was right. I'd get up and—

"Mr. Rickert will see you now."

I heard it somewhere in the distance. Then I was on my feet, stumbling through the inner office, walking down the hall to the big layout in back.

My head was splitting. Larry Rickert smiled at me across the desk.

"Sit down," he said. "Good to see you, Eddie. Be with you in just a sec."

He waved goodbye at me with his left hand and picked

up a phone with his right. He began to talk, and a steady stream of conversation and cigar smoke drifted around the big red folds of his neck.

I lit my next-to-the-last cigarette. The headache was worse now. I tried to remember my canned speech, but I couldn't. All I wanted to do was run away. When he finally hung up and turned to me again, I couldn't even remember to smile.

"Now," said Rickert, "what can I do for you, sweetheart?"

"That's exactly what I want to know," I told him.

"What do you mean?"

"I mean I came in here over two months ago, because your ads say you're a good agent and that's what I needed. You didn't sign me up or anything like that. But you did manage to get over three hundred bucks out of me, for retainer fee and for photographs and audition records. What I want to know now is, when do I see a little action?"

He gave me the same grin he used for his advertising photos.

"Take it easy, Eddie. Relax."

"I've been taking it easy, but I can't relax. I want to know why you haven't sold me or my show idea."

Rickert stopped smiling. He leaned forward and waved the chewed end of his cigar at me. It dripped.

"Listen, son," he said. "This isn't Iowa. That package idea of yours—the Television Psychologist—may have sounded pretty good to you when you dreamed it up back there. And I was willing to give it a whirl. I sent out your audition discs to all the network reps. I've pitched you. But it's just no dice."

My headache was worse. Rickert's face wavered in and out of focus as I answered him. "All right, drop the show idea. But remember, I'm still an announcer. I had a chance to get on in Des Moines, and I'm willing to start at the bottom here. There must be plenty of openings around town."

"In manholes, yes." Rickert lit a fresh cigar. It dripped nicely, too. "Look, sweetheart, here's some free advice. Maybe you're not ready for the big time yet. Why don't you

go back home, take that job? You won't starve. So you're out a couple of hundred on this deal—so what? Maybe you'll click later on. Lots of these executives, they listen to the little stations. Who knows, maybe somebody will spot you and—"

"So I'm not ready for the big time yet, eh?" I stood up and tried to keep my balance in the rolling room. "All right, Mr. Rickert. Thanks for the analysis. But it's a pity you didn't tell me all this before I spent three hundred bucks with you— and two months of my life."

"Hold on, now, sweetheart—"

I was holding on, hard. Even though my head was splitting, even though I wanted to kill somebody, I held on. I knew there was no use getting mad. He'd given me the answer. I was washed up.

"No hard feelings, Eddie," said Rickert. "Go on home and think it over. Maybe something will still break. I'll let you know."

"Only if it's your neck," I told him. "This I'd love to hear about." Then I stopped. "I—I really don't mean that. Sorry, I'm not feeling too good."

I went out and managed to wobble through the hall, back to the outer office. It was like walking under water, and the glass bricks wavered before my eyes.

The little man with the monocle was still sitting there. I swam past him. He looked up and started to open his mouth. Fat little fish, gulping air in the wavering water.

"Pardon me," he said. Voice from far away. Sound under water.

I didn't stop. I couldn't stop. I opened the door and emerged upon the sunlit shore of the street.

He padded after me. "Please—" he murmured.

I shook him off. "Go away." I knew that's what my voice said, but I couldn't control it. "Go away. Can't you see I'm busy? I have to kill somebody."

Rushing around the corner, rushing into the crowd, I wondered who it was I meant to kill.

All I knew was that it was going to happen soon.

Two

The sunshine swept all around me, and so did the people.
These people walking along the Strip were no better or no
worse than those in any crowd, but right now I couldn't stand
their faces: those horrid, impersonal wooden masks which
everyone wears in public.

I see those masks on people everywhere: walking down
the street, waiting on the corner for cars or busses, standing
in elevators, eating in restaurants. All of them trying to pretend they're alone, all of them behaving like toys wound up
to walk, ride, stand or eat.

I saw them now, the hideously animated dolls, and as I
hurried along I turned my head away. I breathed deeply but
I couldn't stop trembling. What was wrong with me, anyhow?

I knew what was wrong. I had nowhere to go.

Stopping in a doorway, I lit the last cigarette, and when I
threw the package away I was tossing Rickert and the photos
and the recordings into the gutter. Everything was gone.

And where did I go from here? The cigarette teeter-
tottered in my mouth as I searched my pockets. I found
crumpled bills and some change. Four dollars and thirty-five
cents. I'd better have something to eat, first.

Eat? I never eat on an empty stomach…

The thoughts kept spinning around, bruising my brain.
Why had I ever come out here, anyway? I was just a hick,
like all the other Iowa farmers who dream of the trip for
years, save up for years, finally travel 2000 miles to get here,
and then have nothing to do but send a souvenir to the folks
back home—a miniature wooden privy with the name of the
city stamped on it.

Yes, I was a hick, but I couldn't go back home. They'd

laugh at me. My brother Charlie would laugh at me. I was laughing at myself.

Eddie Haines, the Boy Wonder. The star of the Senior Play. Just a high-school kid who never grew up. I used to think I was pretty good. They all thought so, then. "You ought to be in the movies. Or on the radio. Or television."

Why not? It sounded great—in high school. And after high school I got this job at the local radio station. Things were looking up. Then came the idea for this Television Psychologist program and I thought I was all set. So I came to Hollywood and went to Rickert and here I was.

Here I was, right now, standing in the bar with half a snootfull. Funny, I wasn't standing on the street any more. I was in this dark, quiet bar, and I kept telling these things to the bartender, and he said, "Sure, buddy," and poured me another.

He didn't care. He was my pal. He knew there was nothing else to do. Nothing else to do when you're down to four dollars and thirty-five cents and can't go back.

Then there wasn't any more money and it was time to go home. Home? That one-room deal on the third floor with the disconnected phone and the mail slit that never had a letter sticking in it? And how much longer would I even have that to go back to?

Well, maybe I wouldn't need it much longer. The important thing now was to get there, fast. Walk a little. Lurch a little. Up the stairs. Easy to find the key—it was the only thing left in my pocket.

Very close inside and dark. Close and dark, like a tomb. Shut the door, click the light against the night. There.

When the light came on, my headache started up again. Something about monocles crept into my brain, something about them staring at me. Did Charlie wear a monocle, or Rickert, or the bartender? I couldn't remember. No, it was somebody else. I wanted to figure it out, but there just wasn't any time left.

I had promised to do something and I must do it in a

hurry. I must do it right now, to get rid of the headache. I walked quickly into the bathroom. The reflection in the mirror hit me in the face. I steadied myself and waited for the mirror to go away. It didn't, but I knew how to make it go away. I pulled back the door of the medicine cabinet and that did it.

The objects on the shelves were unpleasant. I didn't want to see them, but I was looking for something and couldn't help but notice. Aspirin, toothpaste, cold tablets, pills, iodine, scissors—I hated all of it. The melancholy of anatomy…

Everything I saw reminded me of the way you have to fight just to keep alive. Fight with yourself, with your body. There's always something. Like this headache. Or a cold, sinus trouble. Tooth decay. Bad eyes. Bruises, blisters, cuts, burns, aches, pains. An endless round of cleaning, brushing, scrubbing, combing. Cutting of hair and fingernails and toenails. Eating, eliminating, resting, sleeping. Fighting all the time and you can't win.

I reached out and swept everything into the washbowl. Everything except what I wanted. The toothpowder spilled and the iodine splashed, but I didn't care. I had what I wanted, now, in my hand.

That Charlie, that big brother of mine, was a tough egg. Always ready to hand out some patronizing advice. But one thing he told me I never had forgotten.

"There's two things a man should always get straight—his whiskey and his razor."

Well, I'd taken the whiskey. And now I had my razor. I held it for a moment and watched my hand tremble, as I thought of Charlie, and how we'd parted, back in Iowa.

I held a razor in my hand then, too. It was at the height of our final quarrel, and I'd been packing, and the razor had been resting on top of the table. Just resting, until I'd grabbed it up, groping for it through a red haze, and I went for Charlie, screaming, "So I'm no good, am I? I'll kill you for saying that, I'll kill you, I'll kill you—"

Would I have killed him?

Suppose he hadn't caught my wrist in time. Suppose I'd let the razor slash down. Would I have gone through with it and murdered Charlie? I still didn't know. I know that he *did* grab my wrist, knock the razor to the floor, and hold me until I quieted down and the haze cleared away.

But I also knew that whenever I got angry, really angry, the haze came back—and with it, the urge to kill. Perhaps I was a murderer, at heart. Perhaps I could go out again, right now, razor in hand, and run amok in the streets among all the wooden-faced people. I could carve new expressions on their faces with this razor of mine.

I held it in my hand, and my hand didn't tremble now. I was thinking about a whole new way of life. A way of death, rather.

Suppose I took this razor and made it an instrument of Destiny. I could carve faces, I could carve a career with it for myself. All I had to do was stand in an alley and *show* it to most people and they'd give me anything I wanted. They'd give me everything I couldn't seem to get any other way. Just the sight of it was threat enough. I could get money from the men, and from the women I'd take—

No. I was crazy to think of it. It would end in murder, and I'd become a killer, just as I feared. There was a killer inside of me, I knew that now. There's a killer inside everyone if you probe deeply enough; my killer was strong and he sent out a red haze when he wanted to escape.

He wanted to escape now. And the only way to prevent that was to turn the razor on him. This whacky town was full of murderers—torso slayers, rippers, maniacs on the loose. It must be something in the air; perhaps the smog was a red haze in disguise.

Well, my killer mustn't join the rest. I, and I alone, could prevent it, had to prevent it. Because if I went on, sooner or later somebody else would die. I was certain of it.

So I held the razor in my hand and I was ready. It was time to cut loose. Time for the unkindest cut of all. Time to kill the killer—

My headache almost blinded me. It sent sharp pains out against my eyes, but not sharp enough. Not nearly as sharp as the straight edge of my razor, pressing against my throat.

Then the haze was back and I said to myself, "This is the way it feels when you murder, this is what it's like to be a murderer—and lucky for you that you're murderer and victim too."

My hand moved in the haze, and the razor's edge was sharp. As it came down, I was thinking that the edge of a razor is the sharpest thing in the world.

Then it was the only thing in the world...

Three

Then there was something else in the world, after all. Noise. Knocking. Persistent knocking. And rattling. I could hear it somewhere, a million miles away. Knocking on my door, rattling the knob.

I wouldn't answer. Maybe the noises would stop if I wouldn't answer. Then my hand might be steadier and I could go ahead. But not with that thudding— It didn't stop. I heard a muffled voice outside. What right did anyone have to interfere? I still didn't have to open the door. This was my business.

"Go away!" I yelled.

The doorknob rattled again. Somebody was knocking on my door, pounding on my head.

I moved into the living room. The voice was now plainly audible.

"Open up—I want to see you."

"No!"

Silence. I stood there, waiting for the sound of receding footsteps. Another moment now and I'd be alone again. Another moment and I could walk back into the bathroom and— I heard rustling. Something was sliding under the door. Something green slithered into view. I had to move closer, had to look down at it, had to see what it was. I stared. It was a hundred-dollar bill.

I bent down and picked it up in my left hand, the free hand. There was magic in the feel of it; I stopped trembling the moment my skin came into contact with the crispness. I could see it quite clearly and the pain behind my eyes receded. Who said money can't work miracles? Miracles

from outside the door. Opportunity knocks but once…

I turned the bolt, opened the door. He came in. The little guy, Peter Lorre. Only it wasn't Peter Lorre. This man was bald. He had taken his hat off and the light from the bathroom shone on an absolutely hairless skull. If a fly lit on his head, it would slip and break an ankle.

I didn't really think that; there was no room in my mind for a gag then. All I could do was stand there and look at him while I tried to slip the razor into my pocket.

He turned on the living room light, walked over to the sofa, sat down, and pulled out the monocle. This time it didn't hurt my eyes. Nothing hurt my eyes. I could feel the hundred dollar bill in my hand.

The little guy looked up at me and smiled. "You are Eddie Haines," he said. "Delighted to meet you. I am Professor Hermann."

My left hand held the money, and my right hand stayed in my pocket with the razor. So I merely nodded at his introduction. Then all at once I felt that I must sit down. I took the chair. He watched me, still smiling.

"You will pardon my intrusion. I tried to call, but it seems your telephone has been disconnected. And it was important that I see you."

"How did you get here?"

He waved his hand, the one with the diamond ring on the little finger. I wasn't so sure it was a fake diamond any more.

"Mr. Rickert gave me your name and address. You remember, I was in his office this afternoon. You wouldn't talk to me, but I went there for just that reason. I was looking for you, Mr. Haines."

"But why?"

"I heard your voice on an audition record. That is what so interested me."

"Are you in radio, Professor?"

"No. But I am interested in voices. I have something in mind which may also interest you."

He had already interested me. Anybody who shoved hundred-dollar bills under my door interested me a lot. I'm funny that way.

I was sobering up. I started to withdraw my right hand from my pocket and nicked my finger on the straight edge of the razor. I forced a grin as I swabbed at the blood with a handkerchief.

"Afraid I must apologize to you," I said. "You see, I was shaving when you rang. Came out in such a hurry I was still carrying my razor, and I stuck it in my pocket. Forgot all about it just now and cut myself a little."

Professor Hermann nodded gravely. "I see there are some things I will have to teach you. Such as learning how to tell a lie."

"What do you mean by that crack?"

"My dear young man! You'll find it's no use trying to deceive me. I happen to know you weren't shaving. You were getting ready to cut your throat."

I gaped at him and he chuckled. "And that would have been very stupid of you, my friend. Very, very stupid. Because you and I are going to make a million dollars—together."

"When? Where? How?"

"I'll tell you all about it at dinner," he promised.

And that's why I put on my coat and went out with him. That's why we sat in the little restaurant until almost nine, eating and talking.

I did most of the talking, at first. The Professor didn't say much, beyond encouraging me to tell about myself. I was perfectly willing to do so, as long as I could feel the crispness of that hundred-dollar bill in my pocket.

He sat there, nodding and smiling and shaking his head on cue. It wasn't until I had several jolts of coffee inside of me that I came out of my talking jag. Maybe I was foolish in letting him pump me without knowing what he really wanted.

I lit a cigarette and pushed my cup away.

"Seems to me as though I'm doing a lot of talking."

His bald head wobbled. "Go ahead. I like to listen to you. You have a wonderful voice."

"Tell that to the radio and TV executives. They won't listen to me."

"Executives!" I caught the familiar wave of the hand, the glittering arc of the diamond swirling through space. "Your voice is too fine an instrument to be wasted on selling gasoline and laxatives."

"Then what interests you?" I asked.

"I've already told you. It's your voice. I've spent weeks now, listening to voices. Auditioning records and transcriptions with talent agents. I heard your voice by accident the other day in an advertising office. Mr. Rickert must have sent them a record.

"Right then I knew I had found what I was looking for. Because you do have a very fine voice, Mr. Haines. I'm not speaking of diction or phrasing. I'm talking about pitch and timbre. You have a persuasive voice. You sound sincere and convincing. Women like your voice, don't they, Mr. Haines?"

What was the matter with this guy? I stared at him— a fat, ugly, bald-headed little stranger who tossed around hundred-dollar bills and talked about voices.

He smiled. "You don't understand, of course. But you will. I'm sure of that. I like your inquisitive attitude. I like your self-confidence. The way you tried to stare me down in the office this afternoon. I often amuse myself by observing the reactions of strangers. And I've made up my mind that with proper training you will go far. You have the voice, the appearance, the youth and the background. It was no accident that brought us together. It was Destiny."

Professor Hermann wasn't smiling now. He hunched forward over the table and his eyes were glittering to match that big diamond.

"Cut the violin music," I said. "What's your proposition?"

He glanced at the restaurant clock and stood up, quickly. "We haven't time to discuss that now," he said. "It's getting late. We're due at the meeting."

"What meeting?"

"Come and see. It's important that you arrive before the testimony starts."

"Wait a minute. I want to know what I'm getting into here. After all, I can't afford to waste my time—"

He grinned. "You don't trust me? Then I suggest you give me back that hundred-dollar bill and call it quits. I'll go to the meeting, and you—you run along back home and cut your throat."

I stared at him for a long second, and then it struck me. I began to laugh. I was still laughing as I followed him out of the restaurant and down the street.

"So you've decided to come along?"

"Right," I said. "But I still wish I knew where I was going."

"All you need to know," Professor Hermann told me, "is that tonight we take the first step. The first step in the direction of a million dollars."

Four

The professor led me down the street for about half a block and halted before my idea of a beautiful animal—a handsome new black Jaguar.

"Climb in," he said.

"But we didn't come in a car—"

He gave that grin again as he jangled a set of keys before my eyes. "Correct. I parked here before I went to see you. I had everything arranged."

I matched his grin with a shrug and opened the door. I was relieved to know I wasn't getting mixed up with a car thief, but at the same time I didn't quite like the idea of his being so sure of me in advance. A smart apple, the Professor —a smart little bald-headed apple.

We pulled away, headed down the boulevard, then went northwest toward Beverly Hills. Neither of us said anything for a while and the Jaguar just purred.

The Professor glanced at the dashboard clock. "Right on time," he said. "We'll pick her up and then go to the meeting."

"Her?"

"Oh, I forgot to mention that we're bringing a guest. You will probably like her—I don't suppose you've ever met a movie star before."

"Movie star?"

"Well, a featured player. Seven hundred and fifty dollars a week. Lorna Lewis. You know the name?"

Lorna Lewis, the gal with the glamorous gams. The censor's delight. I'd heard of her, all right. This was going to be interesting, after all.

"The movie colony is particularly impressionable," re-

marked Professor Hermann. "I expect great results from them in our future work. For example, consider their interest in astrology. I can name you dozens of stars, producers, executives who won't make a move unless the signs are right.

"I always think of one top name out here—she's been in pictures ever since the original Lassie was a pup—who lives according to a carefully plotted horoscope based on her date of birth. The only thing is, as she gets older she keeps moving her birthdate forward. She's changed her age four times now, and each time she gets a new astrologer and a new horoscope. But she won't so much as sleep with an assistant producer without consulting the stars."

The car climbed a hill. Poinsettias pressed myriad bleeding mouths to a garden wall.

"About this Lorna Lewis," I said. "Is she gone on astrology too?"

Professor Hermann shook his head. "No. Spiritualism."

I blinked and sat up. "Mean to tell me that's what you have in mind for us—some kind of spook racket?"

"Far from it. My dear boy, don't underestimate me. You and I are above such vulgar fakery. Our paths lead to higher things. But we'll speak of all that at another time. Right now your cue is to observe—and be silent."

We entered the driveway on a hillside. Past the palm-bordered path rose a rambling neo-Spanish *hacienda.* I caught a glimpse of a side terrace and a swimming pool in the back. Then we drew up before broad stone steps. The motor whimpered in death.

Professor Hermann led me to the door. The usual buzzer produced the usual chimes. We waited until the door opened.

"Come in," said a voice. I recognized it immediately. I recognized the black jungle of curls, the almost Negroid lips, the slim sweep of the perfectly proportioned legs. Lorna Lewis, in person.

"Be with you in a minute." She waved us to a love seat in the hall alcove and then dashed up the stairs, treating us to a

profile and rear view of one of the finest pairs of peach-colored slacks I'd ever seen.

"Don't stare!" hissed the Professor. "And from now on, remember, take your cues from me." He produced his monocle and bent forward to polish it with a handkerchief as though it were a rare scientific lens.

"Remember, now, not a word. Let me do the talking."

"But—"

She was running down the stairs again, still wearing the peach-colored slacks and a green blouse. I hadn't appreciated the blouse before, but it was even better than the slacks.

"Ready? Let's go, then. Our appointment's for nine-thirty and we mustn't be late." Suddenly she seemed to notice me. She paused and blinked rapidly, just to show me she could do it without knocking any of the mascara off her eyelashes. "Who's he?" she asked.

"Miss Lewis, this is Judson Roberts."

This was me, apparently. I rose and started to open my mouth, but the Professor coughed.

"Mr. Roberts cannot answer you. He is committed to silence until midnight."

This time her blink was genuine. "Oh—a vow or something?"

"Certainly not, my dear child! Mr. Roberts is no fake mystic. He's a scientist. As such, he is engaged in an experiment of psychological conditioning. He has just arrived from the University of Lima and plans to collaborate with me in my work. I'd like to have him tell you about it some time— I'm sure you would be interested."

"I know I will." She gave me a long look and I found out she could do other tricks with her eyes besides the blinking act.

"I've invited Mr. Roberts to accompany us as an observer this evening." The Professor hesitated. "If you don't mind."

"That's fine with me. But I don't know if Mrs. Hubbard will approve. I hear she's very particular about strangers."

"More than likely." The Professor led us outside and slid behind the wheel of the car. Lorna Lewis followed and I

edged into the front seat beside her. The peach-colored slacks pressed against my thigh. I pressed back. Maybe I wasn't allowed to talk, but I managed to make an impression.

The Professor was doing most of the talking as he nosed the Jaguar south, then east. "Your Mrs. Hubbard probably doesn't care for outsiders a bit. I wouldn't, either, if I was working a nice soft racket—preying on motion picture people with phony spiritualism."

Lorna Lewis tossed her head. Jungle-storm.

"You'll see! Mrs. Hubbard is different. She doesn't try to fool anyone with tricks or hocus-pocus."

"No ectoplasm or apparitions? What about rope escapes and raps? Does she produce apports?"

"You're making fun of me." Her fingers caressed a silver cigarette case. "Mr. Roberts?"

"Mr. Roberts does not smoke," snapped the Professor.

That was news to me. I wondered if I also did not drink. Probably I fasted a lot, too. Certainly I had nothing to do with women. Eyeing Lorna Lewis, I decided *that* was one rule which would be changed in a hurry.

"My dear Miss Lewis," purred the Professor, "I am by nature a skeptic and by profession a psychologist. As such I have devoted much time to the investigation of so-called psychic phenomena. I am sorry to report that I have never seen a genuine medium."

"But Mrs. Hubbard doesn't put on a show," the girl protested. "Why, I've only been there once before, and it was just like sitting down for a visit. The lights were on and everything. But the things she told me, the things she knew about me, it was simply uncanny!

"She knew my name—my real name, that is—and my age, and where I lived, and who my folks were, and what my next picture would be and who would direct it. She even told me I'd get Lester Vance opposite me, and I didn't hear about it from the studio until three days later!"

The Professor chuckled. "You're in pictures, my child. Such information is virtually public property."

"But my real name, and my real age—"

"It's all listed somewhere. Your birth certificate is surely available by mail. And certainly an unscrupulous woman would be willing to spend a few dollars on investigation. She probably has a line into the studio, paying someone to feed her advance tips on activities. She hopes to make you a regular client and attract others. Didn't you say your hairdresser told you to go there in the first place? It's all very obvious."

I realized, suddenly, that he was talking to me more than he was to her—trying to tell me the angles. I listened carefully.

"If you are gullible enough, I predict that sooner or later your little ten-dollar readings won't satisfy Mrs. Hubbard. She'll give you some good advice about the future, and some even more intimate information about yourself; feed it to you bit by bit, just to keep you coming back for more. Sooner or later she will find out that you too have mystic powers, that you're clairvoyant, clairaudient, a natural medium. She'll give you slate-writing and then the old psychic force routine."

"Psychic force?"

"Moving inanimate objects without touching them. Waving her hand over fruit, walnuts, coins. They'll obey her, move and follow her hand. Psychic force. I'll show you how it's done, sometime."

"Tell me."

"Simple. She wears a magnetized ring. There's another magnet planted inside the walnut or fruit or fake coin. Naturally, it moves. By varying the weight of the object she can produce anything from a stir to a jump. It sounds simple and stupid and obvious, but wait until she gives you the buildup—in the dim, quiet room with her voice pitched low and the spirits abroad."

Lorna Lewis shook her head. "Mrs. Hubbard isn't like that at all. You'll see."

"Very well. But remember, I'm here to protect you. Just introduce us as friends. I promise not to interfere in any way, but I want to observe what happens."

"That's right, Professor," said Lorna Lewis, with the roguish smile that endeared her to millions. "Just hold your water."

We turned into a street that looked like the butt-end of Tobacco Road. Lawns of brown weeds and sand, withered palmettoes decorated by the dogs, houses sagging behind rusted iron fences.

It was a hot night. On paint-peeled porches, unlovely women rocked and fanned futilely. Towheaded brats peered from behind phlegm-green window shades. Street lights lent a wavering distortion to the flight of myriad flies, but did nothing to cut the stench of shrivelled vegetation, rotting wood, sweat, garbage, and the frying odor of food.

"Here we are." Lorna Lewis indicated a house. She might have been psychic at that; I couldn't have distinguished this particular shack from any of the others. It was a wide two-story house which might once have been painted yellow. The shades were drawn, the door was shut, and the only sign of occupancy was a smear of cat droppings across the broken boards of the porch.

We parked, then swerved across the sidewalk in single file. I stumbled over a battered blue coaster wagon which lay on its side near the fence. Right then and there I almost forgot my vow of silence.

I fancied I saw the shades move slightly in a window to the left of the porch, but I was more interested in the movement of Lorna Lewis's peach-colored slacks. We followed her up the porch steps.

She pressed the buzzer and a sour whine echoed from within the house. A sallow-faced Mexican girl opened the door. She brushed the perspiration from her mustache, wiped her hand on her stringy hair and said, "Yes, please?"

"We've come to see Mrs. Hubbard. We have an appointment."

"I tell her. Wait here."

She ushered us into the hallway and left us there.

The hall was dark and narrow, like a closet. And like a

closet, it smelled of mothballs and mustiness. There were doors on either side of the hallway, and the girl departed through one at our right. Nothing supernatural about that— she opened the door before entering.

We settled down in wicker chairs and waited. My chair was next to a wicker end table piled high with tattered magazines. I picked one up. It was a copy of *Film Fun* for January, 1933.

Lorna Lewis found another cigarette. The Professor polished his monocle. I looked at "gag" still-shots of such forgotten cinema zanies as Harry Langdon, Jimmy Finlayson, Andy Clyde and Edgar Kennedy.

The silence was emphatic. The air was hotter, mustier. The hall became an oversized coffin. Time passed, but what's time when you're inside a coffin? Lorna Lewis stepped on her cigarette. The Professor adjusted his monocle. I sat there listening to the worms bore through the woodwork.

Then the door opened, and we jumped, and the Mexican girl said, "In here, please."

Beyond the door was an ordinary parlor—"sitting room" in the day when this house was built—filled with the usual scrolled oak furniture, upholstered by a contemporary of Queen Anne. The wallpaper was Paris green, obscured in many places by large chromos of the Saviour in meditation, exaltation and agony.

The center of the room was occupied by a "dining room suite" consisting of six chairs and a round table. Mrs. Hubbard sat in one of the chairs, her elbows on the table top. She wasn't exactly Mrs. Hubbard—"Mother Hubbard" would be a more accurate tag. A fat, blowsy, red-faced woman in her mid-menopause, with pork-bristles on her arms and chin. Coarse brown hair nestled in a bun against the back of her high-necked black dress. There was something tragic about her deep-set eyes; here, if ever I saw one, was a woman who had been suffering. From a hangover.

"Greetings."

Her voice was as big as her body. It bounced off the walls and exploded against our ears.

"You are prompt, Miss Lewis. And I see you have brought some guests."

"I thought you wouldn't mind. This is—"

"I know." Mrs. Hubbard smiled slightly. "Please be seated, and I will endeavor to convince the skeptical Professor Otto Hermann, Ph.D., that I am indeed a psychic sensitive."

We selected chairs and sat around the table. The Mexican girl opened the door again and ushered four more people into the room. We turned and stared at the fat little red-faced man with the mustache, the portly matron in the flower-print dress, the pale, bespectacled blonde girl, and the gaunt, gray-haired woman who fiddled with her coral beads.

Mrs. Hubbard, unsmiling, waved them to places at the table. The Mexican girl brought in some extra chairs and then produced a card table which she set up in the corner of the room. Mrs. Hubbard rose and retreated to a seat behind the card table and we sat around the larger one, facing her, in a semi-circle.

Nobody said a word. Lorna Lewis watched Mrs. Hubbard. I watched Lorna Lewis. The Professor was watching me. Mrs. Hubbard didn't appear to be watching anybody. The whole affair began to take on the charm and jollity of an inquest. I was waiting for something to happen. I was waiting for the closing of the blinds, the whisperings in the darkened room, the rappings and the wailings, the screech of chalk moving across a slate, the phosphorescent phantom issuing from the mouth of a moaning woman.

The Mexican girl appeared again. She carried a tablet of cheap blue-ruled paper, a package of envelopes, and a handful of sharpened yellow pencils. This assortment made a nice little mess on Mrs. Hubbard's card table.

We watched and waited as the Mexican girl rotated chunky thighs towards the door. The red-faced man fingered his mustache, the matron played with her purse, the girl with the glasses coughed, the gray-haired woman used her coral beads for a private rosary. The Professor had his monocle to divert him and I had Lorna Lewis. Her black hair

held a living lustre. I wondered how it would feel to dig my fingers into those curls, press that head back, and—

"Will everybody take a pencil, a sheet of paper and an envelope, please?"

Mrs. Hubbard was ready to go into her routine. We rose, filed past the table and returned to our places.

"Because our group tonight is a little larger than usual, and because there is a natural reticence in the presence of strangers, I feel it best to have you put your questions in writing." Mrs. Hubbard smiled.

"I suggest that each of you write down one question, to begin with. If we have time, I shall be glad to work with your further inquiries personally—and privately, if you wish.

"At the moment the important thing, frankly, is to gain your complete confidence. Without it you will have no faith in my power, nor in my ability to help you. Since some of you are here for the first time tonight, I'm going to make use of a rather spectacular method to convince you of my extra-liminal perception."

The deep voice rolled smoothly, easily, persuasively.

"I'm not very much of a showman—I cannot offer you a dark room, table-tipping, ghostly presences. But if each one of you will write a question on a piece of paper, fold it as much as you like, and personally seal it in an envelope— then perhaps I can demonstrate an interesting psychic phenomenon."

There was a pause, a shared feeling of hesitation. Mrs. Hubbard didn't have to be a mystic to sense the indecision.

"Please. It's very simple. I am going to read your questions back to you as you have written them, without opening the envelopes. There's no trickery. You can examine the paper, the pencils, the envelopes. You won't find any carbon or wax or acid-treatments. There will be no waiting and no switches. I'll read your questions back to you immediately and give you the answers as they come to me. So if you'll write—and make your questions sincere—whatever is closest to your mind and heart—"

The red-faced man scrawled something on his ruled sheet and folded it carefully four times. The matron licked the tip of her pencil and frowned. Lorna Lewis pouted. I watched her lips pucker as if seeking kisses—or bites. The spectacle suggested several questions to my mind, but not the kind I cared to have read back to me in public.

I shielded my own paper and wrote, "Will my new venture be successful?"

There was much business of folding and sealing. Lorna Lewis ran her tongue across the flap. She was like a kitten lapping cream. I wondered how it would feel to—

Then I stopped wondering. Mrs. Hubbard lumbered around the table and took up the sealed envelopes. I watched her for obvious reasons; we all watched. But I could detect no switch or sleight-of-hand. She collected seven envelopes, shuffled them carefully, and placed them on the table. She spread them out fanwise before her and frowned. Our chairs scraped back as we faced her. She switched on a lamp behind her and produced a wire filing basket.

"I shall read your questions and answer them one at a time," she told us. "In order to confirm this, I am going to ask the writer of each question to raise his or her hand and let me know if I've sensed it correctly. Then I'll open the envelope containing it. Is that agreeable?"

We nodded. I looked at Professor Hermann. His face was utterly expressionless. I wondered what he was thinking, what he would do if Lorna Lewis seemed convinced by Mrs. Hubbard. So far he hadn't opened his mouth.

Mrs. Hubbard stared down at the envelopes. Her forehead creased. A fat hand reached out at random and lifted an envelope from the center of the fan-shaped assortment. She placed the sealed envelope high against her wrinkled brow. Her eyes closed.

Then she was speaking, and her voice came from far away—as if from inside herself, as if from inside the envelope.

"Should I sell my property to the syndicate or hold out for the original figure?" she whispered.

A red-faced, mustached Jack-in-the-box popped up. "That's it!" he shouted. "By golly, that's my question, all right."

Professor Hermann never blinked. Everyone else was leaning forward, tense with excitement.

Mrs. Hubbard smiled. "Please, control yourselves. It makes it more difficult for me to concentrate." She opened the envelope now, unfolded the sheet, glanced at it carelessly, and I placed it in the wicker basket. And all the while, she continued to talk.

"As it comes to me, Mr. Rogers, this property you refer to consists of a block of eight lots just south of San Juan Capistrano, on the coast highway. This syndicate of which you speak, the—"

Rogers opened his mouth and she paused. "Of course I will not mention their names, if you prefer. But it is true, isn't it, that they plan to build a hotel on this site? And that yesterday they offered you $18,000 cash for an outright sale, while you are holding out for $25,000? I thought so. It appears that if you refuse, they will offer you $20,000 on Thursday. If you still refuse, on Monday they will meet your price."

Without pausing, the plump hand sought another envelope, pressed it to the red forehead. Her eyes closed and her mouth opened.

"Will Mike leave me?"

Lorna Lewis leaned forward. "Yes," she murmured. "That's my question."

Mrs. Hubbard nodded, slitting the envelope. She tossed the unfolded paper into the basket, glancing at it and nodding at the same time.

"Mike will leave you soon—forever. He is preparing to depart right now. He hasn't told you yet, because he doesn't know about it himself, fully. But I see him going away from you, going far, far away—"

The girl's mouth opened. Mrs. Hubbard apparently was used to this reaction, for she hurried on. "I could tell you

much more, but it would not be discreet. Alone, perhaps, and later, if you desire."

Again I tried to pierce Professor Hermann's bland stare. I tried to figure it out. There must be an angle, an answer to all this, but where?

"Will my new venture be successful?"

She was reading my question!

My own mouth opened now. It sucked in air as I watched Mrs. Hubbard carelessly unseal the envelope and withdraw the folded paper. She unravelled it and then—*her mouth opened*.

Something red fluttered to the table; something bold and brazen, with the picture of a half-naked girl emblazoned on its crimson background.

It was the cover of the *Film Fun* magazine I'd been reading in the hall!

Professor Hermann was on his feet, snatching at the cover. "You made a mistake in the envelopes," he said. "My question, I believe."

Mrs. Hubbard's open mouth gulped for words. When they came, they sounded in a sweetly audible cadence.

"You lousy rat!"

But she couldn't escape. We were crowded around the table now and the Professor, inarticulate no longer, was holding forth.

"You see, it's very simple. The whole trick is old as the hills. While the audience is looking for mirrors, electronic detectors, all kinds of elaborate devices, the fake mystic is merely using the old 'one-ahead' system. All she needs for that is a stooge. In this case, it was Rogers, here."

The red-faced mustached man who had popped up like a Jack-in-the-box now looked as though he would collapse like one. But the Professor held his arm firmly.

"Here's how it works. The stooge writes his question and seals it up like all the others, but he marks his envelope by nicking the flap with his fingernail. The medium spots it at a glance. Here."

He held up an envelope—unopened.

"This she saves until the last. But she calls out the stooge's question, first. She knows it in advance, of course. Then the stooge jumps up and makes a big production about hearing the correct question. She opens the envelope she's held to her forehead. Naturally, it's one of the others containing a legitimate question which she reads after opening the envelope. So while answering the stooge's question, in convincing detail, she was actually reading Miss Lewis' question from the envelope she opened. Then, with the next envelope, she answered Miss Lewis. Then she opened the flap and found Mr. Roberts' question.

"But when she called Mr. Roberts' question, she opened my envelope—and that was her mistake."

"All right, fink," muttered Mrs. Hubbard. "What do you want?"

The Professor shrugged. "Nothing at all, really, from you—except your promise to quit working a racket on people who are in need of genuine assistance from reputable consultants. I don't think you'll be trying these tricks around here very much longer."

"Why you goddamn—"

"Careful, now! Watch your language. You aren't very ladylike, Mrs. Hubbard. Of course, appearances are deceptive; you ladies and gentlemen must always remember that. For example, Mrs. Hubbard here does not use ladylike language because she really isn't a lady. In fact—"

The Professor's hand descended to Mrs. Hubbard's head. It rose again, clutching a brown-bunned wig. We gaped down at a fat, bald-headed man who gripped the edge of the table and cursed like the producer of a sustaining show.

Professor Hermann ignored his victim as he turned to us with a little bow.

"My friends," he said. "I think our little session with the supernatural is over."

Five

We drove Lorna Lewis home. It was hard for me to remember that I was "Judson Roberts" and that I was under a vow of silence. But the Professor was in the driver's seat. He drove, I fidgeted, and Lorna Lewis babbled.

"You were so right," she sighed. "And I'm so grateful to you. If that racketeer had found out about me—I mean, if I'd trusted him and really told a lot of things I need advice on—"

She shivered. It felt good against me.

Professor Hermann smiled. "Perhaps in the future you will be more discreet. Only a reputable consultant should be trusted with your intimate problems."

"That's what Mike tells me." She lit a cigarette, and it was agony for me to sit there and smell the smoke flaring from her mouth. "About Mike—there's something I must know."

"Bothering you, is he?"

"Yes. And I want you to help me. I can trust you, now. When could we talk about it?"

"Miss Bauer makes all my appointments. Call her at my office whenever you wish."

He left it at that when we dropped her at the house. She said goodbye to me and hoped we'd meet again. I nodded calmly. As her peach-colored posterior wiggled its way up the walk, I was tearing open a package of cigarettes, fumbling with the matches. I got a light as we drove west.

"Can I talk now?" I asked.

The Professor nodded.

"I don't get the pitch yet, but I can see that you've sold her a bill of goods."

He smiled.

"That was a sweet idea, using the magazine cover. But what if it had been some other racket—were you sure of being able to expose it anyway?"

"Certainly. There is no possibility of failure, the way I operate. You will learn that in due time."

"Where are we going now?"

"You shall see."

"When are you going to tell me about those plans of yours?"

"Soon."

I shut up and watched the lights of Santa Monica flash by. We kept going, hugging the edge of the ocean where, hours before, the sun had dropped into the water like a big California orange.

A lemon moon was in the sky as we neared the flickering street lights of Long Beach. The Professor parked on a side street and led me down a ramp to the boardwalk. We jostled through the late evening crowd and emerged on the midway.

"Follow me," said the Professor, and led the way to a stand down the line.

Sideshow banners proclaimed the presence of SEERO THE MYSTIC—SECRETS OF PAST, PRESENT AND FUTURE. Gaudy horoscopes decorated the sides of the ticket booth. A horse-faced woman with yellow hair and teeth to match smiled at us from behind the glass.

The Professor greeted her. "Is he here yet?"

"Just came in a minute ago. You can come in. There's nobody with him now."

We entered the pitch, going through a short passageway and emerging into a darkened, banner-draped room. A man sat behind a covered table, peering into a crystal ball. He wore a bathrobe and a turban. When he saw us he stood up, went to the door, latched it and returned to his seat at the low table.

No one spoke for a moment. I stared at the mystic and wondered where I'd seen that fat face before. He must have caught my thought, because he took his turban off and laid it

down on the table. I recognized his bald head and then I knew.

The man was "Mrs. Hubbard."

"You got here quick," he said.

"I always keep my promises." The Professor smiled. "Is everything all right, Jake?"

"Yeah, sure. All fixed but the payoff." Jake gave me the kind of stare that would have cracked his crystal ball. "Who's the savage?"

"This is Judson Roberts, my new associate. He'll be working with me from now on."

Jake now favored me with his normal smile, which would scarcely have wilted a flower at three hundred paces. "Please to meet up with you. You a dummy?"

"I can talk," I said. "But I learn more from just listening."

"A wisey, huh?" Jake swung around to the Professor. "Say, Rogers said for me to collect his split, too."

"Very well." Professor Hermann reached for his wallet and laid three engraved portraits of Benjamin Franklin on the table. Jake covered them with one big fist.

"Thanks," he said.

"You did a good job. I'm glad the Lewis question came out before my envelope."

"Kept my eye on it," Jake answered. "I could of given her a cold reading if you'da let me."

"None of that, if you please. Just follow orders when you work with me. I shall call you for something else in a few days. Meanwhile, stick to your pitch here. Forget the Mrs. Hubbard angle. It's washed up. Too risky for such small stakes."

"Gotcha."

"And that goes for Rogers, too. He has other assignments to carry out for me."

"Yeah. Well, be seeing you."

We left. The Professor walked out to the beach and headed for the water's edge. Surf lathered the tan cheek of the beach. He stood frowning off into the darkness.

"Now I understand," I said. "You couldn't possibly fail, could you? Because you rigged it all from the beginning. You planted a phony medium just to pull that stunt, so there never was a chance of anything going wrong."

The wind tore the chuckle out of his mouth and carried it away across the water. "Of course. I never permit any margin for error. And this little affair tonight was more important than you know. Lorna Lewis had to be convinced. She is my opening wedge into the movie colony and the big money beyond that.

"You will find that I plan my projects perfectly. Everything we do will be carefully calculated in advance. That way we cannot fail. I will want your complete confidence. And I shall pay for it. Not with hundred-dollar handouts. I'm talking about real money now—thousands, perhaps millions. For me. For you."

His white face stared up at me. "We can take over this town, you and I. Not with a phony cult or a fly-by-night racket. We're going after the top, the cream. We'll get next to them, get under their skin, get into their minds. We'll start out by advising and analyzing them—but we'll end up running their lives. We're going to own them, body and soul!

"Today you saw me arrange events so that Lorna Lewis would ask me for help. If my plans work out, six months from now, I'll order her to do anything I wish. And she'll do it. She and dozens of others like her.

"That's why I need you. That's why I found you. Because this calls for a front man—young, good-looking, persuasive. He'll work directly with the women and with the men, too. Of course, you must be trained for the role and that will take time. It will not be easy, for there's so much to learn. The arts of social presence. Metaphysics. Psychiatry. Theology. Your personality must be molded for aggression and command. I am the guiding hand—you will be the instrument, ground to perfection for our work.

"I shall demand strict obedience, insist that you follow the program I lay down for you. But in return, you will receive

everything you've always wanted. Fame, wealth, power.

"You'd like that, wouldn't you? I can sense it in you—that drive, that urge for power. Power over them all: the sleek, slim women you've never been able to have, and the hard, smug domineering men who've always ignored you. You can rule them if you wish, make them do anything you desire. Judges, doctors, politicians, financiers—the whole pack will come fawning at your heels, licking your fingers and whimpering for what you can give them."

The surf lashed at my feet, the wind tore at my face, and his voice rode the surf and the wind to beat me down. Darkness and a white face and a voice that hinted and promised...

I had to say something. "But look, you can't do this to people. Maybe they'll fall for a line, but sooner or later they find out. I don't feel right, selling them something phony."

He laughed. "And yet you wanted to be a radio or television announcer."

"That's different—"

"Is it? Is it any more honest to read off gaudy lies about the nonexistent benefits of soap and toothpaste than it is to advocate self-help? You'd be perfectly willing to tell millions of pimply, bloated hags that they can become lovely and alluring if they buy a cake of perfumed fat to drop into their bath water. Isn't that the same thing?"

"Well, not exactly. I mean—"

"Be honest with yourself, now. You'd have no scruples about trying to run people's lives as a radio announcer, would you? You'd sell anything, use any threat or method. Fill poor little adolescent know-nothings with self-conscious fear, droning horrible warnings about acne and bad breath and perspiration odors. Frighten old folks with grave hints about the dreadful dangers of constipation and upset stomach. You'd promise wealth, success and happiness by inference to anyone who obeys your commands—runs down to the corner druggist, the neighborhood grocer, buys this, uses that, eats whatever you want to sell. Yes, and if your

studio handed you the script, you'd use your best voice to shout the merits of a crooked politician, the virtues of a dishonest business policy. And yet you're squeamish!"

I nodded. "Maybe you're right, when you put it that way. But I still don't think you can get away with your plans. There may be a few idiots who want to be fooled—who go for all the isms and ologies that come along. But most people are fairly sensible, after all. And I don't see—"

"You will. Come along and I'll show you."

He led the way back across the beach. We nearly stumbled over a couple huddled on a blanket. The unshaven man in the T-shirt was fumbling at a high-school girl. Without removing his hands he raised his head and said, "W'yncha watch where tha hell ya goin'ta, ya dumb basserds?"

The Professor nodded and whispered. "We're back in the world of normal people, my friend. Look at them."

I looked.

The beach came alive all around me. A brawny, towheaded man passed me, brushing so closely in the darkness that I could see his tattooed arm and smell the stench of tobacco from between his rotted teeth. He was grinning down at a giggling girl whose voice rose to a shriek as he dragged her into the water by her ankles.

"Oooooh, Ernie!" she yapped. "Oooooh, ya *dog!*"

A cannibalistic circle huddled around a small fire, gorging on half-raw weenies and rancid dill pickles. Troglodyte faces gaped in the firelight. A wrinkled, wizened old man's head: white, bushy hair and beetling black brows that moved convulsively as he chewed with his whole face. There was a fat, blobby woman with stringy hair and a red neck; the rest of her flesh hung in dead white folds, broken here and there by bulging purplish veins that stood out like mountain ranges on a relief map. She slapped at a screaming brat with one beefy hand, slopping beer from a punctured can clutched in the other. A bullet-headed youth squatted next to a portable radio, fiddling with the volume control and scratching the hairy recesses of his armpits.

"Welcome to the world," whispered the Professor.

A big kid hit a little kid. A broad-shouldered man whose back was covered with black fur now stood on his hands and walked over a group of three tittering girls who lay on a blanket exhibiting their charms—shaved armpits, vaccination scars, flabby breasts, hennaed curls on pimple-pitted foreheads. Two hulking sailors hurled a beach ball into the group, growling with oafish laughter to compel attention. A baby began to whimper in the darkness. We moved on, away from there.

I had sand in my shoes. I was hungry. I stepped through a tangle of crumpled paper, greasy cardboard plates, broken pop bottles. A small dog rushed up and nipped at my ankles, yapping hysterically.

"You see?" murmured the Professor. "Here are your normal people."

"All right," I said. "I don't particularly care for them. But that doesn't prove anything. It doesn't prove they'll fall for a line of phony advice about their lives and futures."

The wind sent a dirty newspaper flying against my leg. I bent down and pushed it away, glimpsing the red letters of the headline: SEX MANIAC SOUGHT IN HATCHET SLAYING.

"Perhaps this will help to make you understand," Professor Hermann told me. We turned onto the midway again.

Fluorescence and incandescence blinded me. My lungs gulped in popcorn oil, lard, the reek of frying meat, the stink of decayed fruit, and a rancid stench composed of tobacco, sweat, cheap perfume and whiskey.

Banners swirled all around me—before me, behind me, on either side, overhead. CONGRESS OF FREAKS. FLEA CIRCUS. ARCADE. EATS. FUN HOUSE. LEARN YOUR FUTURE. THREE SHOTS FOR A DIME. PLAY THE WINNERS. MAN-EATERS. RED-HOTS. A dozen jukeboxes blared and boomed, a merry-go-round seethed; against this background rose the whirling, rattling, clanking and grinding of the Whip, the Dodger, the plane rides and the roller-coaster. The sharp crack of rifles echoed from the shooting

gallery. Barkers shouted in command, and amplifying systems carried their exhortations, roars, and raucous bawls of invitation. From the rides overhead I heard screams, shrieks, wails, and high, hysterical laughter.

"Close your eyes," said the Professor. "Don't look at them. I won't even ask you to look at them. Just listen. And what do you hear?"

I closed my eyes and stood there, jostled by the crowd.

The harsh music suggested bands, and the boom-boom beat was a marching tempo. I thought of war. Yes, war— with rifle-shots and shouted orders. Grinding machinery: tanks, planes and armored cars, artillery wheeling up for action. And over that, the screams. The screams of the wounded and the dying. The screams of the killers, boring for blood with their bayonets.

Then the Professor was whispering again. "Normal people," he told me. "Normal world. They're out for entertainment tonight. Forgetting their troubles. Having fun, as they call it.

"Having fun! Look at them! Paying money to be locked in cages and whirled through the air upside down. Bolting themselves into cars that lurch and sway until their stomachs turn inside out and the blood churns in their stupid brains. Standing up in roller-coasters and risking death to attract attention. That's all it is, you know. The shouting, the laughing, the posturing and screaming—it's a cry of 'Look at me! Look how brave I am, how important! See what I'm doing, I'm having a good time!' And watch them smash into each other with the cars when they can, watch the play of sadism and masochism that passes for amusement.

"This is an amusement park, my friend. People come here to find what they want out of life—entertainment. They put their pennies into the peepshow slots because they want to do so. They know they're being swindled and they love it. They love the lies, the phoniness, the cheats. They know the freak shows are fakes. They know the spielers are conning them about stepping up and winning the electric

clocks. They don't believe in our friend SEERO THE MYSTIC, but they pay their money and go inside because they want to be fooled.

"It's not a new concept. Your showman, Barnum, said it long ago—and it was known and spoken of in ancient Egypt. But it is a truth that survives, for the desire for self-delusion never dies.

"People long for escape. Some of them pay their pennies to find it here. Others are able and willing to pay fortunes for something a little more convincing. For the sort of escape we will give them. These are the ones we shall rule. The seekers."

"Suckers," I said.

"The seeker is always a sucker," said Professor Hermann.

Six

I showed up at the Professor's office the next morning. Somehow I'd never pictured him in a downtown office. But there was the sign on the door in neat, discreet lettering:

OTTO HERMANN, PH.D.
PSYCHOLOGICAL CONSULTANT

The waiting room was cool and dark, well-furnished without the flash of Larry Rickert's fake modern layout. The receptionist's desk stood right out in the open. Behind it sat a plump, middle-aged brunette wearing a loose white smock and a tight red smile. She smiled up at me and her words filtered through a thick accent.

"You would be Mr. Haines?"

"I would."

"The Professor is expecting you. Please to enter."

I pleased to enter. Bookcases lined the walls of the private office. There was a red leather couch in the corner and a row of filing cabinets beside it. The Professor sat in a chair at the side of his desk. He was wearing the same black suit, or a reasonable facsimile. When I entered, he reached for the intercom.

"Miss Bauer—I do not wish to be disturbed."

He glanced at his watch. Then his gaze ricocheted to me. "You are late."

"Sorry. I overslept. Yesterday took a lot out of me, I guess."

"You are rested now?"

I nodded.

"Good. Then we can proceed to business." He opened a drawer of his desk and drew out a thick sheaf of legal-bond typing paper.

"What's that?" I asked.

"Your book, of course. The one you wrote."

I stared at the title page and read:

$$Y - O - U$$
by
Judson Roberts

"Take it and read it," he said. "Memorize it. After all, you're Judson Roberts, you know."

"I didn't know." I riffled the pages and sat back. "What's it all about?"

"Did you ever read Dale Carnegie? Walter Pitkin? Stuart Chase? They're all in here. And Doctor Frank Crane and Elbert Hubbard, too. Also Madame Blavatsky, Mrs. Eddy, and a little bit of Thorstein Veblen. And of course, Herr Freud and Jung, and Aldous Huxley and Philip Wylie and Ouspensky and Spengler. A little bit of everyone. But with revisions and improvements, of course."

"Did you actually write it?"

"No. Rogers wrote it. You remember, the little man with the mustache, at the seance. He has talent, when controlled. I commissioned him to start the book a year ago, when I began to plan all this."

"What's the point?"

"Perfectly obvious. Now that I've found my Judson Roberts, the book will be published. I can arrange for printing and for distribution. Rogers can set up a direct-mail campaign and we will sell it ourselves. It's good for ten, twenty years. A small, steady income—though that's not important in itself. But a published book is needed to establish Judson Roberts as an authority. That is most desirable. By the way, I've already sent your name in for a course and a diploma."

"Diploma?"

"You're going to be a Doctor of Psychology, just as I am. There's a correspondence school in the East. Fifty dollars gets you a degree, and no questions asked. What are you grinning about?"

"It just struck me funny. All of a sudden I'm a Doctor of Psychology and the author of a book."

"There's nothing funny about that. It's window dressing. And speaking of window dressing—"

The Professor rose and surveyed me critically. "Watch your posture. Your shoulders aren't squared, you have a tendency to slouch. And you slump when you sit in a chair. We'll correct that. You'll need a wardrobe, of course, but that will come later. Hold your head a trifle higher and emphasize your height. You gain a certain advantage when people have to look up to you during a conversation. You might experiment with a different hairstyle. Those sideburns are all right for a cheap salesman, but I want more dignity. But enough of that for now. We have other work to do."

"Such as?"

"Reading your book."

I picked up the manuscript. "I'll run through it this evening," I promised.

The Professor shook his head. "Only the beginning. You'll read it tonight and then you'll read it again. And again. The content is the key to our whole system. It must be correlated with your other reading. For the next three months you're going to sit in that apartment of yours and read. I'll see that you eat, meanwhile."

"Sounds pretty soft."

"It won't be. You're going to study and sweat. I'll quiz you. You'll take tests. By the time I'm done, you'll be able to hold your own conversationally with any occultist, real or phony, and sound convincing."

"Okay. You're the Professor."

"And you're Judson Roberts."

That's how it started. I walked into the office as plain Eddie Haines and I walked out as Judson Roberts, with my book under my arm.

Judson Roberts took his book home and studied it. Then he studied the basic, selected writings of Freud, Adler, Jung, Brill, Moll and Stekel. He subscribed to psychiatric journals.

He read Swedenborg and *Isis Unveiled*. He read Frazer in bed, Charles Fort at the lunch counter, Briffault in the bathroom. He waded through it all, good and bad alike—Lully, Flammarion, Tyndall, Toynbee, Nietzsche.

At first I couldn't make sense out of it all. Nothing seemed related. But gradually Judson Roberts made sense of it. For as I read, Judson Roberts took shape. He was born out of the books, weaned on the Professor's nightly question sessions. Judson Roberts learned to discourse on affects and autistic phenomena. He could give a Rorschach test. He could explain the symbolic derivatives of a matriarchic culture pattern and analyze the inherent masochism of Kafka's works. Roberts could improvise a relationship between the Sung Dynasty, Appolonius of Tyana, and enuresis.

It takes a few minutes to write down, but it took months of doing. Eight hours of reading a day, seven days a week, plus two or three hours of talk—questions and answers. But wading through theories and ideas, I began to understand people a little better. Motivation and compulsion and compensation. Sublimation and projection.

Meanwhile the Professor kept educating me on the practical level. He took me around to astrologers, palmists, phrenologists, spiritualists—men like Jake on the midway and top operators working out of mansions in the hills north of Hollywood. I saw how they worked, who they worked on. I learned that suckers are all alike, and the methods of handling them basically the same.

And through it all, he kept after me with questions. One afternoon towards the end of the third month, for example: "What are the twelve divisions of normal interest?" droned Professor Hermann.

"Time, personal magnetism, sex and marriage, investments, friends, obstacles, enemies, health, money trouble, changes and trips, surprises, and warnings."

"What is yoga?"

"Yoga means unity, right action. Yoga is practiced by a

Guru, or teacher, and a Chela, or pupil. There are five divisions of yoga."

"Name them."

"Raja-Yoga, the development of consciousness. Jnana-Yoga, or knowledge. Karma-Yoga, right action, and Bhakti-Yoga, right religious action. Then Hatha-Yoga, or power over the bodily functions. Govern your body and you govern the universe through Asana, the system of bodily posture, breath control, and the control of the circulation and nervous system."

"Good enough. Now, define Turiya, Dharma, kalpa, mantavaras. And recite the laws of Manu."

"Hey, take it easy!" I stood up. "You've got me so full of that stuff, it's coming out of my ears."

"I know. But there's no time to waste. We must be ready to act soon."

"I'm ready now. Ready for Utter-McKinley's enbalming staff. Have a heart, Professor, I'm only human."

"You must be more than human for this job. You might apply some of the principles of Hatha-Yoga for exercise."

"I don't need exercise. I need a rest, a chance to get out of this damned hot apartment. I haven't had a drink for months, haven't seen anybody to talk to but you."

"That was our bargain."

"Our bargain was for me to make a million dollars, to have anything I wanted. And what do I get? A little cigarette money and enough studying to kill Einstein. Look—I'm not Judson Roberts all the time, you know. I like a little fun once in a while."

"So." The Professor's fingers caressed the nakedness of his skull. "How would you like to go to a party tonight?"

"What kind of a party—another seance in Pasadena?"

"No. I'm talking about the real thing. As a matter of fact, you're invited to attend. She's been inviting you for weeks, but I didn't tell you."

"She?"

"Lorna Lewis. She has inquired about you frequently. Yes, maybe that would work out—if you're interested."

"Count me in. I'll be there with bells on."

"No bells. You'll be there in a nice, conservative gray Palm Beach suit. You'll behave yourself and do the job I've laid out for you."

"But—"

"You'll do one thing and one only. Be nice to Lorna Lewis."

"That," I said, "is just ginger-peachy. I might even teach her a few yoga positions."

Seven

I sat on the sofa at Lorna Lewis' party and played footsie with myself. When I got tired of that, I just watched the crowd.

The movie bunch is peculiar. There are sets, cliques and a definite pecking-order here. The $500 per week mob doesn't mix with stock contract players. The $1000 up-and-coming gang has nothing to do with the $3000 celebrities. Producers, writers and directors spend most of their time with the agents and the money men, if possible.

This happened to be the $500 crowd, with a sprinkling of $1000 eager beavers. I could figure that out after a little observation. Everybody was in there with the good old college try—a bunch of former extras who were now extroverts. The clothing was flashy, the conversation loud and brassy.

Lorna Lewis herself was a typical specimen. It was obvious that she had come to Hollywood via the contest-winner route. Probably she had talent, too—if not necessarily the kind that displays itself before a camera. But her language was coarse, her geniality forced.

I watched her race around the big living room and the miniature bar out on the terrace, displaying the incredible whiteness of those famous legs through a slitted black skirt. She was high on excitement, not alcohol.

I sat on the sofa and the sports jackets wove a pattern of tartan and checks before my eyes. I monitored a parade of sandals, moccasins, brogues. I eyed elkskin and surveyed suede.

The Professor had planted me here half an hour ago and then wandered away, after acknowledging a nod from our hostess. I was a little disappointed with that nod. I hadn't really expected Lorna Lewis to throw herself into my arms and nibble my ears, but even so her cool reception didn't sit well with me after all the buildup. So when the Professor vanished, I sat and fidgeted. All I'd gotten from that greeting was a distinct letdown.

Plump little Miss Bauer from the Professor's office had been on hand, too, at first. It was she who had identified the stocky, freckled, curly-haired man who dug his fingers possessively into Lorna's forearm.

"Mike Drayton. Is her husband."

"Husband? Didn't know she was married."

"Yes. He is a professional player."

"Playboy?"

"No, player. Of hockey."

"Oh, sure. I remember now." Lorna Lewis had talked about "Mike" to the Professor in the car, the night of the rigged-up seance. She had some problem with him. Well, he looked like a problem to me. If we tangled, I'd be a dead duck.

But now it appeared I'd never reach the tangling stage. Lorna was flitting around, greeting leisure jackets and evening wraps, offering glasses to Aloha shirts and gabardine slacks at the bar, being kittenish with a tall red-faced man who was obviously a producer and obviously aware of it.

Mike Drayton, the husband, had disappeared. So had Miss Bauer and the Professor. I caught one glimpse of him as I went to refill my highball glass; he was stalking Lorna Lewis on the terrace. Maybe he'd steer her over to me.

The highballs were good. After my long layoff, the second drink took hold. I had a third, but I was too nervous to enjoy it. What was I doing here? Obviously the Professor had a plan—he always had a plan. But what was it?

A trio of Filipinos wandered around making noises on mandolins and ukeleles—very corny. But most of the guests

seemed to be far past the third drink and they shouted requests. A small group gathered around a blonde who kicked off her shoes for a hula. Another group sat on the stairs and talked shop. Through an archway I saw a fringe of bald, partially bald and gray heads huddled over a card table.

It looked too typical, too pat and according-to-formula for me. Too much like the Hollywood party you read about. I don't know what I'd been expecting—certainly anything but this. And on top of it, I was all alone, ignored. I sat off in a corner with no Lorna Lewis to finger the lapels of my Palm Beach suit.

I thought I'd better get drunk in a hurry and forget it. I thought I might as well get out of here. I thought…

She had hair the color of ripe apricots. She even smelled like apricots—well, apricot brandy, then. Because she was carrying a load.

She sat down beside me and smiled up with green eyes. They were nice eyes, a bit on the glassy side.

"Hello."

"Hello, yourself."

"What's the angle?"

"Angle? There's no angle."

"Come, now—everybody's got an angle. Are you trying to get Himberg's eye?" she asked.

"Who's Himberg?"

"That red-faced character—the producer. You're trying to break into pictures, aren't you?"

"Not me, sister."

"I could never feel like a sister toward you, chum. And you aren't exactly the brotherly type yourself. So why the big isolationist act?"

"Sorry. I just came to watch the floor show."

"Well, you might get me a drink. And seeing as how you're getting so intimate and making advances, my name is Ellen Post."

"No relation to Emily?"

"I'm going now. I can see I misjudged you. You didn't look like the kind who'd pull that one."

"Please, sit down. I'll get you a drink. Let me guess. Would it be bourbon, straight?"

"Extremely straight, if you please."

"I please."

"Quit your bragging and run along."

I went up to the bar and got a straight shot and another highball. Ellen Post watched me as I crossed the room toward her.

"So you're Judson Roberts."

"Who told you?"

"A little bird. A little bald-headed bird, with a monocle. A little sparrow, hopping after Lorna Lewis."

"I see you don't think much of psychological consultants."

"Not much." She downed her shot.

"You in pictures?" I asked.

"No. This is my line." She tapped her glass. "Prescribe me another, Doc."

I finished my drink slowly and made my way back to the bar. Professor Hermann was sitting on the terrace with Lorna Lewis. They glanced at me as I passed the doorway, and the Professor winked. I didn't know what that was supposed to mean, so I ignored it. Right now I liked apricots better, anyway.

"Here we are." I gave Ellen Post a glass and clicked my highball tumbler against its rim. "Forbidden fruit."

"What kind of a toast is that?"

"You be the psychologist and figure it out. It so happens I was thinking of apricots."

"Apricots?"

"Yes. You—your hair, your skin."

She chuckled. It was a husky sound from deep within the throat, but it sounded surprisingly feminine.

"I've been called a lot of things in my time, but that's a new approach. I might add that I like it, Dr. Roberts. Or is it Judson? Or Judd?"

"Whichever you prefer."

She put down her glass, frowned and rose. "Damn it!"

"What's the matter?"

"I'm going."

"Have I said something wrong?"

She shook her head. A scent came from her hair. It was a pleasant scent, but it didn't match her mood. Her face was strained in the semblance of a smile.

"No—you didn't say anything wrong. That's the trouble, they never do. It's always the right thing, and I have the right answer, and the drinks get good and the conversation gets better. Up to a certain point. And then, it's no use. It's just no use. So tonight, I'm going home."

"Could I—"

"You could. But I won't let you." She walked swiftly, a little uncertainly, toward the terrace. "Goodbye, Dr. Roberts. See you in Alcoholics Anonymous."

"But—"

She moved away, and then I became conscious of another scent behind me. Not perfume, but something more vital than that and heavier. Tiger lily. Not golden, but white. I didn't have to turn to know that Lorna Lewis was smiling up at me.

"There you are," she said. "I was coming to rescue you."

"From what?"

"The Post. Miss Pillow-to-Post. Did she ask you to go to bed with her? She always does when she gets a few drinks in her."

"What kind of a person is she?"

"Can't you tell? A lush. One of those rich-bitch society types. She always crooks her little finger, even when she drinks out of the bottle. I can't stand her, but Mike likes her. He would—he's a rummy himself."

Jet-black brows shaped a scowl. More tiger than lily right now. She peered up at me. "You seen him around lately?"

"Your husband?"

"Let's just call him Mike—if you don't mind. I suppose

he's upstairs with a bottle. He always goes into that routine when I throw a party."

"You aren't very fond of him, are you?"

"Let's watch that talk, now. I take my troubles to your pal, Professor Hermann. I've been talking to him about you all evening."

"Do I trouble you?"

"You might."

"All right." And I could see that it was. The way she held my arm and looked up, with her teeth flashing. I caught a heavy gust of Scotch. She'd been working the bar, making up for lost time.

I looked around for the Professor, waiting for a cue, a signal. He'd tell me how nice I was supposed to be, what I was supposed to do now. But the Professor had disappeared. This meant I was on my own. On my own, with six drinks under my belt, and a girl who knew exactly what she wanted. Maybe I should have remembered that I was Judson Roberts, Ps.D. Maybe I should have figured out how to play it carefully, slowly, cleverly.

Instead I looked down at those white legs, looked into the blue, blazing insolence of Lorna's eyes.

"It's hot in here," I said.

"It might be even hotter, outside."

"You're thinking of your husband?"

"Don't call him that. He hasn't really been my husband since the Toronto game when somebody hit him with a stick. All he wants now is his bottle, understand?" She leaned close.

I understood, all right. I understood that she wasn't in love with me, that she wasn't in need of affection or anything else I could give her except sensation. But she had those legs and she was a movie star, or almost a star. And I was Eddie Haines, a nobody from nowhere. I was Eddie Haines, trying like hell to hold my liquor, trying like hell to remember my name was Judson Roberts.

There was only one answer within me.

"Let's go outside," I said.

Dark curls tumbled from side to side. "No, not now. I'm the hostess, remember? Wait until later, when I get rid of this gang. I'll throw them out and check on Mike."

"When?"

"Tell you what. It's after eleven, so you come back about twelve-thirty. Most of these people are in pictures, they go home early during the week nights. Twelve-thirty will do it. I'll wait for you down at the coach house. You know where it is—on the side, behind the swimming pool."

"Right."

"Clear out, now. I don't want us to be seen together any longer—you understand."

I understood. She squeezed my arm and rose. I stood up as I saw Himberg's red face bobbing towards us, then moved away through a maze of low-cut peasant blouses, open sports shirts and drink-spattered jackets.

I made one last attempt to find the Professor. He wasn't in the big room and he wasn't on the terrace. Miss Bauer had melted away like an old ice cube.

Ice cube. I could use another drink. But not here. I made for the door. The night air was cool. I breathed slowly, deeply, evenly. But inside my chest, my heart was going like a dynamo. There was nothing to do for an hour and a half. Just nothing to do but wait…and drink.

I walked down the road a way and before I knew it I'd hit a highway. There was a little neon-lighted place not too far up, and I stopped in for a quick one. It had to be quick, because the bars close at twelve. When I found that out I had another, and another.

Somehow I remembered another bar, months ago, where I'd stood drinking the hours away before I went home to meet the Professor for the first time: Only, when I went, I hadn't expected to meet the Professor. I'd expected to cut my throat. And now, just three months later, I was drinking again. And when I left here, I wouldn't be on my way to cut my throat. No indeed.

I'd come a long way in three months. And I was going a long way. Money...women...power. Luck had changed for Eddie Haines, now that he was Judson Roberts.

Tonight was important to me. I knew that now. It marked the turning point, the real turning point. I'd find out, once and for all, if what the Professor promised was true: if I could reach out and take what I wanted from a world of suckers.

It was a little after twelve. I'd know very soon, now.

I staggered out, lurched up the road, breathing deep. I got my balance under control quickly, but my thoughts were still spinning.

It was a good night. It was a damned good night. Cool, but not too cool, and very clear. Stars up overhead. Millions of them. They went round and round. Why not? What the hell else did they have to do? That's what they got paid for. Going around like that. That's why MGM put them in the sky. I wondered who had the moon concession. Paramount, probably. No, they had stars, too—stars and a mountain. Well, I was also going to have a star.

The house was dark as I approached the terrace. Cars were all gone. Good. I cut across the lawn, went through the shrubbery. There was the swimming pool ahead. Mustn't stumble and fall into the swimming pool. Show up all wet. Stars in the swimming pool, too. Star light, star bright, first star I see tonight, wish I may, wish I might—

Well, I was going to.

Coach house. What the hell kind of a business was that, a coach house? Nobody had coaches. Not this little Cinderella, certainly. But here it was. Here it was in the dark, and here was I, and where was the door?

I found the door and it opened and somebody was waiting for me. Sure enough, I could see her: she was waiting. She came forward. What was I waiting for?

"Everything all right?" I asked.

"Sure. Mike was upstairs. Out cold."

"You're not cold."

"You're not sober."

"Do you mind?"

"What do you think?"

Then she laughed. I wanted to stop that, so I did. My mouth closed down on hers, and her mouth came up to mine, and all of her came up to me. Through the doorway I could still see the stars. Then the stars turned to buttons, and I began to give them my attention. And then—

"Wait a minute. What's that?" she said.

"Forget about it, honey."

"No. I hear something outside. Somebody's coming."

Now I heard it too: the crunch of gravel, then the fumbling and the sudden squeaking of the door.

"Mike!"

He stood there in the doorway, going round and round. I tried to focus my eyes on him. He was a big man, and it was hard to see him clearly or separate his bulk from the monstrous, menacing black shadow on the wall—the shadow of an ape.

He stood there and cursed us. He cursed us in a low, steady, monotonous voice, ripping his words off back-alley fences, off privy walls. He said other things, too.

" 'N now I'm gonna kill ya. I'm gonna rip out ya guts an'—"

He was in the light, I was in the dark, and now was the time, if ever.

I went up to him and he reached out those hairy-ape arms of his. I weaved under them, straightened, and hit him hard. But not hard enough. He backed away and then he came up with one on the side of my head. I felt it, soft and far away, and I wobbled as he hit me again. He turned and knocked me outside.

Then we were both in the moonlight and Lorna said, "No...stop...please..." But it was nothing but cheap dialogue; it was a corny scene, a couple of drunks fighting over a tramp.

That made me mad, so I hit him again. He swung, not to

hit this time, but to gouge at my eye with his thumb. He was good at it. I pushed my knuckles against his mouth, hard. He grunted and tried to tackle me.

All the while he was growling deep in his throat, and he kept coming in. Coming in for the kill. He had meant what he said—he wouldn't stop now until he killed me. And I was beginning to realize he could do it.

Mike was heavy, Mike was strong, and he pushed me back towards the edge of the pool. I could see him gritting his teeth in the moonlight, and the blood running out of the corners of his mouth looked bright and heavy as quicksilver.

His knee came up suddenly, found its target. My loins lanced with pain. His thumbs sought my eyes. I pushed him off, but only for a moment. He growled louder.

Then everything went away, and I felt something tightening around my throat. He had my neck, he was choking me, trying to tear my windpipe out, trying to tear my head from my body.

Lorna whimpered and he growled louder, but I could only gasp from far away. Everything was far away, including life. It was oozing out of my body, my breath was going, my sight and senses. He was killing me.

I kicked up and in. It was a last convulsive movement, but something happened. The tightness suddenly relaxed. I could get to my feet, slowly. There was time to breathe now, time to fight off the pain and regain my awareness, time to watch him. He stood doubled-up at the edge of the pool, waiting for his pain to ease. Then he'd come in again and finish killing me.

I couldn't wait. I moved towards him. He was getting ready, now. He spread his big hands and poised there, crouching to spring. I took a deep breath. I closed my eyes and swung from the waist.

My hand hurt. I stood unsteadily, rubbing my fingers, watching him fall backwards into the pool. It took a million years before he hit the water, another million years before the splash came, another million before he disappeared.

Lorna stopped whimpering. Everything got very quiet. I could hear my panting subside. I could hear a little bird chirping a mile away. I could hear the stars going round and round on their courses. I walked over to the pool and looked down. There was nothing to see in the pool but bubbles. Pretty little silvery bubbles, gleaming in the moonlight.

Eight

The water stabbed me with novacained needles. I gulped, paddled, then dived. Silver pressed my eyeballs, but I could see through silver. I could see something dark and huddled, bobbing down there at the bottom of the pool.

I reached for it, tugged at it. Heavy. Heavy as the weight inside my lungs, my head. I went up for air, got it. Then I dived again, tugged again. This time I could lift. We came to the surface together, live and dead weight. Dead weight. He couldn't be— I had to get him out.

"Help me lift him up!" I panted.

Lorna stared over the edge of the pool. Her lips twitched, and then her mouth tried to run away from her face. But she reached down and held Mike's collar as I pulled myself over the side and then grabbed him under the arms.

I pushed and lifted. He was heavy as lead. Lead. Dead. No, he was all right. He had to be all right.

Then he was sprawled out on the grass, face down, and I was kneeling over him, pressing his back and lifting him, press and lift—

"Is wrong, perhaps?"

I jerked and Lorna jerked. Mike Drayton just lay there.

We stared up at the plumpness of Miss Bauer.

"What are you doing here?"

"She is with me."

Professor Hermann emerged from the shadows of the walk. "What goes on here? We've been looking all over for you. When the party broke up, we left, and I called your apartment from a filling station. No answer, so I came back. Apparently it was wise that I did so."

"We had a fight," I said. "I hit him and he fell into the pool. I fished him out. But—"

The Professor pushed me aside. He knelt and took off his hat. The bald moon of his skull shone down over Mike's face as he turned him over on the grass. A fat hand fumbled beneath the soggy wet shirt. It came to rest there, and it stayed forever.

The wind stopped moving. The grass stopped rustling. The stars stopped twinkling. The trees bent forward, listening…listening for a heartbeat.

"He's dead," said Professor Hermann.

Then everything was moving again, fast. Too fast.

"Steady up." Miss Bauer was holding me.

"But he can't be. We've got to work on his lungs, get the water out! He couldn't have stayed under more than a minute or so—"

"He was unconscious," the Professor said. "It is too bad."

"Too bad?" We all looked at Lorna. Her mouth was twitching again, but this time a torrent of sound gushed out.

"I'll say it's too bad! Wait until the papers get hold of this, wait until Lolly finds out. I'm through! Himberg will tie a can to me. And the cops! God, somebody do something. You got to—"

I shook her. It only jumbled the sounds together.

"Oh God…Himberg…gotta…"

I slapped the mouth shut.

"Cut that out!"

The Professor put on his hat, rose and laid his hand on Lorna's shaking shoulder. "He's right. Hysteria will not help, now. We must be calm. We must think."

"Think? What good will thinking do? Mike's dead, and they'll find out, they'll get us—"

"No. Not if we're calm."

That stopped her for a moment. The Professor's voice gained assurance as he went on.

"Listen to me, Miss Lewis. I may have a solution, but you'll have to help me."

"How?"

"By answering questions. Here."

He gave her a cigarette, lit it for her. He watched it wobble between her lips, then steady a bit as she inhaled.

"Better? Now listen to me and answer. Are there any servants in the house now?"

"No. I told Frieda to clear out when the gang left. The rest were just hired for the party. They went home, all of them."

"Good. Can you remember what Mike did at the party?"

"Mike—No—I don't want to talk about him—"

"You must. It's important. Your life, your career."

He knew how to get to her, all right. Not with "life" but with "career." She sobered at the word.

"What time did Mike go upstairs with his bottle?"

"How did you know about that?"

"I saw him. Miss Bauer saw him. Others must have seen him—that group on the stairway."

"Yes, you're right. Let me see, now. It was around eleven, I guess."

"Was he drunk?"

"No more than usual."

"He drank frequently?"

"He's been lushed up, off and on, for the last six months now, like I told you the other day."

"And people know that? Your friends?"

"Right."

"Did they know why—the reasons he had for drinking?"

"Say, I don't tell people everything. You know and Judd knows, because I told him tonight. But outside of that, nobody. I guess they all thought he was just a rummy."

"But it is established generally that he drank a great deal. That he was moody, anti-social."

"He pulled that stunt at every party I've given, or every one we went to. Not that he'd come with me very often, the

louse. And when he did, he generally sneaked off in the middle of the evening and took the car with him."

"You say he'd get drunk and then leave a party—drive off somewhere alone?"

"Sure. He wrecked the station wagon about four months ago. Drove it into a piling near Santa Barbara. How the hell he ever got way up there I don't know. He didn't know, he was that stiff. It was in the papers."

"That time he wrecked the car—how long was he gone?"

"Two days, nearly. The cops picked him up. He wasn't hurt, but I had a hard time helping him beat the rap. Himberg fixed it somehow."

"Your friends know his habits. You're sure?"

"Yes." She gasped. "Please, Professor, don't ask me anything more. I think I'm going to be sick."

She weaved away and was sick—very sick—over by the trees. I turned and watched Miss Bauer as she worked silently, furiously, on Mike.

"Please," said the Professor. "That is useless. Besides, I have a plan."

He looked up at me. "Did anyone else know of your... visit here at the coach house?"

I shook my head. "I stopped in at a tavern below the hill here, but there was no one around except the bartender. I didn't spill anything to him, of course."

"Good. Then will you please take my car and drive yourself home? I'll get in touch with you tomorrow."

"But Mike—the police—"

"I am taking care of Mike. And there will be no police, if you do as I say. Go, now. I must talk to Miss Lewis alone."

Miss Bauer tugged at the Professor's sleeve. "I do not like this," she said. "Let me continue. The water is leaving the lungs. If we send for a rescue squad, he may yet be alive."

The Professor faced her. "That is for me to decide."

It was more than a statement. It was a command. Miss Bauer bowed her head. The Professor went over to Lorna and took her arm. She sobbed against him and he began

whispering to her. His voice was soft, soothing, gentle. I couldn't hear anything he said, and they both ignored me.

Then I was walking, walking away from the swimming pool; walking away from the thing that lay on the grass, shining white and bloated in the moonlight, like a dead fish. I walked to the car, climbed in, drove away. I went up to the apartment, closed the door. I ripped off my wet clothes and fell down on the bed.

First I was sleeping and then I was watching. I watched my smart-aleck brother Charlie sneering as he read about the murder in the papers. I watched myself run from the cops. I watched them catch me, grill me. I saw myself stumbling up the iron stairs to the cell block. I gripped the rail with hands that left a trail of sweat and blood.

I talked to my lawyer, I talked to all of them: the state's attorney, the judge, the twelve good men and true. They looked like the people I'd seen on the beach. Lorna screamed at them, but they took her out of court.

The matron who dragged her away was "Mrs. Hubbard." She had the same power, and I could see she was able to foretell my future. They could all do that. The jury did and then the judge did.

I saw the Professor at the last. He was better than a priest. I watched myself pleading, couldn't he slip me something? Just one little favor, that's all I asked, just for him to slip me something so I wouldn't have to suffocate.

It was no use. Nothing was any use. No wonder my legs wouldn't work, no wonder they had to drag me, no wonder I fell as they took me into the gas chamber. That gas chamber —nobody could hear me scream, and there was a hissing, and then I coughed. I choked, my meal came up and my lungs came up and my chest burned with a million novo-cained needles. Only this was different.

I watched them carry me and cut me. What was left went into the wagon. The grave diggers get union pay, and it's steady work. The Professor brought flowers. Charlie didn't want my body. But the Professor was kind, he brought

flowers, and he was the only one who came. Then it rained
that night on my grave, and the flowers melted into a soggy
mess. Like the soggy mess inside the box.

But how could I know that if I was dead? I couldn't be
dead. This was all out of my imagination. I was safe in bed in
the apartment. Safe until tomorrow, when they found out.

I opened my eyes, then fell forward into a pool of deeper
sleep. Somewhere in that pool I found the body of Mike
Drayton. We drowned there together...

Coming up out of the darkness, into the sunlight, I felt like a
new man. A man who needed a shower, a shave, breakfast, a
cigarette.

I had them all. But when I lit the cigarette, my hand
trembled. The old yoga wasn't working for Judson Roberts
today.

I wondered if Professor Hermann was working. I wondered whether he had dumped the body in the ocean, tried
to make it look like suicide by drowning. I wondered if
something had gone wrong, if they were looking for me.
Better pull down the blinds, quick, and—

No. That was wrong. I must trust him. I had to trust him.
He told me to wait, that he'd get in touch with me. So I'd
wait.

I read a little bit about totemism and tried to figure out
how Lorna Lewis was taking it, if she'd gone to the studio
today. I took some notes, and all the while I kept thinking
what if Miss Bauer had been right, if resuscitation might
have worked.

I threw down the book and asked myself what her angle
was—why the Professor had hired her instead of a smart,
fast-talking female who was never at a loss for a bright
remark, a file folder, or a fresh box of Kleenex.

I picked up Flugel's *Psychology of Clothes* and began to
read about canes as symbols of personal extension, and wondered what Ellen Post was doing this fine day. Did she have
a hangover? Did she remember me? I tried to picture her,

place her in a setting. A hall bedroom? Obviously not the place. An apartment like this one? Wrong, again. A big house? Room next to her parents? Did she have money, live alone?

Why hadn't I found out more about her, gotten her address, made a date?

Lorna said she was a lush. They were all lushes, according to Lorna—she lived in a world of them. Lushes. Hopheads. Queers. Crackpots. This town was full of them. People with quirks and delusions and dreams. People with money. The kind of people I was supposed to take over the jumps, if I got out of this jam.

But Ellen Post was different. Like ripe apricots. Charlie and I used to eat them when we were kids, a whole bagful at a time. They were soft and sweet.

This was no time to think about it. This was no time to read about canes as phallic symbols, either. I wanted to know what was going on. I had to know. Why, it was past noon already!

I dialed the Professor's office. He'd paid my phone bill for me for just that reason, last month. I listened to the double ring, then heard a click.

"Yes?"

"Miss Bauer, this is—Judson Roberts. Did he—is the Professor back?"

"No."

"Have you heard anything?"

"No."

"I see. If he should come in, you'll ask him to call me at once?"

"Yes."

"Thanks."

I put the little black baby back in its cradle. As I reached for a cigarette, the doorbell rang. I started to get up, then sank back. Once before the doorbell had rung and I'd been afraid to answer it. I'd waited, and a hundred-dollar bill had

slid under the door for me. What would happen if I waited now?

I decided to find out. I sat there, as the bell sounded again. Then came an eternity of silence. I stared at the door.

Something rustled. Something rustled, crept, slithered under the door. It wasn't green, like money. It was white, like paper. A newspaper.

I rose and walked over to the door on tiptoe. I looked down. The newspaper had been reduced to a single sheet, and the torn top portion of a column was inserted under the door upside down. I cocked my head and read a headline:

HOCKEY STAR VICTIM IN TRAIN SMASHUP

I opened the door and let Professor Hermann in.

Nine

"I don't see how you did it!" I shook my head and tried not to shake anything else.

"It was simple. The newspaper tells the story, does it not? A drunken driver, stalled on the tracks near the curve at La Placentia, just outside of town. The express hit the car, dragged it for a quarter of a mile. Michael Drayton, 31, husband of Imperial starlet Lorna Lewis. Wife hysterical at news of accidental death." The Professor shrugged and put down the paper. "End of story."

"Didn't they find water in his lungs?"

"There was no water left, thanks to Miss Bauer's work. I checked on that. Lorna's story about smashing the station wagon gave me the idea of what to do. I told her it would cost her a car. She gave it to me without question. I bundled the body into the back and drove over in time to catch the train that comes through at 4:10 A.M. It was still dark and the side road was deserted. I got out, stalled the motor and propped Mike up in the front seat. Then there was nothing to do but wait for the express to come, and watch it hit. The car was smashed to bits, and I suppose that Mike—"

He saw my face and broke off without finishing the sentence. "I walked a few miles and caught a bus," he concluded. "Then I phoned Lorna Lewis and told her what to say when she was notified. After that I went home to sleep. I slept until I knew it was time to get up and look at the newspapers."

The Professor told it that way, without inflection, without emotion. I began to feel cold all over.

"You make it sound so simple," I said. "But if you hadn't figured it out, I'd be finished. The whole thing is like a night-

mare, from the beginning. It was all an accident, you know. But I could never prove that. Maybe he was no damned good, maybe he had it coming—but I'm still to blame. And you saved me. I don't quite know how to say it—"

He sat there, smiling at me. "Never mind. I understand. You can forget last night. It was just lucky that I happened to be there."

The black hat came off. The bald head bobbed, an animated skull. I shuddered and lit a cigarette. He was right, better drop it. I was lucky, lucky he happened to be there. *Luck...happened.* Something clicked.

"What's the matter?" asked Professor Hermann.

"Nothing. I was just thinking. How come you didn't give me any instructions for the party last night?"

"I don't understand."

"You remember, you were going to build me up with Lorna."

"I did. I spent much time talking of you."

"Yeah. But you didn't tell me what to do with her. You left me alone, disappeared."

"I saw that you were getting along all right. There was no need to stay."

"But you came back."

"I phoned you, from the filling station, after midnight. I got worried when there was no answer."

"Didn't you figure I might be keeping a date with the lady?"

"Yes, of course. But I wanted to check on you." He smiled. "You know, I am very careful about everything I plan."

"You must have been."

"What do you mean?"

I stood up. "I mean, the whole thing looks funny to me now. How did you know where to find us when you returned? How did you know we weren't in the house, upstairs? Yes, and Mike Drayton—he was supposed to have passed out, with a bottle. What made him come to the coach house and surprise us?"

The top of his head had the dull lustre of old ivory. I stared down at him.

"You've told me yourself that you never leave anything to luck. Things just don't happen by chance when you have a hand in them. So it has to be this way. You went upstairs and woke Mike. You told him where we'd be. You sent him to us, knowing there'd be a quarrel, a fight. Perhaps you even planned on murder."

"Sit down—you don't know what you're saying! You sound like Lorna Lewis, now."

"Well, I'm not Lorna. I'm not a hysterical little fool. I know what I'm saying, and I know you. You did plan it this way, didn't you? All of it, from the beginning?"

He looked up at me and smiled. His mouth smiled, but his eyes didn't change. They looked blank, empty: just holes in an old ivory skull.

"Yes," he murmured. "There is no reason why you shouldn't know. I planned it this way."

"But why—why would you do such a thing?"

"Relax. Keep your voice low. I'll tell you. Better still, I'll show you. Next month, on the first, when I get a check from Lorna Lewis for a thousand dollars. Consultation fee. There will be such a check, every month, from now on."

"Blackmail."

"I do not like that word."

"I don't like what you did. I don't like the way you messed me up in this deal. Why did it have to be me?"

"It just worked out that way. It seemed—"

"Never mind how it seemed! Nothing just works out around you. You had a reason. I want to know."

"Very well, my young friend. You will know. I'm sorry you forced me to say this, but perhaps it's for the best." The skull leaned forward. The eyes, dead no longer, bored through my scowl.

"I have plans for you, big plans. I have taught you many things and you will learn more. In a short time now, you will be Judson Roberts—a man with a reputation, with contacts.

You'll be meeting the public and I'll be in the background, and the money will roll in. Just as I promised.

"And I know you. In a little while you'd start getting delusions of grandeur. You'd begin to wonder why you couldn't run the show alone, why you must continue to play Trilby to my Svengali. And you'd try to dump me.

"Mind, I don't say you'd succeed. But you'd try." He nodded slowly, confidentially. "So to protect myself, I planned this. And it has worked. Now you won't try to step out of line. Because you're involved in a murder. You know it and Lorna Lewis knows it. But more important still, I know it. And I'm not afraid to talk if I must."

I smirked. "I can just hear you talking, Professor! Why, you're an accessory—"

"Perhaps. It might cost me a year or two in prison. But you'd get the book thrown at you. And, as you have so aptly remarked, I leave nothing to chance. That's why I brought Miss Bauer along. She's a good witness—an innocent bystander who saw it happen. She would testify as I wish."

I knocked over the ashtray and swept my hand up, trying to keep the sweat on my forehead from blinding me. The skull bobbed up and down before me.

"So now you know, my friend," murmured Professor Hermann. "And now you will never try to cross me. You will never attempt to take over. You will do just as I say and not plan anything rash, like running away."

I stood up again. It was hard, this time, but when I reached my feet the power came back, surging through me. I needed that power, now.

"You think of everything," I whispered. "But did you ever think that I might try to…kill you?"

I was lightning. I was thunder. I struck from the side. My hand went down, aiming for the fat crease in his neck—

But something was wrong. I stumbled. His foot was out. I was going down. And then there was a pressure in the back of my own neck, an intolerable pressure, crushing the spine up into my brain.

His voice found me in the darkness.

"You're a fool! Don't ever try that again. I warn you, I have powers you've never dreamed of! Now, get up—if you can."

I dragged myself over to the chair. My head rested on a red-hot lance that bored through my backbone.

"I told you once before to forget everything that happened last night. That was good advice. You had better follow it. Forget today, too. Because we're starting over again."

He was still sitting there, perfectly calm. The skull still grinned.

"Yes, we're starting," he murmured. "The time has come. I've got the office lined up and the decorators hired. Next month we'll be on our way, both of us—on our way to the top.

"That's why you must forget all this. The past is dead, safely dead. Only the future is alive. I'm going to make those promises come true, for both of us.

"I am your friend, Eddie. Believe that. I'm the only friend you ever had. You can trust me. You must trust me. You will trust me."

It was like something you hear in a dream, something you hear when you're under ether, something you hear when you're under hypnosis. Hypnosis. Those slitted eyes of his, staring and staring at me… "You'll have everything," droned the voice. "I'll stay in the background and you'll get the glory, the fame, the money, the power. That's the way it's going to be. Never doubt it for an instant. You're Judson Roberts, remember? And I'm just…nobody."

I shook off the voice, shook off the stare, and looked at nobody, sitting there in the chair. His head was like a skull, and then it changed. Maybe it was the slitted eyes and the slitted mouth. Maybe it was something else. But all of a sudden, it hit me. For the first time I realized that Professor Hermann looked like the Devil.

He sat there, and his pudgy hands closed over a shadow. It was only a shadow, but he held it tightly now and I knew he would never let it go.

He held my soul…

Ten

The inquest was a routine thing. I didn't even have to get up on the stand. Lorna was there, of course, and she saved the day. She'd learned something about acting all right, and she gave the performance of her life. She sobbed and gasped and murmured at all the right times; she trembled and quivered in all the right places.

After she finished her testimony, it was in the bag. Mr. Himberg said a few words, and so did the Professor, but the verdict was already set. Accidental death. Of course, as the Professor reminded me, a coroner's inquest verdict can always be set aside, pending the introduction of new evidence. But there wouldn't be any new evidence, as long as I was a good boy.

By common consent, we scattered as soon as we got outside. Himberg escorted his starlet through the newspaper gauntlet, and Lorna did an encore of her performance. The Professor drove off with Miss Bauer, after arranging to meet me at his office in the morning. We were going to get started and he suggested I get a good night's sleep.

As for me, I teetered on the edge of the curb for a moment—and then *she* showed up.

The dusty, battered convertible slid to a halt alongside me and she said, "Oh, dear! I'm late again—it's all over, isn't it?"

I nodded. "That's right, Ellen."

"Well, I'm not going to pretend I'm sorry. I missed it on purpose, you know. I—I didn't want to hear about it." She shivered, slightly. "The whole thing just makes me sick. People like Lorna and Mike, ruining their lives. But who am I to talk?" She shivered again. "Can I give you a lift somewhere?"

"Just on my way home," I told her.

"Climb in."

I did so, murmuring my address. She made a U-turn at the corner. She drove expertly, and today the apricot scent came through untainted by alcohol.

"If you came late on purpose," I said, "why did you bother to stop by at all?"

"Please, Mr. Roberts. You shame me." But she wasn't ashamed as she continued. "You know why I came. It was to see you and to apologize for my rudeness the other night."

I blinked. It had been a long time since I'd heard any straight answers.

"You were very kind and patient with me," she continued. "I appreciate that."

"And I appreciate your frankness, Ellen. I'm not used to honesty lately."

"You mean your friend, the Professor?"

She caught me off guard for a moment. "The Professor? What do you know about him?"

"Oh, nothing, really. Except that my uncle tells me he used to run some kind of fake mail-order health cult until the postal authorities cracked down on him. Are you working for him?"

"No. He's just…advising me."

"I see." She smiled. "Sorry, I didn't mean to pry."

"All right." I lit a cigarette and leaned back. I could sense her nearness, could sense how it would be if she were even nearer. She wouldn't be like Lorna, full of gasp and frenzy; her love would not be blind—blind eyes, blind mouth, blind body groping for frantic fulfilment. No, she'd be soft and warm and steady and sure. I could feel the kindness and the comfort here, and I wanted it very badly. I needed it very badly.

But it was not mine to take. So I puffed on my cigarette and moved away while she threaded through the traffic.

"You could say you're glad to see me, you know," she said.

"I could. But I won't."

"Oh. And why not?"

"Because if I did, you'd believe me. And of course, I'd

ask you to dinner tonight. And we'd go somewhere and talk. And because you're honest, I'd want to be honest too. And so I'd tell you all about myself. Then you'd hate me."

"Are you that bad, Mr. Roberts?"

"Worse."

"I must say you administer a very subtle brush-off."

I half-turned in my seat, facing her. "Believe me, Ellen, it's not that. I wish I could explain, but I can't. If I could only have met you three months ago, before all this happened; if you had only slid under my door instead of that hundred-dollar bill—"

She was staring at me curiously, and I didn't blame her. I'd said too much already.

"You're in trouble, aren't you?"

I started a laugh, but it came out as a grunt.

"Trouble? It all depends what you call trouble. Right now I'm getting ready to take my place sitting on top of the world. The throne has already been built. But it's not going to be an easy seat. And there's only room for one."

"I see."

She didn't, of course. All she saw was that she'd made another mistake—come crawling to a guy she hoped would be kind, and found out that he was just a conceited heel. I wondered if she'd get drunk again tonight. I knew I probably would, meeting or no meeting.

We drove on in silence. It was the worst strain I'd ever felt in all my life. I wanted to talk to her, I wanted to confess, tell her everything. Something about her hypnotized me. It was the same reaction I had to the Professor. If she told me to jump out of the car and kill myself, I'd probably do it. She wouldn't even have to tell me—just a look would be enough. *Like the Professor—*

A horrid thought crawled out and leered. Suddenly I was back three months ago, sitting in Larry Rickert's office and trying to stare down Professor Hermann's eyes. Had it been hypnosis then? Had Professor Hermann communicated with me through extra-sensory perception that afternoon, had he planted the seed, told me to go home and kill myself? I'd

always wondered why I'd had that inexplicable impulse, and now everything was falling into place.

He never did anything without a purpose. He left nothing to chance. He'd arranged it all: even timed it so that he'd show up and stop me with that hundred-dollar bill. Yes, he knew how to choose his man. Professor Hermann found me open to the power of suggestion, the power of darkness. He was the Devil, and he had work for idle hands to do.

I opened my mouth. I knew what I wanted to say. I wanted to say, "Ellen, don't stop at my place. Just keep on driving. We can be in Mexicali, you and I, before midnight. We can get married down there and just keep right on going. You need me. I need you. What do you say?"

I opened my mouth, but the Professor closed it for me. What had he said? "You will do just as I say, and not plan anything rash, like running away."

So I didn't tell Ellen. I didn't take her in my arms and bury my face in the apricot fragrance of her hair, seek the ripeness of her lips, enjoy the rich harvest of her body.

She drove silently, swiftly, surely, with never a word or a glance for me. And then came the screech of brakes and we were outside my apartment.

"Thanks," I said. "Ellen, I'd like to see you again—I haven't been able to explain what I wanted to say today. This has been a strain, and perhaps when things settle down a little, we can talk. I mean—"

She turned away, but not before I caught a glimpse of her oddly contorted face.

"Goodbye," she murmured. "And go to hell."

Then she drove off, before I recognized and realized the meaning of her look. She'd been crying.

But she'd said, "Goodbye," and she meant it. And she'd said, "Go to hell."

Maybe she didn't mean that. But she was right, nevertheless. For Professor Hermann was the Devil, and he had my soul. And my choice, my path, was clear from now on.

I was going to hell.

Eleven

A tall young man with wavy hair and a professionally precise
mustache stared at a tall young man with wavy hair and a
professionally precise mustache who stared at a tall young
man with wavy hair and a professionally precise mustache
who—

But you get the idea.

It went on that way, endlessly. The man wearing the soft,
sand-colored suit, the white shirt and the solid black knit tie
gazed at himself in each of the eight mirror surfaces covering the octagonal office walls.

This octagonal inner office was as big as a barn, with a
high ceiling and recessed lighting. The degree of brightness
was controlled by a knee-switch behind the desk. That desk
and its companion chair, set in the center of the room, con-
stituted the only visible furniture. The rest was all space,
light and mirrors—mirrors multiplying the presence and
personality of Judson Roberts. Mirrors that dazzled and
confused the client.

The mirrors caused self-consciousness and self-hypnosis,
too. Of course I wasn't susceptible any more. Three months
here had made me acquainted with the layout, and with the
man in the mirror whom I had become: Judson Roberts.

It had cost Professor Hermann a lot to set up *Y-O-U*—
"Your Opportunities, Unlimited." There was a big nut in the
overhead, too, but already it was starting to come back.

I sat behind the desk and studied myself in those mirrors.
Mr. Judson Roberts smiled back at me from all over the
room. Well, why shouldn't he smile?

The book was selling through direct mail, the ads were
pulling, there was a big play for the weekly lectures at the

hotel, the appointments poured in regularly. Strangers kept calling, mail arrived. And Judson Roberts was taking the suckers over the jumps, just as the Professor had predicted.

I didn't resent the Professor any more, either. He was right, and our successful operation proved it. The Lorna Lewis mess was forgotten—I never saw her any more. For that matter, I saw less and less of the Professor these days. As he had promised, he got me started and then left me alone. He handled his office and I handled mine.

Of course he'd assigned little Sid Rogers to help steer me over the hard spots—and keep an eye on me, too, I suppose. Rogers even took an upstairs room in the new house I'd rented over on New Hampshire near Wilshire. But he didn't intrude on my privacy, and his aid was welcome at the office.

He briefed May, our secretary. He ghosted my weekly lectures. He checked the appointments, sized up clients, studied the backgrounds of potential prospects. He offered me sensible advice.

"Always dress conservatively...flash is out. This isn't the boardwalk. Remember to keep your voice soft, low...make it just a little hard for them to hear you...they'll have to concentrate then, and that's half the battle. Never turn your back on a sucker. Don't give him a second to think about anything else."

Tricks, gimmicks, angles. Always something to learn, something to remember, something to try out.

At first I'd been afraid, wondering if the bluff would work. Now I wondered why I'd ever wondered. The Professor was right: the seeker was always a sucker. And I wasn't finding it difficult to keep up a front any more. The face smiling back at me from the mirrors was different, somehow. It wasn't only that I wore a new mustache; I wore a new look of confidence. I looked like Judson Roberts now, I felt like Judson Roberts, I *was* Judson Roberts.

The phone rang. I lifted the receiver from the concealed alcove inside the round desk. May's voice was crisply confident. That meant business was in the office.

"Mr. Roberts? A Mr. Caldwell to see you. He wishes an appointment."

"Wishes" was a code word. It meant big money. "Appointment" was another code word. It meant a ten- or fifteen-minute stall, until Rogers could finish checking on the client.

"Right," I said, softly. "Tell Mr. Rogers to give me what he can. I'll buzz you when I'm ready. Meanwhile, give Caldwell the consultation routine."

That meant May would phone the Professor's office and ask for Doctor Altschuler. There would be a discussion of psychiatric treatment over the phone. "Mr. Roberts advises— Mr. Roberts recommends that the patient—Mr. Roberts finds indications of—" All for the benefit of the poor mark fidgeting in the handsome but contrivedly uncomfortable chair in the outer office.

I knew what Rogers was doing, too. He was working on Caldwell's name, out of the little office down the hall from me. He and the girl we hired to play "nurse" were tracking down Caldwell's history with the aid of three telephones and an entire wall-cabinet full of city directories, phone books, detailed city and county street maps. They were looking for biographical sketches in *Who's Who*, in business directories, fraternal publications, school annuals. They were phoning for credit ratings, tracing leads to newspaper morgues. They were checking cross-indexed files furnished by the Professor's friends in similar rackets. And they would get results, fast. Sometimes fairly spectacular results.

Given a little luck, Rogers could work even without a sucker's name. All he needed was a glimpse of the license plate of the car he drove. In fifteen minutes, working according to plan and system, he could come up with name, address, occupation, age, financial status…wife's name, names and ages of children, names of parents and close relatives…present residence and previous residences for the past ten years. In addition there were the little convincing touches: hobbies and club memberships, school background and nickname, and a fairly detailed description of his home

and its landmarks. From this it was often easy to guess the character and present problems of the sucker. Yes, Rogers was a good man and he had a good system.

He came in through the concealed entrance behind the rear-wall mirror and laid the typewritten cards on my desk.

"Looks like we've got a live one," he said. "Airline corporation counsel—inherited money, too. But it's all down here."

"Thanks, Sid. You're a fast worker."

"Good luck."

He vanished. I read the *dossier* very carefully. Then I read it again. I looked at my watch. Fourteen minutes since May had called. Time enough.

I put the cards down next to the phone, picked up the receiver and buzzed May.

"Send him in," I said. I leaned back and pressed the light switch. The mirrors seemed to rise out of the walls, glaring and pressing forward.

The door opened and Edgar Clinton Caldwell stepped into the room.

Now there are three ways to use the information I'd just received from Sid Rogers. The first would be to put on the old mystic act—telepathic impressions. It works well with women and with swishes. The second method is the arch, inscrutable approach: "Yes, we have our own sources of information, you know." That's for the wise guys, the loud blusterers.

Looking at Edgar Caldwell, I decided to try the third routine.

He stood there, fat and flustered under the blinding light, gazing at his rumpled reflection in the mirror. He had been sweating, and his coat hung soggily from broad, stooped shoulders. The lower button was open, revealing a wrinkled white triangle with a broad base over a protruding stomach. His gray hair was plastered back over a high, ruddy forehead. He was fat and he was also big—all his features seemed a little larger than life-size.

I could tell he was frightened, but he didn't know I could

tell. He thought he was looking fierce. His eyes glowered. His chin—and its accessory folds—thrust forward aggressively. But I was watching his hands; the large, red, knob-knuckled hands, the hands that clenched and unclenched in unconscious, uncontrolled apprehension. Those hands were looking for something to hang onto in a room of emptiness. Those hands wanted to smash out at the mirrors that multiplied and distorted their reflections. Those hands wanted to come up, cover the eyes and shut out the glare of light, shut out the spectacle of my complacency. But the hands were powerless.

The hands could not grasp. The hands could not destroy. The hands could not conceal.

I looked at Caldwell's hands and decided on the third approach. I'd increase his fright, then reassure him.

"You are Edgar Clinton Caldwell?" *Soft voice, but phrase the question as though the man is on trial.*

"Yes. Mr. Roberts?"

Good. His voice trembled a little on my name. Got him.

"I am Judson Roberts. Won't you come in?"

Get him to cross the room. Make him sweat and falter as he tries not to watch himself in all those mirrors. He'll notice everything he's tried to hide from others and himself: the way he looks in profile, the unflattering angles of his head, his poor posture, his ridiculous waddling butt sticking up from behind. Get him to cross the room and he's licked before he starts.

"Trick layout you got here."

Start the next gambit. Frank, open smile. Look up. Let him feel reassured, just for a moment.

"It's meant to impress the credulous. I must apologize to you, sir. There's no need of any further stage effects."

I dimmed the lights. He blinked his relief, standing there and waiting for me to confide in him.

Third gambit, now.

I reached into the desk recess and drew out the typed notes. I held them out to him.

"Here, Mr. Caldwell—I'm going to ask you a small favor before we go any further. Will you please verify the accuracy of these statements?"

He took the cards and I watched them disappear in the red folds of his huge hands. I watched him read, watched his eyes dilate, watched the eyebrows as they tried to climb his forehead and hide in his hair.

"What the—where the devil did you get all this dope?"

Smile. Let it hit him, let it sink in. Wait until he's sold.

"I could make it sound mysterious, Mr. Caldwell, but the whole thing is really quite simple. I have a trained research staff, you know. The moment your name was announced, they went to work in the files. Naturally, a man in your position has left his mark in many places: newspapers, trade publications, directories. Our references yielded this preliminary data. Undoubtedly a more comprehensive checkup would afford us much more information on your background and position.

"Now the reason for all this is obvious to you, Mr. Caldwell. I am a professional psychological consultant, and as such I am a businessman. I conduct my affairs on a business basis, just as you do. Naturally, it is helpful for me to know as much as possible about a client before I see him, just as you try to find out what you can about a prospect. I'm sure that you also have your sources, Mr. Caldwell."

Watch him grin. He isn't frightened now. He thinks you're taking him into your confidence. He's flattered. You wouldn't pull any tricks on him. He can see that because you've sized him up as an equal. In a word, the poor fish is hooked.

"I might as well be perfectly frank with you, Mr. Caldwell. Our relationship to come will demand such frankness, mutual frankness. Don't you agree?"

He nodded. I wanted to keep him nodding from now on.

Build up a dependency. The patient and analyst relationship. Keep it in that stage. Flatter him with questions, inquire after every detail, endlessly. Everyone wants to talk about

himself. That's Y-O-U, the whole secret of it. Complete catharsis.

"And now, Mr. Caldwell, let's talk about you and your problems. You have a problem, don't you, Mr. Caldwell?"

He had a problem, all right. And now, he was ready to tell me. I listened, but I thought of other things. Problems. They all have problems. Every one is different, and they're all the same. Always a common denominator—the basic fear.

The rabbity little man, Mason, who came on Thursday afternoons. He was afraid of his homosexuality. Mrs. Finch, Mondays and Fridays by appointment in her home, feared what happened to her when she tried stopping or cutting down on her dosage of luminol. Maxwell Solomon, very confidential ("apt to call you anytime I need you"), attempted to conceal in pyrophobia his dread of divine retribution for saving himself rather than his wife and child in the crash of their private plane. Miss Eudalie Vinyer was afraid of me because I was all men and all men were her father and at thirteen she had been too young to understand what her father was doing with that colored woman. Baker feared his boss, Klotscher feared God, Mrs. Annixter feared cancer, which was a polite term for syphilis, which was a polite term for intercourse, which was a polite term for the Sin Against the Holy Ghost, which was a polite term for the fact that she really enjoyed it. By a strange coincidence, Mr. Annixter was a patient too, and he feared—Mrs. Annixter.

It was all very simple, and all very complicated. Some of them knew and some of them didn't know what was wrong. Some of them could be told and some of them didn't want to be told. Some of them needed a doctor, some a psychiatrist, some a lawyer, some a priest, some an executioner. But all of them needed me. They needed an audience, a father confessor, a child, a mother, a lover, to listen and understand and flatter and cajole and condone.

They needed Y-O-U.

Detail. Endless detail. They wanted to tell everything.

They wanted every test I could give them—coordination, color determination, mnemonics, word-association and free-fantasy sessions, work with charts, slides, ink blots and anything else I could think up. I would send them to a pal of ours, Dr. Sylvestro, for a complete preliminary physical checkup, and they loved that too.

That was the answer. They feared and they wanted love. Love in the form of interest, attention, an affirmation of their own self-importance. Y-O-U gave it to them. For Y-O-U, with all the metaphysical and practical psychology hokum boiled away, was simply an extension of the old bromides, "Know thyself" and "Be yourself." The whole routine was built up to flatter the individual, make him think about himself. There were touches of the "charm school" and "expand your personality" routines here: we sent people to beauty parlors and plastic surgeons and dress designers and dancing schools. But in the end, we took them—to the cleaners.

It was fascinating to watch the spectacle. There was only one difficulty: I kept wanting to go outside and vomit.

Now here was Mr. Caldwell and *his* problem. Edgar Clinton Caldwell, 54. Wealthy. A "successful businessman." A typical example of middle-class respectability and sublimated anal eroticism.

Doctor Sylvestro had referred him to me. "Nerves." Also hemorrhoids and constipation.

"But there are some things you can't even tell a doctor—you understand that, Roberts. Like the string. Sounds silly, and I wouldn't even mention it to Mrs. Caldwell. But I save string. Every bit. I have boxes full of it down in the office. In the safe. It's just a habit. I know it's nothing serious. But why do I do such a thing?"

I knew why. But I didn't tell him. I let him do the talking during this first session and at the next. I booked him for twice a week and let him gabble for a while before I took over. First with a routine probing. Then with a gradual, almost imperceptible hypnotic technique. That's something I was picking up from Professor Hermann. I suspected he

used it on Miss Bauer and that he'd always tried it with me.

It worked with Caldwell. He grew to depend on our sittings. And I kept taking notes. Notes about him. Notes about his business dealings. I wasn't quite sure what angle we'd use for the payoff yet. That I'd leave to the Professor.

When I thought I had enough, I took my material to him and asked his opinion.

Professor Hermann read, listened, twirled his monocle. Then:

"Get him to retire. Liquidate his holdings. We'll need cash for this."

"Retire? But he loves his business—I can't take that away from him. Oh, I can probably force the issue, but the results will be bad. He'll just go to pieces. Inside of six months, he'll be a wreck."

"And we'll be rolling in his money." The bald head bobbed, the monocle twirled. "Get him to retire."

So I went back to Caldwell and approached the subject. He listened, then exploded.

"But I don't want to retire, man! It isn't that I don't place any faith in you, Roberts. You know better than that. But here I am, in the prime of life—with a fine position—I own better than fifteen percent of the airline stock. I've worked years to get where I am, and now you advise me to get out. Why?"

"Because you're not happy."

"Damn it, man, who says I'm not happy? I've got a net worth of upwards of two hundred thousand, and no debts. Got a house here in town and one at the beach. Marge and I get along great. The sex part doesn't bother me. You know, I told you about Eve—"

"You're not happy."

"Don't keep saying that! Just because of those goddamn piles and a few dreams—"

"I'm sorry to keep interrupting you, Mr. Caldwell. I'm sorry to keep repeating myself. But you are not a happy man. And you know it. Your very defensive attitude reveals it.

Happy men are under no compulsion to save string. Happy men do not wash their hands until the flesh is red and chafed, the knuckles constantly rubbed raw from frequent cleansing with strong abrasive soaps. Happy men do not require as sexual stimulation, that their mistresses—"

"Please, let's not mention that part again. I wish I hadn't let that slip out."

"You will be thankful some day that you were utterly frank with me. And you will be thankful that I am utterly frank with you." I leaned forward, confidentially. "I want you to retire. These sessions are stimulating, but they are not enough. In order to remake your life, you must devote your life to the task.

"Your present habit-patterns and associations keep you chained to the very reflexes and conditioning which make you unhappy. You will never be free, never emancipate your personality, until you are willing to start fresh and clean.

"I don't wish to be an alarmist, Mr. Caldwell, but unless you undertake the step soon, it may be too late to ever escape. You aren't getting any younger, you know. What you can do today, voluntarily, you will be unable to do five, three, or even one year from now. This is perhaps your last chance."

"I don't see it, Roberts. Don't see it at all. You talk as though I were a sick man. Just because I get down in the dumps once in a while, same as everybody else—"

"Are you the same as everybody else, Mr. Caldwell? Can you say that honestly to me, and to yourself? After what we both know about those dreams, about your relations with Eve, about what happened at the fraternity initiation years ago in college—"

"That was an accident!"

"But your impulses, your desires, were not accidental. They were fundamental, implicit in your disorder."

"You can't frighten me, Roberts."

"Please. I'm not trying to frighten you. Have I ever resorted to any mumbo-jumbo or trickery, since the first time you came to me? Have I ever been anything but straightfor-

ward and sincere? I haven't preached or lectured or put on
any of the cheap front you despise. I haven't attempted to
delude you in any way. That's what makes it so hard for me
to impress you now. But you must be impressed with the
importance, the necessity of taking this step. Or else—"

"Or else what? What are you driving at?"

"There'll be a psychosomatic reaction, to begin with. The
old-fashioned 'nervous breakdown.' You've seen it happen
to others, many times. In your case, with an anal fixation, it
will be most painful. And Eve will take over. She's almost
done so already. From what you've told me, she's practically
blackmailing you right now, as it is. And suppose your wife
were to find out? Suppose something else happens. In your
circumstances, it could easily enough. Then what? Do you
remember the Arbuckle affair—"

When a fat man trembles, his flesh quivers all over. Acres
of gray jelly, quaking and oozing perspiration.

"But what do you want me to do? Suppose I retire, then
what?"

"I'm going to take you back forty years. We'll start all over
again. We'll go back to the time before the initiation and
the scandal, before you had to leave school. You know what
your ambitions were then. We'll recapture that personality,
make it dominant once more, make a young man of you, a
new man."

"How?"

"I'll work with you personally. Every day. Oh, nothing
spectacular and nothing drastic entailed. You love Marge
and the boys—I won't do anything to affect those feelings.
But you must make a major alteration and adjustment. You
need help.

"And you can afford it. Even if you weren't so badly in
need of treatment, I'd advise retirement on the general
principle that any man who is financially independent should
retire from business and begin living. You've tried to retreat
from life into your work, and it isn't successful. So now you
must retreat from work into life again."

"So that's it, eh? I can afford it, you say—meaning here is where you make a killing. Big fees, is that the angle now, Roberts?"

"Please. You're antagonistic—not to me, but to the truth. You know my fees. Twenty dollars a consultation. That is not exorbitant. I shall not be able to give you more than three sessions a week. Our program will take about a year. Say three thousand dollars, at the most. I assure you I do not need your money, nor would I particularly care to undertake this treatment if the prognosis were not favorable. Besides, frankly, I have a personal interest in your problem, Mr. Caldwell. And you know I can help you."

"Yes, I do. I'm going to think over what you said, think it over very seriously. It would be worth it, just to get rid of Eve. Do you think—?"

"That you will be strong enough to give her up? Yes, I can definitely promise you that, Mr. Caldwell. Quite definitely. Eve England is on her way out."

Twelve

There were empty glasses and filled ashtrays all over the small apartment. I could smell scotch and smoke and Tabu and stale food and Lysol—everything but fresh air. Fresh air wouldn't have suited Eve England, anyway.

I didn't exactly suit her, either. I sat facing her on the sofa, pretending to examine my drink while I sized up the tall blonde with the brunette's complexion. Her hair was dark at the roots, her eyes were red at the corners, her mouth was lined at the edges where the lipstick tapered off.

She gave me a look that would have made her a fortune as a glass cutter and said, "Well, now that you're here, what's the big idea?"

"No big ideas. Just little ones."

"Cut the cute stuff. Speak your piece and get out."

"That's no way to handle a customer."

"Say, what is this?" She stood up, bracelets jangling.

"Don't be afraid."

"Afraid? Listen, you—"

She began to impugn my character and reputation in rapid, monosyllabic fashion, and that told me all I wanted to know. She was not a clever woman. Just a pushover. And I knew how to handle her. I kept my voice loud, made it harsh.

"You've come up in the world, haven't you? This Caldwell must treat you all right. Of course, he goes for your little tricks. Where'd you pick up those fancy ideas? When you worked Las Vegas?"

Her earrings quivered and danced. "So it's a shakedown, huh? Well, let me tell you—"

"No. I'll tell you, instead. This isn't a shakedown at all, Edith."

"Eve."

"Edith Adamowski. You see, I know your name. I know all about you. But don't get excited. If you want to know who told me, it was Caldwell himself."

"Caldwell? What kind of a gag is this, anyway?"

I told her what kind of a gag it was. She sat down, after a while, and drank her drink. She even nodded. I went right on talking.

"The important thing is, he doesn't know anything about it. He mustn't know. As I told you, he's willing to pay five grand to get rid of you for good. He thinks he's a new man, that he can frighten you into it. I advise you to let him do just that. Take the five grand and blow. Then stand by for further orders and maybe you can make more."

"Well, I dunno. I got a good setup here."

I walked over to her and sat down. I smiled into her eyes. "Do you mean to tell me you like it?" I asked, softly. "Do you really like it when—"

"Shut up! Don't talk about it! I hate it. Why do you think I'm on the sauce all the time? He gives me the creeps, but—"

"Then do as I tell you. Take the money and wait for more."

"How can I be sure you don't double-cross me?"

"How can *I* be sure you don't double-cross *me* and tell Caldwell I was here?"

She grinned. "Yeah, I never thought of that."

I grinned right back at her. "Well, don't start thinking of it, either. Because if you do sing to him, you're going to have an awful sore throat."

"Huh?"

"Come here." I led her to the window, pushed aside the gray strand of a curtain that had once been white. "See that man down there? The big one, standing next to the car?"

She looked at Jake and nodded to me. "I see him. What about it, who is he?"

"I'm not going to introduce you. I hope I never have to. But he's the man who has orders to see you if you don't play ball."

"So that's it, huh?"

"That's it. Are you in?"

Eve England gulped the rest of her drink. She drank fast, like a bar tramp, and that's what she was. If Jake didn't kill her, some cop or bum surely would. I watched her mouth dispose of the drink and waited for her to form the words I knew would come.

"All right," she said. "Count me in." And then, "When do I get the five grand?"

"Caldwell will have it for you," I told her.

And he did.

I saw him just two days later. He entered, exuding exultancy.

"By God, Roberts, you were right! I did it!" His knobby knuckle slammed against the desk.

"I knew you would. Did you say what I told you?"

"Bet your life. And it was just the way you predicted it would be. She turned on the tears, and then she tried to threaten me. But I remembered what you said, and it worked out."

"Good for you."

"You know something? I almost couldn't go through with it. At one time she almost had me backing out. But I didn't weaken."

"Did you pay her off?"

"That's the important thing. She left town today. I gave her the money in cash."

"That isn't the really important thing."

"No?"

"The important thing is what you've proved to yourself. That you have the courage to start over, start fresh. That you are already beginning to become the kind of man you want to be."

I stood up and looked down at him. "I'm anxious to get started on our regular sessions. How soon will you be through winding up your affairs?"

"Be about three weeks more. They took it pretty hard down at the office, you know. And if it wasn't for your sug-

gestions, I'd never have been able to sell the retirement notion to Marge. But I'll be a free man in three weeks."

"Except for your stock."

"You can't talk me out of that one, Roberts. There's one setup where I'm the expert. Dumping fifteen percent of the company stock on the market right now would sink them. The Imperial outfit is just waiting to close in and reorganize. Besides, as it is, the stuff keeps bringing in dividends. It's a sound investment. And I won't have to watch it, just let it sit. I'm going to be a free man."

"That's right," I said. "In three weeks you'll be a free man." I stood up. "Meanwhile, we might as well begin our sessions. Suppose I meet you at ten tomorrow, corner of Wilshire and Western?"

"All right," he said. "You're the doctor."

We stood on the corner the next morning, bucking the breeze. "What's the big idea of the briefcase?" Caldwell asked. "I don't get it."

"You will, soon enough. Just follow me and obey orders."

"Right. Oh, what the devil—"

His hat blew off. I watched it swirl away over the car tops, then spiral into the street. It rolled on its brim.

He started to rush after it.

I grabbed his arm. "Wait a minute. Let it go."

"Let it go? But that's a twenty-dollar panama, I'm not going to—"

"Hold it. Your first lesson in living begins right now. Look, Ed. Never chase your hat in the street. You might be killed by a car. Besides, who wants to get sweated up and out of breath chasing a hat?"

"But—"

"Let the other fellow do it for you, Ed. Don't you understand? There's always somebody else who's willing to chase your hat for you. Willing? He's crazy to death to do it. It makes him a hero. And if you thank him for it, he'll fall all over you."

I turned and gestured.

"You see? That man without a coat, between those two sedans. He's picking it up for you. Here he comes now. Just wait here."

"This yours, mister?"

"Yes, it is. Thank you very much. I appreciate your kindness."

"Oh, that's all right. Glad to oblige."

"Look at him blush," I murmured, as we turned away. But Caldwell held back.

"Don't you think I ought to give him something for—?"

"Certainly not. As it is, he's happy. He's done his good deed for the day. He feels superior. If you handed him a dollar now it would be like kicking him in the face. He's on top of the world at the moment, and you have your hat back without any exertion. Just remember that principle in the future."

Caldwell nodded. "I guess your theories aren't as impractical as they sound."

"Well, we'll test another one right now. Follow me down this block."

We walked quickly without speaking. At the corner I led him to my car. "Get in."

"We going somewhere?"

"Not yet. First, you've got a job to do. Take this pencil and paper."

"Yes."

"Now, write down everything you can remember seeing during our walk down the block."

"How's that again?"

"It's very simple. Just write down everything you saw as we walked over to the car here. People. Costumes. Faces. The names of stores. What was in the windows. Everything."

"Why?"

"Don't ask questions. I'm trying to find out something about your powers of observation and association."

He grumbled and he sweated, but he wrote. And he was secretly flattered by the attention. *This* was something like it! Here was somebody who really took an interest in what a

man thought, what he could do, what made him tick. Nobody had ever cared about those things before—Marge didn't, that slut Eve didn't, the fellows at the office didn't, even his friends. Why, in the old days his teachers, his father, his own mother hadn't cared.

I watched him, knowing what he was thinking, knowing what he was doing, knowing what I was doing.

In a way, I almost felt sorry for the man. He looked so pathetic, so eager, as he sat there scribbling away like an anxious schoolboy. I was giving him something nobody else had ever bestowed upon him in his lifetime—something few men ever get or ever realize they want—personal interest. I suddenly knew that I *could* do what I had promised: remake him, remold him into a better, more integrated, healthy personality.

But why should I? Suddenly it all came back to me: a picture of Caldwell, dozens of men like Caldwell and what they had done to *me* in the past.

"Sorry, Mr. Caldwell is busy and cannot be disturbed… Afraid there's nothing doing right now…If you'd care to leave your name…No, I haven't time to discuss it with you…"

Yes, there were a lot of Caldwells, a lot of fat, well-fed Mr. Bigs around, ready and waiting to make the little fellows dance to their tune, ready to play God.

Well, I wasn't having any more. From now on, I was Mr. Big and the Caldwells could dance for me.

"All right, that's enough," I snapped.

"But I'm not finished yet."

"Sorry, another time." I looked at my watch. "I've got a new assignment for you."

And so we started.

I gave him assignments galore—went through the whole bag of tricks.

I supplied him with a card, an order pad, and a briefcase full of sample neckties and sent him into a haberdashery shop, cold, to pose as a tie salesman and get an order.

Another day I got him hopelessly lost in the canyons and made him drive us back.

I kept him awake for two days and two nights, denied him food and water for twenty-four hours, ordered him to grow a beard.

It was silly, it was pathetic, it was as simple as A-B-C, and he loved it. Because I kept up a fast line of patter about personality development, exposing oneself to new experience variants, learning dormant skills and realizing and utilizing psychic potential. The very simplicity of the methodology is what made it so effective. I was always at his side, always ready with a new problem, always eager to discuss his reactions, listen to him talk about himself. He was completely sold.

As a matter of fact, it didn't hurt him a bit. It was really good therapy. He dropped about eight pounds in two weeks, took on some color, stopped washing his hands every hour. He was still a string saver, but the change of pace and the absence of Eve combined to restore his sex drive and focus it upon more normal goals.

It surprised me, at first, to see him benefit. But why shouldn't he benefit? The fake religions, the fake healers, the fake mystics, all have a history of success with sufferers and seekers. Sometimes the success is illusory and temporary, often the converts plunge still further into a final morass of maladjustment, but that doesn't seem to matter to them.

Certainly the change made Caldwell happy. He felt free, uninhibited, readjusted.

"I'm ready to start fresh now," he kept telling me. "And thanks to you, I know what I want to do. I was never happy in corporation law, anyway. Handling other peoples' affairs and other peoples' funds—that's living your life secondhand. You've shown me I know how to sell, how to analyze. And I do have a background of business experience. Seems to me I ought to take advantage of it."

"What did you have in mind, Ed?"

"Real estate. There's a boom building up again in the south, you know. Beach development, housing. I've had my eye on some property for a long time, now. But I always kept putting it off, being cautious and afraid. Well, now I'm ready.

"And if I do, Roberts—I'd like to show my appreciation to you. Cut you in on the deal if you want."

"But your funds are tied up," I reminded him. "Everything's invested in that stock, remember?"

He laughed. It was a surprisingly energetic laugh. "That was a lot of nonsense. I was talking like an old woman in those days, wasn't I? Sure, if I sell, the company may have to reorganize and Imperial might take over. But I've got my own life to lead."

This was a new Caldwell talking, and I listened with new interest.

"What do you say, Roberts? Should I go ahead, sell my stock? And do you want in if I do?"

"Well." I hedged. "I don't know if you're ready yet. Give me a little time to analyze the elements involved. I trust you won't do anything rash until we work things out."

"Naturally I wouldn't make a move without your say-so. But I want action."

"All right." I nodded. "I think I can promise you some action very shortly."

And we left it at that, and I went home.

My new place on New Hampshire was a white frame affair, seven rooms and a fireplace—conventional enough, because I didn't operate from here. Rogers had a bedroom on the second floor, and he kept out of my way, using the back entrance. I wasn't usually around much anyhow. I ate out, and the night work didn't give me much chance to try out the fireplace-and-slippers routine.

Once in a while, like tonight, I had a chance to relax. Or thought I did. That's why I set the pint bottle out on the table and poured myself a shot.

I had to be careful. Rogers mustn't see me drink. If he was home, he'd be upstairs, though, with his own pint. The important thing was to keep my occasional indulgence from the Professor.

To hell with the Professor!

I took my first drink on that. And as I did so, I realized I

meant it. Perhaps Caldwell's offer today had started me off. Whatever it was, I felt differently now. I knew I had to get out, get away. If only I could take advantage of his friendly offer, go into real estate or something legitimate. Why, this was the kind of thing I'd always looked for.

And now it came too late. Much too late. Because I couldn't go in with Caldwell. My job was to line him up for the big trimming. And I couldn't run, either. Because they'd bring me back. I'd have company all the way—some brawny dick sitting next to me in a coach car, trying to make conversation and hide the handcuffs.

No, I couldn't run because that would only mean trouble. Besides, I was thinking like Eddie Haines now, not Judson Roberts. Not Judson Roberts, who sat in the driver's seat, who had a fancy office and clients and money rolling in.

Or did he? The Professor was really in the driver's seat. And the money was rolling in to him, not to me. Sure, I was drawing my hundred a week plus expenses—but he was making more, would make thousands on these killings.

Killings. That wasn't a good word to use or think about. I was just a stooge. Professor Hermann had me where he wanted me, and I'd never get out. I couldn't save Caldwell from whatever fate the Professor had planned. I couldn't save myself.

But I *could* have another drink...

"Good evening."

The Professor had come in quietly, using his own key. He stood in the doorway and stared.

"Come in, sit down," I said. "I didn't expect you."

"That is obvious."

"You mean the whiskey? I was just having a nightcap."

He sat down at the table and crossed his arms. The sleeves made a black X on the table. X marks the spot. Black suit again. All that money coming in and he still dressed in the same clothing. Like a minister. Or an undertaker...

"What's the matter with you?"

"Not a thing. Should there be?"

"Rogers tells me you do a lot of this lately in the evening."

Rogers was a little rat. I raised my glass and drank to holes in his cheese. "Not so much. Besides, what else is there for me to do?"

"You might keep up your studies. There is no end to learning, you know."

"I'm doing all right. The money's coming in, isn't it?"

"Yes. I really cannot complain on that score."

"Then I'm entitled to my own way of amusing myself."

"Amusing yourself." The Professor ran a hand across his gleaming skull. I thought of a janitor waxing a dance floor. That was better than thinking about gleaming skulls.

He stared at me across the table. "So you are still interested in amusement, eh? That's the end-all and be-all of your existence, amusement. Your sole purpose in living is to justify and pay for amusement, as you call it. In other words, you have the philosophy of a garage mechanic."

"That would pretty accurately describe my income and status, too."

"You're dissatisfied?"

"What a marvelous analysis," I said.

"But when you think of where you were just seven months ago—"

"I'd rather think about the big promises you made to me. Fame, fortune, anything I wanted. You remember?"

"Yes. Those things will come, if you desire them. Although I had hoped that through your study, you might have developed a genuine interest in metaphysics. Then you and I could have gone on to the next phase together. But I misjudged you, I see. You want, as you term it, amusement."

"Let's just call it more money and be done with it. You'll never get to me with any nonsense about 'spiritual riches,' if that's what you had in mind."

"I've trained you too well, I see. You're always sure of an ulterior motive, aren't you?"

I sighed. "I'm not sure of anything anymore," I told him. "Except this."

I reached for the bottle and he took it away.

"That's out."

"Look, now—"

"Would a guarantee of five hundred a week help to keep you on the wagon?"

"Yes, but—we're not doing that well."

"What about your friend Mr. Caldwell? He'll be ready for the next move, soon."

I straightened up. "That's right. And I wanted to talk to you about that. You know, I'm really helping him."

"Of course you are."

"He wants to sell his stock. That will bring in about a hundred and fifty thousand dollars."

"Excellent. We have uses for that amount."

"He plans to invest in real estate."

"Good. Let him plan. His plans will soon change."

"Look, now, Professor. I've got another angle. Maybe we won't have to touch him at all."

"What's that?"

I talked fast, and as I talked it made sense. "Why not let him take his money and go? He's a new man, he deserves a new start. We don't need his savings. Not with my angle, not with what I know."

"I'm listening," said the Professor.

So I told him what Caldwell had said about his company, about what would happen if he dumped his stock and Imperial took over.

"Do you understand now?" I asked. "I'll get him to sell his stock. His broker is—"

"I know," said the Professor. Of course he *would* know. I realized he had all the details checked.

"Anyhow, the minute he sells, that's your cue. Get all the cash you can lay your hands on and buy Imperial. They'll take over and their stock will rise, probably split and rise again. Why, you can make as much or more than you would from Caldwell, and do it legitimately—no danger of a kickback or trouble. Caldwell's happy and you're happy. Could there be any better deal?"

"It's worth considering." The Professor rose. "I'll think

about it and let you know. Meanwhile, keep Caldwell dangling a few days more."

I faced him. "This is important," I said. "I'd like to see things work out without Caldwell getting hurt."

"I'll worry about that angle."

"But he's going into real estate," I continued. "And he'll cut me in. We can make still more if we let him lead us to profitable deals—"

"I told you I'd decide." The Professor smiled. "But that isn't the big thing, right now. I came to tell you you're going on the air."

"Radio?"

"Fifteen minutes, twice a week. To sell the book, sell your name. I'm having Rogers check on time and costs. Then we might consider an expansion program—train a few assistants for your you and sell consultation over the air. How does that sound to you? Five hundred a week and your own radio show—is it a bargain?"

I hesitated.

"Remember, you handle your affairs, and I'll make the decisions. About Caldwell and all the others. Agreed?"

I took a deep breath because there was nothing else to do. I said, "Yes," because there was nothing else to say.

The Professor nodded. He didn't shake hands. He never shook hands. Somehow, that suited me. He had hands like fat, blind white spiders...

"I'll say goodnight," he told me. "I've got another appointment this evening. Get in touch with me tomorrow and I'll let you know about Caldwell."

He left us alone, then, and there we sat: the bottle and I. I looked at it.

"Did you hear what he said?" I asked. "Five hundred a week. And I'm going on the radio! That's a laugh. I came out here to go on the air, but Rickert said I wasn't good enough. And now—"

The bottle didn't answer me.

Thirteen

Two days later, Caldwell sold his stock.

The evening after the sale, I went into a little bar off the Strip to meet the Professor. I slid into a booth and ordered club soda, straight.

Then I waited. Waited and worried. The Professor was late. Probably cooking up something for Caldwell—cooking up a scheme with Doc Sylvestro, Jake, and Rogers. Hush-hush stuff.

Everything the Professor did was hush stuff. I began to wonder about that.

Professor Hermann was a type. A West Coast type. More specifically, a Southern California type. He wouldn't flourish in another climate.

But this was a land of Messiahs and miracles, of Peter the Hermit and Isaiah the Evangelist; a land where red flowers and green skyscrapers sprang up overnight. A land of fabulous fertility, luxuriant lushness.

The rod smote the rock and gold gushed forth in '49. The rod waved as a magic wand and lo, there was Hollywood. The rod smote the rock again, and oil spewed fortunes to the skies. The rod pointed and there was real estate, and aircraft factories, and an entire civilization that bought cars from Madman Harry, cracked up, and was buried at Forest Lawn. At night, the flying red horse heralded the Apocalypse in advertising from a dirigible. The searchlights stabbed at heaven to proclaim the presence of a new fruit stand.

No wonder the Professor was accepted here! Even I had accepted him, done his bidding. And now, my life was in his hands.

Yet I knew surprisingly little about him. A little fat bald-

headed German refugee who wore black in a land of light, a man who climbed the rungs to money and power, who delighted in dominating. Maybe I'd better use the Judson Roberts technique and analyze him. "It's a hard job," I told the bottle. "A hard job, trying to psychoanalyze the Devil."

"What you need is a drink," the bottle said.

I blinked, then realized the words hadn't come from the bottle. They were spoken by Ellen Post.

She had just come in, and she stood opposite me, at the bar. I looked at her a long time, because I wanted to look at her more than anything in the world. I studied her oval face. That exotic effect was caused by a double-fold of the upper eyelids. A simple explanation made by the practiced observation of Judson Roberts, but it didn't keep Eddie Haines from admiring her features.

Right now I felt more like Eddie Haines than I had in a long, long time.

"Your order?"

I looked at the waiter. I looked at her. Then, "Two apricot brandies."

She slid into the booth across from me and she smiled. Judson Roberts could have analyzed that smile before you could say "Mona Lisa"—but I wasn't Judson Roberts tonight. She smiled, and that was enough for me.

"So you remembered."

"Like an elephant. A pink one." I took another look at her. She was taller than I remembered her to be, and her voice was softer.

"What brings you here?" I asked.

"My convertible."

"Nuts."

"Why Doctor Roberts, what you said!"

"I mean it. Let's not be smart tonight. I want to know all about you. I've been wondering. Who you are, where you live, why we hit it off so miserably after such a brave beginning."

The drinks arrived. She stared at her glass as though she

was looking into the Grand Canyon. When she spoke, her voice was almost a whisper.

"We were both upset, I guess. About the party, and Mike's death—everything. We should have seen each other. I know that now."

"What have you been doing?"

"Not drinking, mostly. For quite a while. I went down to the beach and took some more lessons."

"What kind of lessons?"

"Voice. But I didn't stick at it this time, either. I'm just not good enough. As with everything else, I'm a might-be. That's not even as good as a has-been. Apparently my only talent is for liquor."

"So you're starting again?"

"Yes and no. I haven't gone out for months. This was just an impulse." I watched her pick up the drink. Apricot brandy, apricot lips. She swallowed, made a face.

"Brrr!"

"Then why do you do it?"

"What else is there?"

"You were going to tell me about yourself," I said, patiently. "About the house you live in, the clothes you buy, the things you like to eat. How you wore your hair when you were a little girl. Do you like fireplaces? And sunsets? And does your nose get red when you have a cold?"

"Really, I'd like to, but I have to run along now." She rose.

"Sit down."

"Say you really mean it, don't you?" She sat down again and waited.

"Why do you always run away when somebody asks you about yourself?"

"That's my business."

"You told me once that drinking was your business. Is it a part of the running away, too?"

"Good old *Doctor* Roberts! Do you think, in your benev-

olent, homespun way, that you're going to *help* me? I've heard that line before, too."

"All right, so it's a line," I said. "I can't help you. Nobody can help you. You help yourself. Either that, or you keep on drinking. And in two hours you'll be up at the bar, telling everything you wouldn't tell to me. Spilling drinks and intimacies in front of the bartender. He'll help you."

She wrinkled her nose. "You know something? I like you when you get mad. You drop that phony front, then. I made a mistake when I walked out on you. We could have had a lot of fun together."

"Sure," I nodded. "A lot of nice clean drunken fun. We're adults, aren't we? We know what we want. A great big bottle and a chance to suck on it. A chance to drool our way back to infancy. Babies don't know what they're doing, they're not responsible if they go to bed with each other and make messes. Yes, we could have had a lot of fun. And I'm damned glad we didn't."

"So am I."

She leaned forward. I smelled apricots. The suntan had ripened her.

"Another drink?"

"No. Let's talk. If you've been trying to scare me off drinking, you've succeeded."

"Good. Try and pretend I'm God for a change."

"I don't get it."

"Your God is the bartender. The bartender is always God, or haven't you noticed?"

"I hadn't, but go on. You will, anyway."

"Drinkers are all alike. They go to the bartender for peace, for release. They tell him their troubles in confessional. Like God he dispenses wisdom, judgment, guidance. He rules supreme in his own world. He is quick to punish the transgressor. He can also reward with his favor—or with free drinks. He is omniscient and all-powerful. He knows everything about everybody within the microcosmic universe

of the tavern. He is the source of solace and consolation.
And he is worshiped in libations, with sacramental wine that
produces divine intoxication. He is also, I might add, the
father-image. Or more exactly, an idealization of the father.
The infantile regressions of the dipsomaniac fit into this
pattern of unconscious symbolism."

"Funny you should say that. I never drank until Dad was
killed."

"And after he died, you kept away from men."

"That's right." She looked at her glass. "He was one swell
guy. Drank a lot himself, though. Geoffrey Post—industrial
designer. You recall the name? He got into plane building
in the thirties. That's how he died, piloting one of his own
planes. Cracked up."

"So you cracked up. No mother, and the father-image. He
drank, so you drank. You couldn't have anything to do with
men, either, because of the part he played in your psychic
fantasy. You drank and were attracted to men, but that made
you feel guilty, so you drank again. And—"

"Wait a minute. I'm not crazy."

"They call it dipsomania, you know. And rightly so. Most
psychotic states are rooted in some sexual aberration."

"Why do you drink, then? Are you in love with your
mother?"

"I'm an orphan." I grinned. "But seriously, doesn't it make
some kind of sense to you?"

She nodded. The empty glass between her fingers nodded
with her.

"I guess it does. I was beginning to figure some of those
things out for myself. We were always together, Dad and I,
traveling around and never stopping long enough in one
place to make real friends. When I was eighteen he'd take
me dancing, we went to parties together. Strangers took us
for—" she bit her lip "—lovers."

"They were right in a way, weren't they?"

"Yes. Although neither of us was conscious of those feel-

ings. It wasn't until after Dad died that it hit me. Then I went to pieces, and now I'm trying to put those pieces back together."

"You can't do it alone very easily. You'll need help."

"Are you suggesting professional treatment?"

"Non-professional. Please, Ellen. I want to help you."

"But you said you had to go your way alone. That there wasn't room for anyone else in your life."

"That's all changed now. It has to be. You trust me, don't you?"

"We'll see. I want to think things over, first." She rose, and this time there was no dissuading her.

"When will I see you again? I don't even have your address."

"I'll call you. At your office."

"Goodnight, Ellen."

"Goodnight—Judd."

And she left, taking the light with her, leaving the shadows and the empty glass.

I shook my head, raised it in response to a sudden sound.

"That girl, who is she?"

The Professor shot up out of a trapdoor or appeared in a burst of flame.

"Her name's Ellen Post. We saw her at the Lorna Lewis party."

"That's right. She was attracted to you, I remember. Have you seen much of her since?"

"This is the first time since the inquest, and our meeting was accidental. But I hope to be seeing more of her."

"Good. She may be useful."

"Useful?"

The Professor slid into the booth, removed his hat, and gave me a glimpse of how his skull looked under dim blue neon lighting.

"I've checked on her. Something Lorna Lewis let drop one day aroused my interest. She's Geoffrey Post's daughter, isn't she?"

"Yes."

"Well-fixed?"

"I don't know." I was wary. "She probably has a small income from the estate."

"That doesn't matter. But she's the niece of Leland Post— his only niece. He takes an interest in her, and it helps. Leland Post is a state senator, with ambitions and connections. He'd do a lot, out of love for her and self-interest, to keep her from getting mixed up in any scandal."

I leaned forward. "Now wait a minute. If you think—"

"Please. Restrain yourself and hear me out. Leland Post is owned by one of the oil syndicates from Long Beach. He's going to make a bid for Congress next year. Right now he's very much in the public eye."

"Hold it, Professor. I've got a—a personal interest in this girl. No funny business."

Those eyes, those unblinking eyes, burned up at me. They burned a hole through the upholstery behind my head. But I met the gaze.

"Very well," he said, softly. "It was only a thought. Nothing important. We'll abandon that gambit, as long as you have a personal interest."

We talked of other things, then. I learned that the radio program would be ready in a month or so, as soon as Rogers could do the scripts. We discussed current cases, current sales figures. And, inevitably, we discussed Caldwell.

"We're going to have a meeting tomorrow night, at your house," the Professor told me. "We'll decide on our next move there."

I nodded. "What about the stock deal?"

"You were right. He sold, and I bought Imperial today. As much as I could lay my hands on."

"Then you'll leave Caldwell alone?" I asked.

"Why leave him alone?" The Professor smiled. "After all, he's got a hundred and fifty thousand dollars in cash, just floating around."

"But you said—"

"I said I'd think about it. And I have. You'll get the full

story tomorrow night. Make it nine, sharp." He stood up. "Goodbye, Roberts."

Judson Roberts nodded goodbye. Eddie Haines just sat there, wondering if she'd call, when she'd call, when he'd see her again. There were definitely two of us to consider, now. Eddie Haines and Judson Roberts. Just a couple of the boys. Eddie Haines hadn't been around very much lately. He was stuck on Ellen Post, but he never came around any more. Judson Roberts was always available, though. He was everywhere. Seen in the best places these days. A fast, smart operator, this Roberts. He knew how to handle himself and everybody else, too.

Telling the old ladies at the lectures, "Remember the first principles of Y-O-U. Your Opportunities, Unlimited. Cultivate yourself. Allow the seeds of your personality to take root and flower. If your soul is thirsty, drink deeply." Straight out of the old seed catalogue, that's the way Judson Roberts worked.

Sitting down with the shy ones, explaining, "There is a homely wisdom in the expression, 'a diamond in the rough.' For the personality is a jewel, and like a jewel it must be cut and polished. Experience is the cutting edge that brings out the facets of personality. The more facets, the more brilliance." Courtesy of *Mootbeck's Cut-Rate Diamond Supply Co.* The whole spiel.

And Judson Roberts wasn't just a spieler. He got around. He knew more about human nature than a towel girl in San Diego. A deep thinker, this Roberts. There was always study and analysis and observation, the sort of thing that helped his personality to flower like a beautiful cluster of poison ivy; gave him more facets than a rhinestone garter.

Sometimes he played God. Sometimes he went out into the streets and worked on his cold readings. He got so that he could size up a stranger at a glance. He lectured, he autographed copies of *Y-O-U*. He dressed well, he was in the chips, he looked like a million.

Of course, there were little wrinkles forming around the

corners of his eyes these days. Once in a while, when he get angry, his mouth crawled out from under his mustache—and it was the kind of mouth that bites the heads off canaries. But why worry? Everything was sailing along smoothly now. Sailing along on the *S.S. Schizophrenia*—passengers Judson Roberts, first class, and Eddie Haines, steerage.

That's the way it was, and that's the way I thought about it that night and the next day, until Ellen Post finally did call me up at the office.

She was at her beach house, at Malibu, and would Mr. Judson Roberts care to run down tomorrow afternoon?

"I'll be seeing you," said Eddie Haines.

Fourteen

Eddie Haines had a date for tomorrow afternoon. But Judson
Roberts had a date for tonight—nine sharp, at his house.

They joined me around the big table in the dining room:
the Professor, Rogers, and Dr. Sylvestro. I had all my notes
on Caldwell ready, and they kept passing them around and
making notes of their own.

I sat there and watched my companions: little Rogers
with his hypersensitive twitchings; the Professor, an ivory
Buddha in a black suit; Dr. Sylvestro, a gaunt gargoyle whose
specialty was stony silence.

The Professor finished reading and sat back. We all
watched him.

"You've done a good job," he said.

"Thanks. As I told you, I'm actually helping the man."

"Fine. And now we're ready to take over."

"I see he's sold his stock," Rogers commented.

"Right."

"That leaves our string-saving friend in possession of a
cool hundred and fifty thousand in cash, does it not?" Sylvestro's deep voice rolled out. I stared at his unnaturally pallid
face, at the unnaturally red lips. He sat there smirking like a
vampire, saying, "You have plans for that money, Hermann?"

The bald head inclined slowly. "Naturally. In fact, my
plans are already in effect. When Jake gets here—"

I was sweating, but I had to make one last try. "Look,
Professor. What about my idea? Buy Imperial stock and cash
in. Then let me play along with Caldwell for a while. He's
going into real estate and he trusts me. I'll be able to advise
him, check every move he makes. Who knows, if we wait we
may make as much or more without any risk. Now suppose

you were to arrange a tie-up with some promoters who own beach property, and we could split the profits—"

A fat hand rose and pushed the rest of the sentence back down my throat.

"That is too slow and too uncertain. I have found a better way. With your friend, Eve England."

"Eve? But I paid her off, she went away."

"Before Caldwell broke with her, before the payoff, there was a lapse of several days during which he continued to see her. You know that."

"Yes."

"But what you do not know is that Rogers also contacted Eve England for me—right after you did."

I sat up. "Meaning you didn't trust me to handle the deal?"

"No. We checked on you, naturally. That is my policy. But we had something else in mind. We anticipated this situation." The Professor got his monocle into position, held me with his glittering eye. "Has it ever occurred to you, my friend, that if a man is willing to pay five thousand dollars he may be willing to pay a great deal more?"

"I don't get it."

"Let Jake tell you. That sounds like his ring."

I got up and answered the bell. It was our Neanderthal friend, all right—the man whose forehead was voted most likely to recede.

"How's tricks?" he grunted.

"You're the mystic, you tell me," I suggested. "Come on in and sit down." Our little family circle watched impatiently as he extracted an envelope from the pocket of his sports shirt.

"Here they are," he said.

The Professor opened the envelope. Five small photographic negatives and an equal number of prints shuffled fanwise through his fingers. His face bore the blank stare of a professional poker player who holds a winning hand.

"Well," said Rogers, "what'd he get?"

"See for yourself."

Rogers grabbed at the photos. Sylvestro got up and leaned over his shoulder.

"Hey!" Rogers whispered. "How the hell did you manage to get this?"

"The babe cooperated."

"I'll say she did! But where were you?"

"Closet. I used that new-type flash the Professor got me. No light, see? When she heard how much she could get out of the deal, she fixed me up. Got 'em all the night before Caldwell told her he was through."

"Boy, what a masochist!" Rogers breathed. "Look at those ropes and—"

Sylvestro's gargoyle grimace deepened. He beckoned to me. "Care to look?"

I looked, then hastily turned away. I hoped the Professor wouldn't see my face. I heard myself saying, "But what are you going to do with this?"

Jake knew. "We're going to shake down your pal Caldwell for about fifty G's, to start with. Either that, or we take these pictures to his wife. And then we get another fifty, with duplicate negatives. And then another—"

"Never mind." The Professor silenced Jake and retrieved the photographs. "I think you understand our plan now," he said. "Jake will go to him later tonight. Come on, gentlemen, let's be on our way."

They filed out—Jake, Rogers, Dr. Sylvestro. I just sat there, waiting. The Professor lingered behind.

"Well?" he queried.

I shook my head. "No," I said. "You aren't going to pull a dirty trick like that! You don't expect me to take a hand in such a stinking, rotten setup."

"Oh yes I do," smiled the Professor. "And you will."

"Count me out." I stood up.

"Where are you going?"

"I'm phoning Caldwell right now. I'm telling him to have the police there when Jake contacts him. Evidence of blackmail."

The Professor was still smiling. "You might also ask them

to send a squad around here, then," he suggested. "For evidence of murder. Don't forget Mike Drayton, my friend."

It should have stopped me, but it didn't. I kept moving for the phone. "All right, Professor," I said. "I'll do just that. I'm beginning to think I deserve a rap for all the dirty things I've done lately. And it will be worth it if I can save Caldwell."

He was still smiling. "What about saving Ellen?" he murmured.

That *did* stop me. "Ellen? What's she got to do with all this?"

"Nothing—yet. And she needn't have, if you agree to be sensible. But remember what I told you the other evening. We could use Ellen Post nicely, in order to get to Leland Post and some big money. For your sake, I agreed to abandon the notion.

"If you promise to cooperate with Caldwell, I'll keep my bargain. No frame-up for Ellen Post. But if you don't, I'll see to it that she's the next victim. And you know me well enough to realize I don't bluff or make idle threats. Go to that telephone now and Ellen Post will pay for it."

All the while he was smiling, smiling because he knew he'd win. He was crazy, he was the Devil, but he was no fool.

I walked over to the sofa and sat down. I put my head in my hands, but there was nowhere to hide.

"That's better," the Professor told me. "Now, tomorrow morning, you can probably expect a visit from Caldwell. Here's how you handle him—"

He told me, and I sat there waiting to obey. Then he went away and I continued to sit there, waiting for morning to come.

The next morning I sat in my office and waited for Caldwell to come. And I handled him.

"My God, Roberts, say something!"

Caldwell shook my shoulder. Maybe he just put his hand on me, but he was trembling so that he shook anything he touched.

"Don't you understand?" he panted. "This woman—she

came back. She wants fifty thousand. She says she'll go to Marge… And this man has those pictures, he's in with her—"

I shrugged his hand off. "I can't help you. If you'd only taken my advice and broken with her the very day I suggested it, this couldn't have happened."

"I know, I was a fool, a damned fool! But it has happened, and something must be done." He gulped. "Couldn't you see her again, talk her out of it?"

"Please, Ed. Obviously she's determined. And I can't afford to get mixed up in anything like this. You understand my position."

"But can't we fix up a trap or something, with the police?"

"Then they'd see the pictures, wouldn't they? And Marge would hear the whole story."

"God, what can I do? What can I do?"

"I'm afraid you'll have to pay her off."

Silence.

"Look, Roberts, you're sure there is no other way? I'd make it worth your while."

"It's too late now."

"Well, will you come with me tonight when I meet her and that man?"

I gave him a refrigerated smile. "That would be very unwise. And I'm afraid, until this matter clears up, that we had better not see one another."

"But who can I go to now? Who else is there to help me?"

He waited, but I didn't answer. I couldn't answer. There was no answer left for him. I could only sit there and watch him cry, watch his jelly-flesh dissolve in his clothes, watch the red hands as they scrabbled and twisted across my desk, endlessly ravelling and unravelling a piece of dirty string. A string saver.

He got up, finally, and shuffled out. I sat there and kept thinking about that piece of string. Suddenly I knew what was going to happen to Edgar Clinton Caldwell. Tonight he'd pay the fifty thousand. Then, in a few weeks, they'd put

the bite on him for another fifty, with the duplicate negatives. And sometime later, they'd be around again for the last fifty. Maybe they'd want him to sell his house, too.

Somewhere along the line he'd crack. He'd crack and look to a bigger piece of string to save him. Caldwell would end up by hanging himself. I knew it as surely as I knew I was sitting there. He'd follow the unconscious pattern to the end. Once a string saver, always a string saver.

And it was my responsibility. Oh, he'd be no great loss to the world. He'd done his share of despicable things, and his behavior with Eve England wasn't pretty. He deserved some punishment.

But I had no right to do the punishing. Or to execute him. He saved the string, but I'd tie the hangman's knot. I'd place the noose around his neck; I'd kick the chair away and leave him dangling there, gray jelly quivering on the end of a rope, gray jelly jerking and then the rope cutting into his chin, cutting into his neck and stretching it long and thin. They say, sometimes, when they cut down a corpse, the neck is no bigger around than a child's wrist—

Still, it was the lady or the tiger. Ellen or Caldwell. One of them had to go, because the Professor said so. I'd kept my bargain, and now I could go and claim my reward. I could go to Malibu this afternoon.

I walked out of my office and down the hall. As I passed Rogers' little cubicle in back, I suddenly remembered the lecture for this week. He'd be finishing it up, now, and I could take it along for study.

Rogers had his door open. I went in quietly, not wanting to disturb his work. He sat hunched over his desk, going through some papers: pictures and clippings from newspaper files.

I caught a glimpse of a leonine head and a caption:

LELAND POST WINS STATE SENATE RACE

That stopped me.

Rogers looked up. "Oh, it's you," he said, scrabbling his clippings together in a heap. "How'd you make out with the sucker?"

"He took it all right. He'll sail for the fifty G's, I think."

"Good."

I sat down on the desk, casually, and tried to keep my voice from trembling. "Thought you had my speech. But I see you're working on something else."

"Yeah, that's right. Didn't the Professor tell you yet? We're rigging up a frame for this politician, Leland Post. He's the key to some important dough. You'll be in on it, of course—guess you know his niece. Well, she's the key."

"So." I stood up and clenched my hands behind my back, to keep from strangling him. "What's the setup?"

"That's what I'm doping out now. The Professor'll tell you himself, I suppose."

"I suppose."

I walked out of the room, somehow, under my own power. I made it through the hall, taking each step slowly. With every step I took, I called myself a new name.

What a fool I'd been to trust the Professor! Of course he wouldn't keep his bargain, he had no intention of keeping it. He was out after money and power, and he'd get everything he could. Nothing would stop him. Even while *he* was playing with *me*, he'd already set the wheels in motion to take care of Ellen and her uncle.

And now that I knew, what could I do about it? For the moment, nothing. I'd just have to wait and see how he'd approach me, what he'd say, what the scheme was. Then perhaps I might find a way out. But I doubted it. The Professor never left any holes—with him, there was no way out. Except the way Mike Drayton took, the way Edgar Caldwell would take soon.

Maybe, some day, I'd be taking that way out, too. Right now, there was only one place for me to go. Malibu.

Fifteen

The sun was warm at Malibu, so Ellen and I sat in the shade of the little beach house. Only two days had passed since our meeting in the tavern, but here we sat, and I had my arm around her waist. Just a whirlwind romance. Only there was no whirlwind about it, no romance. We merely sat and talked. We had so much to talk about.

Fireworks, for example. The way they look to you as a child. Jewels sprayed on blue velvet. That's what she said.

"No, my dear, children don't think that way," I told her. "Try hard to remember, now. You're seven. You're standing on the top of the bluff, at the park, looking up at the sky. You sense the puff from the ground, hear the swish. You try to decide where the burst will emerge, guessing with your eyes. Then it comes. The arcs shoot out. And something inside your throat moves with them, your mouth opens, and you go—"

"Oooooh!" She squealed. "Of course, I remember, now!"

I faced her. "I'd like to ask you a very personal question, if you don't mind."

"What is it?"

"Did you ever experience the supreme thrill, the ultimate attainment—of riding on a merry-go-round *twice* in a row?"

"Three times."

"Now you're bragging."

"Dad took me. And he used to give me money for the movies, on Saturday. Eleven cents. Ten for admission and a penny for—"

"Gum?"

"Yes, or licorice whips, or suckers. But sometimes I got

a chocolate mint, because if you picked out one with a pink center you won a free candy bar."

She sighed. "It's all so far away, so long ago. But sometimes I wish I could—"

"No you don't," I said. "You don't want to go back. You like it right here."

"What about you?"

"Guess?" I squeezed her in the most convenient place. "I don't want to stir. Maybe you are right, at that. There isn't much fun any more because there's no sense of personal participation left. In order to have fun nowadays, a kid pushes a button or twists a dial or drops a nickel in a slot. And his fun-integer is noise. Noise from TV programs. Noise from jukeboxes. Noise from portable radios, carried into the woods on picnics, carried down here to the beach, carried into the country to provide a constant background of mechanical voices frantically commanding the purchase of deodorants. I used to be a part of it myself, heaven pity me."

"You were in radio?"

"Yes. Back in Iowa. I—"

"Come on. I've told you about me. Now it's your turn."

I stood up. "Getting late."

"There's time. You haven't an appointment?"

"No, but—"

"Then you can't wiggle out of it. Talk."

I sighed. We walked arm-in-arm into the beach house. The large living room held nothing but divans and a chaise longue set near the fireplace. Rousseau reproductions graced the walls. I sat down on a sofa and stared at *The Snake-Charmer.* Dark figure, staring eyes…like the Professor.

"Come on. What's the matter?"

"Look, Ellen, this isn't going to be easy. I'm trying to make up my mind. I want to tell you, yes. But right now it's a risk, wondering how you'll take it. And I must tell you the truth."

"Yes. You must." She came over and sat next to me. She lit two cigarettes and placed the first in my mouth. It was

somehow, to me, the most intimate gesture in the world. We puffed and sped smoke in silence.

"Judd." She came close, very close. "You said you wanted to help me, didn't you?"

"Right."

"Well—one of the things that will help me most is to know the truth, about you."

She called me "Judd" because she thought I was Judson Roberts, and if I was Judson Roberts I'd tell her something all right. It wouldn't be the truth but she'd believe it. Then she'd put her arms around me—those soft sun-ripened arms—and I'd taste apricots and I'd have what I wanted. Only I wouldn't have it really, because I wasn't Judson Roberts but Eddie Haines. And Eddie Haines would rather tell her the truth and take his chances.

"All right," I said. "Here goes."

I took a deep breath and exhaled. Then I talked.

Half an hour elapsed between the time I said, "My real name is Eddie Haines," and my last sentence, "Here I am."

In between there were two cigarettes—the second one left in the ashtray to burn unheeded—and a grateful deepening of dusk that hid my face in shadows.

I didn't want her to see my face. There was enough nakedness as it was, because I held nothing back. The failure, the suicide attempt, the meeting with the Professor, the Y-O-U setup, what we did to people like Caldwell, everything.

Everything except the murder of Mike Drayton, that is. I couldn't tell her that. I wanted to, but I knew what her reaction would be. What I did say was bad enough, and I expected the awkward silence, the stiff, impersonal phrases, the cold, "We'd better go," with which she'd conclude our relationship when I finished.

What I didn't expect was the scent of apricots, the strong arms around me, the leaping fire of her lips.

"And I thought I had troubles," she whispered.

"Then you don't—?"

Her mouth answered me first, then her voice. "Of course not. Oh, I'm so glad you told me, Eddie! I knew I'd never get used to spending the rest of my life with a man named 'Judd'!"

It got dark fast, after that.

It was black as midnight when I came home. In fact, it *was* midnight. There were no lights shining inside the house, not even from Rogers' upstairs room. I let myself in and clicked the living-room switch.

Immediately, the phone jingled.

I answered. The Professor's voice snapped across the wire. "Where have you been? I've called many times."

"Sorry. Just got in."

"Answer my question, please. Where were you?"

"Visiting Ellen Post."

"Good."

"I'm glad you approve."

"I do. By the way, we collected the first fifty thousand tonight. No trouble."

"Congratulations."

"And that brings up another matter. I've got to invest the money, right away. I'm leaving for San Francisco for a few days, perhaps a week. Taking Rogers with me. You'll carry on as usual, with one new assignment."

"What's that?"

"Keep on seeing Ellen Post."

"Very pleasant assignment. I intend to."

"You might enjoy going out and doing the town with her. She likes to drink, doesn't she?"

"Now wait a minute. You sound as if you have ideas. And you promised me—"

"Nothing to worry about, I assure you. I just think you're in need of relaxation. The tension of recent weeks seems to be wearing you down. Why not have some of that amusement you're always talking about?"

Sure. The Professor was right. Live it up a little. He was

my friend. My friend, who wanted me to get Ellen Post drunk in public, preparatory to working some new blackmail scheme I wasn't supposed to know about. He and Rogers would go away and line it all up, and I'd be here laying the groundwork. But suppose I double-crossed him and wouldn't play?

He answered that without my asking. "Don't worry while I'm gone. Miss Bauer will communicate with me regularly. And I've told Jake to keep an eye on you."

"That was thoughtful."

"You ought to know by this time—I think of everything."

"All right." I kept my voice even. "Have a good trip."

"Thank you," said the Professor. "Enjoy yourself, while I'm gone."

Click.

Well, there it was. Mike Drayton was dead, Edgar Caldwell was framed and not long for this world, and Ellen Post was next on the list. Everybody I touched was marked for doom. Because I was a puppet named Judson Roberts, and the Professor pulled the strings.

Only he was going away. I'd have four or five days to work. Four or five days to straighten things out, pull out forever, with Ellen. It was my only chance. I'd have to make my plans and execute them quickly.

I switched off the light. I could think better in the dark. Picking up a cigarette en route, I walked over to the window and stared down at the street. There was a beat-up old Ford parked before my door. It was empty. But lounging in the shadows, staring up at me, watching and waiting patiently, was Jake.

That's how the nightmare began...

Sixteen

Maybe he went away before dawn. Maybe he slept in the car. All I know is that when I went downstairs the next morning, he was standing there.

"Hi," he said.

"Hello. What are you doing around here?"

"Oh, I'm just gonna stick around for a while, if you don't mind. You know, the Professor's going away and he sort of hinted you might need a little protection. In case this gay Caldwell hollers copper or somethin'. If it's all right with you." He grinned.

I grinned back. "Sure, Jake. But you needn't bother."

"No bother. I'll come along to the office with you now."

"I'll be there all day. I can call you when I decide to go anywhere."

"Thanks. But I'll come along. I like hanging around your office. That May, she's a dish all right."

"Suit yourself."

He rode with me to the office and I got inside my private room and closed the door. I picked up my personal phone and dialed Ellen at the beach house. I had to watch what I said in case the Professor had thoughtfully tapped the wire for May to record my conversation.

"Darling, when can I see you? About two be all right? No, I'll come on out. Like to talk to you. No, I'm not upset. Everything's fine. Goodbye until then."

No, I wasn't upset. Merely petrified. But I had to figure something out, and I had to move fast.

Jake had a time keeping up with me in his battered Ford, but he managed.

"Why you going to drag me off to Malibu?" he grumbled.

"I'm going to see a woman. And you're going to sit out in the hot sun and sweat. Professor's idea, remember?"

He called me a name and I gave him a sweet smile. Then we were off.

The same sun shone over the beach today, shimmering in Ellen's hair. Jake stayed up on the roadway. But even if he'd seen us, it wouldn't have stopped me from taking her in my arms.

"My! You did want to see me, didn't you?"

"Let's go inside," I suggested.

"Good idea."

"No—I must talk to you."

"You disappoint me greatly, sir," she said.

"Listen, Ellen, this is serious."

"All right. What's the matter, Eddie?"

Funny how the little things count. Even then, I wasn't sure I'd have the nerve to go through with what I planned. But she called me "Eddie." That was enough. That did it.

I told her everything, then. I told her the Professor had plans to blackmail her uncle through her. I told her that I was to be a part of the scheme. I told her what I suspected.

She shook her head. "But that's utterly insane! People don't go around doing such things. Imagine him thinking that you would go for such a scheme!"

"I did go for it, Ellen. I'm taking you out tonight and getting you drunk."

"You're *what?*"

"It's the only way. I think I've figured an angle. If we go to some place like The Gin Mill—"

I explained my angle to her in detail. She nodded.

"This is our only chance, Ellen," I told her. "I've tried to figure it all out. The Professor is gone, but Jake is tailing me. I've got to shake him sometime during the next few days, without his realizing that I'm shaking him.

"Then I can get hold of whatever cash is available and disappear with you. We'll go down to Mexico together, and further south if necessary. We'll run away for good."

Ellen pulled away from me. "For good?" she said, softly.

"I don't understand. Can it be that you don't want to go away with me?"

"You know I do, Eddie. But we can't run. You'll never be safe or sure."

She was right. She didn't even know about Drayton's death, but she was right. I sensed that.

"No, there's another way. A better way. You told me about this man, Caldwell, and those pictures."

"Yes."

"The Professor and his friend Rogers will be gone. Jake is trailing you. Where do you think those pictures would be?"

"At the Professor's office—no, wait a minute, that would be too risky. Probably at his house."

"And where does he live?"

"Way off someplace. Vista Canyon. I've never been there. Come to think about it, he's pretty cagey where his private life is concerned."

"Eddie, I'll bet those pictures are at his house. And while he's gone, if you can get away from Jake, you can go out there and find them.

"Then you'll have a real weapon! Turn those photos over to Caldwell. You'll save him, and you'll also save yourself. Because once Caldwell has the pictures, he can threaten to expose the Professor if he makes trouble for you over leaving. Don't you see? You can turn the tables and blackmail the Professor!"

She would have said more, but I was kissing her.

"Darling," I said, "you're on the first team. Now, go change your clothes. You've got an important date to go out and get stinking drunk."

The Gin Mill was one of those fake "atmosphere" joints—with singing waiters complete with false mustaches, steins of beer, a "free lunch" which you paid for, and sawdust on the floors. There were also cuspidors alongside the booths.

That's what I needed—the cuspidors. Jake shambled

over to the bar and roosted there for three hours, while Ellen and I kept the waiter rushing to our booth with refills on scotch.

We drank a lot. At least, Jake thought we did. He'd glance in the mirror out of the corner of one bloodshot eye and catch a glimpse of us raising glasses. But he never noticed us as we emptied the shots into the cuspidor.

As the evening progressed our voices rose, and we began to muss each other up. That part was fun—and there was no need to fake. Around eleven I suggested a little singing. Ellen had a nice voice, but when she cut loose on some old favorites it was murder. Even I couldn't stand it.

"Stop, you're overdoing the act," I whispered. But she kept right on singing. She was singing as I dragged her out of there. We staggered over to the car. Jake lumbered along behind at a discreet distance.

I drove Ellen up Wilshire to the apartment hotel where she stayed when she planned to be in town. It was her uncle's place, but right now the legislature was in session and she had it all to herself.

"You coming in?" she asked.

"I wish I could," I said. "But I've got work to do." I watched Jake's Ford in the rear-view mirror, but Ellen pulled my head around.

"Don't try anything foolish, darling. That big gorilla could tear you to pieces."

I shook my head. "I'm not going to bother Jake at all. He'll see me home, watch me stagger up the steps and call it a day."

My prediction proved correct. I dropped Ellen, helped her lurch into the lobby, returned to my car and wove my way home to New Hampshire. Jake pulled up behind me.

"How'm I doin', huh?" I yelled. "Some number, isn't she? Some number, isn't she? Some—"

"Not so loud!" Jake was actually embarrassed. "Look, you better turn in. You're loaded to the eyeballs."

"Good idea. See you tomorrow, same time, same sta'shun. 'Bye now."

He watched me locate the keyhole. I stepped inside, went upstairs and turned on the bedroom light. Then I went into the darkness of the bathroom and peered out of the window. Jake's car was pulling away from the curb. Good. So far, everything checked. I looked at my watch. 11:35 by radium paint. Late, but not too late for me.

It was going to be a long drive to Vista Canyon. But that's where the Professor lived. I didn't know exactly where, and I didn't know how I'd locate his place in the dark. But he was gone, Jake was gone, and now was the time. Now was the time to go back downstairs and drive away very quietly. Now was the time for speed, across town and out of town. Now was the time to wheel and climb and twist and turn through the Canyon passage.

Now was the time for midnight, and a moon, for skirling winds that clawed the clouds to phosphorescent shreds. Now was the time for silence on winding trails, for whisperings in woods, for howling in the far-off hills. Now was the time to park the car on the shoulder of the road, out of sight; to crunch through gravel and inspect the crooked signboard at the roadway's fork.

Names, meaningless names, names of the wealthy, names of the reclusive. No Otto Hermann. Hills rose crazily all about me, leering and looming in the moonlight; huge, white wrinkled faces bearded by titanic trees. They watched and waited, watched and waited, while a little ant crawled along the road. Me.

I was a fool to feel that way. I was a fool to come here. Melodramatic nonsense. But if it was nonsense, why did the Professor hide his house?

Little beads of conversation began to string themselves on a single thread of recollection.

"It's on the very top of the hill…the windlass and cable is convenient because we lower a little car down the hillside for groceries, and you can even ride in it yourself if you like."

And, "It was built back in Prohibition days. Porch on three sides, wonderful view, completely private. But the big

secret is the fox pen just below the house. You see, the bootleggers had to have a place to cache their liquor, and guess
what they did? They set themselves up as running a fox farm,
and—"

It hadn't seemed important at the time I heard it. But
now everything came back to me. Hillside. Look for a cable
from the top of the hill. Three-sided porch. A fox pen in
back, just below the level of the house.

I began to climb, to crawl. Crickets stopped their chirping
and listened. I hit a winding trail that ended up before the
door of a three-car garage. An owl hooted—derisively, I
thought. I went back down to the road and started up another
path. The wind laughed at me. Look for the cable, fool!

I found it. I followed it, through a tangle of scrub. I clung
to the heavy wire as the going got tough. What was the
legend—string in the lair of the Minotaur? But this wasn't
fantasy. It was all panting and sweat and dizziness. Then the
house looked down at me over the edge of the hillside, and I
stared back.

There were no lights on the porches, or inside. I walked
around to the front door, using the gravel path as little as
possible. The door was locked, of course. I contemplated
the wire mesh of the screened-in porch. I felt for my pocket-
knife. Once a Boy Scout, always a Boy Scout.

Supposing the Professor hadn't left? What if somebody
else was here—Dr. Sylvestro, for instance? There were no
answers. There was only a duty to perform. *A Scout is
Obedient*...

It takes about twelve seconds to break-and-enter a house,
according to the movies. Working without director, lights or
camera, I managed it in twenty minutes, with the aid of
scraped and bleeding fingers. My trouser legs ripped as I
wriggled through the wire mesh and dropped to the porch
floor with a dull thud.

I got up and waited for an echo, a response from within
the darkened house. Crickets punctuated the silence. The
door opened to my hand. I was inside, groping for a light

switch. I found it, then hesitated. But, *a Scout is Brave...*

The light went on. I don't know what I expected to see. A bubbling cauldron, a heap of skulls, the heads of children floating in alcohol—

It was a perfectly conventional room in a perfectly conventional home: unpainted furniture, covered with cushions; a round dining-room table, a stone fireplace and a pile of logs, bookcases made out of boards and bricks. A single touch of luxury was the grand piano that dominated the alcove of the living room.

I walked over to the bookshelves. It's the first thing I do when visiting strangers. I looked at titles: *Romola, Helen's Babies, When Knighthood Was in Flower, The Little Shepherd of Kingdom Come, Man Drowning, Five Little Peppers and How They Grew.*

Professor Hermann hadn't chosen these books. Maybe I'd made a mistake, maybe he didn't live here at all. There were bedrooms and a kitchen to investigate now.

I walked towards the hall, and as I did so the cricket chirpings deepened, blending into croakings. Frogs. Frogs, out in back of the house, below. Below...I remembered something about a fox farm, a fox pen. Where they kept the liquor in Prohibition days—

Abruptly altering my course, I went out to the rear porch. I switched the light off as I departed, and then allowed the moon to guide me. The view was magnificent: silver trees on platinum hills. But I wasn't here to prepare a prospectus on mining stock. I sent a stare down at the levelled area in back of the hilltop house. More wire netting, thin-meshed and held together by strutwork. A concrete flooring. This was the fox pen, all right. I didn't see any foxes inside. I didn't see the Professor, either.

Going down the porch steps, I listened carefully to the frogs. Were they trying to tell me something? If they were, they gave it up. As I fumbled with a latch and entered the fox pen, the croaking ceased. Silence. Silver silence. I stood inside the pen, but I didn't feel very foxy. The frogs told me

nothing, the silence told me nothing. I didn't know what I was looking for, but I had to find it.

"The bootleggers had to have a place to cache their liquor and guess what they did?"

They stacked it right out here in the open, in the fox pen. No, they couldn't do that. There'd be foxes in the pen, to make things look right. But—I saw it over in the corner, shadowed by the house above. A black circle: the metal lid covering a cistern.

Of course! That's where they hid the liquor in the old days—down below, in the hollowed-out hillside! Lift the lid and climb down the stairs to the storage rooms, the vaults. That's where they hid the liquor, and that's where the Professor would hide whatever he wanted hidden.

The frogs croaked a triumphant chorus as I walked over to the iron cistern cover, bent down and reached for the ring in the center. It was heavy. I tugged and I had trouble. I couldn't seem to move my shoulder. That's because something was holding it back, gripping it tightly in restraint.

I glanced around at my shoulder and saw what rested there. It was a hand...

Seventeen

"Mr. Roberts—what are you doing?"

I looked up into the plump white face of Miss Bauer.

"Come away," she whispered. Her hand left my shoulder, traveled to her lips. "He will hear you."

"He?"

"Otto. He works down in the vaults tonight." She urged me to my feet. "Do not fear. He will sleep below. Come to the house, eh?"

I followed her out of the pen, up the porch steps. She kept whispering. She had been asleep in the bedroom, she said, and when she heard me prowling around she thought at first I was the Professor. Then she finally tiptoed out to investigate and found me.

All this I learned in the kitchen. Gradually the story filtered through her accent, her idiom, her fear. For Ottilie Bauer was afraid.

She did not know, at first, what crazy business Otto had in mind when he urged her to come and live with him here in the Canyon. This Dr. Sylvestro, he was partly responsible—Otto had been his patient, once, years ago when he'd first come to America, after the war. Otto had been a brilliant man in the old country, but something went wrong. He got crazy ideas about making money, about success, about his power.

Now he was going too far. All this extortion, and threats, and the wild talk—Miss Bauer had warned. Miss Bauer had coaxed. Miss Bauer had pleaded. But he wouldn't listen.

"Now I do not know what will come. He is preparing more of those horrible photographs. I have wanted to see you, to warn you. This must be stopped. And if you can not

stop it, it is better for you to go away while you can. While he is—"

We both heard the sound, both turned. But it was only the wind. I smiled at her, but my hands clenched. She smiled at me, but her lip quivered.

"I can't go away," I said, softly. "You see, the Professor knows I killed Mike Drayton. You know it, too."

Her lower lip quivered, stopped, quivered again.

"No. You did not kill him. That was a lie."

"But—"

"He made you go away. You saw nothing after that. How I worked on the lungs in the car, how he revived."

"He *revived?*"

"He sat in the car and Otto, he drove him away. For air, he told me, and I must go home to bed. It would be all right. So I went home, thinking how lucky we were, and next day in the papers—"

I stood up. "So the Professor murdered him and pinned the rap on me! You're a witness, you can testify. You're sure you saw Drayton alive after I left?"

She nodded, and I saw the part in her straight black hair.

"Yes. I can testify. I do not wish to tell this, but he must be stopped for his own good. You go away."

"You bet I'll go away, and fast!" I stepped around the table, then halted.

"But what about you—isn't it dangerous for you to stay? If the Professor knew that you had tipped me off—"

"He will not harm me, Mr. Roberts." She smiled. It was a very old smile, borrowed from the Sphinx. "You see, he is my brother."

I drove back before dawn, slept until noon, then called Ellen.

"Go home and start packing," I said. "We're getting out of here."

"When?"

"Tomorrow or the next day, as soon as I can clear up a few odds and ends."

"You really mean it?"

"Cross my heart and hope not to die. Have you ever wanted to go to Niagara Falls on your honeymoon? Or do you prefer the Zambezi? That's in Africa—Southern Rhodesia, I think."

"You sound high."

"I'm right up there, and you'll be, too. Now, listen to me. I've just come from the Professor's place. No, I didn't see him, but I did see Miss Bauer. She turns out to be his sister. That's right.

"The Professor didn't leave town at all. That was just a cover-up to fool me. He's actually getting ready to start his campaign on you and your uncle, and lining up Caldwell for another touch. So he's still around, but don't worry.

"Miss Bauer just supplied me with enough information to quiet the Professor—put him behind bars, if necessary. But he's her brother, and naturally she doesn't want to see that happen unless it's absolutely necessary.

"So instead, I asked her for the file and the photos on Caldwell. These she agreed to get. They're hidden out there at the house, she thinks, down below in a concealed basement. Some time this afternoon, if she's alone and gets the chance, she'll get the stuff and bring it over to Caldwell."

"Caldwell?" Ellen's voice rose.

"Of course. That's where I'll arrange to meet her—and you. Let's say four o'clock. I'll call him now and tell him we're coming over. Once Caldwell has his photos and negatives, we can thumb our noses at the Professor and leave whenever we like."

"You're sure there won't be any hitches?"

"How can there be? Nobody's going to suspect Miss Bauer of double-crossing her brother. Nobody's going to trail her to Caldwell's place. That's what makes it all so safe."

"But Eddie—you're being trailed. By Jake." I paused. I'd forgotten that little detail. "Don't worry about Jake. I'll handle him this afternoon. Now, get busy and pack. Bring

your things over to Caldwell's house. Here, I'll give you the address." I read it off to her, made her repeat it. "Take a cab so there'll be no slip-ups. And I'll see you at four. Meanwhile, in case you happen to be interested, I love you."

"You say the cleverest things."

I hung up, not feeling clever. I'd forgotten about Jake. Well, that problem would be faced shortly. Right now there was the question of Caldwell.

I called him at home. A tired woman answered the phone. At first I thought it might be Marge, but it turned out to be the maid. Yes, Mr. Caldwell was there. He wasn't feeling very well, but whom should she say was calling? I gave my name and waited.

Mr. Caldwell wasn't feeling very well. I could imagine why. He'd just had another little phone call from Jake, about more pictures. And perhaps tonight or tomorrow he'd be taking a trip with a little black bag full of bills.

Perhaps a mention of my name would do the trick, though. I hoped so, anyway.

It did.

"Roberts! My God, I'm glad to hear your voice!" He didn't wait for a reply. "I'm in trouble again. I got another call from—"

"I know. And that's why I phoned you. I think your troubles will soon be over. Now, listen carefully to what I'm going to say."

He listened and I told him everything.

"Got it straight?" I concluded. "Ellen Post and Miss Bauer should both be arriving at your house sometime before four o'clock. I'll be there promptly at four on the head. And that's that."

"Roberts, I don't know how to thank you for all this. You've saved my life. You know, I was seriously thinking of…doing away with myself."

"You'll live to be eighty, I guarantee it! By the way, is your wife at home?"

"Marge took a run down to Venice to stay with her aunt for a few days. Nobody here but the maid."

"Maybe you'd better give her the afternoon off."

"Right. See you at four, then?"

"Four sharp."

And that wound it up. Except that I wasn't feeling high any more, because I remembered Jake. Faithful old Jake.

I glanced at my watch. 12:30. I had about three hours in which to shake him. And I didn't know how. No brilliant ideas came to me as I locked the door, descended the stairs and emerged to find Jake sitting on the steps.

"You sure must of hung on a beaut, the way you slept," Jake greeted me.

"You been here long?"

"Over three hours. This sun's murder."

"You needn't have bothered."

"Boss's orders. He wants to see you."

"The Professor? I thought he was out of town."

"Me too. But he called this morning, big as life. He's going to be waiting for us at your office."

I went to my car and he went to his. We started our parade downtown.

So the Professor was waiting for me, too. That was going to make things harder. My half-formed plans of ditching Jake in traffic went out the window and bounced off the curb of Wilshire and LaBrea. Anyhow, one thing was certain: if the Professor was at my office, then Miss Bauer would have a free hand out at his house.

But the next move? I'd just have to wait and see.

He was in my office, all right, sitting at the desk when I opened the door.

"Come right in," he said.

Yes, come into my parlor, said the spider to the fly—the black spider with the white skull, the black spider who knew by the tiniest tremor just what had wandered into the web he spun.

Or did he know? The stolid face told me nothing.

"Thought you were out of town," I said.

"I had to change my plans. I shall be leaving today, instead. Sit down."

I sat down on the edge of the desk and swung my leg. It felt good, even though it looked too much like a pendulum, ticking off the minutes, ticking off the seconds before he came out with it—

"Jake tells me you did a good job last night."

"If you had my hangover, you'd know what kind of a job I did."

"That's fine. I want you to keep it up. Tonight and to-morrow night. I'll return Friday and take over."

"Take over?"

"Yes. I know how you feel about the girl, and I've arranged to spare you completely. She will never know of your con-nection in the matter. Friday you will take her out for the last time."

"I will?"

"You will pass out. A friend of hers will be present to take her home. That's all."

"Only she isn't going home. I get it."

"No need for you to worry. I promise she will not be harmed in any way. And she'll not blame you for what hap-pens after that. But her uncle will prove to be extremely cooperative from then on, I can assure you."

He stood up. "In a few weeks it will all be over. Completely forgotten. No harm done. Take her out every night between now and Friday. I'll get in touch with you then and give you your final orders." He smiled. "Jake will keep an eye on you meanwhile."

I smiled right back at him. "You certainly think of every-thing," I said.

"That's correct."

"Well, think of this for a moment. I'm not taking Ellen Post out tonight, tomorrow, or Friday. And Jake isn't going to play Boy Detective with me any more, either. Because I am quitting this business, as of today."

"So?"

"Just so. And get this, while we're on the subject—if you try any funny stuff on Ellen Post or her uncle, I'll rip your head off and stuff it down your throat."

"Dear Doctor Roberts!" He grinned, slowly. "Is this all you have learned of tact, the diplomatic approach, the psychology of personal relationships? You need a refresher course in Y-O-U."

"I'm not fooling. I mean what I said."

"That is quite apparent. But may I remind you that you are acting under my orders? And for a very good reason?"

I watched him now. I wanted to see his face.

"Mike Drayton's murder? But I didn't kill Mike Drayton. You did."

I wanted to see his face and I did. It wasn't worth it. He had no reaction at all.

Then, and only then, did I realize the value of his advice. I should have been tactful, diplomatic, tried to find another way of wriggling out. But no, it was too good to miss, telling him off. And in telling him off, I had told all.

He'd guess, instantly, where I got my information. There was only one possible source. And now...

There was a paperweight on the desk. I slid off the edge of the desk slowly, meeting his blank stare with a smile. Then all in one motion I grabbed, grasped, swung.

He toppled forward in the chair very slowly, like a big, bald-headed doll. The doll was bleeding from a cut behind the ear. Out cold, and for a long time.

I stepped over to the door and peeked out. May was behind the glass, at her receptionist's desk. Beyond the glass I saw Jake, lounging on a sofa and reading a magazine.

"Jake!" I called. "Come in here a minute. The Professor would like to see you."

He came over, waddled through the door, waddled right into the paperweight. He didn't fall like a doll—he fell like a ton of bricks.

I left them decorating the inner office, and locked the door on my way out.

"They're in conference in there," I told May. "Don't want to be disturbed. I'm going out—back later."

"See you," said May.

I hoped not. Glancing at my watch, I found it was almost 3:30. Just enough time to make it out to Caldwell's by four o'clock. I climbed in the car and headed up Wilshire for Beverly Hills.

I swung into the driveway at five minutes to four, got out and ran up the steps.

Caldwell opened the door immediately.

"You're here," he acknowledged. "Good!" We went down the hall to the library. Ellen Post stood up and came over and confirmed the look in her eyes with her lips.

"Nobody's following you?" Caldwell asked.

"Not likely," I said. I told them what had happened at the office.

Ellen nodded. "But Eddie, you took an awful risk. Suppose they come to, and go out after Miss Bauer?"

"Couldn't make it in time. She must have left there about the same time I left the office. All it means is we'll have to hurry. I'm going to have her sign a statement when she arrives—just in case something happens later on. Then we'll take the photos and negatives, and that ought to prevent anything from happening, ever.

"After that, we'll be leaving. I think we've got this whole thing licked at last."

"Certainly hope so." Caldwell paced the room, glanced up at the mantel clock. "Shouldn't Miss Bauer be here by now, though? It's almost ten after."

Tick-tock. Tick-tock. Tick-tock.

We listened to the clock, and nobody said anything. The clock was suddenly quite loud.

"Where's the phone?" I asked.

Caldwell gestured towards the next room. I went over,

picked up the phone and dialed Information. I got the number of the Professor's house after a two-minute delay, and the clock kept going louder and louder. Tick-tock.

The phone buzzed. If there was no answer, I could assume Miss Bauer had left. If there was an answer—

"Hello."

It was a man's voice. There was something familiar about it. I hesitated until I placed the speaker. *Dr. Sylvestro.*

"Hello?" he repeated, questioning.

I hung up without answering. Sylvestro was out there. And if the Professor had revived and called Sylvestro before Miss Bauer got away, then...

"Did you get her?" asked Ellen.

"No, but I'm going to."

"What do you mean?"

I glanced at my watch. Twenty past. "I mean I've got to get out to the Professor's house, right away. She may still be coming, delayed by a flat tire or something. But we can't take that chance. Sylvestro answered the phone just now, and that can mean anything. So I'm on my way."

"I thought you weren't taking any chances. What do you call that? If they find you there, you'll never get away."

"I've no choice. Miss Bauer is my alibi, our alibi. Besides, I can't leave her in the soup."

Ellen put her arms around my neck. They seemed to belong there.

"All right, Eddie. But I'm coming with you."

"Me too." Caldwell clenched his big hands.

"No you're not. You can't. Miss Bauer may still show up here. You'll have to be on hand when she arrives, get her statement and the pictures and the negatives. Wait for me to call. I will call, as soon as I can."

"If you can."

I kissed her. "Yes, darling. If I can."

It wasn't very heroic, and there was nothing heroic about the way I kissed her. I didn't want to go, didn't want to stick my neck out, or in.

But I had to, and I went.

I went fast. The walls of Vista Canyon flashed by, the roadside signs blurring before me. "DRIVE SLOWLY" meant nothing to me. And "DANGER—FALLING ROCKS" was kid stuff. I wasn't afraid of falling rocks. I was afraid of seeing the Professor's car, or Jake's, in the rear-view mirror. I was afraid of seeing Doc Sylvestro waiting for me in ambush with a sawed-off shotgun.

As I approached the heart of the Canyon I slowed down. Just before the turn which brought me to the crossroads beneath the hillside, I pulled over to the shoulder and stopped the motor. I climbed out and walked cautiously around the bend. A car was parked up against the trees—a strange car. I inspected it, noted the familiar AMA seal. Dr. Sylvestro's heap, all right. That meant he was still up there.

I returned to my car and started the motor. A U-turn was dangerous here, but it was more dangerous to leave the car standing where it could be seen. If Sylvestro recognized it, or if the Professor and Jake arrived, it meant, as they say in the drapery business, curtains.

So I drove back slowly down the road until I hit another side path in the Canyon. I pushed the car up the dirt roadbed until I found a spot under some trees, out of sight. I parked here and walked back on foot. I kept looking over my shoulder, in case somebody came along. And I kept looking ahead, anticipating Doc Sylvestro.

My neck got sore in a hurry. It was hot, but sunset wasn't far off. I came abreast of the crossing again, glanced up at the hillside house far above me, and then found a clump of bushes to screen me. Then I sat down, lit a cigarette, and let the sand fleas have dinner. The cigarette smoke didn't rise above the bushes, nor did I. I sprawled out and watched the sunset.

Pretty soon it was twilight on the trail, and the ranch-hands were gathered around the fire swapping yarns, the rich and poor alike lolled at their ease before the festive board, and I still sat in the prickly weeds, turning my flea-

bitten face to the hilltop. I leaned back and closed my eyes. I began to doze…

Muffled sound from far away: door slam, crunching, footsteps. Dr. Sylvestro descended interminable stairs. I caught glimpses of him through the trees. He minced down, carrying the inevitable black bag. He stopped at the bottom, mopped his forehead and pulled out a cigarette. He lit it, and a little red eye moved through the dusk towards his car.

The car started, rolled down the road, out of sight. I waited until the sound of the motor died away in the dim distance, and then I got up. I said goodbye to the fleas and crossed over to the wooden stairway.

I climbed. There was no handrail, and the Canyon depths loomed below. A crowd of bats, courtesy Universal Pictures, flew out of an old vampire movie and chittered at me. The sky darkened. I sweated. Up and up and up. I looked down at the gray ribbon of the road. No cars coming. I went on. Then I stood on a level, stone-set patio, before the porch. The windlass for the little cable car occupied part of the area. I occupied what was left. The house before me was dark. This time I knew what to do. I went around to the porch and looked for the place where I'd slashed the screen. It accommodated me promptly. I entered through the porch and walked into the parlor.

The house was more than dark—it was empty. There were no signs of a struggle, nothing to indicate what Dr. Sylvestro might have been doing. Perhaps I'd been mistaken. Perhaps Miss Bauer had left. She might be at Caldwell's place right now. Best thing to do was call and find out, at once.

I looked around for the phone and couldn't find it. I walked through the hall and peeked into the bedroom. Nothing there. The bed was made, no signs of packing or confusion. I was relieved. I walked on, into the kitchen.

Even before I entered, I could smell it: the strangely familiar odor, the instinctively recognized reek. An attempt had been made to mop up. But there were stains on the

table, on the floor all around it. I thought of an operating room—Dr. Sylvestro and his black bag! But then, where—?

Humming. Humming from the corner. Something huge and white and gleaming, something that hummed and purred as it crouched next to the refrigerator. I walked over to the deep-freeze, tugged the handle, raised the lid of the freezer chest.

I saw the packages wrapped in heavy preserving paper— six of them. I lifted out the top one, the round one. I unwrapped Miss Bauer's head.

Eighteen

There was nothing else for me to do, then. I closed the freezer and left the kitchen, left the humming and the odor and the stains. I found the phone in the dining room to my left.

I clicked the receiver, sharply. I said, "Give me the police department, please."

An answering voice came. "What are you doing here?"

It was Rogers who spoke.

Here?

I dropped the mouthpiece. Rogers wasn't *here*. How did he get on the phone? Then I realized. The phone was connected with the vaults under the fox pen!

I knew it now. I knew there wouldn't be time to make a call, because Rogers was climbing out of the cistern. I heard a clang as I ran toward the porch door. I stood on the patio, at the head of the stairs. I gazed down into darkness. I'd have to take those stairs in the dark now, and I'd have to move fast.

Feet thudded behind me. The porch door banged. Then I saw the flash, heard the sound of the shot. It went *sprang!* And it was close, too close. I ran forward. The windlass loomed. I could use the cable car.

There was another shot, another flash and *spang!* I jumped into the car and reached over to trip the windlass. A knife slashed at my wrist. It was too dark, too close for Rogers to use a gun. He had a knife now, and he was cutting the cable.

I reached out, groped, grabbed. He kicked at my face. I found his leg in the darkness, held on. He toppled but I was a second too late. Something snapped, and suddenly the car was plunging down through a gauntlet of branches that

stabbed my face. Rogers squirmed in my arms. We were crashing together, clattering, ripping, roaring in a flimsy wooden car that was like an orange crate.

He still had his knife, and the blade grazed my throat. I twisted his arm. He grunted and bit into my shoulder. I pushed him forward in the swaying car. It was black, no moon shone, and the trees clawed me as we rumbled down. He stood up, trying to kick. The car tipped forward.

I threw myself against him. He screamed and went down. Down and over the side of the car. It went over him. And then it began to turn.

I hurtled down through the treetops with his scream in my ears. I fell and rolled, fell and rolled, and the car crashed past me, and then I hit bottom and lay there, covered with a blanket of black.

A long time later, I opened my eyes. That hurt. But it didn't particularly matter, because everything hurt. My head and neck ached. For a moment I lay still and tried to keep my eyes shut while I sorted and catalogued the varieties of pain.

I raised up, bracing myself on my hands. I was on the ground, but needles were lacerating my hands. Pine needles. Could I stand up? I could try. There was a tree trunk far away: light-years, pain-years away. I hunched forward and my fingers clawed bark, braced the broad surface. I got to my knees, embracing the tree trunk. It must have looked silly, and it hurt like hell.

I stood up, raising myself by degrees. I could hear something snap. It might be twigs; it might be my vertebrae. But I had to stand up, lift up that load of pain. Weary totin' dat heavy load. And where was the lonesome road? I found it. I walked very slowly, very softly. I bumped into bushes, and it hurt. I bumped into trees, and it hurt. But I kept right on walking, through the thick underbrush.

Deep darkness and crickets all about me. I was walking along the dry bed of a little gully. It was dusty. I smelled the dust when I stumbled and fell. I coughed and got up and

walked again. I wiped dust from my face and something sticky came away in my hand. I kept moving. I had to find the car on the side road. Once I found it, I had to drive it. And that would only be the beginning of this night's work.

The car was parked where I left it. I managed to open the door and climb in. Then I sat for a moment, waiting for my strength to come back. After a while I realized I'd have to wait for a long, long time. So I just started the car and drove away.

At first I drove very slowly and then I drove fast. The road kept winding and winding and I wound with it. Finally I was out of the Canyon and back on the highway. I checked my watch. Only 9 P.M. *Only?*

But that meant I'd been gone from Caldwell's for over four hours. And during that time, anything could happen. Miss Bauer was dead. Where was Dr. Sylvestro and the Professor and Jake?

I thought I knew, but I had to make certain. There was just one way to find out. I pulled in at the first filling station. I went to the washroom, first, and cleaned up—trying not to look at my face in the mirror. The cold water felt good on my face and neck and wrists.

Then I lit a cigarette, came out, and used the wall phone. It rang and rang for a long time before somebody picked it up at the other end. I didn't say anything, didn't even breathe until I heard the voice. Then I relaxed.

It was Caldwell, all right.

"Hello," he said.

"You all right?" I asked. "You and Ellen?"

"Yes."

"Thank God for that! I was afraid the Professor might have figured things out and paid you a call."

"What happened?"

"It's too long a story," I told him. "Tell you when I see you. Miss Bauer is…gone. That's all you need to know right now. But listen to me carefully. This is important."

"Right," he said.

"I want you and Ellen to stay where you are. Call the cops at once—tell them you just had a threatening phone call, or anything you want. Just so you get them to send a squad over to watch your house. The Professor might still show up. Will you do that?"

"Yes."

"I'm going down to Long Beach, to the boardwalk. The way I figure it, that's the logical place for the Professor to hide your pictures and negatives. He'd never leave them around his home once he thought I'd be up there. So I'm on my way now.

"Tell Ellen not to worry. If I see the Professor or Jake I won't go in. But I've got to make a search and move fast. I'll call you the minute I'm finished."

"Right."

I hung up and went out. I drove away quickly. From now on, everything would depend on timing. Timing and luck. I circled Venice, kept on going. I was beginning to feel better, now. No bones broken, and at least Caldwell and Ellen were safe and under police protection. All I had to do was find the photos. Timing and luck.

Long Beach loomed ahead. I parked, headed for the boardwalk through the tunnel. I kept my eyes open. No sign of Jake, no sign of the Professor, no sign of Dr. Sylvestro— just the usual evening crowd. I thought of my first visit here, months ago. I'd hated the crowd, then. Now I wanted to reach out and touch people as they passed by—touch them, stop them, tell them I needed their help. Well, they couldn't help me. I didn't deserve help. This was something I had to do on my own. I had to do it and succeed, so that I could take my place among people once again.

I stood in front of the pitch. The horse-faced woman nodded at me—she'd seen me often enough, by now, to be friendly.

"Anyone around?" I asked. "Jake, or the Professor?"

She shook her head. "Haven't seen them all evening. I'm just taking it easy until closing time. Jake said he probably

wouldn't show up tonight but I should stick, just in case he needed me." She turned the page of a comic book.

I moved past her.

"You going in?"

"Just for a minute," I told her. "Rogers left my script here yesterday, he tells me. I'm on my way into town. Thought I'd stop by and pick it up."

It was a simple, logical excuse. She looked up from the page and said, "Want I should help?"

"No, that's all right. I think I know where it is."

I headed for the entrance, and then I was going down the short, dark passageway. My skin began to tingle in anticipation—I didn't like dark passageways, however short. But there was no one waiting for me.

The inner room was empty, too. The banners hung listlessly in the background and when I snapped on the dim overhead light I saw nothing but the covered table and the crystal ball. I didn't expect to see more. There was a second room in back. Here Jake retired when business was slack and brewed himself a pot of coffee over a hot plate.

I poked my head around the corner tentatively. Nobody took a crack at my skull, so I went inside. Chair, cot, chest of drawers, hot plate, shelf—my eyes inventoried and appraised. Where would he hide the pictures?

I went to work. I turned the chair upside down. I overturned the cot and felt the padding thoroughly. I took all the drawers out of the chest. I swept the plates and cups off the shelf. I even inspected the inside of the coffee pot and the bottom of the hot plate. I drew nothing but blanks. Then I went back into the other room. I kicked over both chairs, ripped out the padding. I yanked the cloth off the table, holding the crystal ball carefully in my hand. No photos, no negatives.

I was wrong. They weren't here, after all. Sighing, I set the crystal ball back on the bare surface of the table. The clouded crystal ball. Too bad it wasn't real—then I could stare into it and find out where the pictures were.

I could stare into it and—

My fingers scooped it up, twirled the base. It came free. And there, inside the rounded hollow, I found what I'd been looking for: five pictures. Negatives, two sets of negatives. The works. My hands trembled as I set them down on the table and fumbled for a match. It was very hard to strike a light, but I knew I'd make it. The match flared up. Then, all at once, the flame wavered. The flame wavered, because something came up with a rush and a swoop behind me. I tried to turn, but the match went out.

Something came down on the back of my head, and I went out, too.

Nineteen

"Eddie, are you all right?"

It was Ellen's voice. I opened my eyes and stared up into her face. My head was on her lap. She massaged the side of my neck. The back of my head throbbed. But I could forget about that, as long as Ellen was with me.

Ellen was with me. But that meant—I tried to sit up and almost made it.

"Take it easy," she said. "Wait a minute."

But I didn't have a minute to wait. I had to sit up, even though the walls spun round and round. I had to sit up, focus my eyes, and stare at my surroundings. I had to find out where I was, where we were.

I managed. Ellen and I were on a couch in a small room. The walls were of unfinished board, nailed loosely in slats over a base of stone. I could see the stone through the boards because some of them were badly warped by dampness. The air smelled damp and musty. A low-watt naked light bulb dangled from the ceiling, its wire connection trailing off to another room beyond a low door.

There was only one other piece of furniture—a chair—and Caldwell slumped forward in it. He looked at me, nodded, but did not smile. Ellen wasn't smiling, either. Come to think of it, neither was I.

Quite a reunion. Quite a surprise. I'd always been senti-mental about reunions, but this wasn't the time or the place. I could see that at a glance.

"So they got you, eh?" I said.

"That's right," Caldwell sighed, heavily. "The way I figure it, Jake or the Professor came to and called Doc Sylvestro

out at the Canyon. He took care of Miss Bauer. They didn't figure you coming back out, so you surprised Rogers.

"They thought you'd come to me. And that's where they went looking. We had the door locked, but Jake got in through the cellar. Before we suspected anything, he had a gun on us and then he and the Professor took over."

I shook my head, trying to shake off some of the pain and not succeeding very well at it. Apparently this wasn't my day for success.

"Might have figured it if I hadn't been so stupid," I said. "Then I suppose they were already there when I called you?"

"Yes," Caldwell told me. "They were there, all right. Jake had his gun in my back all the time I was talking to you. I wanted to warn you, somehow, but—he had his gun in my back, and…"

His voice trailed away in a sigh.

"Not your fault," I said. "What else could you do? So they knew I was going to the boardwalk and they came after me."

"Sylvestro did," Ellen said. "The Professor and Jake brought us here in their car. Sylvestro took you."

"Just where are we?" I asked. Then, "Don't tell me. I already know. Well, I always wanted to find out what the Professor's hideout looked like. I always wanted to get down into the cistern. Looks like my wish is granted."

"Take it easy, Eddie."

I stood up. The room whirled, but I waited until it was steady once more. "Where are they?" I asked. "And what are they up to? They didn't tie us up or anything. Maybe we can—"

"Forget it."

I recognized the shadow even before the bullet head poked around the side of the door. Good old Jake. Good old Jake and his big fat .45.

"The dame's right," he said. "Take it easy. Doc and the Professor are having a little conference. They'll be ready for you in a minute."

I grinned at him. He grinned back. Then he slouched into the room. I watched him, watched the gun. Both kept coming closer.

"You know something?" Jake asked. I could smell alcohol on his breath, and I could also smell that acrid, metallic odor common to guns. I didn't like either one, and both were close.

"What's that?" I watched him and the gun, but I didn't move, didn't dare to move.

"That was a dirty trick you pulled on Rogers. We found him in the bushes. A dirty trick. I don't like dirty tricks."

The gun was moving, now. It moved fast. I tried to dodge, but he brought the butt down hard on my shoulder.

Ellen gasped and stood up. He swivelled the gun around. "Sit still, sister," he said. "This'll only take a minute." And he brought the gun-butt up again.

"I kind of liked Sid," he muttered. "That was a dirty trick." The butt was coming down and I could only watch it. I couldn't grab the gun, couldn't move away. I could only stand there and try to shut out the pain as this drunken ape beat me up in front of Ellen. This time I tried to claw at his arms, but the gun came anyway. I braced myself for the stunning blow, gritted my teeth, and then—

Jake grunted. There was a splintering sound and a crash. His face hung over my shoulder for a moment, frozen in numb surprise. Then he toppled to the floor.

Caldwell stood behind him, panting and holding the splintered back of the chair. He'd moved fast and quietly for a man in his condition. But I wasn't giving him my attention at the moment. I had my eye on the gun. It lay on the floor, next to Jake's limp hand, right at my feet.

I stooped to pick it up.

"Hold it!"

They were in the doorway, now—the Professor and Doctor Sylvestro. The man in black and the man in white. Both of them had convincing arguments pointed my way.

I stood up again. Doctor Sylvestro came forward and

picked up Jake's gun. Then he knelt and went into his bed-
side manner. "Bleeding pretty bad," he said. "Ought to take
care of this right away, Otto."

"Never mind." The Professor spoke to Sylvestro, but he
looked straight at me. "He deserved what he got. I told him
to stand guard. He disobeyed. There's no room in my plans
for disobedience."

The Professor made a courtly gesture with his gun. "Will
you all come this way, please?" he solicited. "I have something to say to you."

We left the room single file and walked down a short corridor. The Professor was in the lead, walking backwards so
that he could watch us with his three eyes—the two in his
head and the third, deadly little round eye pointing at us
from his hand. Sylvestro brought up the rear, and for the
second time today, Caldwell had a gun in his back.

We passed a second room at the end of the corridor. I
managed to stare into it. A yellow light bulb disclosed the
contents of a photographic darkroom, complete with running
water and piles of raw film, chemicals and spools of finished
negatives.

I thought of the blackmail photos and wondered how
many others might repose in this businesslike little estab-
lishment. But there was no time for further speculation. We
turned the corner and entered the main chamber.

It was nothing but a low-ceilinged vault, carved out of the
rock. The cistern stairs were in the corner, and again a single
light bulb gleamed. Its radiance was almost lost in the dark
curtains that covered the walls from floor to ceiling. I didn't
quite understand their significance until the notion suddenly came to me: the drapes would muffle all sound here
and prevent anything being heard in the fox pen or house
above. As a matter of fact, part of this layout—the other two
rooms and the corridor—would be directly under the house.
The roof there wasn't stone, but the solid wood flooring of
the basement.

This wasn't the time for architectural speculation. It was a time to file around the big round table in the center of the room and take chairs. Sylvestro and the Professor sat on one wedge; the three of us occupied the remaining chairs as a group.

The Professor stared at us. I don't know what he saw—fear, hopelessness, resignation.

I stared at the Professor. I saw a little, bald-headed psychopath. I saw a brilliant psychotherapist gone wrong. I saw an immobile basilisk carved out of solid ice. I saw the Devil. And then I saw a small, fat, middle-aged expatriate who had somehow broken under suffering; who had taken a twisted road years ago and could not go back. He drove others because he was driven, he issued commands because he was commanded, he meted out punishment because he was punished. All men were suckers to the Professor, because he'd been a sucker, once. And he was still a sucker now. Even if he killed me, even if he killed all of us, he was a sucker. I almost pitied him.

There was no pity for me in his face, in his voice, when he spoke. "There is not much time," said the Professor. "I will be brief."

The gun gestured. "No need to discuss the circumstances which bring us together. I regret them as much as you probably do. Mr. Caldwell had no business to get mixed up in this matter. Miss Post, I had hoped to spare you as much as possible. But now there is no choice."

His eyes were on me again. I didn't flinch. "As for you, what can I say? I offered you everything, and you betrayed me. From this night on, Y-O-U is finished and your usefulness is at an end. Both Doctor Sylvestro and myself will have to seek another field of operation."

"Come on," said Doctor Sylvestro. "We don't need a funeral oration, do we? Thought you said you'd be brief."

"Allow me please to explain," the Professor answered. "I must tell these people what we have worked out, in order that they may…cooperate."

"They'll cooperate, all right," said Sylvestro. "I guarantee

that." He gestured with his gun for emphasis, although it was unnecessary.

"The Doctor and I have spent some time discussing just what we can do and how we can move to rectify tonight's mistakes. I think we have found a solution." The Professor smiled.

"It will require your assistance, however. Mr. Caldwell, you will play the role of witness."

Caldwell's knuckles gripped the table. "Witness to what?" he muttered.

"A murder."

"Now, look here—"

"Might I remind you that I still retain possession of certain pictures and negatives? Besides which, you have no choice. You're here, and you'll have to watch. The chances are, you'll never need to testify as to what you see."

The Professor turned his gaze to Ellen. "As for you, my dear, your role is equally passive. You are to be a murderess. Oh, you needn't look so shocked—you won't actually kill anyone. It's just that you'll have to put your hand on the gun for a moment, after it is used and safely emptied. We shall require your fingerprints."

Ellen's eyes entreated me. I half-rose, but Doctor Sylvestro's gun was watching me.

"Again, the chances are you will never be brought to trial for the crime. Because I have good reason to believe that I can sell the murder weapon quite promptly—to your uncle."

The picture was beginning to take shape, now. He had his blackmail scheme worked out after all. In spite of all that had happened, all the obstacles in his path, the Professor never faltered or failed. He'd use Caldwell as a witness, frame Ellen with a murder, and then go to her uncle and bleed him dry. A quick touch and then he'd run.

All he needed now was his victim. And that answer came, too. The Professor looked at me.

"I don't need to tell you what role you're going to play here tonight," he murmured. "It is not something I had

intended—but you've chosen the part yourself. Your actions make it imperative and inevitable."

Ellen began to sob. "Do something, Eddie. Don't let him kill you. Do something!"

Caldwell patted her shoulder. The Professor's gun followed his every move. Sylvestro kept me covered.

"Let's get it over with," he said.

The Professor nodded slowly.

"Whenever you're ready," he murmured.

Sylvestro's gun came up. The hand holding it across the table was steady. I watched his left eye. It was beginning to squint. I watched his index finger. It was beginning to squeeze. I watched the muzzle of the gun, waited for the explosion to come.

Then I braced my feet and my knees went up, hard, and my arms shot under and the side of the table rose in the air.

Ellen screamed as the gun went off, and then Sylvestro screamed. The flash blinded me for an instant, but I caught sight of the red blur which had once been Sylvestro's face. The Professor was on the floor, his shoulder pinned by the table. Caldwell bent over him, and the Professor tugged his arm free, fired. The shot went wild, found another target—the light bulb.

Suddenly we were in darkness. I grabbed Ellen's arm. "Quick!" I panted. "Over here." We could hear Caldwell gasping, struggling with the Professor. Then came a thud and silence.

"Caldwell!" I shouted. "You all right?"

The answer was a burst of flame. The shot echoed down the narrow corridor. I ran for it, dragging Ellen behind me. We crouched in the corner of the photographic darkroom. I smashed the yellow bulb.

I could hear Ellen gasping. I could hear slow footsteps dragging across the floor. They came down the corridor, closer and closer.

Ellen and I moved back against the table. I groped amidst the chemicals in the darkness, hoping to find something to

use as a weapon. The hanging negatives brushed the back of my head.

I picked up a glass jar, held it ready. The footsteps were close, now. They paused in the doorway.

"I give you one chance to come out quietly," said the Professor. "Otherwise I must shoot. And at this range, I will not miss."

He was telling the truth. I thought of Ellen beside me. I thought of a .45 slug tearing into her flesh, ripping and rending. Better to come out quietly, take my medicine. I'd done my best and failed. The Professor never failed.

"I'll count to three," said the Professor. *"One…two…"*

I didn't wait for *three.* I threw the glass jar forward with all my might. At the same time I pulled Ellen down on the floor; at the same time the Professor's gun shredded the darkness with a fountain of flame. He screamed.

The jar had either hit him or smashed on the wall behind him. It didn't matter. The acid, whatever it contained, had splashed. Splashed over his face and throat and chest, splashed and eaten. He writhed on the floor, and we could see him.

We could see him. I turned, swiftly. The bullet had struck the dry negatives hanging from clips on a wire. They flared now. One of them dropped to the table, and a thread of fire ran to the photographic paper.

"Get out, fast!" I shouted. "This place is full of chemicals!"

We ran back into the other room. Caldwell was groping in the darkness next to the cistern stairs.

"Can you make it?" I panted.

He mumbled an assent. "Then hurry, start climbing." I boosted Ellen up the rungs. A muffled explosion sounded from behind us, and suddenly the darkness was suffused with acrid fumes.

Caldwell was at the top of the cistern now. The lid came off. The rush of fresh air swept through the chambers below us. The fire billowed and rose. Caldwell took Ellen's arms and I lifted her legs from below. She was out. I climbed

swiftly, half-suffocated by the rising smoke. Another crash sounded from below.

Then I was out, I could breathe fresh air, I could look up at the stars as they whirled around calmly and coldly, calmly and coldly.

Whirling calmly and coldly, I passed out.

Twenty

Ellen drove me to the beach house and put me to bed. I stayed there for the next two days. I had a fever, and nightmares, and a constant need for her hand on my forehead, her voice in my ear, saying, "It's all right, Eddie. Go to sleep, now, and rest."

Gradually I managed to pull out of it. On the third day she showed me the newspaper stories about the fire at Vista Canyon.

The house had burned: the fire had risen through the basement over the photo lab, and by the time an alarm was given it was too late. Jake, Sylvestro and the Professor were presumed to have perished in the flames. As for Miss Bauer —they must have disposed of her remains immediately after I found the deep-freeze, because there was no mention of her at all. Rogers was at the bottom of the hill, his neck broken. They surmised he'd been fleeing from the fire in the cable car when the cable broke.

Of course an investigation was in progress. Police were "linking Otto Hermann, well-known psychological consultant, with an organized cult-racket run from his hideout in the Canyon house."

Apparently they hadn't found much to go on. The fire had taken care of that. My name wasn't mentioned. Judson Roberts wasn't tied into this deal, and Eddie Haines never had been. He never need be.

I've gone back to the office and closed it up. May, the secretary, had already shown enough sense to disappear. She left the Judson Roberts record file behind, though, and I destroyed it completely. Since there's no connection between Judson Roberts and Eddie Haines, officially, I'm in the clear.

I can leave town with Ellen now, and nobody will ever know what happened. I can even go to work for Caldwell if I like—he's grateful enough, and he has reason to keep his mouth shut. On the other hand, I can spill the works. I can go to the authorities and lay the whole mess on the table.

There's no need to "confess" anything. I don't feel that compulsion. My own part in the racket was no better and no worse than the role played by thousands who still operate their phony "self-help" swindles today.

But that's just the point. I've been doing a lot of thinking lately. Maybe it would help someone if I told the truth. Maybe it would make it a little easier for the suckers and a little harder for those who prey upon them. I have no illusions about breaking up the whole system, but it might do some good.

Ellen and I can go away, today. Or I can stay here and face the music, risk taking a rap if they want to pin one on me for what happened. Writing it all down here, the way I have these past weeks, I've been trying to make up my mind. I can turn it over to the authorities tomorrow. Or I can burn it, the way the Professor was burned, the way the past was burned.

What should I do? Will I be a seeker or a sucker? And which is which? I think I'm going to leave those questions for Ellen to decide. She'll know what's best for me and for both of us.

Yes, I'll ask her. And whatever she says, I'll do. Just as long as she remembers to call me "Eddie."

THE
END

Get Hard Case Crime by Mail...
And Save 43%!

☐ YES! Sign me up for the Hard Case Crime Book Club!

As long as I choose to stay in the club, I will receive every Hard Case Crime book as it is published (generally one each month). I'll get to preview each title for 10 days. If I decide to keep it, I will pay only $3.99* — a savings of 43% off the cover price! There is no minimum number of books I must buy and I may cancel my membership at any time.

Name: _____

Address: _____

City / State / ZIP: _____

Telephone: _____

E-Mail: _____

☐ I want to pay by credit card: ☐ VISA ☐ MasterCard ☐ Discover

Card #: _____   Exp. date: _____

Signature: _____

Mail this card to:
HARD CASE CRIME BOOK CLUB
1 Mechanic Street, Norwalk, CT 06850-3431

Or fax it to 610-995-9274.
You can also sign up online at www.dorchesterpub.com.

Everyone is Raving About

HARD CASE CRIME

Winner of the Edgar® Award!

USA Today exclaimed:

"All right! Pulp fiction lives!"

The New York Times wrote:

"A stunning tour de force."

The Chicago Sun-Times said:

**"Hard Case Crime is doing a wonderful job...
beautiful [and] worth every dime."**

New York Magazine called us:

"Sleek...stylized...[and] suitable for framing."

Playboy called our books:

"Masterpieces."

Mickey Spillane wrote:

**"One hell of a concept. These covers brought me
right back to the good old days."**

And Neal Pollack said:

**"Hard Case may be the best new American
publisher to appear in the last decade."**

Find Out Why—and Get Each Book for

43% Off the Cover Price!

(See other side for details.)